DEADLY WEBS

JAMES HUNT

---

*P*uddles lined the potholed street. A light rain fell from the night sky, and Mallory Givens flipped the collar of her neon-orange raincoat up. The wind gusts brought a biting cold and made the raindrops sting. Though covered, her feet and hands were frozen, along with the tip of her nose, but she adjusted the backpack straps over her shoulders and trudged on.

The stores Mallory passed were closed, the late hour keeping everyone tucked in their beds. The windows to the shops were barred, and the cracked pavement and garbage-littered sidewalk matched the broken streetlights above. The lights that did work flickered, and despite their guidance, the path she walked was still darker than she would have liked.

It wasn't safe for her to be out this late, but despite the danger, there was a certain level of excitement to beginning a new adventure and leaving a life she never wanted behind. The only part that made her hesitate about the future was her mother, who was back in their apartment, bundled under the covers because their heat was turned off (again), sleeping between her shifts at the diner.

Mallory loved her mom. But she was never around. And even though she worked all of the time, they always seemed to be late on bills. It was something her mother tried to shield her from, but she wasn't a kid anymore. She hadn't been for a long time. Between her mother's twelve-hour shifts and no siblings or family members in the area, Mallory practically raised herself. She didn't blame her mom for their circumstances, but how could her mother blame her for wanting to leave?

Still, in the back of her mind, Mallory knew that her mother would worry. She left no note and gave no hint of her departure. Her mother would be devastated when she woke to find her gone, and that thought alone nearly prompted her to stay. But telling her mom where she was going wasn't part of the deal. That was the price of a new life.

Mallory would leave it all behind. No more teasing, no more name-calling, no more mean remarks from the kids at school. She hopped in excitement at the prospect and lifted her head to the light drizzle and smiled. Never in all her twelve years did she feel more free.

She paused at the corner of Wurth Street and Thirty-Fifth Avenue near the park's entrance. She checked the time on her digital watch that she received for Christmas last year. They couldn't afford a cell phone, so the watch was deemed a suitable replacement so Mallory could at least know when to come home.

The pickup wasn't for another twenty minutes. The corner of a bench stuck out from behind a cluster of bushes and sat protected by an overhang from the rain. Mallory decided to wait there. It couldn't be seen from the street, and she didn't want to draw any unwanted attention.

The rush of the moment kept her on the edge of the park bench, and after she sat, Mallory removed her backpack and then opened it. She pulled out a black spiral notebook, the twirling metal curves bent in awkward places from being shoved in and out of the bag.

Mallory opened the notebook to the first empty page and reached for the outer pouch of the pack to retrieve her pen. The moment ink and paper made contact she became lost in her own mind. The rain, cold, and nauseating smell of whatever garbage the homeless left behind suddenly disappeared. She traveled to another place, her favorite place.

It rested on the side of a mountain. The air was crisp and cool, and the sun was shining. From the balcony of her cabin she had a breathtaking view into the valley where the river cut through the gorge. A forest thick with green trees circled the cottage, and a scent of pine floated in the air. She had cocoa in her hand, the mug warm against her palms, with marshmallows floating on top.

This was the place where her stories were born, where she whispered all of her hopes and dreams of the future, the only place where her thoughts came to life. All the bad and the fearful was cast aside and left behind in the real world. This realm belonged to her, and nothing in it existed without her consent. It was perfect. And that was exactly how she hoped it would be with him.

When the idea first popped into her head she thought it was crazy. He was handsome, and she was plain. He was funny, and she was dull. He was charming, and she couldn't say two words to him without getting tongue-tied. She thought of him every night before she went to sleep, and he filled her mind through most of the day. And the more she fantasized, the more real it felt.

"Hey."

The voice was haggard and violent and yanked Mallory from the mountainside. She suddenly found herself back in the park, where the drizzle had transformed into a steady rain, and she shivered from the cold.

The homeless man in front of her was tall and gaunt. The jacket and pants he wore were torn, several holes visible in the dark. His left foot wore a boot, and his right, a sandal. Long black whiskers sprouted from his cheek and chin in wild tufts. The rain had flattened his mangy hair to his skull but did little to help with his smell.

"What are you doing out so late?" the homeless man asked.

Mallory pressed the notebook tight to her chest, where her heart pounded against it quickly. She opened her mouth but lost the ability to speak. He was so tall, and the darkness only intensified his ominous features. He moved forward until the water from his beard dripped down onto her lap. He pointed to the backpack next to her.

"What's in there?"

Mallory took a swallow and then finally mumbled a word. "N-nothing." She reached for the bag, but the beggar snatched it off the bench before she could stop him. Mallory hopped off the bench and extended her arm as the homeless man stepped back out of reach. "Please, no. It's all I have."

The homeless man kept the bag by his side, and his body between it and Mallory. The way he looked at her sent a chill stronger than the cold through her bones. She knew that a lot of the homeless people used drugs, and she wondered if he was on them right now. She remembered from a news segment that specific drugs made people angry. And violent.

"It's not safe to be out here at night," he said, his voice so deep it sounded like it hurt him to speak.

Lightning flashed in the sky, followed quickly by the crash of thunder. Suddenly, everything Mallory had hoped for seemed silly. It was foolish to come out here this late. It was stupid to think she could have done this, and now it was all going to end.

"What's that you have there?" he asked, pointing to the notebook clutched tight in her arms.

Tears formed in the corners of Mallory's eyes, but they blended seamlessly with the rain. She trembled, shaking her head. He couldn't have this too. Let him take the bag, let him take whatever else he wants, but not this.

Mallory retreated, the backs of her legs smacking into the bench, and her knees buckled as she fell hard onto the seat. The man reached for the notebook, and she twisted away from his hands, the meaty poke of his thick fingers clawing for her last possession. She spun off the bench before the man could grab hold.

"Give it to me!" The homeless man snarled and moved quicker than he looked as he lunged again. This time he ripped the notebook from her grip, and she screamed as a pair of headlights flashed to her left. The homeless man sprinted away into the rain and darkness while Mallory collapsed to the ground.

A million thoughts ran through her mind at the sight of those headlights. If it was the police, they'd take her home and she'd have to explain to her mother what happened and why she left. And then she'd have to tell her about *him*, and her life would be over.

Mallory wiped her face, unable to feel the difference between the rain and her own tears, and her sleeve was so wet that she couldn't tell if it even helped. She was stupid. Stupid for thinking that she could do this. Everyone at school was right. All she was good for was reading books and daydreaming.

The bright headlights finally shut off, and Mallory slowly craned her head toward the car. She blinked rapidly, her eyelashes batting away the water. Someone stepped out of the car and walked toward her. Mallory's heart pounded faster, and the existential dread of exposure triggered another wave of sobs.

"Mallory?"

The voice sounded far away, but it was one she recognized. She sniffled and then crawled forward. "I lost my bag." She looked down at her clothes, which were now soaked, despite the raincoat, and filthy from dirt and debris. "Someone took it, and my notebook I—"

"It's fine. Just get in the car, hurry."

Before she could argue, the car door shut and the engine sprang to life. Mallory pushed herself off the ground, and with her head lowered she shuffled toward the car. Maybe there was still a chance. Yes, she thought, of course there was. She could get new clothes. And he wouldn't care what she wore. At least she didn't think he would.

True love didn't care for such things. And that was exactly what this was. Mallory reached for the door handle of the car and yanked it open. When she climbed inside she felt better. This was her new life. This was a new beginning. She shut her eyes and found herself back in the cottage on her mountain. She wouldn't be there alone for much longer. And she couldn't wait to start fresh.

2

---

*I*t had started last night just like it always did. The sour pit in Detective Chase Grant's gut always worsened right before a bust like this. Even after a decade on the force, he still couldn't stop the butterflies. A part of him didn't think they'd ever go away. Another part didn't want them to.

Grant pumped his left hand a few times, closed his eyes, and focused on his breathing. More nerves than poor health. Grant was on the closer edge of six feet, and while the job had added a few pounds over the years, he was still in good shape. Better than most of the cops at his precinct anyways. And at thirty-five he still had a thick head of wavy black hair that refused to gray, giving him a look much younger than his years. The only real signs of his age were the wrinkles when he smiled. Public opinion agreed that he could still pass as someone in his twenties. Though emotionally, he felt more like someone in his sixties.

When Grant opened his eyes, he glanced down to the watch on his left wrist. The digital timer ticked closer and closer to the twelve-hour mark. That's all most abduction

7

cases lasted. The first six to twelve hours were the most crucial. Though on this particular case, he found himself at a disadvantage since he was brought in a week after the girl was already taken. But he treated it just like a new case regardless of the original timeline.

The driver of the van hit a bump, and Grant smacked into the S.W.A.T. officer to his right. There were a dozen FBI agents riding with him, all covered in tactical gear, with masks over their faces and assault rifles pulled protectively to their bodies. Everyone was quiet.

The officer in front of Grant kept his eyes shut, and his left knee bounced up and down like a jackhammer. He was a younger man, couldn't have been older than twenty-two. Grant was willing to bet that he had a few butterflies of his own.

"Three hundred," Grant said.

The young officer opened his eyes, and his knee stopped bouncing. "What?"

"That's how many hours your tactical training lasts, right?" Grant asked.

"Just about, sir."

Grant nodded slowly, and grinned. "I was part of an exchange program with Seattle PD five years ago where I cross-trained with our S.W.A.T. unit. Some of the best offi-cers I've ever worked with."

"Hell yeah!" The boast came from further down the van and triggered a series of hoots and hollers. The young man cracked a smile.

"Trust the man next to you," Grant said. "Once you start moving, your training will override everything else."

The young officer nodded quickly. "Yes, sir." The boy's knee remained steady the rest of the trip.

"Detective Grant, you'll follow the medical team inside once the house is secure." FBI agent Chad Hickem was the liaison Grant had been working with for the past twelve hours. He was a mountain of a man. Served in the Marine Corps and was deployed twice in the Middle East. After an honorable discharge he went back to school and received his degree in criminal justice, and then worked his way up the ladder to lead agent of the missing persons unit for the Northwest Division of the FBI. In Grant's humble opinion there wasn't anything more terrifying than a big body controlled by an even larger mind.

"I could cover the back," Grant said. "I might not have my three hundred, but I got close."

"And have Seattle PD up my ass for getting their top detective killed in action?" Hickem shook his head. "Hell no." He turned and adjusted the rifle strap on his shoulder. "You did your job, Detective. Now let us do ours."

While Grant didn't like being sidelined, Agent Hickem was right about one thing. Grant did do his job, and he did it quickly. The past week had left the FBI chasing its tail, and it only took Grant ten hours to identify a suspect. And it couldn't have happened a moment too soon.

The abduction of the ambassador's daughter had been the only thing the news had covered for the past week. Speculation about who took the girl and why fueled an already increasingly political divide across the country. Pundits on both sides of the aisle pointed fingers, yet no one seemed concerned about what happened with the girl—aside from her parents.

The van squealed to a stop, and the sourness in Grant's stomach ended. All the nervousness, the anxiety, the fear that accompanied a life-and-death situation that the foundation of these raids was built upon was wiped away. All the pieces were in place now. The hard part was over.

"Team is on me!" Hickem said, his voice booming the orders from the front of the S.W.A.T. van. "Priority is extraction. If we can take him alive, fine, if not, then that's the way the head rolls." Hickem opened his door, and at the same time, the agents that Grant had rode with spilled out the back.

The gray colors that plagued the sky just before dawn fogged the world outside. On Grant's suggestion, Hickem had decided to take the suspect early in the morning. Their suspect was a night owl, according to Grant's profile.

Grant watched through the front window of the van as Hickem busted down the door and the second and third teams on the other sides of the house stormed inside. Glass shattered, screams were shouted over the radio, and Grant instinctively reached underneath the FBI jacket to the 9mm Glock in his shoulder holster. It was a natural response to the heightened action, and it was hard to force himself to stay in the van, but he did.

Grant pumped his left hand again, doing his best to stem the adrenaline coursing through his veins, and then winced from a sharp pinch between his fingers. He glanced down at the gold band around his ring finger, which had caught a piece of skin. He gave the ring a little twist then quickly returned his focus to the house as the radio chatter died down.

"House secure," Hickem said. "We have the girl, send in the medical team."

Grant planted both boots on the ground and jogged toward the house, falling in right behind the stretcher and two paramedics.

Inside, the house smelled like piss, and Grant saw Anthony Myers flat on the floor with his hands cuffed behind his back and at least three rifles trained on the back of his head.

"You're not supposed to be here!" Myers gave a few heavy, labored breaths, his face sweaty and red and his long black, greasy hair clinging to his forehead. "I just needed more time! I could have saved us! I could have done it!"

"Shut up!" One of the agents pressed his barrel harder into Myers's skull, and the rant ended.

"Detective Grant." Hickem was farther down the hall and motioned for him to come. He passed the girl as she was loaded onto a stretcher. She looked pale and weak, but unharmed. The pair of medics strapped her down and wheeled her out of the house.

Hickem stood at the entry to a room, his mask off, shaking his head. "Looks like you were right. He was planning on doing it tomorrow. Had the date circled on the calendar, and everything ready to go."

Grant craned his neck around the door to get a look for himself. Plastic sheets lined the floor and walls. A series of knives were displayed on a white cloth, increasing in size from left to right. A mattress with white sheets and a single pillow was in the middle of the floor. The bastard even set candles out.

"I didn't think he'd be so theatrical about it," Hickem said.

"People who twist words and their meanings often do so because of an already twisted mind." Grant took a single step inside the room but didn't dare to go farther. If he lingered too long it would become too real, and he'd seen enough of these things in his career.

When the ambassador's daughter was taken, Myers had killed both members of her security detail, and then with their blood he had written on the sidewalk where they were slain, "Truly, truly, I say to you, unless one is born again he cannot see the kingdom of God."

"I'm glad we brought you on board when we did," Hickem said.

But Grant was still staring at the bed. He wasn't sure if Myers would have raped the girl before he killed her, but it wasn't out of the realm of possibility. He was just thankful that it was nothing more than a could-have-been.

"You'll need to put him on suicide watch," Grant said. "He's failed in his mission, and he'll want to join his heavenly Father as quickly as possible."

Hickem glanced back into the living room where Myers was being pulled outside and whisked off to the nearest detention center to await booking and then the inevitable trial.

"I don't think that would be such a bad thing," Hickem said.

"It would be," Grant answered, watching Myers disappear into the back of a squad car. "He doesn't deserve to get anything he wants."

Hickem clapped Grant on the shoulder, and the two walked outside. "You know with the success of this case there'll be a lot of talk about bringing you on board," Hickem said. "Hell, they might even want you to try and take my job." Hickem laughed, but there was always a shred of truth in humor.

"I've got a caseload back at my station that needs attention," Grant said. "You'll have to handle the next political abduction by yourself."

The pair shook hands, and Hickem departed to have a word with the forensic team sweeping the building. With the girl safe and the suspect apprehended, Grant looked down at his watch and hit the stop button. Eleven hours, fifty-eight minutes, thirty-nine seconds. With the clock stopped, a weight lifted from Grant's shoulders, but when the phone in his pocket buzzed with "Mocks" plastered across the screen, he knew it wouldn't last much longer.

"How'd you find out so quickly?" Grant asked.

"I could tell you, but then I'd have to kill you." Mocks kept her tone serious and her volume quiet.

"Already make the news?" Grant asked, walking over to one of the vehicles about to head back into town where his car was parked.

"The FBI made an official statement on Twitter," Mocks answered.

Grant would bet his last dollar that they had two versions of that tweet ready. He climbed into the passenger seat, then the officer who was acting liaison for the local sheriff's department pulled onto the highway.

"You on your way back?" Mocks asked.

"Yeah, I'm about two hours away once I get to my car."

"Good, because I just had a mother call about her daughter. Says she skipped school today. I've got one of the rookies bringing her in now."

"Get the paperwork started," Grant said, his shoulders feeling instantly heavier. "I'll start making calls to the offices. Get them ready in case we need to press forward." He paused. "You think it's serious?"

"I don't know. She sounds like it's serious."

"They always do. I'll see you in a bit."

Grant hung up and winced from a very faint churn of the intestines just below his belly button. He glanced down to the wedding ring and then to his watch. He drew in a breath, cleared the timer, then started the countdown once more.

* * *

THE STATION WAS busy for midmorning. The shift change had already happened, but the news of the kidnapper's arrest had permeated the ranks of the department. A series of high fives and applause followed Grant all the way to his desk.

Officer Banks sat at the desk behind him, and Grant tapped the rookie on the shoulder. "Where is Mocks?"

Banks pointed toward the back. "She's in Interrogation

Room Three. And, hey, nice work with the ambassador's daughter. That's gotta win you some brownie points, huh?"

"Yeah," Grant said. "Thanks."

The congratulations slipped off him like water on a seal. Grant's mind had already shifted gears to a new case. The well-wishes and applause wouldn't help him now. Once the clock restarts, the score goes back to zero.

"Sorry I'm late," Grant said, stepping inside the room.

The woman turned, dabbing a tissue at the puffy skin underneath her eyes, which were bloodshot from crying. The features of her face were pulled in tight, and her skittish movements reminded him of a shrew, scared of anything that moved too quickly.

Grant extended his hand. "Mrs. Givens, my name is Detective Grant." He lowered his voice. "I'm sorry to hear about your daughter."

"It's Miss," she said, sniffling. "But thank you, Detective Grant."

Grant placed a comforting hand on Dana Givens's shoulder. "Please, you can call me Chase."

Dana nodded quickly, a taut smile accompanying a whimper through closed lips. Grant took a seat next to the mother rather than across the table where Mocks sat. His partner was a brilliant detective, but she lacked the human touch that was often necessary in their line of work. Though he did notice she managed to get the mother something to drink and the box of tissues. Then again, that was in the training manual.

Detective Susan Mullocks was a small woman, barely clearing five feet and a hundred pounds. Petite was the word most used to describe her, but she was anything but. Mocks leaned back in her chair, no notepad, no recorder, every answer from Ms. Givens's mouth retained in her memory. The only tool used in her interrogation was a green Bic lighter. She flicked it on and off between questions. It helped her think. And it was a reminder of a past that kept her looking forward.

The woman had been through a lot, a history littered with pain; it was one of the reasons why she always wore those long-sleeved shirts, even in the summertime. It was a different kind of pain than Grant had experienced, but he always believed you never know about the rocks in other people's shoes. She brushed the dark-brown bangs from her forehead to behind her ear, exposing the massive rock of her wedding ring, and gave the lighter another flick.

"I know you've been answering a lot of my partner's questions, so I won't waste time repeating some of the things I'm sure she's already asked, but I just want to let you know I've already reached out to state and federal officials, and I've already spoken with my lieutenant about scheduling an Amber Alert if it's needed," Grant said.

"Of course it's needed!" Dana blurted the words out like a machine gun, and the sudden outburst surprised even her, as she quickly covered her mouth and shut her eyes. "I'm sorry. I'm sorry. I just—" She drew in a quick breath, and her lower lip quivered. "It's just that this isn't like Mallory. She doesn't just skip school. She doesn't run off. I'm telling you someone took her."

Grant placed a hand on Dana Givens's arm and nodded. "And we're going to do everything we can to find out what happened. In the meantime, do you have anyone that you can call to come and pick you up, Miss Givens?"

"No. I'll just take the bus home."

"I'll have one of our officers take you back." Grant reached into his pocket and removed one of his business cards and handed it to Ms. Givens as he helped her up and out of the room. "If you need anything, that card has my cell number on it. Any updates that I have in regards to your daughter I'll let you know personally."

"Please, you have to find her." Dana clutched Grant by both arms and squeezed tight, her nails digging through the cloth of the sleeves on his shirt. "You have to."

"We'll do everything we can," Grant said then motioned to Banks, who came over and took Dana by the shoulder. Banks escorted Dana through the office, and Mocks gave Grant a gentle shove on the arm.

"You wanted to say it, didn't you?" Mocks asked.

Department protocol was clear when it came to missing persons cases. No matter the circumstance, no matter the evidence or testimony, an officer of the law never told a victim's family that they would catch the individuals responsible. It provided nothing but a false sense of hope, and it put the department in libel territory, especially in the digital age of social media where anything could go viral.

"When I'm not here I need you to take notes," Grant said.

"Why? You can just read the report when I'm done." Mocks reclined in the chair and stretched her arms back, her left hand still clutching that lighter.

Grant raised both eyebrows, waiting for his partner to speak. "Are you going to keep me in suspense?"

Mocks rocked forward in her chair quickly, her forearms thumping against the table. "Dana Givens, twenty-nine-year-old mother who got knocked up when she was seventeen. The girl's father is Chet Hoverty, some bum that never stuck around. Girl is twelve years old and a sixth grader over at Southside Middle. Mother works over sixty hours a week at a diner in downtown Seattle, barely makes ends meet. Classic case of a single parent who isn't in touch with her kid. No boyfriends, no family in the area."

If the girl went to Southside Middle, then she lived in a

rough area, but Grant imagined the mother's waitressing job didn't provide the best income. "Anything on the dad?"

Mocks looked up, the harsh fluorescent lighting of the office exposing the freckles that dotted her pale cheeks. "I ran a query on him before I took the mom into the room. The nutsack that provided the needed sperm for their union has a rap sheet like an encyclopedia. And you never answered my question."

"What question?" Grant asked.

"Why you didn't promise her we'd find her daughter," Mocks said.

"Your realism has rubbed off on me, Mocks," Grant said. Though the truth was that he'd tossed those promises around too frequently when he first joined the missing persons unit. And he found out quickly that he couldn't keep all of the promises he made. At the time the promises were just something he had to do. It was his way of coping. It was how he worked through his own broken promises.

"You know I never skipped school," Mocks said, lifting up the picture of Mallory Givens that her mother had brought in. "Until the first time."

Grant took a seat and prepped the media package for the Amber Alert. "And I'm sure it wasn't your last time." He lifted the sleeve of his shirt and exposed his digital wristwatch and saw the timer already approaching the three-hour mark. The first six to twelve hours of a missing persons case were the most crucial. And if they wanted to find Mallory Givens alive, then they were going to have to pick up the pace.

3

*A*lready into hour four, Grant completed the description of the girl and attached Mallory's picture as the finishing touch. Mallory had short brown hair, freckles on her cheeks, green eyes, and according to her mother would have never left the house without her pink backpack and orange rain slicker. Though if someone did take her, Grant wouldn't imagine those things would be around for very long.

All of the information had to be pried from Mocks's mind vault, and she always reveled in the knowledge of things she knew that Grant didn't. In a lot of ways she was the younger sister he never had or really wanted.

"You all caught up?" Mocks asked, taking a bite out of her frosted strawberry Pop-Tart. It was her midmorning snack. She said they helped her think better.

"Yeah," Grant answered, finishing up the report and sliding it into the folder. "I think we've got all of our t's crossed and our i's dotted."

Crumbs sprinkled onto Mocks's shirt, and she brushed them aside as she took another bite that quickly replaced the

Pop-Tart particles she wiped away. "So how do you want to handle this one?" Despite her God-given ability as a detective, and at times her inopportune mouth, she still looked to him for guidance.

"I'm heading over to the school," Grant said, sliding his arm through his jacket sleeve. The last night's rain had brought with it a new cold front, and even at the end of March it wasn't going to get above fifty today. "I need you to go to the Givens's house and scope out the girl's room, see what you can find."

"You hear back from any of the agencies?" Mocks asked.

"No, but I'll call you when I do." Grant walked backwards and pointed a finger at Mocks. "And be nice to Ms. Givens when you get there, all right? She's unlikely to have made any progress in calming her nerves."

Mocks devoured the last bite of her Pop-Tart, smacking her lips loudly, talking with her mouth still full. "I'm always nice. It's just not always perceived that way."

There were a few more congratulations on the way out the door from his previous case, all of which were ignored save for one, which came from the captain, who had stepped out of his office to shake Grant's hand personally.

"Fantastic work, Detective." Captain Hill was pushing retirement age and had accepted his fate as a desk jockey for however many months he had left. "You've made this department look very, very good."

"Thank you, Captain."

"Just got off the phone with the mayor, and they want to give you some type of award." The captain gave a hearty laugh. "Seems that ambassador fellow from—say, where was the girl from again?"

"It was the ambassador to the Philippines, sir."

"Yes, well, he wants to thank you personally for the matter. You have a date with him tomorrow morning."

With the fresh case on his desk, it was hard to get excited about something that would interrupt the new investigation. Under normal circumstances he would have declined, but with the political persuasion the ambassador carried, he didn't think it was something he could avoid. And in those situations, especially when it came to politics, he found it best to go with the flow.

"Thank you for letting me know, sir," Grant said.

"We'll see you tomorrow."

The captain waddled back to his office, and Grant lingered in the station's foyer. "Yeah. Tomorrow."

Grant stopped by the lieutenant's office, and his direct supervisor wasn't at his desk, which was a rarity. There were times when Grant thought the man was a part of the desk and chair he always sat at. It was hard to imagine him doing anything else other than paperwork, but the lieutenant had his own history with the department, one that involved a shootout from fifteen years ago. A bit of a taboo subject no one spoke about, and because of the hush-hush nature, the lieutenant had developed into a bit of an urban legend. Grant tossed the folder with Mallory Givens's paperwork onto the lieutenant's desk then went outside and hopped in his car.

The ride over to Mallory's school took longer than he expected, the traffic already in full swing from the lunch crowd. The middle school was a more modern structure among the decaying neighborhood that surrounded it, an effort from taxpayers' dollars to help perk up the zip code, though the new school didn't fix the homeless or drug epidemic that was consuming the area.

With all of the kids still in class, the hallways were large and empty. Lockers lined the walls on the way to the main office, and when Grant stepped inside he was greeted by an elderly woman with thick glasses and knobby, arthritic fingers. She looked up from behind the receptionist's desk with an expression that was no doubt intended to make kids feel like they were in more trouble than they actually were. "Can I help you?"

Grant flashed his badge. "I need to speak with the principal."

"Yes?"

Grant turned and saw a woman dressed in slacks and a business jacket. She had short-cropped blond hair, wore no jewelry, but still looked like she could attend a high-price-ticket gala event somewhere, and looked nothing like the principal he remembered having as a middle schooler. Not in the slightest.

"I'm Detective Grant with Seattle PD," Grant said, extending a hand that the principal shook firmly. "I was hoping I could take a few moments of your time and speak with you about one of your students."

"Of course." The principal's heels fell silently on the carpet, and Grant followed her back into her office. She gestured to the seats in front of her desk and then shut the door. "I'm assuming this is about Mallory Givens?"

Grant reached inside his jacket and removed a notepad and pen. While Mocks didn't have to take notes, he did. "What do you know about the situation"—he glanced down at the nameplate on the desk—"Principal Tanner?"

"You can call me Michelle." Her red lips spread wide in a smile and contrasted heavily against her pale skin. She reminded him more of an attorney than a principal. Her eyes were focused, never straying off him. And they were bright blue. Beautifully blue.

"Michelle," Grant said. "What do you know so far?"

"Mallory's first-period teacher informed me that she wasn't in class," Michelle said. "When a student isn't accounted for we notify the front office, and then Mrs. Harlow"—who Grant was betting was the old crow at the front desk—"cross-references that against any callouts from parents. If the student isn't on that list, then we notify the parents via phone call. The same procedure was followed in this scenario, but after the parent is notified, that's where our job ends."

Grant scribbled a few notes down, nodding along while Michelle spoke. When he lifted his head again she smiled. His cheeks flushed, and he removed his coat. He was suddenly sweating. "Was Mallory in trouble often?"

Michelle shook her head, clasping her hands together, and Grant stole a quick glance at the bare left ring finger. "Mallory was an excellent student. Honor roll all year long. Never acted up in class. As principal you get to know the really bad students, and the really good ones." She smiled. "Mallory was the best."

"Has your resource officer noticed anything out of the ordinary in regards to adults in the area? Any irregular visits or sightings?" Grant asked.

"I have weekly meetings with him, and he's never mentioned anything," Michelle answered. "I can have Mrs. Harlow pull the visitor log if you'd like."

"That would be very helpful." Grant paused, and for a moment he forgot where he was.

"Anything else?" Michelle asked.

"Um, yes," Grant said, tucking the pen and notepad into his jacket pocket, hoping that this second wave of heat didn't flush his cheeks too much. "I wanted to speak with some of Mallory's teachers."

"I'll have Mrs. Harlow print out a schedule. I'm sure one of her teachers is on their free period right now."

It turned out there was a teacher on her free period. And it had been the same teacher that had alerted the principal that Mallory was not in class. Ann Colthern was a mousy woman and fit every stereotypical version of the eccentric

English teacher. Her hair was wild and frizzy, sprouting from her head in random, untamed directions. She wore glasses as thick as coke bottles, and she curled her body inward as if opening up would expose her to an inescapable doom.

"I just can't believe this is happening," Mrs. Colthern said, dabbing a tissue under each eye, neither of which looked to be wet. "She was such a sweet girl."

Grant ignored the show. He'd interviewed enough people in his lifetime to know when someone was playing it up. Not that he doubted the woman's distress; he just didn't think it was as bad as she was letting on. "And did Mallory mention anything to you about trouble at home?"

"No, but I do know her mother works a lot." Mrs. Colthern shook her head. "Single mother. I heard the father is a deadbeat. Poor thing doesn't even know him. That sort of thing can cause a lot of trauma, especially in the mind of a young girl."

"Mallory told you this?" Grant asked.

"Well, no, but you know how people talk."

"I do," Grant replied, ignoring the scowl Mrs. Colthern made after the remark. "Is there anyone else she was close with here at the school? Friends? Other teachers?"

Mrs. Colthern shook her head, again adding a few dry dabs beneath her eye with the corner of her tissue. "She kept to herself a lot. Many things have changed since I was a student, but the intelligent loner as an outcast isn't one of them." She reached for a stack of papers on her desk, shuffled through them, then handed one of them to Grant.

A red A+ was circled at the top, accented with a smiley face, and Grant saw the name Mallory Givens written across the top.

"She was such a talented writer," Mrs. Colthern said. "Always scribbling in her notebook. She was one of those students a teacher comes across maybe once a decade that makes you remember why you got into the profession in the first place." She smiled. "Such a treat."

Grant had never excelled in writing, but he could appreciate a good yarn. And from the small snippet he viewed of Mallory's prose, he admitted that it was entertaining.

"Do you have any more of her work?" Grant asked.

"Of course!" Mrs. Colthern spun around and opened one of the drawers of a filing cabinet behind her desk. She shuffled through the folders and then pulled one out that was four inches thick. Still smiling, she handed over the documents. "Mallory was always doing assignments for extra credit. Not that she needed it for the grades. She just enjoyed the challenge."

"Thank you for your time, Mrs. Colthern."

"If you need anything else, please, let me know." Mrs. Colthern grabbed Grant by the arm, her small hands unable to curl all the way around his bicep, which she squeezed tightly.

Grant gave a curt nod. "I will. Thank you."

When Grant stepped out of the classroom and back into the hallway, there were a few dings over the PA system which signaled the end of the current period, and a few seconds later the empty hallway was flooded with middle schoolers.

They traveled in packs, clusters of friends discussing anything but school. They chased after one another, the hall a cacophony of shrieks, laughter, and chatter. For a moment Grant was transported back in time, almost twenty-five years, to when he walked the halls of his own middle school. He could still remember his friends, the excitement, the drama, the fear that accompanied growing up in the jungle that was the public school system. He remembered students like Mallory, and while he didn't participate in their ridicule, he didn't do anything to stop it because it would have exposed him, and if there was one thing kids held onto during this phase in their life, it was safety in numbers.

Grant shuffled his way through the hordes of students and found Michelle speaking with Mrs. Harlow in the office. She stepped out of their glass-encased box of an administration office and handed him a folder.

"This was everything she had," Michelle said. "If you need any—Jimmy! Slow down!" The boy did as he was told, and she turned back to Grant, giving a nervous laugh. "Sorry about that."

"Remind me to never run in the halls," Grant said then kicked himself for the stupid line. "I appreciate the help." He reached into his pocket with his left hand and extended his card. "If you think of anything else, just call." He paused. "I'd love to hear from you."

And now it was Michelle's turn to blush, but as she took the card from his hand, she paused when her eyes caught the gold band around Grant's ring finger. He noticed her pause and then followed her line of sight to the ring. She let go of the card and took a step back.

"I can just call the department if I have anything," Michelle said, crossing her arms. "I'm sure they can put me through to you." The bell chimed, signaling the end of the transition into the next period. "Have a nice day, Detective Grant."

Michelle Tanner disappeared into her office, and Grant remained frozen in the empty hall as the last few classroom doors shut, with his hand still extended with his card. Finally, after a minute, he lowered his arm and then trudged out of Southside Middle and into the parking lot.

Grant flexed his hand, looking down at the ring. He'd forgotten it was there, which was easy to do since he never took it off. And even if he did, that gold circle would never disappear. It represented a past that he couldn't shake. When he reached his car door, a gust of wind gave an abnormal chill that seeped into his bones. He got inside the car quickly, and then his phone buzzed. It was Mocks.

"What'd you find at the house?" Grant asked.

"Not much," Mocks answered. "There weren't any signs of forced entry, and the girl's room had a window that led to a fire escape. The window was still unlocked, so it looks like she may have left of her own will."

"Yeah, that fits with what I'm thinking as well. Both the principal and one of her teachers confirmed that Mallory was a loner. I think her English teacher may have been her best friend."

Mocks snorted. "Yeah, I don't think she was winning any popularity contests."

"Did you find a notebook or journal anywhere in her room?" Grant asked.

"A lot of books, but nothing like that. Why?"

"Her English teacher said she always had a notebook she was scribbling things down in. If we found that, we might have a better idea of where she went and who went with her." And the more and more Grant thought about it, the more he started to think that Mallory really did leave of her own accord. It seemed like the only thing going for her at the time was the fact that she was good in school. Her mother was never at home, and anyone that spent time with her would have realized that. Especially adults who could use that to their advantage.

"Listen," Mocks said, breaking Grant's train of thought. "The dad's probation officer got back to me. It looks like our father-of-the-year broke parole. He hasn't heard from him in over a month. But I pulled some old property records, and it looks like the dad's uncle has some property upstate."

Grant arched his eyebrows. "Upstate from Seattle?"

"Yeah, so you can probably guess who just jumped up on

our most wanted list."

"I can."

Seattle had a few growing problems. The first was the number of sex traffickers using ports to smuggle bodies from Pacific nations. Most were young girls, poor and desperate and tricked into thinking that they were heading for a better life. The second was the homeless epidemic. And the third was drugs, specifically opioids and meth that had manifested and been cultivated in Washington State's northern border. It was an easy location to smuggle drugs from our great neighbors to the north and into the wooded areas where drug labs had popped up like camping sites.

"We should ride together," Grant said, getting into his car. "You head back to the station, and I'll pick you up on the way."

"My money's on deadbeat dad," Mocks said. "Nine out of ten times it's always family."

Grant started the engine. "We'll find out when we find him."

* * *

CIVILIZATION DISAPPEARED the farther north they drove. Every mile Grant saw fewer buildings and more trees. But that was the way the people who lived up here liked it. There were times when Grant pondered the life of isolation. He imagined it was incredibly simple. Simple could be good. But if he was alone, then he'd be stuck in his own mind all day, every day. And that would drive him mad.

Mocks flicked her Bic lighter. It was her own way of dealing with the nerves. Grant didn't mind the quiet though. It gave him time to think.

But there was a roadblock that kept appearing: Principal Tanner. No matter how hard he tried, he couldn't get the woman off of his mind. And with the case in front of him, that distraction was dangerous, both personally and professionally.

"How did they communicate?" Mocks asked, peeking out from behind her shroud of silence. "Mallory and her dad?" She turned to face Grant. "She didn't have a phone, and the dad's background didn't strike me as someone who would become a pen pal."

Grant shook his head, ridding himself of Michelle's smile. "They could have met somewhere. The mom worked really late. It gave Mallory plenty of time to leave and come back without Mom being the wiser."

The turn off the highway was onto a dirt road, which was still wet from the morning rain, and Grant was forced to slow his speed down the one-lane path. They passed two trailers on their journey deeper into the woods, and their inhabitants scurried from their lawn chairs and back inside the moment they saw the car.

"Looks like they've seen cops up here before," Grant said.

"I didn't think we were that obvious," Mocks replied.

"Radio dispatch, give them an update on our location and have a unit on standby in case we need it." Grant reached for his phone and checked the reception. "My phone doesn't have a signal."

There had been a few cases of missing persons that had led Grant this far north before, and he discovered that the folks who enjoyed living on their own did not enjoy others meddling in their affairs. And when push came to shove, they were not afraid to shove back.

They arrived at the trailer that matched the address Mocks found from the property records, and the brakes squeaked when Grant stopped the car.

"You think he'll run?" Mocks asked, unclipping her seat belt.

"He might," Grant answered.

The sky was overcast, which only made the cold linger. It was worse up in the mountains. But the cold wind also carried the sounds of nature: birds, insects, and the light rustle of leaves. Grant would have considered it peaceful if not for the purpose of their mission.

Both Grant and Mocks kept one hand on the butt of their service pistols as they approached the trailer. There were a few chairs in the yard, along with the truck that towed the trailer up here. The hunk of junk didn't look like it ran anymore, but Grant made sure to box it in with his car anyway. The windows were taped over, a telltale sign that it was a drug lab.

A rusted awning sat above the front door, and Grant pounded hard enough to shake the whole trailer and loosen some rust flakes that drifted to the ground. "Seattle PD! Open up!"

Mocks kept her head on a swivel, her eyes scanning the area while Grant watched the door. It was quiet for a few seconds, and just before he pounded his fist on the door again, there was a loud crack that came from the back of the trailer. Mocks sprinted around the side, and Grant bust down the front door.

A wave of heat and the stench of chemicals flooded his senses, stinging his eyes and nose. He blindly stumbled into the trailer and, through the back door exit where the suspect had fled, saw Mocks chasing him down, and he joined the pursuit, sprinting into the woods.

The thick trees provided plenty of cover for their suspect to hide, and as the man darted between the trees, Grant thought he'd lost their man at least a half-dozen times.

"Freeze! Police department!" Both Grant and Mocks repeated the order on their sprint, but Mr. Hoverty didn't stop.

A rock formation appeared, and Mr. Hoverty climbed over it to the other side with ease. Grant motioned for Mocks to stop, but his partner continued forward.

"Mocks, no!" Grant said.

Hoverty emerged at the top of the rock's ledge, now armed with a rifle, and fired. Bullets disfigured the tree Mocks ducked behind, and Grant raised his 9mm Glock in retaliation.

The ring of the gunshot, along with the recoil, paralyzed him for a moment. It'd been two years since he'd fired his weapon in the field, and he'd forgotten how harsh the sound of the gunshot was without ear protection.

But the bullet did its job as Hoverty ducked back behind the rock while Grant and Mocks exchanged a glance from behind their respective trees. She motioned to curve around to the back side and take him by surprise. Grant nodded, the ringing still piercing his ears.

Grant craned his neck around the tree trunk, his right shoulder scraping against the rough pine. He immediately directed his eyes toward the cluster of rocks which provided plenty of juts and mounds for Hoverty to maneuver.

Two leaping steps and Grant ducked behind the cover of the next tree, repeating the process of ensuring Hoverty was still behind the rocks before each adrenaline-fueled sprint. Between runs, another gunshot thundered from the rocks, and Grant saw Mocks crouched low behind one of the thinner trees where Hoverty had pinned her down with gunfire.

Grant stepped around the trunk of his own tree, exposing himself to gunfire, and managed to squeeze off three shots that sent Hoverty cowering behind the rocks. Grant glanced left and saw a clear path up the left side of the rocky protrusion. He sprinted up the uneven slope, his lungs catching fire from the cold air. His eyes stayed glued to the ridgeline, knowing that any moment Hoverty could appear over the side and blow him off the face of the earth. But he didn't.

Grant leapt over the ledge, Hoverty too busy reloading his rifle to notice the detective barreling down on him. Grant tackled Hoverty, and the pair rolled down the back side, elbows, knees, and limbs smacking against the hard and jagged edges of rock, the cold amplifying the pain by ten.

Their tumble ended at the base of the rocks, and Grant and Hoverty rolled onto the soil and leaves. Both the Glock and rifle had left their owners' hands, and Grant did his best to corral the pain from the collisions down the mountain, searching for the pistol.

Finally, Grant spied the Glock in the dirt, and he scrambled on all fours toward it until a heavy weight flattened him back to the earth.

Hoverty rammed his fist into the detective's lower back and left side. Grant jammed his elbow into Hoverty's rib and knocked him off. A gunshot rang out, and for a moment Grant thought Hoverty had gotten hold of his rifle. But instead of pain, he heard Mocks's voice.

"Grant! You all right?"

The combination of the punches and the fall from the rocks left him groaning as he pushed himself off the ground slowly. "Yeah." He retrieved the pistol, holstered the weapon, and then removed his handcuffs. Grant manhandled Hoverty onto his stomach and pinched the steel around his wrists nice and tight. With the suspect apprehended, Grant took a moment to catch his breath while Mocks finally lowered her own weapon.

"You're sure you're all right?" Mocks asked.

"Just need to catch my breath." Grant nodded toward Hoverty. "Let's get him back to the trailer. See why he was in such a hurry to run."

4

*G*rant's inquiry into why Hoverty had run didn't take much investigation. The inside of the trailer was filled with enough drug paraphernalia to supply meth to the entire state of Washington. And in addition to the drugs, Grant found a trove of unregistered firearms, along with a filing cabinet filled with documents that seemed out of place.

Mocks poked her head inside just as Grant started sifting through them. "Backup is on their way. Might be a while though since the closest unit is in another county." She gestured to the cabinet. "What'd you find?"

Blank forms with legal jargon plastered over the pages. "They look like government forms." Grant shook his head. "It's nothing I recognize though."

Mocks stepped inside, and Grant handed her a stack of the papers. "Christ, the whole cabinet is full of them."

Grant stepped outside, a handful of the papers still in his hand, and made his way to the car where Hoverty sat in the backseat, handcuffed. He flung the door open and shoved the papers into Hoverty's face. "What are these?"

Hoverty kept his face forward. His cheeks were thick with a matted beard, and his forehead and neck beaded sweat, despite the frigid cold. Grant figured he must have been coming down off of something. The man wouldn't stop shaking.

"You've got a trailer full of drugs and firearms, and you assaulted two police officers," Grant said. "You don't have a lot of leverage right now."

"All that stuff was in the fuckin' place when I got there, man." Hoverty kept his head low when he spoke. "All I do is show up and make the drugs. They don't tell me nothin' else."

"Who's they?" Grant asked.

Hoverty chuckled. "Like I'm gonna tell you, shithead?"

Grant glanced down at his watch, the timer just now reaching the five-and-a-half-hour mark. Once they crossed into six-hour territory, it was a race to find Mallory before it hit twelve. After that the chances of finding her were cut in half every subsequent hour. There wasn't time for delicacy.

Grant one-handed the back of Hoverty's neck and yanked him from the car. The man couldn't have weighed more than a buck-fifty, and Grant tossed him to the ground with ease. Hoverty smacked the dirt and let out a loud groan. "What the fuck, man?"

Every cop had a threshold. Some were shorter than others. Grant had always considered himself to have a very long one, but there were a few times where he dared to peek over the edge. He'd seen what the bottom of that cliff looked like, and the last time he inched his toes over the side he nearly killed himself. It was the farthest he'd ever gone. There was always great perspective when faced against the finality of death. He hadn't been there for over two years, but he wasn't afraid to at least toy with the idea. And that was always bad for suspects.

Grant towered over Hoverty, who lay pinned on his back

like an exposed turtle. Grant thrust a finger in his face, and he felt blood rush to his cheeks from the sudden burst of anger. "Who's your boss?"

Hoverty lifted his head from the dirt, his beard smeared in soil. He shook his head in defiance, so Grant wrapped his hand around Hoverty's throat. All the while Mocks just leaned against the car and crossed her arms. She knew him. She trusted him.

"You tell me right now, or I'll take you back into the woods and beat you with your own goddamn rifle," Grant said.

Hoverty's cheeks flushed a crimson red as Grant tightened his grip. "You don't have the balls."

Grant looked to his partner. "What do you think, Mocks? Is Mr. Hoverty resisting arrest?"

Mocks tilted her head to the side, while Hoverty choked for air. "Why, yes, I believe he is."

"Bullshit!" Hoverty said, a small spray of spittle ejecting from his lips.

Grant slammed his fist into the left side of Hoverty's rib cage, and a raspy scream escaped the choke hold Grant had clamped on his throat.

"Who are you working for?" Grant asked.

Hoverty kept his mouth sealed, but one more punch to the ribs and he nodded furiously. Grant released his hand, and Hoverty hacked and coughed, wheezing as he inhaled, and Grant wiped the snot from under his nose with his sleeve. It'd been a while since he had to work someone like that.

"Christ, man," Hoverty said. "I'm working for Baez's crew, all right?"

Unfortunately it was a name that every officer in the state of Washington knew. His gang had helped the drug epidemic become so bad in Seattle that the DEA had set up a command post in the city. Baez had turned Seattle into the northwest drug hub of the United States.

"How the hell did you guys even know I was here?" Hoverty asked. "My probation officer didn't even bother to come looking for me!"

The longer Hoverty spoke, the more Grant realized that the man had no idea what happened to his daughter. Grant stepped toward Hoverty, and the man recoiled.

"Your daughter is missing," Grant said. "Have any of the people you work with threatened to take her? Owe any bad debts you can't pay off?"

Hoverty scrunched his face up. "What? Hell no! I don't fuck around with these people. Shit, no one even knows I have a daughter. I don't ever see her. I don't call her. Whatever happened to that girl isn't my problem."

Grant picked him up and shoved him into the backseat and slammed the door shut. Mocks followed Grant back to the trailer, both of them quiet until they reached the awning.

"You've had a lot of excitement for one day," Mocks said. "You turning into an adrenaline junkie on me?"

"I don't think I have the stomach for that sort of thing," Grant said, and now that he had retreated from the threshold, his body grew tired. He leaned against the trailer for support and wiped his forehead with the back of his hand. "What are the odds that this guy got in too deep with the drug cartel and they took his daughter as leverage?"

"Slim, considering there wasn't any ransom note," Mocks answered. "Not to mention that the guy doesn't give a shit what happens to his daughter either way."

"The two possibilities here were family or a child predator. And I think it's safe to say we can cross this guy off the list," Grant said. "Someone has been working Mallory Givens for a while and finally convinced her to hop on board."

"Which means our guy is still on the loose."

ONCE BACKUP ARRIVED to case the scene and log evidence, Mocks and Grant took Mr. Hoverty back to the station for processing. Normally they would have dropped him off at the local precinct, but seeing as how they claimed jurisdiction over the case, as well as Grant's desire to make sure the piece of crap got what he deserved, they took care of him personally.

Hoverty demanded to speak to a lawyer for nearly half the trip back and vowed that both Grant and Mocks would lose their badges for what they did to him, but the moment they stepped into the station, the gusto ran out of him.

Grant stopped at the front desk on their way inside and motioned for Mocks to go ahead with processing. "Give the DEA a call and let them know we found a lab they can take a look at. They'll have more resources to deal with that mess than we do. Once Hoverty is processed, we're done with him. I wanna follow up with the lieutenant about the Amber Alert request."

"Tell him he better speed up the process," Mocks said. "You want me to call the mom and give her an update on her ex-lover?"

"No," Grant answered. "He's a dead end, and I don't want to cause the woman any more grief." Grant walked to the lieutenant's office and this time found his CO at his desk, buried in paperwork. Grant knocked to grab his attention.

"Yes, come in." Lieutenant Furst didn't even bother lifting his head.

"Sir, have you had a chance to look over the Amber Alert request I submitted earlier today?" Grant asked.

"Yes." The lieutenant remained quiet for a moment before he lifted his head. "I heard about the case with the ambassador. You keep that up, and pretty soon they'll make you sit at my desk." He smiled, and when he did, it accentuated the scarring on the left side of his face. It spread from the top left of his eye all the way down to his jawline. A constant reminder of just how dangerous their line of work really was.

"You know I'm not much of a desk man, sir."

"No," Lieutenant Furst answered. "You're not." He reached for a stack of paperwork and shuffled through it until he found the request Grant submitted. He scanned it a few times, flipping over the pages, pausing to reread certain sections. "And what's your opinion on it, Detective?"

Grant took a breath, running through the information already in his head, the pieces of a puzzle starting to come together in the early stages of investigative work.

"The girl fits the description of a classic loner," Grant answered. "No real friends. Mom works a lot so the two never talk. Loved by her teachers, but shunned by her peers. We just brought her father in, and while he is into some bad stuff, I don't think he is involved, at least not directly. All in all she's the perfect target for a pedophile." He took another breath and then nodded. "So, yeah, I think someone convinced the girl to run away and now she's being held against her will. Clock is running out on this one, Lieutenant."

The chair squeaked when Furst leaned back. He was a young man, only slightly older than Grant. There had been speculation that if Grant hadn't taken his leave of absence two years ago and stayed in Homicide, that seat would have been his. He was an exceptional detective, he got along with everyone, and he knew how to handle himself in front of the press. Ideally, he was the poster boy for the department, and the chief would have loved to groom him to climb the ranks.

And there was a time when Grant saw that for himself. But those ambitions died years ago.

"You've already got a media package ready?" the lieutenant asked.

"Yes, sir," Grant answered, absentmindedly rubbing his thumb over the gold band on the same hand.

The lieutenant flipped to the last page and then scrawled his signature onto the paperwork. "Just make sure that all of the agencies are up to speed. I'll schedule some overtime for any officers who want to help with the call-ins. Any leads?"

"Not yet," Grant answered. "But once we get eyes out into the field we will." He tapped his knuckles on the doorframe and then left the lieutenant to the rest of his paperwork, a renewed spring to his step. Amber Alerts weren't anything the department took lightly. The coordination between local, state, and federal officials made it a bear to manage, but it was highly effective. With the number of eyes in the street and the widespread use of social media, Amber Alerts gave a boost to the likelihood of finding the kid before it was too late. And when it came to life and death, any percent increase of success was welcome.

When Grant returned to his desk, Mocks leaned forward, her eyebrows arched as she opened another strawberry Pop-Tart. "The verdict?"

"We're good to go," Grant answered. "I'll let Homicide know." He walked backward, still talking to Mocks. "You call the DEA?"

"Our hands are washed clean," Mocks answered.

"Good, because once that alert goes out, we'll be in watch mode on the hotline and social media."

Mocks rolled her eyes. "My favorite part of the day." She bit into her cardboard pastry and then picked up the receiver on her desk phone.

Homicide was always notified during an Amber Alert for

preparation in case the child was found deceased. Minors involved in homicides always jumped to the top of the priority list. Aside from the simple fact that officers felt a certain moral obligation to bring justice to victims that were children, with all the press and media attention they garnered it was impossible to ignore them. They were always Grant's most hated cases during his time with Homicide.

Both Marcus and Franz were at their desks, the two slouched so low in their chairs that they were practically lying down. He'd worked with Marcus just before he'd left the unit, and while they never had anything against one another, they never spent enough time together to be friends. And during Grant's last days on the unit, he wasn't exactly the most pleasant individual to be around.

"There he is," Franz said, taking a quarter-turn swivel in his chair and spreading his arms wide with an accompanying flabby grin. "Seattle's soon-to-be favorite son. You have your eye on becoming mayor in the next few years or something?"

Grant gave a lighthearted grin as Franz collapsed his arms to his sides. "Sounds like my perfect nightmare." He turned to Marcus. "The lieutenant is about to initiate an Amber Alert. Wanted to give you guys a heads-up."

"Shit, really?" Marcus asked, letting out a sigh. "How old?"

"Twelve. Female. She's a sixth grader over at Southside Middle."

"How long has she been missing?" Franz asked.

Grant glanced back down at the watch, the timer just now passing six hours. "Too long." The detectives nodded gravely, and Grant left before he was forced to reminisce about old times.

In Homicide there was only one guarantee with every case, and that was the fact that your victim was dead. At the start of his career in law enforcement, Grant wanted to join Homicide because he wanted to stop murderers from killing someone else. But as his schooling and career progressed, he found it rare to find a serial case.

Most murders were passionate, violent one-offs. It was by someone who was drunk, or jealous, angry, bitter, you name it and Grant had seen it. Five years ago when the vagrant problem was at its peak, there were gangs that would force new members to kill a homeless person as initiation. It was the only case Grant ever received in terms of serial killings. And what was worse was that it barely made the evening news. Twenty homeless men and women were murdered, and no one cared.

The missing persons unit was the fresh change that Grant needed when he came back from his leave of absence. While his work in Homicide may have provided closure for the victims involved, he was tired of receiving the cases too late. In missing persons there was always the chance, no matter how grim or how small, that he could find the person and bring them back before something worse happened to them. The fires of hope that he stoked for those families helped keep his own lit. A man needed hope. People needed hope. He needed hope.

Mocks set the phone down and reached into one of her drawers and removed a candy bar. She peeled the wrapper off the top of the Snickers and took a bite before she spoke, mumbling her words between chews. How the hell she snacked so much and stayed so skinny was a mystery he'd never solve.

"Parole officer thanked us for finding his guy." Mocks swallowed and then chomped off another large bite. "Said his boy will be going back on the inside for at least ten years this time. It's his third strike out on parole." She held up a fist like an umpire. "He's outa here!"

"Better finish that before the press conference." Grant checked his watch and then poked his head around toward the front desk where the first few news vans were already gathered. "We won't have to take questions yet, but the lieutenant will want us presentable."

Mocks flashed a nugget, caramel, and peanut grin and then reached for her coffee. "I'm presentable."

5

𝓘t wasn't but five minutes into the Amber Alert's initiation that the calls and messages started coming through. Everyone and their mother had seen Mallory Givens since the broadcast went live. But that was standard. With the number of tips they received, some of them were bound to be inaccurate. The obstacle now was sifting through the fake leads to find the real ones.

Another stack of call-ins at least two inches thick was dropped on Mocks's desk by the receptionist, and she slumped her shoulders slightly like a kid who couldn't stand the homework and wanted to go and play outside before the sun went down.

"The next time we need to have a department fundraiser, I say we just call it an Amber Alert," Mocks said, reaching for the fresh pile of leads. "We'd hit our quotas in no time at all."

Half listening with a phone to his ear, Grant hung up and jotted down a note. "I think I've got something. A bunch of kids on social media were posting about Mallory's disappearance, and at least ten of them were talking about some group she attended at a church on Wednesday nights."

Mocks frowned. "The mother never mentioned anything about the girl going to church every week." She arched an eyebrow. "And I thought church was on Sundays."

Grant slid into his raincoat and tore off the address he'd jotted down. "The kids that were talking about it had pictures of Mallory at the event." He dove his hand into his pocket to retrieve the keys. "And church does happen on Sundays, but most churches have youth events on Wednesday nights."

Mocks reached for her jacket and leapt out of her seat. "Well, I don't care if it's an event for free prostate exams, if it gets me out from behind this desk, I'm going."

Both Grant and Mocks ignored the questions from the reporters on their way out of the station, using the ever-popular phrase, "We cannot comment on an ongoing investigation." It made both of them smile, and it drove the reporters nuts.

A few of the questions were in regards to Grant's previous case with the ambassador, all of which he declined to comment. He was sure there was some kind of confidentiality agreement he signed with the FBI in regards to the case details. When it came to the press, he had one rule that he followed very rigorously: keep your mouth shut until it's not news anymore. Grant understood that the press were just doing their job, but that didn't mean he had to like them.

Rain sprinkled on the windshield just as Mocks's phone rang. The ringtone was from some band she liked. Grant couldn't remember the name of it. While Mocks was more rock 'n' roll, Grant had always enjoyed the classics. He flicked the windshield wipers on as she answered.

"Hey," Mocks said. "Yeah, it'll be a late one... We can talk about it later... No, you don't have to wait up.... Bye." She tucked the phone back into her pocket and immediately started playing with her wedding ring.

"Everything all right with you and Rick?"

"You know how it goes," Mocks answered. "Our hours aren't exactly marriage friendly." She shifted in her seat and crossed both legs, sitting Indian style. She was small enough to get away with it.

"No, it's not," Grant said, his voice quiet but his tone firm. "But you have to make time for it. Whatever you two are going through, just talk to one another."

Mocks reached for her Bic. "Sharing feelings isn't my strong suit."

"It only gets worse when you don't talk."

Mocks exhaled a breath riddled with stress. It was an exhale Grant knew well. "I know." She flicked the lighter on, then off. "You miss talking to her?" The question came out sheepish, almost like she was afraid to ask, and when Grant looked over, her eyes were wide like saucers.

"Every day," Grant answered.

After that it was quiet for a while, and when Mocks flicked her thumb raw on the lighter she pocketed the Bic and zipped up her jacket. "What's the name of the place we're going?"

Whenever Grant drove he rarely used the A/C or heat. There was a part of him that liked the naturally dreary weather that Seattle provided. There was something about the ominous overhang of an ever-looming storm that challenged him.

"New Faith Church," Grant answered, turning on his blinker and merging onto the expressway that would shoot them across town. Mocks remained quiet, and Grant stole a glance over and saw that her arms were crossed. "What? You've been there?"

With her gaze still focused out the window beside her, she nodded. "They used to host meetings there. I went a couple times when I first moved out here."

It was always dangerous footing when Mocks brought up her past, or if it was brought up for her by someone else. She'd been clean for five years, but it was like they always said in those meetings: You never stop being an addict.

Mocks actually took Grant to one of the meetings after they'd been partners for a year. It was the first time Mocks had opened up about it. When she'd asked him if she could take him somewhere after their shift was over, he actually thought it was a date. And after she burst into tears from laughing, she promised him that it was definitely, certainly, not a date. She was married, and she reiterated that he was definitely not her type. Too melancholy, she said. He'd be lying if he said that his ego wasn't hurt.

"I can take you back if you don't—"

"It's fine," Mocks said.

Grant tossed her a glance. "You sure?"

Mocks finally turned from the window, grinning. "Yeah. I'm sure."

The rain had stopped by the time they arrived at New Faith Church, and the place looked more like a compound than a building for worship, and it was the ugliest color purple Grant had ever seen. Mocks informed him that it was one of those megachurches where people who don't really identify with any specific sector of the Christian church get together. The sermons had roots in the Bible, but it was more feel good than it was factual Scripture.

A van was parked near one of the side entrances close to an unloading dock, and Grant spotted a young man stacking pallets of drinks onto a dolly. He gave a friendly wave when he saw Grant pull up and walked over as they parked and stepped out of the vehicle.

"Afternoon! Can I help you folks with something?"

Grant and Mocks flashed their badges, and the handsome face in front of them immediately expressed concern.

"Is everything all right?"

"I'm Detective Grant, and this is my partner, Detective Mullocks," Grant said. "We were hoping to speak with a Mr. Glenn Paley. Is he around?"

The young man straightened up a little bit, his prominent Adam's apple bobbing up and down. "I'm Glenn. What's this about?" His voice cracked on the last word, and a few beads of sweat broke out on his forehead.

"Do you know a Mallory Givens?" Mocks asked, taking a sidestep toward the van.

"Y-yeah, she comes to my youth group on Wednesday nights. Sweet girl. Is she all right?"

Mocks spun around after checking the inside of the vehicle, Grant making a mental note that the vehicle had no decals on it that signified it was a church van.

"Is this your vehicle, sir?" Grant asked.

Glenn spun around, his right arm twitched, and his lips quivered as he spat his anxiety-riddled answers. "N-no, it belongs to the church. I checked it out today to run up to Costco and grab some supplies for our event this week. Can you tell me what's going on, please?"

A woman appeared from the entrance to the loading dock. She looked the same age as Glenn, and when she sidled up next to Mr. Paley, it was like looking at the real-life versions of Ken and Barbie. The woman lowered the scarf wrapped high on her chin to protect herself from the spurts of icy wind blown in from the coast, and offered a polite but confused smile.

"Sweetheart, what's going on?" she asked.

"I'm trying to figure that out," Glenn answered.

It could have been the arrival of his lady, but Glenn's demeanor shifted to more of a defensive tone as he embraced the girl with both arms, which she reciprocated. Their stance reminded Grant of a pair of lovers that had been caught in the act, fearful of the repercussions of their affair.

"What's your name, miss?" Grant asked.

"Stacy. Stacy West."

"And how do you know Mr. Paley?" Mocks asked.

The girl frowned at Mocks. Stacy was half a foot taller than Grant's partner and looked down on Mocks with a holier-than-thou attitude. If the pair were back in high school, Grant didn't think Mocks and Stacy would have run in the same circles.

"I'm his fiancée." And as if to prove the point Stacy removed her glove and, even in the gloomy skies of Seattle, Grant saw the shine of the ring. Hell, he was confident the astronauts on the International Space Station could see that bling.

Mocks circled behind the pair like a shark, which only worsened their anxiety. "Congratulations."

Finally, Mr. Paley stepped forward, hands clenched into fists as his spine stiffened. "I have a right to know what is happening, and if not, then I demand to see a warrant."

"Mallory Givens, that girl who attends your youth events on Wednesday nights, has gone missing," Grant answered.

Stacy gasped and quickly covered her mouth with the hand that sported her rock, and Glenn's face quickly drained of color, his shoulders and back slowly rounding.

"Oh, my God," Glenn said, his words soft.

"When was the last time you were in contact with Mallory?" Mocks asked, jumping in sync with Grant. When the two got on the same wavelength, they could put a lot of suspects off-balance. Grant had never had that with any partner on the force before.

Glenn pressed his palm into his forehead, shuffling his feet from side to side as he gave his head a light shake. "Um, last Wednesday? When she attended youth group." His eyes misted. "She walked in with a few of the friends she'd made over the past school year and left with them. I haven't seen her since."

"When did she go missing?" Stacy asked, gripping the removed glove tightly with both hands.

"Early this morning," Mocks answered. "We'd like the two of you to come down to the station, answer a few questions."

Both Glenn and Stacy nodded aggressively. "Yes, of course. Whatever we can do to help." Glenn gestured back to the van and the drinks still inside. "If you can just let me finish up here, we can meet you in less than an hour."

Grant reached inside his jacket and removed his card. "The station's address and both our cell numbers. If you get lost or something comes up, please, let us know."

"We will," Glenn said, a nervous grin appearing on his face. "This won't take long at all."

"Thank you, and God bless," Stacy said, walking back to the van as both Grant and Mocks returned to their vehicle.

Once the doors were shut and they were out of earshot, Mocks fidgeted in her seat. "I didn't like how that smelled."

"We'll get a warrant for his phone records, see if he made any calls to the Givens household," Grant said.

"A young girl, outcast by society, warmed by the good Lord and a handsome man," Mocks said. "If she's been coming here without her mother knowing for the past year, then that's been plenty of time for Mr. Paley to lay down his groundwork." She grimaced. "That one's good at pretending."

"We'll know more soon enough," Grant said, shifting into drive as their radio demanded attention.

"Unit thirty-five, this is dispatch, over."

Mocks picked up the receiver. "Go for unit thirty-five." She let her thumb off the receiver and then looked at Grant. "When did you put both our cell numbers on your card?"

Grant shrugged. "Can't remember. It was whenever I had my last office supply order. Is that all right?"

Mocks grinned. "Am I listed as your emergency contact too?"

Grant scoffed. "I'm not that stupid."

The radio blew static, and dispatch's voice came in garbled and unintelligible.

"Say again, dispatch," Mocks said.

"We have a hit on your missing girl. Multiple witnesses have her heading northbound on Interstate 5. Suspect is male, balding, late forties, and the vehicle is a gray 2002 Buick Regal. We have units in pursuit."

Grant flipped on the lights and slammed on the accelerator. The tires spun out on the church parking lot asphalt, and Grant swerved back onto the main road toward the nearest I-5 on-ramp.

Traffic diverted left and right, and Grant weaved around the few cars that either refused to move or were too oblivious to the speeding, flashing, siren-blaring bullet rocketing past.

"See if the chopper is up?" Grant asked.

Mocks reached for the radio, turning the knob to another channel. "This is unit thirty-five heading northbound on I-5 in pursuit of Amber Alert suspect. Do we have air support?"

"Negative, unit thirty-five, bird has not taken off yet."

Mocks tossed the radio on the floorboard. "Shit!"

The sedan's V8 hummed, and Grant glanced down at the speedometer, which tipped over one hundred miles per hour. Thankfully, traffic was sparse, which let Grant keep the dangerous pace to catch up. The adrenaline brought with it the twisting feeling in his gut. Chases never ended well. For anyone involved.

The radio continued to blare sporadic updates, including a notification of a roadblock that shut down the entire northbound side of the interstate. A million thoughts raced through Grant's mind during the chase, many of which included the safety and well-being of those still on the road, but at the very top of his list was Mallory Givens. A little girl who had no idea what was happening.

Whenever Grant spoke to the victims afterwards they all said the same thing, nearly word for word, the moment they were free: I thought he was going to kill me.

The suspect's motives varied from case to case. Some wanted to kill the victims they abducted, but others, much like the man who'd taken the ambassador's daughter, had darker intentions. Acts that if spoken in the light of day in a public place would get them beaten to death. Grant just prayed that whatever intentions were meant for Mallory Givens had not yet been practiced.

Grant finally caught up to the growing caravan of police cars in pursuit of the Buick. Dozens of blue and red lights flashed, taking up all four lanes of traffic. The roadblock was set up four miles down the road. But the Buick quickly swerved off on the nearest exit ramp, and the horde of police vehicles bottlenecked while trying to keep pursuit.

When Grant passed the exit and the police vehicles keeping pursuit, Mocks whipped her head around so fast and hard that it sounded like she snapped her neck.

Grant pointed toward the sky before she could utter anything, and that was when she saw the chopper overhead, which could track the Buick from anywhere now. "We'll take the next exit and cut him off on one of the crossroads. Follow the updates from the air."

Mocks shook her head and changed the channel to the air cavalry circling overhead. "I swear sometimes I think you're telepathic."

"I just pay attention."

The chase continued for another twelve miles, passing

through a no-name town in the middle of nowhere before the driver cornered himself. Either out of desperation or planned efficiency, he veered into the dirt lot just outside an abandoned canning factory. Grant and Mocks were the sixth car on scene, and when they stepped out another five police cars pulled up behind them.

A perimeter was quickly established as Grant and Mocks hopped out of the car and jogged over to one of the officers yelling into his radio over the hum of the chopper overhead. The Buick was parked in the center of the lot with the driver side door and trunk still open.

"He went inside?" Grant asked, his badge dangling in the open space of his jacket.

"Yeah, we're calling S.W.A.T. now to handle extraction," the officer said.

Grant shook his head. "This guy is desperate." He pointed to the trunk. "If he had the girl in the trunk, then he doesn't give a shit what happens with her life." Grant removed his pistol from his holster, and Mocks did the same. "I need two officers with me and Detective Mocks."

The officers froze, and Mocks stepped forward, her presence much larger than her tiny frame suggested. "Now, gentlemen."

"Yes, ma'am!" A pair of officers at the lead car separated immediately, and the four of them started their path toward the rundown structure.

Grant kept his feet as light as possible, and while the normal steel-winged butterflies still fluttered, the continued adrenaline had also given him a light tremor in his right hand. Between the events of the morning and now, the day had provided more excitement than Grant had intended.

The foursome paused at the broken door that the suspect had entered, and Grant and Mocks were the first inside. It was dark, the overcast sky and dirty windows providing poor visibility. Grant reached for his light, and when he flicked it on, the beam highlighted rusty equipment and floors covered in thick layers of dust and animal droppings, sprinkled with mildew caused from leaks through multiple holes in the roof.

Everyone was quiet, and Grant hand-signaled for each officer to check a quadrant. They moved slowly, steadily, and surely, their sweeps methodical. They had to squeeze the suspect out of hiding without spooking him enough to hurt the girl.

"Stop!" The panicked voice rang out just as Grant's flashlight found the tip of his shoe sticking out from behind one of the office walls meant for the foreman on the job when the old factory was still operational. "Don't move any closer or I'll shoot her."

The suspect quickly thrust the girl around the corner and revealed the barrel of the .38 special revolver pressed against the girl's head. The man's arm covered her face, and Grant couldn't confirm if the girl was Mallory Givens.

"It's all right," Grant said, raising his voice an octave higher. "We don't want anyone to get hurt. Not even you."

"Bullshit!" The outburst rang high in the vaulted ceilings. The violent outcry was filled with a desperation that accompanied the knowledge of one's own finality. "You'll put a bullet in my head the moment I hand over the girl."

"No," Grant said. "As long as the girl isn't harmed, you still have a way out." Grant crept closer, inching forward slowly. "You never really wanted to hurt her, did you?"

The man swayed back and forth, the gun's barrel still pressed against the girl's head. Grant glanced back at the officers and motioned for them to hold back. He didn't need to add to the man's growing anxiety. But when he squinted in the darkness, he couldn't find Mocks.

"I just want to get out of here," the man said, his voice still wavering.

"And I just want the girl," Grant said. He took a step forward. "You give her to me and we can work that out."

Movement to Grant's left out of his peripheral caused him to dart his eyes in that direction, and it was there he saw Mocks creeping around to the back side of the office. He quickly returned his gaze to the suspect, praying he didn't give her away. He just had to keep talking. Keep the man focused on him.

"Listen, I'll tell you what," Grant said, again taking a few steps before stopping. "You don't want to give up the girl because you need a bargaining chip, right?"

A pause. "Yeah."

"So why don't we do this," Grant said. "You send out the girl, and then you can take me instead?"

"No, you have a gun."

"I'll leave the gun behind, see?" Grant extended the pistol and placed it on the floor where the suspect could see it, then Grant kicked it with his foot, and the weapon skidded across the concrete. He extended both hands, palms out. "No more gun. No more weapons." He reached around for the hand-cuffs as he caught the last view of Mocks just before she ducked around the backside of the office. "I'll even let you cuff me so you know I won't give you any trouble."

As Grant drew closer he had a better view of the man and girl, but her face was pressed into the gunman's stomach. She was about the same size as Mallory Givens, same hair color.

"I-I don't know," the man said. "What about the rest of the cops. What'll they do?"

"They'll do exactly what I tell them," Grant answered. "I'm the one in charge. And if you control me, that means you're the one in charge."

From the silence that followed, Grant knew the man was

mulling it over. His panic-stricken mind grasped at any hope of getting out of this situation alive, and it was exactly what Grant wanted the man to think.

Mocks was out of view now, the building blocking Grant's line of sight. His heart rate was jacked, and he had no idea when she would make her move. The tremor in his right hand had worsened, and his mouth had gone completely dry. He kept his eyes locked on the lunatic still pressing the revolver to the girl's head.

"It's a good deal, buddy," Grant said.

"Don't rush me!"

Grant inched closer, wanting to draw the man's rage and focus on him and off the little girl. "Tick-tock. What's it gonna be?"

"Stop yelling at me!"

Grant took another step. "Take me. It's the best way out."

"Don't tell me what to do!" The man trembled, but the pistol was off the girl's head and now pointed at Grant.

"Last chance," Grant said.

The man pulled the hammer back on the revolver, and his face flushed red. "Fuck you!"

Grant shuddered from the gunshot but dove forward in the same instant, ripping the girl from the man's clutches while simultaneously knocking him to the floor. Something warm grazed Grant's cheek, and he felt nails dig into the sleeve on his arm, and as he lay on the floor with his eyes shut, he was afraid to open them to survey the aftermath. It was a split-second decision, a coin toss. He just hoped the girl was on the winning side.

6

"*D*etective Grant!"

The words sounded muffled after the ring of the gunshot, and Grant wondered how much more abuse his eardrums could take.

"Detective Grant!"

He opened his eyes and saw one of the officers hovering above. He then looked down to his arm and saw the young girl kicking and punching him, screaming to be let go. When he released her he finally got a good look at her face. It wasn't Mallory Givens.

One of the officers led the girl away, and Grant turned around to see Mocks handcuffing the kidnapper with his belly on the concrete and a bloodied wound covering his shoulder.

"We need a medic," Mocks said, slightly out of breath, then looked to Grant. "You all right, partner?"

A stab of pain radiated from Grant's left hip down the side of his leg as he pushed himself off the floor. When he stood and put pressure on it, the pain worsened, and he leaned against the wall for support before he collapsed. "I think I tweaked something."

The factory was flooded with officers now, and a pair of them relieved Mocks of the suspect and whisked him outside. Mocks walked over and helped Grant walk out, him leaning against her like a crutch. She was surprisingly sturdy for her size.

"You were working that distraction pretty hard," Mocks said.

"Wanted to make sure you had enough time," Grant replied, the pain lessening the more he moved. "You could have given me a heads-up beforehand though."

"I figured you'd catch on eventually," Mocks said.

Outside, the police force had increased tenfold, and helicopters hummed overhead. Mocks helped Grant over to one of the medics to get him checked, but after a few more practice steps on his own, the pain in his leg disappeared, and the paramedic couldn't find anything else wrong with him.

Another drizzle started, and Grant and Mocks returned to their car to avoid the wet. The windows fogged, and a biting cold caused Mocks to disappear into her jacket.

"So, that wasn't Mallory Givens," Mocks said, zipping the jacket all the way up to her chin. "Guess that means our date with Mr. and Mrs. Faith is still on."

Grant massaged his left hip with his knuckles and grunted a "mm-hmm." "We need to trace the tip that led us to this guy. See if there was anything unusual about it."

"Unusual how?" Mocks asked.

"In the decade-plus I've been with Seattle PD, I have never seen an instance where a tip came in the middle of an Amber Alert for a kid that looks exactly like the missing person, and then that individual ends up being the victim of another abduction. Have you?"

Mocks stayed quiet for a moment, and she reached for her lighter, flicking it on as she answered, "No."

"I don't think that has ever happened in the *history* of the Seattle PD," Grant said.

"So what now?"

"I'll drop you off at the station so you can interview the youth pastor and the fiancée. While you're doing that, I'll head over to Mallory's neighborhood and see what I can find from the neighbors. If she left on her own accord, then there may have been someone that had seen her." Grant drew in a breath, checking the timer on his watch. "I'll call the mother and let her know what's going on before the news spins any information that sends her into a speculation nosedive." And considering the girl was most likely in a similar situation as the girl they just rescued, that speculation was probably very accurate.

* * *

WHEN MOCKS STEPPED out of the vehicle at the precinct, she was immediately swarmed by the flock of reporters that had roosted outside, jamming microphones and cameras in her face, asking about the car chase.

"We apprehended the suspect, and we're discovering more information as we go along. Thank you." Questions still buzzed about her ears and followed Mocks all the way to the door, which she could barely open from the cluster of reporters engulfing her, then she squeezed inside, glad to be rid of them. Like Grant, she had no desire to speak with them. Ever.

Mocks weaved through the precinct and back to her desk, where she was forced to prepare the paperwork for discharging her firearm. She hated paperwork. It was so monotonous and tedious. If she had known that most of her detective career would be spent filling out forms, she might have changed career paths.

But despite the piles of paper, she still loved the job. And she was lucky enough to have a partner that felt the same way. She and Grant shared a deep-rooted connection in that regard. They shared a past that was soiled and fertilized in despair. Though she understood his pain differed from hers.

One of the first things Mocks learned about Grant before she even met him was the series of events that led to his 'voluntary' leave of absence. But when she found out they were to be partners, she ignored the rumors and gossip and went straight to the source. She was surprised at the truth and even more heartbroken. How Grant had pulled himself out of that hole was more than she could understand. But as an addict, she could empathize when it came to making the wrong decision.

"Detective?" The voice was high-pitched and echoed more of an adolescent than the grown man standing in front of her.

"Mr. Paley," Mocks said, looking up from and setting aside the paperwork. "Thanks for coming in." She looked behind him. "Is your fiancée joining us?"

"She's parking the car. It's a bit of a madhouse out there."

"Abductions are hot news topics," Mocks said, leaning back in her chair, folding her arms on her stomach. "Really spikes the ratings."

Paley stood there quiet and uncomfortable until Barbie showed up at the reception desk. Despite the rain and deplorably mucky weather, the woman still looked like she was ready for a night out dancing. Not that Mocks suspected she was the type of woman who danced. There was an anal retentiveness behind that mask of makeup.

Mocks led them into one of the interrogation rooms, and

once everyone was settled, Mocks went to work. "How long have you known Mallory Givens?"

Mr. Paley flexed his grip over his girlfriend's hand and cleared his throat. "Um, the first event she came to was in November of last year. She came alone, said she saw one of the flyers I posted at a restaurant downtown." He looked anywhere but Mocks's face.

"What's an event on Wednesday nights like?" Mocks said, reaching for the lighter in her pocket. It helped keep her mind calm and working. It always received odd stares, but when it came to interviews, she wanted to throw people off their game.

"I'm sorry, shouldn't you be writing all of this down?" Stacy asked, both eyebrows arched. "We came here to make a statement and to help, but you're not writing anything down."

Mocks flicked the lighter on, the flame wiggling. "We have a recorder in the room. Takes down everything we say. I can play it back later if I need to." But she wouldn't need to. It was her go-to response whenever she was asked that question. It was easier than explaining how her memory worked. And the answer satisfied Stacy's inquiry, which let Mr. Paley continue.

"It's mostly fun stuff." He gave a half-smile. "I try to keep the preaching to a minimum and only at the end. Tweens can only take so much of that, and most of them go to church on Sundays anyway, so…" He shrugged, as if his half-explanation was enough.

"What's the age range of children you deal with?"

"Middle school through high school, so anywhere between eleven and seventeen."

"What happens when the kid turns eighteen and they're still in high school?"

"They shift over to the young-adult groups that we have at the church."

Mocks leaned forward, her left hand still playing with the lighter. She examined the youth pastor's movements, looking for nervous ticks, microexpressions of the mouth and eyes, anything and everything to form a well-rounded opinion. "And you're the only adult at these youth events?"

"No," Stacy said, cutting in. "I'm there as well." She smiled and leaned over for a kiss. "It's how we met."

It could have been the overload of soon-to-be marital bliss, or the fact that both seemed more absorbed by their own self-interest than finding a little girl who had gone missing, but Mocks decided it was time to make both of them uncomfortable.

"And both of you adhere strictly to the sanctions of marriage?" Mocks asked.

"What do you mean?" Mr. Paley asked.

Mocks rocked her head side to side, enjoying the cryptic confusion on each of their faces. "You know? Waiting until the big night for the holy union?" She bounced both brows. "Going toes to Jesus?"

Stacy held up her hand. "I understand the question." She lifted her chin and threw her shoulders back. "Both of us have remained pure for one another and will consummate our marriage on our wedding night the way God intended us to."

Mocks flicked the lighter. "That sucks." She let her thumb off the igniter and consumed the Bic in her fist. "If I don't get any for a week I start to get antsy, and you guys are what, twenty-four? Twenty-five? Talk about some pent-up aggression." She turned to Stacy and lowered her voice. "If I can give you a piece of advice for the night of? Make sure you have plenty of tissues for cleanup."

The expression that slowly spread over Stacy's face could

have been described as apoplectic, and there was a solid ten seconds where Mocks was one hundred percent certain the woman was going to punch her in the face.

"This is incredibly inappropriate," Stacy said, her face now as red as Mr. Paley's. "I demand to speak to your supervisor."

Mocks ignored the request and turned her attention back to Mr. Paley. "Were you aware that Mallory Givens's mother had no idea she attended your church group?"

Mr. Paley's mouth hung loose by the hinge of his jaw, and he stuttered out a few phrases that sounded like another language until he finally managed to form coherent sentences. "She told me she never had a relationship with her father and that her mother worked a lot, but I was unaware Mallory was there without her parents' permission."

"You never found it odd that she never showed up to church on Sundays? Or the fact that her parents never dropped her off or attempted to reach out to you and see who her daughter was spending time with?"

"If you push a child—"

"No!" Mocks slammed her fists on the table. "You don't get to make this Mallory's fault! She went to those events because it made her feel connected and safe. She didn't feel like she was an outcast, so don't tell me you didn't know. Don't tell me you tried everything you could. Because if you had, she probably wouldn't be missing in the first place!"

The pair went silent, cowering into a sheepish retreat. Mocks pushed herself out of the chair and stepped out of the room. If she stayed in there any longer she would have leapt across the table and choked both of them, and she had enough paperwork to deal with.

Once she cooled off she returned to the interrogation room, where Little Miss Priss looked to have shoved that stick up her ass just a little bit farther. She struck Mocks as the type of person that would cause a stir if she really wanted, and this wasn't the kind of publicity that the department needed right now. As much as Mocks hated it, she had to swallow some shit.

"I apologize for my outburst," Mocks said.

"Well, I think you should be ashamed of yourself." Stacy glanced back up to the corners and around the room. "And when this tape gets reviewed, I hope you receive the fullest—"

"Stacy, please." Mr. Paley held up his hand. It was the first sign that showed the youth pastor had any balls. "Look, Detective, we all want the same thing. We all want to do our best and help bring Mallory home. And you were right, I should have looked for more red flags. I minored in social work, so I did have some training in regards to looking for things like that."

Mocks took a seat. "And did you notice any red flags?"

Paley paused to think about it before he finally responded. "She was very quiet in the beginning. She opened up the more she visited, but there was always a wall. She'd let you peek over to the other side occasionally, but it was rare."

"Did she ever open up to you?" Mocks asked, noting Paley's blond hair, tan skin, and come-take-a-swim-in-my-deep-blue-eyes.

"A few times." Paley smiled. "She was very eager to learn about the Scripture, and she picked up everything so quickly. When she mentioned to me that her father wasn't around, I told her about the heavenly Father. It seemed to cheer her up."

"Did she ever mention any contact with her father?" Mocks asked.

Paley took a moment to think it over and then furrowed his brow. "No, not to me. She did talk a lot about how she wasn't very popular at her school. Said she was teased. I told her to keep her chin up, and that eventually the students would see her the way her friends at youth group did."

"Was she close with any of the other kids at youth group?"

"Mary Steeves," Stacy said, butting in. "The two were inseparable on Wednesday nights."

Despite the pair's willingness to come to the precinct and give a statement, Mocks was starting to think this was all she was going to get from the two of them. "Well, I appreciate you coming. If I have any more questions I'll be in touch."

"Of course," Paley said. "Anything you need."

What Mocks needed was a confession from someone or an actual tip that would lead to whoever coaxed Mallory Givens to leave her room in the middle of the night without telling a single soul. But perhaps her friend from youth group knew something she didn't.

Mocks walked the pair out back where they could avoid the hordes of media waiting to take their statement, and the fiancée shot Mocks one last snarl before disappearing into the same van she'd seen earlier at the church. As they drove off, she hoped that Grant had better luck than she did.

7

The rain wouldn't let up, and neither would Grant's bad luck. Every door he knocked on either remained shut or its inhabitants knew nothing. After another door slammed in his face, Grant flipped up the collar of his jacket and tucked his hands inside the warm pockets in an attempt to stay dry. But Seattle rain always had a way of creeping inside. Just like everything else.

While his thoughts were always on the case at hand, the meeting with the ambassador tomorrow started to seep through the cracks. It wasn't the meeting itself that worried him but the inevitable newspaper article and report that would come the next day. With such a high-profile case like this there was bound to be mention of his past, and Grant preferred to keep certain elements buried.

It was amazing how one night could impact the rest of your life. One event, one second, one moment in time and everything is turned upside down. He knew he'd have to face those questions sooner or later. It was inevitable. He thought by now he'd be ready. He wasn't.

Grant passed storefronts on his walk, and it was the

64

guitar in the window that made him stop. A Gibson Les Paul. It had a mahogany body with a five-piece walnut neck, rosewood fingerboard, and a pair of Humbucking pickups. It was beautiful, and with a price tag of seven grand, the custom-built axe didn't come cheap. He wasn't sure if Mallory Givens played music, but the shopkeeper may have seen something.

The bell chimed when Grant opened the door, and a father with a little girl stepped past him. The girl was smiling, carrying something in a case. A young musician ready to go and find her own voice. Grant remembered that feeling. The first time he picked up a guitar was the first time he felt good. That hardly ever happened anymore.

"Can I help you?" the cashier asked, wiping down the glass case that displayed the latest and greatest digital tools that helped aspiring musicians leave their digital footprint on the world wide web.

Grant flashed the badge and then the picture of Mallory Givens. "Have you seen this girl before?"

The cashier examined the photo and adjusted the small rimmed glasses on his nose, shaking his head as the bell chimed, signaling another customer coming inside. "Nope. She must not be in Mrs. Claret's class over at Southside Middle. I can tell you the name and instrument of every kid in her class."

"Ben likes to brag."

Grant turned around and saw Principal Michelle Tanner with her coat on, her purse clutched with both hands in front of her. Rain droplets covered her shoulders and hair. The tiny bits of water sparkled in the shop's light. Her heels padded the carpet softly on her way over to the cash register.

"Southside kids have been coming here for thirty years," Michelle said. "And we're thankful you've helped guide our young musicians."

Ben smiled wide. "Happy to do it, Principal Tanner."

Michelle reached into her purse and handed Ben a stack of papers. "Everything should be all set for the spring order. We appreciate your help with everything."

"Yes, ma'am," Ben said. "It'll be shipped and arrive in four to six weeks."

Grant stood, slack jawed as Michelle smiled at him. He was staring. He knew it. She knew it. And he couldn't do anything about it.

"Any news on the case, Detective?" Michelle asked, breaking the silence.

"No," Grant said, quickly. "But we're following up on a few leads."

"Well, good luck." Michelle turned to Ben. "Good seeing you again, Ben."

"You too, Principal Tanner."

The door chimed on her way out, and when she was gone, Ben let out a whistle. "I will tell you it is rare to find a woman like that coming around a place like this."

Grant snapped his notepad shut and ran out the door. He skidded on the slick sidewalk on his burst outside, and saw Michelle still walking on his left. "Michelle!" He jogged to catch up, and she turned around, her collar flipped up to shield against the rain, which started to come down more heavily.

"What is it, Detective?"

Grant pulled her under an awning, but the space was small; intimate. "About earlier today, I wanted to explain."

Michelle shook her head. "It's all right, Detective. I'm sure I'm not the first woman to have flirted with a married man."

"I'm not married," Grant said, looking down to the wedding ring, which he twisted in a fidgety jerk.

Michelle kept her guard up, her arms crossed, and she

cleared her throat. "Detective, if this is some sort of game you play with women, I can tell you I'm not interested."

"It's not a game," Grant said. "My wife died. Two years ago. It was a car accident." He paused. He hadn't said it out loud in a long time, and the words felt odd on his lips. "I was working one night, and she went to visit her parents down in Portland. I was supposed to meet her down there the next day, but—" He lowered his head. "I just didn't want you to think I was that kind of person."

"Well, I'm sorry to have come across as prickly as I did," Michelle said. "I'm very sorry for your loss, Detective."

Grant raised his head. In heels they were the same height. It felt good to look someone in the eyes, be on the same playing field, as equals. "I meant what I said though, when I gave you my card. I'd like to see you again."

Michelle blushed, and did a poor job of hiding it. Not that she could have. The woman had skin like snow. But it was like fresh snow when the sunlight hit it in the morning. "Going on a date with a man who still wears his wedding ring seems to be a bit of a red flag for me."

Grant deflated. "I understand." But at least now he knew. "I'm sorry to have stopped you in the rain like this. Please, let me help you get back to your car." He offered his arm, and she took it.

She wasn't parked far, and luckily the rain hadn't picked up any worse. Grant opened her door for her, and she climbed inside. "Thank you again, Detective. And I apologize for what happened earlier."

"It's okay," Grant said. "Drive safe."

She shut the door, and drove off.

It was probably for the best. If he still wore the ring, that meant he wasn't ready to let go. And that wouldn't be fair to anyone he chose to be with right now. Grant swallowed his pride and returned to canvassing the neighborhood.

A convenience store with bars on the window sat on the street corner. It sat across from a park, which was nothing more than a patch of grass with a bench and swings.

An electronic bell chimed when Grant stepped inside the store, and the cashier behind the counter didn't even bother looking up from the magazine he was reading. Grant had to actually knock on the counter to get the man's attention.

"What?" The cashier had a scraggly beard and saggy bags under his bloodshot eyes. He was high as a kite, something he immediately tried to hide the moment Grant flashed his badge.

"Did you work last night?" Grant asked.

Baggy Eyes cleared his throat and straightened up. "Y-yeah, I did."

Grant fished the picture of Mallory he'd copied from the one Ms. Givens gave him out of his pocket and held it up to the man's face. "Did you see a girl walk by here?"

The cashier squinted, feigning an attempt to actually look at the picture. "No." He shook his head adamantly and then added with a stutter, "B-but I wasn't really paying attention last night. We're open twenty-four hours, and I'm more concerned about the people who actually come in the store. Lot of crazies around this neighborhood, you know?"

Grant tucked the picture back in his pocket. "Anyone in particular that gives this place problems?"

"Drug addicts mostly." The cashier gestured over to the park, which could barely be seen through the iron bars on the window. "There are a lot of homeless people hopped on some kind of shi—stuff." He swallowed hard after catching himself. "And they can get violent sometimes."

Grant pointed to the park. "A lot of them hang out there?"

"Yeah," the cashier answered.

"Thanks." Grant left the store, and the rain had picked up even more. His head, pants, and shoes were soaked. It was like ice smacking him in the face, and he was two seconds away from giving up and returning to the warm, dry car when a pink flash caught his peripheral to the left.

Grant turned in time to see a man with a backpack dart behind a bush in the park and out of sight. Living in Seattle, and pretty much anywhere on the West Coast really, you're bound to see a lot of strange sights and a lot of people making some questionable fashion choices, but he had a feeling the backpack he just saw wasn't one of them.

He broke out into a jog, the rain viciously pelting his face as he easily caught up to the man with the pack who'd tucked himself under a structure made of crates and boxes. He gave Grant a wild look. "What the fuck do you want?"

Grant flashed his badge and reached for the handle of his pistol. "Sir, I need you to step out of there, right now."

The homeless man had a scraggly beard, and black holes appeared where teeth should have been. His clothes were torn and tattered, and the structure he called home had more holes than actual cover. Eventually, the homeless man submitted, and when he did he revealed the cache of hidden gems that he kept in his shambled home.

Grant reached for his cuffs and then grabbed the soggy sleeve of the homeless man, who gave slight resistance to the arrest. The rain refused to let up and so did the stubbornness of the vagrant, no matter how many times Grant repeated his questions.

"Where did you get that backpack?" Water dripped from every point on Grant's body, and despite the long shower the rain provided his suspect, the man still stank. It was hard to wash away years on the street, no matter how hard you scrubbed.

"If you're not gonna charge me, just let me go!" The vagrant sat cross-legged on the ground, rocking back and forth. The never-ending twitches told the story of withdrawals. He wanted another fix. And Grant's presence was the only thing stopping him.

"I'm deciding," Grant said. "Possession. Resisting arrest. Maybe kidnapping."

The vagrant erupted. "What the hell are you talking about? I didn't take no kid!"

Grant crouched to eye level with the Seattle trash. "Where did you get the backpack? I know you didn't pick it up at the mall. And that color doesn't seem to go with the rest of your apparel. Start talking now or you'll spend what's left of your life in an eight-by-eight box."

The vagrant scowled and rocked back and forth. He kept his lips closed tight, and for a moment Grant didn't think that the man would talk. Finally, the dam burst. "I stole the pack, okay?"

"From who?"

Frustration built. "I dunno, man, I was high when I did it. I figured the kid had some food or shit in there that I could sell, maybe there was some money in there. Kids always got money on them from their parents."

Grant retrieved the picture from his pocket and held it up in front of the vagrant's face. "Is this the kid you stole it from?" Grant cupped one hand over the top of the picture to try and shield it from the rain, though with the heavy downpour it wasn't useful.

The vagrant studied the photograph for a minute but then shook his head. "I don't know, man, I told you I was high. I just took the pack and ran, okay? I didn't hurt anyone, I didn't kidnap anyone. Just let me go!"

Grant stuffed the picture back into his pocket. "That's not gonna happen anytime soon." He lifted him off the concrete and shouldered the man forward to the car, taking the backpack and every single one of the man's possessions.

* * *

THE RIDE back to the station wasn't a pleasant one. Aside from the screaming and random autism-esque fits the vagrant provided, the smell was unbearable. What made it worse was Grant knew the damp body odor would linger. It was one of the few times he turned the air on.

Grant tossed the man over to Processing and kept the sack with the backpack and other belongings with him. He found Mocks at her desk, flicking the lighter on and off so quickly that he thought she'd catch fire herself. She tossed a glance to the homeless man he'd brought in and raised her eyebrows.

"You first. What'd the youth pastor have to say?" Grant asked, dropping the bag and shaking out the rain on his coat, flinging a few drops on Mocks's desk.

Mocks threw him a glare as the water droplets soaked in, but quickly resumed her thumb work with the Bic lighter. "Aside from the fact that they love God and pretend to love each other, it seemed that Paley had developed an interest in the girl. He knew about her father. And if Mallory had a crush on him, which I'm pretty sure she did, he could have used that to his advantage."

"Yeah, I could see that." Grant had a younger sister, and Glenn Paley possessed that uncanny mix of classic boyish looks and manly handsomeness that drove young girls wild. He was willing to bet that Mallory had a few boy-band posters on her wall just as his sister did.

"So who's the friend?" Mocks asked, not looking up.

"Vagrant at thirty-fifth park," Grant answered, then lifted the bag of evidence onto his desk where it landed with a heavy thud. "I think I found Mallory Givens's backpack."

Mocks snapped her head up. "You what?"

"Yeah," Grant answered, taking a seat and slicking back

his thick mop of wet hair. "Said he stole it off of some kid. I showed him Mallory's picture, but he didn't recognize her. Told me he was high when he took it."

"Holy shit." Mocks's jaw remained slack. "You think we'll find something in there that can help us?"

"There's no telling what the guy had already thrown away and what's still inside," Grant said. "I'm gonna find an empty interrogation room and spread this stuff out. Wanna help?"

Mocks pocketed the lighter and nodded.

Interrogation room two was open and Grant dumped everything onto the table. All of the vagrant's possessions amounted to little more than a clearance rack you'd find at Target or Walmart. Grant focused on the pack, while Mocks carefully pulled apart some clothes, both wary of any used needles. The homeless weren't experts on medical disposal methods.

There was only one thing that Grant was looking for when he opened the pack, and that was the notebook her teacher had mentioned. He set aside the clothes and small packets of makeup and felt something thick at the bottom. When he pulled out the notebook and set it on the table, Mocks stopped what she was doing.

"Is that what I think it is?" Mocks asked.

The bottom half of the notebook was wet from being stuck in the rain for so long, but the pack of clothes had managed to keep the top portion dry.

Grant opened the first page, and the deepest, darkest, secret inner thoughts of twelve-year-old Mallory Givens appeared on the page. The first thing Grant noticed was the handwriting. It was incredibly legible and beautifully written in cursive, which he didn't even think was taught in schools anymore. It was handwriting derived from pages and pages of practice. Even Mocks was impressed, and that was no small feat.

"A lot of short stories in here," Mocks said, her eyes speeding over the page faster than Grant could turn to the next. "And they're not half-bad either."

"She definitely doesn't show her age," Grant said, taking a seat in the chair so he could concentrate. He had to look between the words and what Mallory was trying to say. Most of the stories were romantic, but a few revealed a heroine adventurer, escaping from her ordinary life to travel the world in search of treasures. Grant found it an interesting mix of Lara Croft, Indiana Jones, and Sherlock Holmes. It was one of the longer pieces, but he found it enjoyable.

By the time they reached the soggy pages, Mocks had lost interest and started rummaging through the rest of the pack. She found a few more interesting items, including a key that wasn't attached to any ring. She held it up between a pinched glove. "Spare for home?"

"Maybe," Grant said, carefully peeling back the wet page and trying not to tear the paper. "With Mom working, it would make sense for her to have her own key." The pencil faded the deeper he went, and the words on the page grew harder and harder to read.

"I'm gonna grab some coffee. Do you want another?" Mocks asked.

"Yeah, thanks."

Alone, Grant tried to make sense of the words on the page. The entries had suddenly shifted from stories to diary. If he could get anything that linked Mallory to Paley, then he could get a judge to provide him a warrant for arrest, or at the very least a search warrant for his place.

The entries described the bullying at school, the fact that she didn't know who her father was (though Grant thought that to be a blessing in disguise), and feelings for someone that she'd never felt before, but the individual wasn't mentioned by name.

Grant flipped to the next page too eagerly and tore a portion of the paper. He cursed as Mocks returned with two cups of coffee, steam rising from the mouths of both. Grant ignored the cup as he continued to read, forcing himself to slow so as not to rip anything else.

Mallory described the strange, overwhelming feelings a young girl hitting puberty would experience, though unsure of how to act on those urges. He turned the pages until he finally found the name he hoped to snag. "Got you."

Mocks leaned over Grant's shoulder and slurped from the rim of her cup. "Time to call the judge?"

"Almost," Grant said, still scanning the pages. "We'll need a little more than just—"

A paragraph caught Grant's eye, and he paused to reread it. Mocks smacked him on the shoulder, but he still wouldn't speak. It was the last entry in the journal, and it was also where the water damage was the worst. He held it up for Mocks to see.

"Is that what I think it is?" Grant asked.

Mocks carefully took the notebook from Grant and held it closer, directly under the light. She squinted hard, inching her face closer to the actual paper, and then nodded. "Yeah. It is."

"I'll get this over to evidence and have everything logged." Grant carefully removed the journal from Mocks's palms and tagged the page. "Get on the phone with Judge Harper. He'll expedite the warrant for us. I'll get with the lieutenant to have S.W.A.T. on standby."

"On it," Mocks said, reaching for the phone.

Grant looked down one last time at the page. A date was circled with hearts drawn all around it and excited phrases of "omg I can't wait!" and "It's really happening!" It all told the story of a young girl ready for an adventure of her own instead of just writing about one. The date she was so excited about happened last night. And the person she was excited to meet was Glenn Paley.

* * *

THE SOUR PIT in Grant's stomach made another appearance, and the multiple hits on his nerves over the course of such a short time was starting to take its toll. The three cups of coffee did little to clear his fatigued mind, its only contribution a random left eye twitch that drove him mad.

But Grant shoved all of it aside and focused on the task at hand. Mocks drove, and Grant glanced back at the S.W.A.T. van that followed close behind and felt a little better about the encounter. Still, he couldn't turn off the spigot of his mind pouring out the dozens of scenarios of how this could go down.

"Unit thirty-five, this is Seattle-One, do you copy?" The radio gargled static after the announcement, and Grant reached for the radio.

"Go for unit thirty-five," Grant said.

"We have officers stationed on the south side of the block to intercept in case of a foot chase, but the closest street is still a few hundred yards away, how do you want us to proceed?"

"Stay put. I don't want to spook him. Tell them to hold their position and wait for command over the radio."

"Roger that, thirty-five."

The neighborhood was middle class filled with small single-family homes that lined the streets. Tiny yards were fenced in by waist-high wooden boards, and a mixture of furniture and fixtures decorated the suburbia. None of them probably would have ever suspected that there was a predator living among them, let alone the conniving youth pastor that lived across the street.

Mocks parked the car a few houses down from Paley's residence. Both she and Grant exited the car as the S.W.A.T. van pulled up behind them. The officers spilled out in orderly fashion, and they all huddled near Grant's trunk.

"The girl is twelve years old, and we have reason to believe she's in that house," Grant said, holding up a picture of Mallory and then pointing behind him. "I want two officers on every exit, and I want two with me and Detective Mullocks near the front. If or when we need backup you will hear it over the radio. Sometimes these guys get desperate, and we don't want to spook him. Understood?"

A series of nods answered, and Grant and Mocks led the charge. The S.W.A.T. team followed and then all but two broke off down the side of the house, heading to the back and side doors. Both Grant and Mocks had their weapons out, and Mocks positioned herself on the left side of the door with Grant on the right. The pair raised their pistol and then the two S.W.A.T. officers stepped up with the door knocker; a heavy, flat fronted battering ram that would level any door.

Grant took a breath and then screamed. "Police Department! Search Warrant!"

The S.W.A.T. officer thrust the ram into the door. The frame cracked and Grant led the charge inside. Subsequent crashes of glass and wood echoed from the other teams around the house as every entrance was infiltrated.

A frightened Glenn Paley stepped into the front hallway from the kitchen. "What's going—"

"Down on the ground!" Grant aimed his weapon at Paley, and the man threw his hands in the air and stumbled backward.

"What is this?" Paley's face had drained of color except for a small pink spot on each cheekbone.

Mocks lowered her weapon while Grant kept his trained on Paley, and she cuffed him. Mocks knocked Paley to his knees after the cuffs were placed on him, and Grant holstered his service weapon.

"Where is she, Paley?" Grant asked. "Where's Mallory?"

Paley's head swung back and forth like it rested on a swivel. "W-what are you talking about?"

"The girl, dumbass," Mocks said, wrenching his arm back so far that it triggered a yelp. "Where is Mallory?"

Shouts of 'clear' echoed through the different rooms along with the sound of heavy boots as the tactical team checked every nook and cranny inside. When the sergeant appeared by the front door with the rest of his team, Grant felt his stomach twinge again.

"No girl, Detective."

Paley was trembling, tears streamed down his face, and snot bubbled from his nose with each uncontrollable, heaving sob. "P-please, I don't know what's going on. What are you doing?"

Grant crouched to eye level with the youth pastor, and a flush of raging heat covered his face. He gripped Paley by the collar and lifted him off the floor and slammed him against the wall. The force of the movement caused a mirror to crash and shatter on the hardwood floor.

"You were supposed to meet her last night," Grant said, baring his teeth. "You knew the kind of girl she was, and you knew she was an easy target, so you brainwashed her over the past year, didn't you, you little creep."

"Grant," Mocks said, tapping him on the shoulder. "Put him down."

But the only thing Grant heard was the pit of rage that had transformed from the bundle of nerves in his stomach. All of it could have been exacerbated by lack of sleep, the number of times he'd been shot at today, or the fact that there was still a missing girl somewhere in this city that he wasn't even sure was alive anymore.

"Where is she!" Spittle flew from Grant's mouth as he slammed Paley's body against the wall again, which triggered another shrill scream and flow of tears from the pastor. Hands and bodies pulled the pair apart, and Grant had to stop himself from swinging at the officers that removed him. In the end, it was Mocks who finally calmed him down as she shoved him out the front door and into the yard.

"What the hell was that?" Mocks asked.

Grant paced a tight circle, glancing down at his feet, the anger still steaming. "He took her, Mocks. You know it, and so do I."

Mocks stepped up in his face, which wasn't an easy feat considering he was almost a foot taller than she was. "The only thing we know is what Mallory Givens wrote in her journal. And that's it." She gave him a little shove. "You know better than to paint the picture before we have all of the colors. You're jumping the gun, and if he did take the girl, then you're giving his attorney an excuse to get him off for police brutality. Is that what you want?"

"No," Grant answered, quick and short like a child who knew he was in the wrong but didn't want to admit it. But he knew Mocks was right. He was getting ahead of himself. He looked down at his watch, which just sped past the eighty-hour mark.

"Get forensics in here," Grant said. "I want the house searched from top to bottom."

orensics was on scene in less than twenty minutes, and they immediately went to work scouring the house while Paley was kept in the back of a squad car. Grant watched Paley from the front porch, still seething anger.

The youth pastor kept his head down, tears streaming down his face. If the pastor was faking it, then he was doing a hell of a job.

"Grant," Mocks said, poking her head out of the front door.

"Yeah," Grant said, keeping his eyes on Paley.

"We've got something."

The nail in the coffin. Grant followed her inside, past the swaths of forensic members sweeping every inch of the house, and they stopped at a computer nook where an officer had his hands on a laptop, scouring through pieces of data.

"Go ahead, Sam," Mocks said, tapping the officer on the shoulder. "Tell him what you told me."

Sam cleared his throat. "Well, I've been checking the search and browser history on the laptop, and I found a few sites that he frequented. Most of them were harmless: shopping, his church website, social media, things like that. But I did find a site that was visited every day for a month about six months ago."

"And?" Grant asked, when the officer didn't finish.

"And it's underground," Sam answered.

"I never paid attention in my digital literacy class, Sam, so you'll have to catch me up to speed," Grant replied.

"There are two Internets out there for everyone. The first is the normal Internet that ninety-nine percent of people use that comprises the commerce and social media sites that most people visit. The second Internet is the underbelly, a series of servers and dark sites that most people don't even know how to access. It's where a lot of black-market deals go down, and where a lot of communication happens between black hats."

"Hackers?" Grant asked, the phrase stirring a memory in the back of his head.

"Yeah," Sam answered. "The problem with the site I found is that it has a pretty decent firewall around it, which means unless you have the access code to enter, it's very difficult to break through."

"But not impossible?" Mocks asked.

"No," Sam answered. "If I can get this back to the station, I'll have more tools to work with to see if I can crack it."

"What about pictures, letters, notes, anything child related?" In the world of the digital age, molesters and perverts had access to troves of deplorable images. On nearly every child abduction case that involved a stranger, ninety percent of them always had some dirt on their phones or computers.

"I haven't found anything yet, but that doesn't mean there's not a ghost drive hidden somewhere," Sam answered. "But trust me, if there is something on this computer, I will find it."

Grant slapped Sam on the shoulder. "Let me know the moment you find anything." He walked over to the lead forensic investigator to check in. "How's it look?"

Barry Ingle was a short man, barely clearing five feet. His head was far too large for his body, and his torso was squat like his arms and limbs. But if there was a better forensic tech on the West Coast, Grant had yet to find him.

"There are definitely multiple sets of prints everywhere in the house, including the bedroom," Barry answered. "We're checking toothbrushes, combing for hairs on clothes and furniture, and sorting through the dirty laundry to see what we can turn up. Right now though I'd say the place looks pretty clean."

"Find any compromising equipment?" Mocks asked.

"Nothing. No rope, no duct tape, no drugs other than over-the-counter cold medicines," Barry said. "We checked the basement but couldn't find anything but a few boxes and old workout equipment. We'll keep looking, but so far nothing is standing out."

Grant nodded, hope slowly sifting away. "Make sure you expedite those DNA samples and prints for the lab. I want them back ASAP."

"Will do, Detective."

Grant pulled Mocks outside and watched the squad car carrying Paley disappear down the road. There was still the matter of the computer and whatever site Paley had accessed, but there wasn't a guarantee that Sam would be able to break through the security.

"What are you thinking?" Mocks asked.

"The first call he's going to make will be to his fiancée," Grant answered. "We need to figure out what she knows before the two can collaborate on a story."

"You think he brought her in on it?" Mocks asked. "The

stick-up-her-ass didn't strike me as someone who would stay with someone like him if he did."

"You'd be surprised what someone's faith can drive them to do," Grant said. "I once had a case where a mother drowned both her children because she was convinced they were possessed by the devil, and that the only salvation they could find was in the arms of the heavenly Father."

"Christ," Mocks said. "She confess?"

"She left a note," Grant answered. "After the kids were finished she wrapped her mouth around the end of a twelve-gauge that belonged to her husband. The note said she wanted to see her kids again in heaven." He still remembered the way the little bodies floated in the bathtub, facedown. "They were one and two." It was the last homicide case he was assigned before his leave of absence.

"Hey," Mocks said, her voice soft. "You all right?"

"I'm fine," Grant answered. "Let's go and have a chat with Stacy and see what she already knows."

* * *

THE HOUSE RESEMBLED the one Grant and Mocks had just left, though the immediate reaction for both of them was that it was most definitely decorated by a woman. The light accents on the front porch of table and chair, combined with the immaculate flower garden that lined the grass in front of the porch, told a story of a woman who kept a very tidy household.

Lights shone from the windows through thin curtains as Grant parked on the street. He flicked off the engine and unclicked his seat belt. "We don't need to tell her what happened to her fiancé. I'd like to keep her in the dark as much as possible."

"No complaints here," Mocks said.

Side by side they walked the stone path through the small front yard and ascended the front porch steps. The scene was eerily similar to the one they had just left, and Grant found himself with a case of déjà vu. Minus the S.W.A.T. team of course.

Three quick knocks at the door and, after a moment's pause, the light patter of footsteps moved quickly toward them. It opened without so much as a groan, and Stacy West stood there in a light-yellow blouse and jeans, her makeup and hair just as immaculate as the front yard.

"Detectives, can I help you?"

"We had a few follow-up questions for you," Grant answered. "Could we come inside?"

A tight, forced smile spread across her face. "Of course." She stepped aside, and the two entered, the door quickly shutting behind them.

"You'll have to excuse the mess," Stacy said. "I was just getting dinner ready."

What mess the woman was referring to Grant had no idea, but he suspected it was something she would have said if she'd just spring-cleaned the entire house. "It's not a problem at all." He noticed the additional setting at her small kitchen table set up in the living room. A pair of long-stem candles burned, and from what he could tell the silverware that was set out looked like it was only used for special occasions.

"Glenn coming over for dinner?" Grant asked.

Stacy raised both eyebrows and then looked to the romantic scene she had constructed herself. "Oh." She chuckled. "Yes. Have to keep the flame fanned." She gestured to the living room. "We can chat in here until he arrives."

Mocks held back a scoff, and Grant shot her a sharp look as the three of them took their seats. Mocks and Grant opted for the couch, while Stacy took up an armchair across from them. A vase of roses had been placed in the center of the coffee table between them.

The stems were a hearty green, and the petals themselves still a gorgeous red, firm and bouncy. A card sprouted from the middle with words that Grant couldn't read from his current distance. He pointed to them. "I can see he's kept up the romance too."

Stacy blushed and then gave an "oh, stop it" wave with her hand. "One of the many reasons why I'm marrying him."

Mocks leaned forward, ending the lovebird talk and cutting straight to business. "Does Glenn do a lot of work at home on his computer?"

Stacy tilted her head to the side. "Why do you ask?"

"I'm just curious as to the stress levels he might be under at the church," Mocks said. "It seems like a big place, and with him as the only youth pastor I could see how it might be overwhelming."

"I help him with anything that he can't handle." Stacy's tone became increasingly stern. "We're a team. We share everything together. Our successes and our failures. It's a woman's place to help support her husband."

While the pair continued to spar, poking barbs into each other's sides over the female role in a domestic partnership, Grant took stock of the rest of the house. Aside from its incredible detail for cleanliness, he noticed the fine artwork on the walls, the crystal in a kitchenette that was the price of a used car, and the security systems on the windows and by the door. The alarm gadgets looked top of the line, but he didn't see a sign out front that marked the security firm that installed them.

"And what do you do for a living, Ms. West?" Grant asked, interrupting some type of explanation on how God created woman and man in His vision.

"I'm sorry?" Stacy asked.

"We never got that down in the original report when you and your fiancé came down to the station," Grant said. "Your employment."

"Oh, well, I dabble in a few things," Stacy said, dancing around the actual question. "My mother always told me how important it was to be able to handle your own business."

"Is she the one who also told you about the woman's place in the kitchen?" Mocks asked, more teeth on this particular bite.

Before Stacy could respond, Grant cut in. "What kind of dabbling, Ms. West?"

"Well, I actually help out a lot with the systems at the church, making sure everything remains properly organized and—"

"What specific systems do you work with?" Grant asked, trying to cut through the bullshit.

"Computers." But before Grant could push the topic any further, the timer in the kitchen went off. "Excuse me."

The moment she was gone, Mocks sprang up from her seat. "No way she doesn't know something. We need to bring her to the station right now."

His partner was chomping at the bit, and Grant felt it too, but if they pushed too hard they might lose her. "We'll make something up. Get her to come with us."

"Paperwork?" Mocks asked, smiling.

"That'll work."

"Would you two like any refreshments?" Stacy asked, calling from the kitchen.

"No, thank you," Grant answered, yelling from the couch. His eyes caught the roses once more, and while he still heard the clanking of pots and pans in the kitchen, he reached for the card in the middle of the roses and plucked it from its holder.

It was folded in half, and when he flipped open the card,

there was something immediately familiar about the handwriting. It was smooth and practiced, beautifully written on the small business-size card. The steel-winged butterflies made a surprise visit when he saw the name written at the end, circled with a heart. It was Mallory Givens.

Wordlessly Grant dropped the card and reached for his firearm, but before he had his hand on the butt of the pistol Stacy West appeared from the kitchen with a gun in her hand, aiming it between both Grant and Mocks.

"Don't move," Stacy said. "I want both hands on the coffee table, palms down."

Neither Grant or Mocks moved, both frozen in shock at the fact they'd been had.

"Now!" Stacy said, both arms shaking, her finger on the trigger.

Grant and Mocks complied, Grant's mind racing with questions but only asking one. "Is Mallory still alive?"

A smile twitched up the left side of Stacy's mouth. "Yes. She's alive. I wouldn't kill my first. I wanted to enjoy the fruits of my labor."

"You fucking bitch," Mocks said, not hiding the disdain in her tone.

But the comment only revealed an even larger smile across Stacy's face. She stepped farther into the living room, the barrel of the gun growing closer, and Grant finally noticed the suppressor on the end of the muzzle. He was betting she purchased it underground on those black sites that Sam was talking about.

"Clever, clever, clever detectives," Stacy said, taking a few more steps and stopping just out of reach from Grant's wingspan. "I thought I'd have at least a week before any of the fingers started to point my way, but in less than a day?" She shook her head. "You really are good at your job, aren't you?"

"You need to let the girl go," Grant said. "Think of her mother—"

"The one that's never home?" Stacy asked, cutting in. "The one who doesn't know about what really goes on in her own daughter's head? The thoughts of fear and betrayal. The lust she feels for my fiancé? The fact that while her mother lives with her, it's like she doesn't have any parents?"

Grant pinched his eyebrows together, confused. "It was you she was writing about?" He shook his head. "But she wrote Glenn's name down."

"Maybe not as clever as I thought," Stacy said. "You should have just stuck with your gut and brought a case against Glenn. I left a few pieces of evidence at his place to seal the deal. A hair, fingerprints, some of her clothes. You should have just followed the bread crumbs where I placed them."

It was all too surreal. But Grant didn't think he'd live very long to regret his mistake. Stacy's body language screamed she would get rid of them. Now it was just a question of the most efficient manner of how.

"We're going to take a little ride," Stacy said.

9

*T*he pressure from the end of the pistol Stacy pressed against Grant's head held steady the entire drive. Stacy sat in the backseat directly behind Grant, who drove, while Mocks rode in the back with her, handcuffs around her wrist and pinned behind her back with her own pistol aimed at her.

More than once Grant thought of pulling off the road and slamming into a tree or parked car, or anything that would give them a chance, but he didn't have a hard time questioning Stacy's resolve now that he knew she was the one behind Mallory's abduction. The only question that remained now was how to get the girl out alive. But first Grant had to think his way out of this.

Stacy directed Grant to the coast, and their final destination was a small marina twenty miles north of the city. From the rusted gates, crumbling boathouse, and decrepit vessels that littered the yard on concrete blocks, the place looked like it had been closed for a long time.

"Shut off the engine and cut the lights," Stacy said. Once

Grant complied, she removed the barrel of the pistol from the back of Grant's head and then opened her door. "Get out, Detective Grant."

Slowly, Grant reached for the handle, and as he stepped out, so did she. One pistol remained trained on Mocks while the second was kept on Grant. "Now," Stacy said. "Let your partner out, but keep her cuffed."

Again, Grant complied, and Stacy walked the pair to the only dock still standing, which jutted out a few hundred feet into the bay. The wooden boards groaned with each step and were slick from years of ocean spray. Wind gusted from the Pacific in cold bursts, and more than once Grant thought they were going to plunge into the freezing ocean.

Stacy walked them all the way down to the end of the pier, and once they reached the edge Grant and Mocks turned around, both staring down the pistols meant to kill them.

"So what now?" Grant asked. "Shoot us and then dump us in the ocean?"

"That was the plan," Stacy answered. "The tide will take you out, and you'll be lucky if your body comes ashore tomorrow, maybe the next day. By then you'll be bloated and difficult to identify, which means a DNA test must be performed, and that could take up to three days. Though I'm sure your brothers in arms will be able to connect the dots once you don't show up for work tomorrow. Oh, which reminds me. Badges. Both of you."

Grant took off his own and tossed it at Stacy's feet then removed Mocks's badge and added it to the pile. Mocks looked like she was ready to charge, so Grant made sure to keep half his body in front of hers to avoid any mishaps. And besides, if someone was going to do something stupid, it was the woman with the gun.

"Did you date him just to get close to the kids, or did you actually love him?" Grant asked.

"More for the kids," Stacy answered. "And talk about the perfect cover!" She laughed, the stick up her ass suddenly removed, now that she could be herself. "It's not hard playing the little church girl when you're attractive. Hell, it's not hard doing anything when you're attractive. Not that everyone here would know."

"Fuck you," Mocks said.

"You're not my type, sweetheart," Stacy said then smiled, and the fading evening light made her eyes look bloodred. "If you only knew what I knew, Detectives. There's a world you can't even imagine out there."

"Underground," Grant said, trying to keep her talking, trying to stall, trying to figure out how he would keep Mocks afloat with those cuffs on. "You're talking about the site you visited on Glenn's computer."

"Your cyber team will eventually find a ghost file with some stalking pictures I put on there of Mallory, but they won't be able to crack the site." She smirked. "No way some government pencil pusher could do that."

This time of year the water was close to freezing. With Mocks in tow it was at least a five- to ten-minute swim to the shore from all the way out here. More than enough time for hypothermia to set in, and the wind would only make it worse when they finally made it out... If they made it out.

"We will nail you, bitch," Mocks said. "I promise you that."

"No. You won't," Stacy said, fingers curving over the triggers. "Turn around."

"Can't look us in the eye and do it?" Grant asked.

"Now!" Stacy said.

Slowly, the pair complied. Once they faced the water, Grant felt the barrel of steel once again return to the back of his skull. And judging from Mocks's shudder, he guessed she had one on the back of hers as well. He knew she was scared. So was he.

"Goodbye, Detectives," Stacy said.

It was now or never. As quick and as hard as he could, Grant shouldered Mocks forward and to the right, sending both of them crashing to the waves below. Gunshots thundered, but when Grant smacked into the icy waters, his whole body went into shock. He could have been shot a dozen times and he wouldn't have been able to tell the difference between the bullets and the thousands of knives piercing his skin.

Underwater, Grant opened his eyes, the cold stinging his eyeballs. The water was dark and murky, and he groped in front of him but couldn't find Mocks. His lungs choked for air, and he clawed toward the surface. He broke the plane of water and was met with an icy burst of air that burned his cheeks.

Gunshots fired from above, and Grant splashed frantically for the cover underneath the pier, then plunged back under to search for Mocks. His heart rate was jacked and his muscles stiff and sluggish, but the initial shock had lessened a little.

Again, his lungs choked for air, and just when he was about to paddle back toward the surface he saw a figure in the murky depths. He plunged deeper, his muscles cramping from the lack of oxygen, and as he drew closer he saw Mocks kicking both legs and the last few bubbles of breath escaping her lungs.

Grant grabbed her under the left arm and shoved her toward the surface, both kicking with maddening fury. The last few inches felt like it would kill them, but when they broke the surface they gulped the icy, life-giving air.

Mocks coughed up a mouthful of water, her lips almost blue, but whatever reprieve they hoped to have was spoiled by the continued gunfire from above. Bullets splintered the old wooden boards of the dock, sending lead and wood raining over their heads.

With Mocks still cuffed and disoriented, Grant took hold of one of the pillars and shielded her from the gunfire. Stacy screamed unintelligible words, but it wasn't long before she was out of bullets as well as patience. Footsteps scurried back toward the shore, and then there was the faint sound of Grant's car starting then driving away.

Grant spun Mocks around, struggling to keep the two of them afloat. "You all right?"

Mocks's teeth clattered together, and she wouldn't stop shivering. "Bitch still has my gun."

Grant laughed and then kissed her forehead. "Humor is a good sign. C'mon." The next ten minutes were grueling. The waves and cold battered him as he kicked and clawed to the seawall, looking for any ladder or rope the pair could ascend.

The longer Grant stayed in the water, the more his limbs turned into immovable pieces of lead. His joints stiffened, and halfway to the dock Mocks had run out of steam. He was lucky she was so small. If it was anyone else he didn't think they would have made it.

His shoe scraped barnacled concrete from an old boat ramp, and Grant sighed relief. He dragged Mocks out of the water, and the pair collapsed on the ground and wheezed, trying to stave off hypothermia a little while longer.

The cold seeped through everything: clothes, skin, muscle, all the way to the core of Grant's bones. "We... need to... radio... for backup," Grant said, chattering through clanking teeth. He clawed his fingers into the dirt and pulled himself over to Mocks, who had stopped shivering; a very bad sign.

Mocks's lips were blue, and her eyes were half-closed. He gave her body a gentle shake. "Mocks, stay with me." He pressed his fingers against the side of her neck and felt the faint bump of a pulse. Ice formed in her hair and eyebrows, freezing from the cruel coastal winds.

Grant looked around for anything that could warm her and noticed an empty oil drum on its side along with a cluster of trash that had spilled out of a dumpster. With two shaking legs, he pushed himself off the ground and forced himself to walk to the empty oil drum.

Every step felt like his bones were going to snap in half. Numbed fingers flipped the empty drum barrel right side up, and then he grabbed as many old papers from the dumpster as he could, tossing them inside the drum barrel. With it about a quarter of the way full, he dragged the barrel over to Mocks and then patted her down to find the lighter in her pocket.

He pressed his thumb against the starter, but no spark flickered to life. He repeated it a few times, frustration building as he gritted his teeth and did his best to steady his shaking hands. Sparks finally ejected from the lighter's barrel, then flame, which he held to paper.

It smoldered for a minute but caught fire even in the cold. He dropped the makeshift tinder into the can, and the rest slowly caught fire. Embers flew from the drum barrel into the fresh night sky, and Grant dragged Mocks's body to the barrel to keep her warm.

Grant reached for his phone, but the cold bay waters had done their work well, leaving him nothing but a black screen. He patted Mocks down, who was now shivering, a better sign, but when he found her cell phone, it was in the same condition as his. He cursed under his breath and then hobbled away from the warmth of the fire and deeper into the biting wind that had picked up speed.

When Grant reached the road there was no sign of Stacy or his car, or any other vehicle for that matter. It was nothing but asphalt as far as the eye could see. He glanced down at his watch, which had survived the plunge, and the timer ticked up to ten hours. The next thirty minutes were crucial. He knew Stacy would transport herself and Mallory somewhere new now that she had been found out. It was the only play she had left.

Grant stumbled down the road, his ragged and tired brain trying to remember any buildings or stores they passed on the way over. But every time he got close to a thought, it was quickly snuffed out by a blast of icy wind.

Exhausted, Grant collapsed to his knees. The timer on his watch continued to tick away seconds. And every second that passed was one more where Stacy had time to get a head start. Mallory, the girl who had wanted an adventure, was now going to take a trip from hell.

Grant closed his eyes, and he saw his wife then suddenly felt warmer. Ellen smiled, and he reciprocated, his face tight and numb. She was in the living room, playing the piano. She was so good, and he loved to watch her play. It was her hands. She had the most beautiful hands.

A pair of headlights appeared down the road, and Grant lifted his head. It looked more like a mirage at first, but the longer he stared and the closer it moved, the more he realized it was real. He waved his hands in the air, stepping out into the road, forcing the car to stop.

Grant reached for his badge but quickly remembered that Stacy had taken it. He leaned against the hood, his hands warming against the engine as the driver rolled down his window. He wore a jacket and beanie, squinting through a pair of small glasses that rested on the bridge of his nose. "Damn, buddy, are you all right?"

"I need… your phone."

* * *

BY THE TIME medics and the police arrived at the old marina, Grant had run out of paper to burn in the old oil drum, and Mocks had slipped into unconsciousness. The prick who let Grant use the phone bolted the moment the call was over. Had he a coherent mind, Grant would have gotten the license plate number and paid a visit to him later. He had at least been able to take the handcuffs off Mocks though, the key managing to stay in his pocket after the plunge.

A change of clothes was brought for Grant, and a liaison from Seattle PD arrived to take his statement, though the officer moved a little too slowly for Grant's taste.

"It was your squad car that was stolen, Detective?" the officer asked, repeating what Grant had just told him.

"Yes," Grant answered, a space blanket wrapped around him and the growing warmth fanned by the flames of frustration. "You need to get on the horn with dispatch and put in a request to lock down my vehicle's GPS coordinates. It's registered as an undercover vehicle, so it will have LoJack."

The officer asked him something else, but the sound of Mocks awakening on the stretcher in the back of the ambulance stole his attention. He jogged over, his knees still stiff from their icy swim.

"Let me off this thing," Mocks said, trying to sit up, but the paramedics kept her down. "I'm fine."

"Ma'am, please," one paramedic started. "You need to—"

"It's all right, guys," Grant said, walking up. When Mocks saw Grant, she relaxed a bit. "Give us a minute, will you?"

The paramedics nodded and begrudgingly hopped out of their ambulance and into the cold. Once they were gone,

Mocks finally collapsed onto her back. Ice still lingered in her hair, and her skin was white as snow. They'd managed to get most of the wet clothes off and replaced them with frumpy wool blankets that made her look like a kid lying in a bed that was much too large for her.

"They want to take me to the hospital," Mocks said.

"And that's where you're going," Grant replied.

"Like hell I am." Mocks lifted her head, reaching for the sheets. "I'm going with you."

Grant placed his hand over hers. Her skin was still ice to the touch.

"You're going to the hospital," Grant said. "And you don't have a choice in the matter." A burst of color returned to her cheeks, and before she had a chance to rebuke his comment, he added, "You told me two years ago that we had each other's backs. You made me promise that neither one of us would let us do something we knew we couldn't handle, because it's not about our stats, or our records, it's about the people we help." He placed a hand on her shoulder, and her muscles relaxed. "Remember?"

Mocks looked away. "You're a pain in the ass sometimes, you know?"

Grant smiled. "I know." He gestured for the paramedics, and they climbed back inside.

Mocks raised her head to look at him before they closed the doors. "Find her, Grant."

"I will."

The doors slammed shut, and the ambulance honked its horn, and the driver pulled out onto the road, the lights flashing brightly against the fresh night sky. Grant turned back to the officer who had made his way to his squad car and, much to Grant's delight, was on the radio. He walked over just as the officer set it down.

"All right, Detective, I put in the request to track the

squad car, and it turns out it only made it about a mile down the road before it was ditched and switched out for another vehicle."

"Any traffic cameras nearby?" Grant asked, holding on to the one thread of hope.

"Just one," the officer said. "Looks like your girl is driving a 2004 white Toyota Corolla. An APB was put out, and it was sighted outside an apartment complex. Turns out one of the apartments is registered in Stacy West's name."

Grant nearly jumped behind the wheel of the squad car himself. "Let's go!"

* * *

DOZENS OF POLICE cruisers had circled the old apartment building, blocking off exits, officers establishing a perimeter. The spotlight from the helicopter circling above highlighted the fifth floor, where Stacy's apartment was located.

The whole neighborhood was lit up with red and blue lights, and nearly every person in the surrounding houses and duplexes had stepped out of their dwellings. Grant just hoped they wouldn't get the show they expected.

Grant pushed his way to the front of the line, where he found the officer in charge, and thanks to a radio command from his captain, the sergeant knew he was coming. His celebrity from the ambassador case didn't hurt either. There wasn't a cop in the city who didn't know who he was.

"Any visual on Mallory Givens?" Grant asked.

"Not yet, Detective," Sergeant Moynahan answered. "We're still waiting on establishing some form of contact. We've tried her cell phone, as well as the apartment's land-line, but haven't had any luck."

"She's not going to answer," Grant said, sliding on the bulletproof vest he fished out of the squad car. "We'll have to get the girl out ourselves. Give me a rundown of the building."

The surrounding officers didn't move, their jaws still slack as they looked to one another. It was the sergeant who finally spoke first. "Detective, we don't have the authority to do that." The spotlight from the helicopter flashed briefly overhead. "We have to wait until we hear word from the chief."

The hours and stress finally caught up with Grant, and he wrenched the sergeant by the collar. "You know the average statistic of a predator keeping a child alive during a stand-off?" He didn't wait for a response. "Forty percent. Now I don't know how well you did in math, but I think we can agree that anything below one hundred percent is too low." He pointed to the building. "That woman is smart, she's armed, and she's dangerous. She knows what's coming." Grant let the sergeant go and then turned to the others. "We need to throw her off-balance. We wait, and we lose."

Sergeant Moynahan looked to the rest of the officers and then glanced down to the radio receiver still in his hand. The others waited for his action, and Grant knew that if he wasn't on board with the plan, then he'd be going in alone.

Moynahan set the receiver back inside his squad car. "Officers Milks, Petty, Richards, and Grantham, you're with us." He looked to Grant. "We'll follow you inside."

Grant backed toward the building as weapons were being drawn, addressing the men following him. "How many people do we still have in the complex?"

"At least sixty," Moynahan said.

"Where are we at with cutting the power?" Grant asked, gradually gaining speed as he led the six of them to the building's south entrance. Moynahan radioed for a response, and utilities informed them that power would be off in two minutes.

The group paused by the stairwell door. News helicopters swarmed overhead alongside the police choppers, the heavy thump of blades overshadowing Grant's pounding heart. His arms and legs shook with adrenaline. He didn't feel cold anymore.

With thirty seconds until power was cut, Grant found himself retracing every step of the case. He'd followed it to the letter in regards to protocol and profiles. And yet, here he was, facing a female abductor who had taken a young girl and used that very same book against him. It was like she knew his moves before he was even going to make them. It was nothing but chance that he found her in time, and when investigations came down to chance, events grew chaotic.

The light above the stairwell door cut off, and Grant flung the door open, leading the charge inside. The illuminated circular ends of flashlights revealed the narrow staircase and the five flights of stairs they needed to ascend.

Boots collided against the steps silently but quickly. The stairwell retained a damp coldness worse than outside. The light drip of water into a puddle signaled a leak somewhere, and judging by the warped guardrail to the stairs and the graffiti sprayed on the walls, this place was one building inspection away from being condemned.

Empty beer cans and liquor bottles huddled in the corners. The smell of human waste drifted past Grant's nostrils a few times, and each whiff agitated the sour pit in his stomach. They passed the second floor, then the third and fourth, and when Grant's flashlight highlighted the number five on the wall to the right of the floor's exit, he paused.

The officers clustered at the door and lowered their flashlights along with their pistols. Grant motioned the sergeant close.

"What's the apartment number?" Grant asked.

"Five-twenty-two. It'll be on the left when we exit into the hallway."

Grant nodded. "You do not fire until we have the girl, and you do not fire unless you have a clear shot. Understood?"

Nods answered in response, and Grant slowly reached for the door handle. "Let's move." He pulled the door open and stepped into the hallway, the light from his flashlight bouncing across the floor and walls in time with his steps.

Even with the aid of the flashlight, his eyes strained in the darkness as he counted down the apartment numbers on either side of the hall, all of which still had people inside, sitting in their living rooms or bedrooms and scared to death.

All it would take was one stray bullet through one of the paper-thin walls of the complex to trigger a chain of events that would lead down a bloody path. But in the time frame given, they couldn't measure all the variables. They had to act. They had to get the girl now.

Five-twenty-two finally appeared on Grant's right, and he held up his hand, halting the advance of the officers behind him. He approached slowly, checking the doorframe for any cracks or breaks, any sign that the woman may have laid a trap.

Once cleared, he motioned the rest of the officers close. Three officers stacked up against one another on either side of the door. Grant curled his fingers around the door knob and gave a gentle twist. The knob gave way, and Grant paused one last time, drawing in a breath. This was it.

Grant thrust the door open, leading the charge through a narrow hallway that opened up into a living room. And the first thing his flashlight fell across was Mallory Givens sitting on a worn and tattered couch with duct tape over her mouth, and her wrists and ankles as well. But what caused

Grant to lower his pistol and flashlight were the bricks of C-4 strapped to the twelve-year-old girl's chest.

Sitting next to Mallory on the couch, as calm and still as water, with her arm stretched out and holding a detonator with her thumb over the trigger, was Stacy. "Everyone except the detective out, or we all go up in flames."

The officers froze. Every person in the room was one breath away from pulling the trigger, or in Stacy's case, letting go.

"Detective Grant?" Sergeant Moynahan asked.

"Do as she says," Grant answered. "And get as many people out of the building as you can." Slowly, one by one, the officers obeyed, retreating out the door and closing it once they were gone.

With the three of them alone, Grant turned his attention to Mallory, who shivered uncontrollably. She sniffled through her nose, and her red eyes and puffy cheeks revealed she'd been crying. "It's going to be all right, Mallory. I promise."

The girl gave her head a gentle nod but then shuddered when Stacy touched the back of her neck.

"She's doing just fine," Stacy said, stroking the girl's hair. "This is something she's been looking forward to for a very long time." A single tear rolled down the little girl's cheek as she shut her eyes. Stacy turned back toward Grant, her arm still outstretched with her finger over the trigger. "You're a difficult man to get rid of. But I suppose I only have myself to blame. Keeping the flowers was reckless." She shook her head. "I didn't adhere to the rules. If I had just waited one more day like everyone else—" She shut her eyes. "It doesn't matter now."

Grant's heart rate and blood pressure skyrocketed. Despite his eyes adjusting to the darkness, black crawled over his vision. It was the first warning sign just before someone passed out or had a heart attack. He gritted his teeth and leaned up against the wall, the only way he could stay upright.

"The website you visited," Grant asked. "What was it?"

Stacy inched closer to Mallory on the couch and put her arm around the girl like the two were friends. The intimacy triggered another spasm of revulsion from Mallory as well as Grant. "It's a gateway into a world that was once shut to many, but is now open." She leaned forward and placed her hand on Mallory's leg. "For me it was a way to learn how to get what I wanted. A class of seduction"—she dug her nails into Mallory's bare flesh—"and law. I even learned about you."

"That's very thorough of you," Grant said.

"The website suggests researching the missing person detectives in the areas where you're going to abduct," Stacy said. "See how good they are, learn their patterns, their history. And you have quite the history, Detective Grant. Fifteen years on the force. Ten as a detective, eight in homicide." Stacy frowned, feigning concern. "But then two years ago something happened. Your wife died. Car accident, and you went off the deep end."

Grant tightened his grip over the pistol and flashlight.

"But there was something odd about the sudden shift in your career," Stacy said. "You were great in Homicide. And while the death of a spouse is tragic, your behavior went beyond normal grief. Which meant that there was more. And I was right."

Grant trembled, the black spots growing larger over his eyes. His heart pounded in his chest. "I should have been in that car with her."

"That's right," Stacy said. "And then you could have died along with your pregnant wife, like one big happy family."

The gun and flashlight dropped to the floor, and Grant

fell to his knees. Tears filled his eyes, and he sobbed. He still remembered the call he received at the precinct. He still remembered how brutalized Ellen's body was on the coroner's table when he identified the body; her eight-month pregnant body. And he still remembered how his heart cracked when the doctor told him that the injuries to Ellen's womb were so severe that the baby inside was pulverized beyond anything recognizable. There wasn't anything left to bury.

Grant wiped his eyes, and Stacy laughed. "Don't look so glum, Detective."

"So what now?" Grant asked, sniffling and trying to recompose himself. "The game is over. No matter what you do. You escape, you'll be hunted. You kill the girl, you'll receive the same treatment. You let your thumb off the trigger, and we all die. Was that the point?"

"The point is to extend the inevitable," Stacy said. "That's always been the point." She shook her head in frustration. "It's what you do every day in your job. You try and extend people's lives." She turned and smiled at Mallory. "Like hers." Stacy stood and took two steps closer to Grant but was mindful to stay out of reach should he decide to make a move. "You're going to walk us out of here. Then, we're going to get in your car and drive until we either run out of fuel or the authorities stop following us."

"And if they don't stop following us?" Grant asked, already knowing full well that they wouldn't, no matter what she did.

"Then we start all over," Stacy said. "Stand up, take four steps backward, and leave the gun."

Grant complied, and he watched Stacy pick up the gun and then aim it toward Grant.

"Now, undo the tape around Mallory's legs," Stacy said.

Grant knelt and fiddled with the duct tape with his nails,

but eventually had to tear it with his teeth. Once on her feet, Mallory kept close to Grant, and he had a better look at the device strapped to her chest, but the new proximity wouldn't help him defuse it. If he wanted to stop it from blowing up, then he had to get his finger on that detonator.

"Move," Stacy said, keeping the pistol aimed at the back of Grant's head.

The trio emerged into the hall, and Grant noticed the open doors they passed, which told him the officers had cleared anyone still inside the building. He was glad for that.

By the time they reached the stairwell for the descent, Mallory could barely put one foot in front of another. She whimpered through the piece of duct tape and trembled violently.

Grant knew he was running out of time. The moment they stepped outside, things would only worsen. There would be a chase then a standoff, and then Stacy would be backed into her last corner and blow all three of them off the face of the earth.

"How many others have taken this class of yours?" Grant asked, his voice echoing in the stairwell as he took the first step down.

"It's not my class," Stacy answered. "I don't know who runs it. And even if you were to survive all of this, you'd never find out either." She sounded disappointed. "I am very good with programming code, and I can tell you that whoever designed the site was a genius. The security algorithms would make anyone's head spin."

"You admire him?" Grant asked as they reached the fourth floor, his eyes scanning the corners for those empty glass bottles. "This teacher?"

"Could be a her," Stacy said. "Though statistically that's not likely. I recognize I'm a bit of an anomaly, but I'm not the only one." There was a hint of a smile in her tone. "You'd be surprised how many people search for the ability to live out the fantasies they keep to themselves."

Grant kept one hand on Mallory's shoulder and made sure his body shielded hers from Stacy's aim, not that it mattered if he couldn't get the detonator. They passed the third floor, and if he remembered correctly, there was an empty fifth of Jack Daniels on the second floor. If he could get it without her noticing, then he might have a chance.

"Getting quiet on me," Stacy said. "Whatever you're thinking, I would recommend against it."

Grant made sure to keep the flashlight off as they neared the second floor, and he squinted, praying he could find the bottle in time. He'd only get one shot at it.

"I am thinking," Grant said. "I'm thinking about how you did all of this work and you're so willing to accept the outcome of losing."

"I told you I—"

"I know what you told me. I just think that all of this is useless to avoid the inevitable. At least my inevitable has a chance," Grant said, goading her forward. "Yours doesn't. They know who you are now, and they'll never stop hunting you, no matter how far or how long you run."

"Shut up," Stacy said, taking a step closer and pressing the gun against the back of Grant's skull.

"I mean, for you to just lose everything and for it to come apart so quickly after all of that planning, I can't imagine that you'll have any peace once this is done," Grant said.

"I said shut up!" Stacy pressed the barrel of the pistol against the back of his head even harder.

Mallory placed her left foot on the platform of the second floor, and Grant eyed the Jack Daniels bottle from earlier. With his hand still on Mallory's shoulder, Grant stepped on the back of her foot, and she tripped forward. He stumbled in the same motion to help catch her, his body blocking the view of him snagging the empty bottle in the process.

"Get up!" Stacy said, her shrill scream echoing over the dark walls.

Grant made sure Mallory didn't hit the floor hard, and when he helped her up he kept the bottle tucked in the hand that held her shoulder, which he still blocked from Stacy's view.

"Are you all right?" Grant asked, giving Mallory a light pat on the shoulder. "That could have been bad." The pressure point from the end of Stacy's pistol returned to the base of Grant's skull.

"What the fuck are you doing?" Stacy asked.

For a moment Grant was sure that she'd seen him reach for the bottle and that it would erode the last piece of sanity from her mind and send all three of them to hell. But how could have she seen it? It was dark, his body was in the way, there were too many—

"I said what the fuck are you doing!" Stacy repeated, screaming.

Grant tried to keep his voice calm. "She fell. I was just helping." He remained still, the pressure from the gun keeping him in place. Mallory froze as well and whimpered through the duct tape.

"Well, keep her upright, or I'll put a bullet through your brain here and now," Stacy said.

But Grant knew different. The moment she fired the gun, the entire police force would come raining down on her head, damn the consequences of what happened next. Someone would shoot. Someone would get trigger happy. And then boom.

"I will," Grant answered then nudged Mallory forward, the bottle still clutched tight in his hand. The bottom floor neared, and Grant knew he'd have to make a move quickly.

The best bet would be when they reached the door. It would provide more movement than Stacy could keep track of. It all came down to him just getting his hand over the detonator before she could let go. No matter what.

Mallory reached for the door handle, her hand shaking, and every muscle in Grant's body tensed. Grant purposely held Mallory back, slowing her down and making all three of their bodies cluster at the door. Grant was waiting for one moment, just the right one where he had a half-second jump on her. That was all he needed.

"Go on!" Stacy said. "Move!"

Stacy thrust the pistol forward past the left side of Grant's face, and that was his chance.

All in one movement, Grant smashed the heavy glass bottle to the side of Stacy's face while his free hand closed a fist around the thumb that held the detonator in place. A gunshot fired, and the percussion reverberated so loudly Grant thought his eardrums would burst. The only thing he concentrated on during the one and a half seconds of contact was making sure that thumb didn't come off the button.

Grant and Stacy dropped to the floor, and Grant felt a pop in his left shoulder in the collision. A white flash blinded him, followed quickly by a sharp pain down his entire left side. The muscles in Stacy's arm had gone limp, and blood covered the right side of her face where the bottle had made contact. She lolled her head back and forth, and while the sharp pain in Grant's shoulder kept him frozen in place, he reached his left hand to the detonator.

But Stacy aimed the pistol at Grant the moment he moved, and he was forced to divert his effort to snatch her wrist as the two grappled for the gun. With her finger still over the trigger, Stacy fired three shots into the air until a cluster of S.W.A.T. officers barged in.

Assault rifles spat bullets, and gunshots thundered like

fireworks. In the midst of the firefight, Grant felt another sharp pain, this one on the right side of his abdomen. But through it all he focused all his strength on his left hand, keeping it clamped over Stacy's, over the detonator. When he looked at her face her eyes were open, but nothing except a lifeless expression looked back. She was dead. The bomb didn't go off. Mallory was safe.

10

$\mathcal{T}$he moment Dana Givens saw her daughter in the back of the ambulance, Grant didn't think a reinforced steel door would have held the mother back, let alone the two officers watching over the girl as the paramedics examined her. The pair embraced, then cried, kissed, and cried some more.

When it was all said and done, the girl was unharmed. The emotional scars would take a long time to heal, but Grant was glad nothing physical happened to the girl. It could have been a lot worse.

Grant watched the reunion unfold from the back of his own ambulance. The pain in his right abdomen turned out to be a bullet from one of the S.W.A.T. members that barely grazed his love handle, and the crack in his left shoulder was nothing more than a dislocation. It hurt more going back in than it did coming out.

One of the officers from the raid walked over to the Givens girls and escorted her and the mother to a squad car. Neither were aware of anything other than each other, and Grant was glad the two were reunited. There would be time to question them later, but for now it was best to let the girl go.

The phone in Grant's pocket buzzed, and he jumped from the vibration. It was Mocks. Before he answered, he turned back to the paramedic. "Am I all set?"

"You're good," he said.

"Thanks," Grant lowered his shirt and answered the call. "I didn't think hospital patients could have cell phones?"

"They make exceptions for officers," Mocks answered. "And also for people who raise hell."

"How are you feeling?" Grant slid off the back of the ambulance and wobbled forward. His legs felt like wet noodles.

"Better, but I heard I missed a lot of excitement," Mocks said, her voice tired. "So is the ambassador going to give you two medals tomorrow or what?"

Grant grinned. "Maybe. I'm on quite the streak."

"Well, let's hope your hand stays hot."

He didn't like Mocks's tone or the phrasing. "What are you talking about?"

"Remember the website that was blocked on the youth pastor's computer?" Mocks asked.

"Yeah," Grant answered.

"I just got off the phone with Cyber, and they managed to get through. It's some kind of class where you can learn how to abduct kids. It's got everything from how to seduce them, where to look for them, and how to make it look like you're not doing anything wrong."

"Jesus Christ," Grant said, whispering to himself.

"And that's not even the worst part," Mocks replied. "The site has a subscription list with the usernames of all the 'students' that come to learn."

Grant didn't want to ask the question, but he had to know. "How many?"

"Over one hundred," Mocks answered.

The normal sour pit and steel-winged butterflies that filled his stomach at this type of news returned in full force. Grant looked down at his watch, where the timer for the Givens case was still running. He stopped the timer then cleared it, resetting everything back to zero. What came next would be a different beast, one that he'd never encountered before.

Parker read the address one more time, making sure he had it right. He wiped his palm onto his pants. He couldn't stop sweating. The writing on the paper had faded. He didn't know why he wrote it in pencil.

He crumpled the piece of paper and reminded himself of the five grand that was waiting for him after he was done. It was a lot of money for one job. And there was the potential for more if he was successful. It dark money though. Real dark.

Parker grew up Catholic. His grandfather and grandmother had raised him and forced him to go to church twice a week. Each visit warranted a confession of his sins. He repented and the priest would absolve him, and Parker would leave.

Parker never understood how the priest just sat there and listened to all the terrible things that people did. He imagined it was a hell of a weight to carry, knowing everyone's secrets and keeping them to yourself. If Parker was forced to listen to everyone's troubles, he imagined he would have blown his fucking brains out a long time ago. He could barely handle his own issues, let alone that of a whole community. But that was why he never went into the priesthood, a piece of disappointing news for his grandmother. She'd be rolling in her grave if she saw what he was doing now.

The parking lot mall was busy. Saturday was always a big

shopping day. Parker sat in his truck and leaned back low in the seat. He was a big guy, nearly filling up the whole cabin, and he grew more uncomfortable the longer he sat. He was wedged in a spot between a sports car and a minivan, but his truck was high enough to see over both, giving him a three hundred sixty-degree view of the cars that passed and jock-eyed for what few parking spaces remained.

One altercation prompted a man to leave his car and threaten another driver that took his spot. It was all just words though. The moment Parker got a good look at the guy, he knew there wouldn't be any trouble. He always knew who was a pussy and who wasn't afraid to bleed.

Parker glanced down to his hand and the white gauze that covered his fresh ink. He patted the puffy bandage with his finger and winced upon contact. He'd gotten it earlier this morning, sealing his fate. He was part of the group now, and the only way out was six feet under. But this wasn't his first go-around with dangerous company.

The rap sheet filed somewhere in his probation officer's cabinet told the same story of most parentless kids. Spent some time in juvie for burglary and destruction of property, did a stint at the state pen a few years back for grand theft. But he couldn't put all of that blame on the back of his nowhere-to-be-found parents. And it wasn't like his grandparents didn't try and do their part. The old crows loved him, were good to him, gave him every opportunity in the world. But he just didn't listen.

Booze, girls, and rock 'n roll were all he cared about during high school, which he didn't hang around long enough to finish. Once he dropped out, his grandparents stopped trying so hard. He figured they finally understood he was a lost cause. That was fine with him.

They let him stay in the house until he was eighteen. There wasn't much talking that last year together, but there was always food in the fridge and leftovers waiting for him on the stove with a note from his grandmother that had his name on it circled in a heart.

Parker's stomach soured at the memory, and he pressed the back of his hand to his mouth to keep the vomit at bay. He was a long way from those days.

It was funny how he still remembered all those things so vividly. He guessed he was lucky that the drugs and booze hadn't rotted all of his mind, though he figured it wouldn't be much longer until it did. Maybe he wouldn't live long enough to find out. There was something comforting about that notion.

The sun grew higher and hotter in the sky, warming the inside of his truck. Parker cranked the manual lever to lower the window and caught a cool breeze that drifted by. It was a gorgeous day outside. A rarity in Seattle for the month of March.

Hordes of people funneled in and out of the mall's entrance, and it became harder for Parker to keep track of all the movement. If he missed her, then he would have to do it somewhere else. But that went against the plan, and the new tattoo on his hand was a reminder of what happened when those plans changed. Best to do what they had told him to do in the first place.

A gaggle of girls in the middle of the crowd exiting the mall caught his attention, and Parker leaned forward. There were a few bodies blocking the face, and when the fat man in the Seahawks jersey finally shuffled out of the way, Parker saw her.

Annie Mauer was in the middle of her friends, all of them holding bags from whatever teeny-bop store had the hottest trends these days. All four of them held coffees, smiling and giggling about nonsense. They followed the crowd toward the bus stop on the other end of the parking lot where they would catch their ride home, and Parker started his truck to follow.

With Parker's attention focused on the girls, he missed the white sedan speeding down the parking lot. A horn blared and Parker slammed on the brakes.

The driver behind the wheel of the white sedan waved his hands in circles, mouthing something that would have gotten him shot if Parker wasn't in a hurry. The sedan passed, and Parker returned to his search for the little blonde girl amidst the sea of bodies.

Parker sped through the parking lot, hoping to reach the bus stop before the girl did. He would have snagged her while she was walking in the crowd, but that opportunity was lost. He had to improvise now.

The truck screeched to a halt in a parking spot right behind the bench where the bus stop was located. Parker kept the engine running as he turned to look for the girl. His heart beat faster the longer he didn't see her, and he squeezed the steering wheel so tight that the bandage on his left hand popped off, exposing the black spider web tattoo that was still bloodied from the morning's session.

Parker pressed the bandage back down over his skin. He looked to his left, and there walked Annie Mauer and her friends. He turned his head away and reached for the hat that he tucked low over his head. He flipped his collar up and opened his door just a crack.

Annie would pass right by him, so caught up in her conversation about boys, or music, or whatever kind of shit that little girls talked about, to even notice the fact that he was near. She stayed in the middle, which wasn't ideal for a quick grab, but Parker had a long reach. She didn't look heavier than seventy pounds.

The sweats worsened, and Parker kept his eyes locked on Annie in his side mirror as she stepped within reach. He thrust the door open and knocked over the closest two girls to the asphalt.

Parker wrapped his meaty hand around Annie's arm and pulled her toward him. She was heavier than he expected, but even with his sensitive left hand, he managed to get her over his lap and into the passenger seat.

The girls screamed, and Annie kicked and thrashed inside the truck. Parker shifted into reverse, balancing one hand on the wheel while the other was busy subduing the girl, and caught a glance in his rearview mirror.

The girls had their phones out, recording him. Distracted, Annie kicked him in the ribs, and Parker slammed on the brakes. He backhanded her so hard she slammed into the passenger side door.

"Stop it!" Parker said, shifting into drive and pulling out into traffic as he ran a red light that nearly wrecked him.

The girl's eyes welled up with tears, and a red lump appeared on her cheek. She curled up into a ball in the farthest corner away from him and cried.

Parker kept both hands on the wheel, adrenaline rushing through his veins. His chest raised and lowered with each heavy breath, and he changed lanes, quickly getting off the main road, and slowed his speed. He had the girl. Now he just had to get to the drop off point.

"What do you want?" Annie sniffled through choked sobs, her knees tucked into her chest with her feet on the seat. "I didn't do anything."

"Shut. Up." Parker cast her a hard side-eye, and the girl shriveled up into nothing. "The more you talk, the worse it will be for you. Got it?"

The girl trembled, silently sobbing to herself. Parker reached for the crumpled paper with the address on it one last time. It was in the middle of nowhere, and a place he would learn to know well if today was successful. But there were a few snags now.

People saw his truck, hell, maybe people saw his face. No doubt those little bitches had already called the police. Plus they had him on video. He had to ditch the truck.

Parker spotted a van parked behind a seafood restaurant. It looked old enough for him to hotwire without any problems. He pulled up next to it, and the abrupt stop jerked the girl into the dashboard. He shoved her out of the way and reached into the glove box. He removed the pistol and searched for anything with his name on it. He paused for a moment as the girl's eyes were locked on the gun, and then he remembered what they had said.

Scare them to the point of torture. We want to break them so we can mold them into whatever we want. The event needs to be traumatic so it changes them. Do whatever it takes.

Parker pressed the end of the pistol's barrel against the side of Annie's head, and the girl moaned with grief. He grabbed her chin with his free hand and squeezed hard, keeping the pressure from the pistol against her skull.

"Listen to me very carefully," Parker said, the tears from the girl's eyes causing his grip to loosen on her chin. "You are going to meet some bad people. They're gonna do things to you, and it's better to just go with the flow from now on, all right? The more trouble you cause, the more they will hurt you. And I'm not talking a spanking like mommy and daddy used to give you. Real bad stuff. Real pain. Understand?"

The girl trembled. Parker pulled the little girl's face closer to his until they touched noses. Freckles spotted her cheeks, and even with her eyes bloodshot, he saw the rich brown color they were. "Do. You. Understand?"

Annie shut both eyes, two more tears streaming down the corners, and nodded.

"Good," Parker said. He slowly removed his hand, and

then the pistol. "Get out." He retreated, and the girl did as she was told. Parker pocketed the truck keys and then stuffed Annie in the middle row of van seats. He pulled a roll of duct tape from his cargo pants and bound the girl's tiny hands together, then did the same to her feet. He sidled up to the driver's side door, which was unlocked, and pried open the dash underneath, exposing the wires.

It'd been a while since he'd hotwired a car, and it took a few tries, but he finally sparked the engine to life. He looked back in the middle row of seats and saw that the girl had lain down, curled up into a ball. Her face was wet and her eyes were still red, but her expression was stoic.

Parker had seen that look before. He'd even worn it a few times. Your mind reached a threshold where it just couldn't take any more, so you burrowed inside yourself. It was the only way to cope, because the alternative was insanity.

As they drove to the meeting point, Parker's mind drifted back to the priest of his childhood. He wondered if the holy man ever heard any of the really bad stuff, stuff like he'd done over the past few years. And if the priest did, Parker wondered what he thought of those people that he saw on Sundays. All of those vile creatures sitting in his church, filling his pews, nodding and singing and chanting all of that bullshit. It was all just a show. Just a game people played to make themselves feel better. The only god and devil in this world were the ones people created for themselves, and Parker had already chosen sides.

11

_____

The crowd turnout was larger than expected and turned the auditorium into standing room only. Guest speakers, press, politicians, anyone who was anyone was at the ceremony. Congratulations were thrown around, all the appropriate agencies patting themselves on the back. It wasn't every day that an ambassador's daughter was rescued. But the longer the ceremony continued, the more anxious Detective Chase Grant became. He didn't like the spotlight. Loathed it, really.

Grant was the youngest man on the stage by at least ten years and, standing at six feet, was the tallest. Still, at thirty-five years old, he understood he was no spring chicken, but he'd kept in decent shape, unlike the public servants surrounding him. However, Grant's complexion was much paler than his fake-tan counterparts. A bi-product of Seattle's weather and basking in a fluorescent glow for hours at his desk.

The press in the front row snapped pictures. Grant didn't smile. It was hard to think about anything other than the new case he'd stumbled into just the day before. It was unprecedented.

Grant twirled the gold band on his left ring finger and tried to ignore the tie choking his neck. He glanced to his left and examined the exit just off stage. He'd need to get there quickly. The line of politicians to his right, which included the ambassador, Senator Pierfoy, and the mayor himself would be eager to extend the event with photo-ops. Grant intended to avoid it.

"And so in closing," Mayor Brugsby said. "I want to thank everyone involved in the successful rescue of Ambassador Mujave's daughter and returning her safely to her family. None more so than Detective Chase Grant, whose input and expertise brought a speedy end to a horrible nightmare. And for his efforts, I present to him Seattle's highest honor, the Medal of Valor."

Grant gave a light bow as the medal was ceremoniously placed around his neck. Applause. Pictures. More congratulations, and then a slow exhale as Grant ducked off stage and headed toward the exit, his hand in his pocket to retrieve his phone. He'd kept it on silent, so if Mocks had called him with an update—

"Detective Grant!"

Grant stopped and closed his eyes. *So close.* He turned slowly as the mayor's press secretary, Stephanie Gutz, jogged toward him with a clipboard and headset.

She grabbed Grant's arm and tugged him back toward the front of the stage. "You need to say a few words to the press."

Grant stood his ground. "The department has already made a statement." He placed a gentle hand over hers and carefully removed her claws from his jacket. "I have to get back to work."

Grant made it one step before she blocked his path, hands clasped together, begging for him to stay.

"Please! Your picture tested so well with our focus groups. You have no idea how good this will make the mayor look, especially with his campaign for re-election kicking off next week. We need the momentum." Stephanie paused and then leaned in closer. "The mayor doesn't forget things like this, Detective. It could be beneficial for you in the future."

There were a number of reasons that Grant could have given Stephanie to avoid the dance of Q&A with the press, but there was only one that mattered. Reporters liked to dig, and the more they dug into Grant's past, the more they would find. And it was a past Grant preferred to keep buried.

"I appreciate the offer, Ms. Gutz, but I really have to be going," Grant said, subconsciously grabbing the wedding ring still on his left hand. "There's another case I'm working on, and it really can't wait."

Stephanie's eyes grew wider. "Anything you'd like to share? You've been on quite the roll lately."

"Have a good day, Ms. Gutz." Grant left the woman with her arms flapping at her sides, exasperated. He headed toward the rear exit door where his undercover sedan was parked when another voice bellowed his name.

"Detective Grant!"

Grant sighed, turning around. "I really don't— Mr. Ambassador. My apologies."

"I was hoping to catch you before you left." Ambassador Mujave was the shortest on stage, but his booming voice and warm grin compensated for what he lacked in stature. He was the only politician that Grant had ever met that didn't make his skin crawl.

"What can I help you with?" Grant asked.

The pomp and circumstance faded, and the tone of a father emerged as he pulled Grant aside. "I just wanted to thank you again for what you did." He rolled the tips of his fingers together as he spoke, looking down at his shoes. "My wife wanted to be here to thank you personally as well, but she hasn't left Dalisay's side since she was returned to us." He swallowed. "Since *you* returned her to us."

"It was a group effort," Grant said. "The FBI laid some solid groundwork."

"The FBI had no idea who took her or where to look," Mujave said. "Even their lead investigator told me that he couldn't have done it without you."

Grant remembered the special agent in charge, Chad Hickem. He was a mountain of a man, but friendly enough. "That was kind of him to say."

"Detective, the motivation for my attendance here today extended beyond expressing my gratitude." Mujave paused, his hands clasped together, his brown eyes intently focused on Grant. "I've spoken to a number of your coworkers and commanding officers, and it appears you have quite the reputation with the Seattle PD." He smiled. "You're very good at your job. The best."

Grant ran a hand through the thick and wavy head of hair that was as black as the ambassador's suit. "I've been fortunate with some breaks."

"I'm not sure fortunate is the right word, Detective," Mujave said. "Your superiors call you the bloodhound." He tapped the side of his nose. "They say you're relentless."

Grant shifted uneasily. He could only take so much praise in one day, and he was itching to check his phone to see what Mocks had learned. "Most of the missing persons I deal with are children. Abductions by strangers are typically traumatic. The quicker I find those kids, the faster they can start healing."

"A parent's grief is a powerful tool," Mujave said, his words slow. "Perhaps that's what propelled you to switch departments and join missing persons. Your wife was pregnant when she passed, yes?"

It was the very same question Grant had hoped to avoid with the press. "Eight months." Grant's voice caught on the last word, and he cleared his throat.

"I'm very sorry for your loss," Mujave said. "It was a car accident?"

Grant nodded. "A semi-truck driver fell asleep at the wheel. My wife and daughter were killed on impact."

Mujave gripped Grant by the arms and stepped intimately close for a pair that had only met twice. But there was a genuine concern on the ambassador's face, and it was very calming.

"Your pain has helped many other families," Mujave said. "Mine included. But I want you to do more. I want to offer you a job."

Grant furrowed his brow. "I'm afraid I'm not much of a politician."

Mujave smiled. "No, you're not." The ambassador stepped away from Grant, his head down, again quickly rolling the tips of his fingers together. "My country has a terrible problem, and I'm afraid it's become intertwined with your own." He spun on his heel, looking up at Grant. "Right here in your very city in fact."

"What problem?" Grant asked.

"Every year, hundreds of women and young children are taken from the Philippines, plucked from their homes and families, some as young as eight or nine, and sold as sex slaves that are trafficked around the Pacific, including the United States." Mujave's eyes misted, but his voice didn't break. "It would be a great opportunity for you. Both professionally and financially."

Grant covered the wedding ring on his left hand with his right. "I appreciate the opportunity, Ambassador, but I have plenty of work here in Seattle."

Mujave nodded and reached inside his pocket. "If you

change your mind, give my office a call. Do your best to not misplace the card." He leaned closer and pointed to the number. "It has my personal cell." He flashed that wide political grin. "Thank you again, Detective Grant. You have done more for me than I could ever repay."

Grant nodded his thanks and escaped the auditorium without further obstruction. He flipped his collar to shield himself from the cold wind blowing outside. Despite the sun, it hadn't warmed past forty degrees, though Grant was thankful the rain finally stopped. He flipped over the card Mujave had given him and read the scribble on the backside. There were two words written on it: Polaris Project.

Grant had heard of it. The organization had an office based here in Seattle. He had heard reports through some of the other precincts of the sex trafficking issue the ambassador mentioned and how it had quickly turned into an epidemic along the West Coast.

The individuals that were kidnapped in the Philippines and other parts of Asia were funneled through Seattle's port. After they were given fake identification, they were shipped down south. Massage parlors were the biggest cover up. Almost all of them operated without a license, and they popped up like weeds choking the communities where they were housed.

When Grant was still with Homicide, he stumbled into one of those places from a case he was working. The women were packed inside the tiny buildings like sardines. Sleeping bags and piles of clothes lined the floors. They were all Asian and scared to death.

None of them spoke any English, and even when the translator arrived, they kept silent. The people who owned them had threatened them into silence. The girls were whipped, beaten, verbally abused, whatever it took to ensure their obedience.

After the raid, Grant turned the case over to the Special Victims Unit and the FBI. A few days later, he heard that three of the women they brought into custody had committed suicide. They were so desperate to escape their captors that they believed death was their best way out. Grant couldn't imagine a monster like that, but he wouldn't mind finding the person responsible.

"Detective Grant!"

Grant's hand froze on his car door handle. He turned slowly, only his eyes visible behind the upturned collar, bracing for the hordes of reporters.

But it wasn't paparazzi. It was an older gentleman shuffling after him, waving his hand in the air. He wore a dark suit with a bright purple tie. As he moved closer, Grant also noticed a flag pin on the man's lapel. It didn't take long for Grant to fill in the rest of the blanks.

"Senator Pierfoy," Grant said. "What can I do for you?"

The old senator consumed Grant's hand with his own and gave it three hearty pumps. "I just wanted to thank you again for all that you've done." He leaned in closer and lowered his voice. "Maybe have you come around to the front so I can snap a few pictures with the press while standing next to Seattle's favorite son?"

Grant gave a light-hearted smile and pulled his hand back from the senator's. "I'm afraid I'm in the middle of something right now." He turned, but the senator leaned his heavy body against Grant's car door to keep it shut.

"I saw you speaking with the ambassador. Most likely about that job?" Pierfoy asked. "I hope you haven't given him an answer yet."

"I have," Grant said. "It was no."

Pierfoy sighed. "Well, that's a relief." He straightened his jacket and lifted his chin. "I'll make this brief then, seeing as your disdain for this kind of talk is well known. I want to promote you. To Captain."

Grant's jaw went slack, and Pierfoy laughed.

"I'm glad I can still surprise people," Pierfoy said. "My wife says I'm too predictable. Glad I can prove the old cow wrong."

Grant held up his hand. "Senator, I don't feel comfortable taking that large of a leap. Especially over Lieutenant Furst. He's well liked by the officers. Me included."

"Oh god, no," Senator said, his guffaw exaggerated. "You wouldn't take over your current precinct. No, no, no. What I'm talking about is something new."

"Senator, I appreciate—"

"The ambassador's heart is in the right place, but there is a more pressing issue in our city that needs to be addressed, and that's the drug epidemic," Pierfoy said. "We are the hub for opioid use and production for the entire western United States. It is an epidemic that is eroding the very foundation of our communities, and it won't be long before they collapse under their own weight."

"Sir, I don't have much experience with drugs," Grant said.

"No, you don't," Pierfoy replied, then lifted his finger and pressed it against Grant's chest. "But you're skilled in finding people. And with your previous background in Homicide, I know you have the stomach for the more violent crime scenes. And during the department exchange program, you logged more hours with S.W.A.T. than any other detective in the state. I know you don't have any trouble banging on doors. Both on and off the clock."

Grant shook his head. "Off the clock?"

Pierfoy lowered his voice and raised an eyebrow. "I'm quite familiar with your past, Detective. Even the unsavory parts."

Grant stiffened. He should have known better. You couldn't outrun time. The seconds ticked away like drops of blood from an IV, and once it was done, so were you.

"I want you to end this war on drugs, Detective," Pierfoy said. "Help me give the communities back to the people who want them to be a safer place for their families. Help me end this violent war we have raging across our entire state. I know you could do a lot of good."

Before Grant answered, the senator held up his hands and backed away. "Just think about it. I know you have a lot on your plate, but it would be a disservice to give your answer so quickly, like you did with the ambassador. I'm in a hurry to get this done, but I'm willing to wait until I get the right people." He flashed a grin, but it lacked the well-natured smile of the ambassador's.

Grant lowered himself into the driver seat of his cruiser, his mind sifting through the morning's events and the past twenty-four hours. Grant knew offers like these were inevitable. He was aware of his skill at the job, but no matter how low of a profile he kept, he couldn't hide the results of his work. Work which required his attention.

* * *

THE PRECINCT WAS BUSY. More movement than usual. There hadn't been any call-ins yet, but Mocks felt it brewing. And it made her nervous.

Detective Susan Mullocks leaned back in her chair, which practically swallowed her whole. She'd always been small, and it had always pissed her off, though she'd reached a level of acceptance now that she was pushing thirty. She rocked slowly back and forth as she flicked the lever of the green Bic lighter in her left hand. The flame appeared and disappeared in rhythmic strokes. Mocks's hand performed the ritual involuntary. Old habits died hard.

She tucked her shortly cropped brown hair behind her ears, which exposed a small, pretty face. Freckles spotted her pale cheeks, and she kept her green eyes on the phone. In her two years with Missing Persons she'd spoken to dozens of parents, but this time felt different. This time she knew it was coming, and that knowledge only worsened the anxiety.

Mocks pocketed the lighter and reached into the bottom drawer of her desk. She removed a fresh pack of strawberry Pop-Tarts and discarded the wrapper on the growing pile of trash on her desk. The other officers joked that she ate like a NFL linebacker but never put on any weight. She cursed that when she was younger. Now she clung to it for dear life.

She opened her mouth to take a bite when her cell phone buzzed in her pocket. She hesitated when she saw the name on the screen. She wasn't in the mood to open this particular can of worms right now. But she knew that putting it off would only make it worse. She set the pastry down and leaned forward on her desk.

"Hey," Mocks said.

Rick paused. "I wasn't sure you'd answer."

"I'm waiting for Grant to get back from his award show," Mocks said. "I've got some time."

"I don't really want to do this over the phone, when are you going to be home?" Rick asked.

"I don't know," Mocks said.

A sigh. "Honey, I—if you're not willing to take the time to talk about this I don't know what we're going to do. We need to figure this—"

"Look, I've gotta go," Mocks said, and then hung up. It wasn't the most tactful goodbye, but her mind hadn't changed. And she didn't know how to tell him that without crushing him. It had made them so distant. They were like

JAMES HUNT

roommates who didn't get along anymore. They hadn't even touched one another in over a month.

Mocks chomped a huge bite out of her Pop-Tart when the desk phone rang, and she reached for it with a cobra-like strike. "Neheckhive Mullhocks." She swallowed the pastry, and repeated herself. "Detective Mullocks."

"I've got a mother calling in, Detective," Officer Banks said. "Says her daughter was taken at the mall. Her friends even have video."

Mocks leaned forward, her forearms crunching over the empty wrappers on her desk. "What's her name?"

"Hannah Mauer," Banks said. "Daughter's name is Annie Mauer. That was all I was able to get out of her. Good luck."

A beep, and then the call came through. "Hello, this is Detective—"

"Please, you have to help me." The woman's voice was quick and panicked. "My daughter, someone took her."

"Okay, ma'am, I need you to calm down for a second—"

"She was at the mall with her friends and they showed me the video of her being taken. It was some man, he was driving a truck," she gasped for breath, and then swallowed. "Someone took my daughter!"

Mocks sandwiched the phone between her shoulder and her ear and broke off another piece of Pop-Tart, nodding along and remembering to keep her voice as neutral as possible. "I understand you're scared, Hannah. But I need you to hang with me for a couple minutes and just answer some basic questions, okay?"

Hannah's breathing slowed, along with the pacing of her words. "O-okay."

"Great." Mocks popped another piece of strawberry-frosted deliciousness into her mouth. "Now, what was the mall you dropped your daughter off at?"

Mocks nodded and replied with affirmative grunts as she

devoured the pastry. She squinted her eyes shut, the rambling in her ear so shrill she had to lean away from the receiver a few times to avoid a pierced eardrum. She didn't bother with a pen and paper to jot down notes. She didn't need to.

Everything Hannah Mauer said into Mocks's ear was permanently recorded in her brain. Annie's description, the clothes she wore, birthmarks, age, birthdate, all organized neatly into the computer that was her brain.

"Okay, and that's the mall on the east side?" Mocks asked, flicking a crumb of hard icing off the top of her wedding ring. "Did her friends mention anything else?"

Malls were busy on the weekends. Made for good conditions for snatching kids. Only a small percentage didn't make it home. And that small percentage found their way to her desk with parents sounding just like her. Well, maybe not *just* like her.

"I-I-I don't know what to do," Hannah said, and she started cry. "I don't know where my daughter is."

Mocks halted the next piece of pastry to her lips and set it down, brushing the crumbs from her long sleeves. "Hannah, I know exactly what you need to do. Do you have a pen and paper? Or anything to write with?"

"Y-yes, just… Hold on, I…. Okay. I'm ready."

"Good," Mocks said. "Get a ride to precinct eighteen in downtown Seattle. That's where I work. Once you get here, we'll have you fill out an official statement. By the time you arrive, I'll have all of the paperwork ready to give my boss to gather the resources to find your daughter. And I'll need you to bring a few things. A recent picture of Annie, and any health records you have. And the video your daughter's friends took. Okay?"

"Yeah," Hannah answered. "I can do that."

"Now, is there anyone that would have taken your daughter?" Mocks asked. "Family members, the father, anyone like that?"

"No. I-I don't know who it could have been," Hannah said.

"That's all right," Mocks answered. "Just get here and ask to speak with Detective Mullocks and Detective Grant. My partner and I will be handling your case."

"Thank you, Detective," Hannah said. "I'll be there soon."

Mocks set the phone down and devoured what remained of the Pop-Tart. She exhaled through her nose and tugged at the long sleeves that concealed the marks in the crook of her arms.

She rose from the desk and walked back to Cyber. She weaved between the officers in the halls, the cops scurrying to get out of her way. When she was a rookie she had been bulldozed. But it only took one chop-block on an unsuspecting traffic cop to get everyone's attention. At five foot nothing and one hundred pounds, she used what leverage she could to her advantage. Thankfully the cop escaped with only a bruised ego.

Cyber was tucked away in a corner office at the very back of the building. They didn't get a lot of foot traffic; in fact, they preferred no traffic at all. It was a request that Mocks was happy to abide by, but Grant always liked doing things face to face and she thought the situation called for his tactics. It was something she admired about him and simultaneously drove her nuts.

Their last missing person case had landed them in some type of abduction conspiracy. Or at least the start of one. The perp from the same case had been logging into a website designed as an online class for abductions. It was how she learned all of the techniques. And if it hadn't had been for Grant, then she would have gotten away. Cyber had been trying to crack the site's source code to find out who created it, but it was tough sledding.

"Hey," Mocks said, knocking on the door. "Where are we at with the website from the Givens case?"

Four bodies turned in their chairs, slowly. The dimly lit room made the motion ominous. Three of them returned to the glow of their computer screens, and only Sam remained. He grabbed his laptop and walked past her without a word, turning into a small nook behind their office.

The site was already up on Sam's laptop when they turned the corner. He typed a few lines of code, sighed, and then leaned back in his chair. "I spent most of last night trying to work my way through the firewall, but haven't made a lot of progress." He crossed his arms over his stomach and chewed on his lower lip. He looked up at Mocks, the fluorescent lighting not doing any favors to the dark circles under his eyes.

"We need progress, Sam," Mocks said. "I just got an abduction call. A little girl at the east side mall."

Sam's face went pale. "You don't think the people who logged in here are—"

"Starting to apply what they've learned?" Mocks asked. "Yeah. I do. So I need to know everything you do."

Sam exhaled a shaky sigh and placed his fingers on the keyboard, drumming them over the letters without striking down. "We know that there were one hundred and seven users that signed into the site since its creation, which was six months ago. I know there are at least seven users who have logged into the site within the past forty-eight hours, and I also have the usernames of eighty of the one hundred and seven individuals who have logged in."

"That's our starting point," Mocks said. "Cross reference those usernames and see if we get a hit on anyone."

"I've tried, but with only a username as my only data point it's hard to find any type of match," Sam said.

"What about the site's contents?" Mocks asked. If she knew what the abductors were taught, then they might be able to get a step ahead.

"It's impressive," Sam answered, typing a few commands to pull up the site's coursework. "I have taken a lot of online courses over the years. Most of them were just 'read this' and then 'answer these.' Nothing but regurgitated thoughts. Whoever made this site put a lot of care and thought into it. The creator intended for their students to become the best. They cover everything in regards to an authority's response to an abduction: search efforts, negotiation techniques, S.W.A.T. formations for home invasions, media response, coordinated efforts across multiple agencies, our entire play-book is on here." He paused a moment, and then cleared his throat. "There was one thing in particular I found I thought you should know." He hit a few keys on his laptop, and the website uploaded a schematic. For explosives. "It seems that our abduction instructor has a scorched earth policy when their students are caught by police. The site suggests either rigging a vest to blow for the kid, or wiring the safe house that they're staying in to explode."

"Master abduction artists who dabble in explosives. Fantastic," Mocks said. "So they know the type of kid to look for, when to take them, and how to get away with it." She clenched her fists. "What kind of sicko would make some-thing like this?"

"Someone who's grown bored."

Mocks and Sam spun around and saw Grant standing in the hallway, staring down at the computer screen.

"How long have you been standing there?" Mocks asked.

"Long enough," Grant answered, switching his eyes from the computer to Mocks. "Banks said you had a call-in."

"Mother says her daughter was taken at the East Side Mall," Mocks said. "Where's your medal?"

"It's in the car," Grant answered, then turned to Sam. "What's the timeline on finding out who created the site?"

"If I can find the root IP, then maybe twenty-four hours, but that's going to be tough," Sam said.

"All right," Grant said, giving Sam a pat on the shoulder. "Let us know when you have something." Grant disappeared down the hall.

Mocks lingered behind. "Let me know if you find anything on that cross reference. And Sam, this is a priority."

He gave a nod, and Mocks chased Grant back to their desks, which sat directly across from one another. She pressed her knuckles onto her desk while Grant sifted through a few notes.

"Did you already take down the report for that girl?" Grant asked.

"Working on it," Mocks answered. "Mother is on her way now. But we've got some time before she gets here."

"Get a package together for Lieutenant Furst," Grant said, reaching for the squat filing cabinet he kept all of his cases inside. "I want to follow up with the Givens girl." He gestured to her Pop-Tart box. "Hand me one of those, will you? I didn't eat breakfast."

Mocks tossed him a packet, and he tore it open and took a big first bite as he scanned the file.

"Anything exciting happen at the ceremony?" Mocks asked.

"No," Grant answered, then closed the file and returned it to the drawer. "You stay here while I go and speak with the Givens girl."

Mocks placed her hands on her hips. "Why can't I come?"

"Because you didn't take any notes from the phone call,"

Grant answered, then looked up. "Or did you actually decide to write something down this time?"

Mocks grunted and plopped down in her chair. "Imprisoned by my own mind."

Grant placed the remaining chunk of strawberry pastry in his mouth, and then slid on his jacket. "I'll call you when I have something. And you let me know what happens with the mother. What was the name of the girl that was taken?"

"Annie," Mocks answered.

Grant froze. The color drained from his cheeks, and for a moment Mocks thought he was going to pass out. But after the momentary glitch, he wiped a few of the crumbs from his mouth and looked down at his watch. He squeezed one of the side buttons, and it beeped, starting that timer of his. It was a ritual, one that he performed with every new case. He always seemed to be fighting time, but she never really understood why. Maybe it helped keep him focus. After all, she had her lighter.

"We're already behind in the first hour," Grant said. "Get the paperwork to Furst ASAP. I'll call you when I'm done with the Givens girl." He nodded to the mess on her desk. "You keep eating those damn Pop-Tarts and you're gonna turn into one."

Mocks raised a fresh one and smiled. "One can only hope." She watched him leave, and that same ominous feeling from earlier clouded her senses. It was like a bad taste in her mouth that she just couldn't rid herself of, no matter how many frosted strawberry treats she ate. She looked at her phone, knowing the next time it rang, it was going to be for another abduction. The only question was when.

* * *

THE PARK WAS BUSIER than usual for a Saturday afternoon.

Craig Johnson blamed the weather. The sun had finally made an appearance after nearly a week of clouds and rain.

Children sprinted around the playground, chasing after one another, their high-pitched squeals of laughter carrying across the park. Kids played on the swings, the jungle gym, glided down slides, indulging in all the activities with friends. There was so much joy. So much life.

Craig came here often, but not too often. His rusted beater of a car had the potential to attract unwanted attention. And he made sure that he always parked in different locations and mixed up his times throughout the day and week. Saturdays were always a special treat he saved for himself when he'd been good.

It was a type of elated torture when he parked his 1986 Toyota Corolla one hundred yards from the park's entrance. He cut off the engine, slouched low in the driver seat, and zoomed in on the kids with his phone to get a better look, keeping an eye on the parents at the park's perimeter.

Sometimes he recorded the kids with video, or snapped pictures, and other times he would do nothing but watch. But today was special. Today was different.

The crowded and chaotic scene made for perfect conditions. He glanced over to the notepad that contained all of the scribbling he'd written from the class online. It was a godsend. All the tricks and tools to perform a successful abduction, all laid out in perfect detail.

Craig was wary about the website at first. There was no guarantee that it was real. What worried him most was that it was a trap to find people that were troubled. People like him.

Police and authorities were always fishing, looking for ways to snag adults who wanted to meet with children. Cyber divisions had grown more sophisticated in catching child predators. And with Craig's lack of technical understanding, he shied away from computers and chat rooms. Old school worked just fine for him.

Still, it was hard being so close and not able to touch. He came close a few times to giving in to his desires. They festered in his mind like glowing coals; never flaming but always hot.

But regardless of how bad he wanted it, for forty-seven years, Craig played it safe. He never risked exposure because he knew what happened to people like him when they were caught: branded evil, wicked creatures, tortured and raped in prison. They were experiences he wanted to avoid. And if it came at the price of forgoing his desires, then so be it.

So, this was Craig Johnson's life. He lived alone in a shitty studio apartment with rotting walls, dirty carpet, and failing appliances. He worked as a janitor for a hospital on the south side of Seattle where the pay was just as bad as the stink of its sickly patients. He had no family in the area, no friends, never went on dates. His only source of joy came from these visits to the park. It was days like this that kept him going. And today was going to be the best day of all.

Craig reached for the notebook and examined his check-list one last time. That was rule number one: check, then re-check. Mistakes could get you caught, and he didn't plan on having come this far only to lose everything.

He glanced in the back seat where the milk crate he'd stolen from work housed food, drinks, and blankets for his drive north. He had enough supplies to last for three days. A second crate sat behind the passenger seat. It was covered with a blue tarp. It was his backup plan, one that he hoped he wouldn't have to use. It was expensive, but he knew if he got caught, then it'd be worth it. That's what the website said at least.

Because he lived alone and never went anywhere, never did anything, his savings account had grown into a nice chunk of change: thirty thousand dollars. Over the past four months, Craig had withdrawn small, random amounts every week to avoid suspicion in draining his account. He reached for the money bag and recounted his cash; all accounted for.

Craig flipped through his documents: passports, Social Security card, driver's license, and bank account information. All of them had a different name: Dave Holgram. It was Craig's new identity. If this was going to work, then he would have to start over, and so would the boy.

A second set of documents sat next to his own. Craig removed the rubber band holding them together and double-checked to ensure everything was in order. The second forged passport had a picture of a young boy. His Tommy.

The child's passport was harder to forge, seeing as how there were specific pictures required for passports to be legitimate. But the school's website where the kid was enrolled had photos from school events, and Craig found plenty to choose from.

Once he had all of the necessary information, Craig sent it to the contact the website had mentioned, along with a check for ten grand. It was pricey, but the website said that it was the real deal. And they were right.

The first three days would be the worst, particularly the first six to twelve hours. That was when the police would be out in full force. Roads would shut down. The boy's picture would be plastered everywhere after the inevitable AMBER Alert, which meant anyone with a cell phone could spot him and call the cops. But because Craig knew all of it was coming, because he knew what the police would do before they even did it, he was prepared. Now it all came down to execution.

Craig lowered his head and drew in a breath through his nose. His stomach was a ball of nerves. He grabbed hold of the steering wheel to stop from shaking, but it didn't help very much. He shut his eyes. This was it.

Craig stepped out of his rusted car and flipped up the collar of his jacket. He slid on his sunglasses and hat and tucked both hands inside his jacket pockets. He was thankful for the bulky coat, as he hoped that it hid his trembling.

Two girls sprinted past on Craig's approach to the jungle gym and startled him, both so close that their little hands grazed his left pant leg. A jolt of adrenaline rushed through his veins from the contact, and he two-timed it toward the boy.

Tommy was in the center of the park, and through the dark lenses of his sunglasses, Craig kept a constant bead on him. He already knew what he would say. He already knew how he would get him to the car. Craig knew because he learned everything he could about the boy.

Tommy was always at the park alone. His mother would drop him off for a few hours while she went drinking at a bar down the street. She would return drunk, stumbling out of the car and reeking of booze.

Craig's mother drank a lot too. She also touched him. But that was a long time ago. Craig could save Tommy from that. He could give the boy something better. And in return, Craig would fulfill his own fantasies.

The cluster of children was thickest at the park's center, and Craig struggled to avoid contact. The adrenaline continued to build, and the bundle of nerves in Craig's stomach rumbled, followed by the slow crawl of acid up his windpipe. He swallowed the bile and pressed on. He couldn't lose it now. He was too close.

Tommy's blond hair reflected the sunlight as he climbed to the top of the slide. Craig smiled as the boy lifted his arms in the air and slid down. Tommy tumbled into the grass, then laughed and returned to the ladder for another slide when Craig called out.

"Tommy!"

The boy spun around at his name. When he saw Craig, he froze. He was frightened. So was Craig.

"Who are you?" Tommy asked.

Craig looked nervously to the left, then the right. They were the only pair in the center of the park that weren't moving. And what was worse, Craig was the only adult. A mother stood up from the bench she was sitting on to his left. He was drawing attention to himself. He needed to move quickly.

"I'm a friend of your mom's," Craig said. "She wanted me to come and pick you up."

The boy remained where he was but didn't exhibit any signs of an outburst. He simply arched an eyebrow. "I've never seen you before."

"I know," Craig said, taking another step forward. "But you need to come with me, and quick. Your mom is in trouble, and we need to go and help her."

The boy flashed concern. "She is?"

"Yes, and it's important we go now." Craig held out his hand, and the culmination of his entire life dwindled down to a few seconds. If the boy backed away or made any type of commotion, then the game was over. But if Tommy placed his little paw into Craig's massive palm, then all of that waiting, all of that sacrifice, all of that time and energy expended into this one moment would pay off. But Tommy had to play along. "And we have to hurry."

Slowly, Tommy grabbed Craig's hand. The moment their skin made contact, Craig clamped down around the boy's paw and walked back to the car. It was too surreal. A mixture of terror and excitement rushed through Craig's body.

"What happened?" Tommy asked as they neared Craig's Corolla. "Is she hurt?"

Craig opened the passenger side door, and the hinges squeaked. He helped the boy climb inside and then offered a reassuring smile. "No, but it's important we get out of here quickly. She wants to meet us somewhere, but if we're not quiet and we don't go fast, then she might be hurt. Do you understand?"

Tommy nodded.

Craig shut the door and saw the woman from before, now breaking out into a quick stride toward his car. She looked like she was reaching for her phone. He struggled to keep a natural pace to the driver side. He fumbled the keys and broke out into a sweat.

The woman waved her hands and broke out into a jog. Craig finally jimmied the key into the starter, and cranked the engine to life, keeping his head down as he shifted into reverse. Tires screeched when he floored the accelerator, the whole car vibrating from the speed.

Once clear of the park, he took a moment to look at the boy now sitting in his passenger seat. The same boy that he'd taken so many pictures and videos of on his phone. The same boy who Craig had watched and fantasized about from this very car. He had dreamed of this moment. But this wasn't a dream. It was real. The boy was his.

$\mathcal{N}$ ormal procedure warranted a successful missing child case to have the victim questioned about the circumstances of their abduction within three hours after being cleared by a medical team, and it was one of those rules that made Grant scratch his head.

It didn't take him long during his stint as a detective to understand that the people who wrote the manuals didn't measure the impact on the individual. Sure, statistically that was how a detective would retrieve the most accurate information while the events were still fresh in the child's mind, but that was the other half of the equation that wasn't measured: it was still fresh in the child's mind.

And the parents' minds for that matter. The kids were still in shock, and Grant always felt a predator himself trying to pry information from them. Out of anyone, he understood the desire to forget the past.

Grant did his best to try and keep his mind focused on the task in front of him with the Givens girl on the drive over, but his mind kept wandering back to the new case and the missing girl's name.

After the accident that killed his pregnant wife, Grant went into a tailspin, and he did everything he could to outrun the pain of his loss. He changed divisions within the department, moving from Homicide to Missing Persons. He sold his house, car, anything and everything that reminded him of Ellen.

But now, two years later, Grant found himself with a new case, and a new missing child. A girl with the same name he and his wife were going to give to their daughter. Annie.

Grant pushed the thought out of his head and parked outside the Givens's apartment building. He pounded on the door and after a few minutes, Dana Givens answered. The single mother wore a ratty robe, and her eyes were bloodshot. She'd been crying. He just hoped they were happy tears.

"Detective Grant." Dana spoke his name softly, and it was accompanied with a light smile. "One of the officers at the hospital said you might be stopping by this morning." She stepped aside. "Please, come in."

"Thank you." Grant bowed and entered. Their apartment was small, with the entrance hallway too narrow for more than one person to pass at a time.

"You can go ahead down the hall and into the kitchen," Ms. Givens said. "Mallory is still upstairs asleep. Do you need me to go and get her?"

"Please," Grant said.

The space in the kitchen didn't improve. The table for two was jammed between the end of the kitchen counter and a wall. The cabinets were crooked, some of the doors completely off the hinges. But Grant knew it was the best a waitressing job downtown could provide with six twelve-hour shifts. The Givens didn't have much, but they still had each other. A fact he knew they would appreciate even more now.

Ms. Givens entered the kitchen, alone, hugging herself

closely and rubbing the frayed sleeves of her robe. "She's getting dressed. She'll be down in a minute."

They stood quietly in the kitchen. Only the refrigerator hummed its opinion, along with the random bark of a dog. A few nervous smiles were passed about and when Mallory's footsteps were heard from the hallway, Grant gave a friendly wave as she entered.

"Hi, Mallory," Grant said.

The girl leaned up against her mother. She wore a similar frazzled robe, and her eyes drooped; either from a night of dead-to-the-world sleep, or a restless one. Grant hoped it was the former.

"I wanted to talk with you if that's all right?" Grant asked.

The girl looked to her mother, who rubbed her shoulder.

"You don't have to do anything you don't want to, sweetheart," Ms. Givens said.

"Your mom is right," Grant said.

Mallory looked at her feet, then lifted her head and looked straight at Grant. "You're going to ask me questions about what happened?"

"Yes," Grant answered.

"Will it help stop it from happening to other people?" Mallory asked.

"It usually does," Grant answered.

Mallory paused, then walked over to the tiny chair jammed up against the wall and wiggled under the table, her hands folded over the top. "Okay."

Grant smiled. "Thank you." In an effort to appear more relatable, Grant slid into the chair where he managed to cram all of his six-foot frame without breaking the table. "Mallory, before we get started, I just want you to know that at any time you feel uncomfortable, or if you want to stop, just let me know and we will."

Mallory drew in a breath and then nodded, exhaling

slowly. Her left hand shook and she steadied it with her right. Grant reached across the table and covered both of her hands with his.

"Everything is going to be fine," Grant said. He slowly removed his hand and then gently placed his elbows on the table, which leaned toward him from his weight. "I wanted to know how everything started. Between you and Stacy."

Mallory swallowed. "She was there on my first trip to the youth group. She was the first person to talk to me. She made me feel welcome. She made me feel like... like..."

"You were important," Grant said.

"Yeah," Mallory said. "Like I was important."

"And what did you guys talk about when you communicated with one another?" Grant asked.

And from there, it was textbook predatory behavior. Stacy would tell Mallory something secret about herself to help establish a bond and trust, and then Mallory would do the same. Grant had seen it before. It was all about layering, making sure the victim was eased into the relationship, making the victim think that all of this was their idea, then once that seed was planted, ensuring that it was only the predator that could save them from a doomed fate.

Mallory teared up twice during the retelling, but Grant admired the courage she gathered to push through it. Despite the terrible trip down memory lane, Grant discovered little that he didn't already know. The woman who kidnapped Mallory Givens was formidable, and she had learned all the tricks and secrets of abduction through the course she took on the website Grant and Mocks discovered.

"You did great," Grant said, his lips curving in a gentle smile. "Thank you so much for telling me."

The color from Mallory's cheeks had gone pallid, the conversation just as physically draining on her as it was mentally and emotionally. She nodded and leaned back in the chair as her lip quivered. Her eyes were focused on the table, but when she looked up at Grant, that courage from earlier vanished and all that remained was a frightened young girl.

"She's dead, right?" Mallory asked, the quivering growing worse. "She can't come back and get me? She won't come back and take me?"

"No, Mallory," Grant said, reaching for the girl's hands once more. "She won't ever come for you again."

Mallory broke down, tears streaming down her face, and Ms. Givens rushed to her daughter's side. The pair cried together and Grant leaned away from the tender moment between the two, excusing himself to leave. But when he stood, Mallory blubbered something while her face was still pressed against her mother's arm.

Grant turned back to the girl, leaning forward over the table. "What was that?"

Mallory lifted her head from her mother's arm, strands of her bangs glued to her forehead in stringy lines. "The spiders. They won't come either, will they?"

Grant shook his head, confused. "Spiders?" Grant asked. "Was that something you and Stacy spoke about?"

Mallory nodded. "It was after things got really bad, right before she put that vest on me."

That 'vest' had ten pounds of plastic explosive wired inside with Stacy West's thumb over a dead-man trigger. If Grant hadn't wrestled it out of the woman's clutches, the pair wouldn't be having this conversation right now.

"What did she say about the spiders?" Grant asked.

Mallory sniffled, finding that courage once again, calming her frayed nerves. "She said that it was better that she got me instead of the spiders. She said it would have been worse with them. That they would have—" She pulled her lips into her mouth, afraid to even speak the words. "Hurt me."

"Did she say anything else?" Grant asked, biting on the new lead, hoping to get more, but Mallory simply buried her face back into her mother's robe.

Grant expressed his thanks and walked himself out, leaving Ms. Givens and her daughter to sort through the process of healing. He mulled over what Mallory had said inside his car, trying to piece it together, but he had as much of an idea about what it meant as Mallory Givens did.

It had to be connected to the website somehow. Grant needed Sam to pull more data from the site. He rubbed the wedding band, his wife creeping into his thoughts for a moment when the radio came on.

"Unit thirty-five, this is Dispatch, over."

Grant reached for the receiver. "Go for unit thirty-five."

"Lieutenant wants you to come back to the precinct. Says it's urgent."

"Copy that, Dispatch." Grant set the receiver back on the hook and arched an eyebrow as his cell phone buzzed. It was Mocks. A light twinge soured Grant's stomach. Something was wrong.

* * *

PRESS VANS CLUTTERED the outside of the precinct when Grant returned. They swarmed his squad car on his approach, and when he finally found a parking spot, the horde circled him, thrusting microphones and cameras into his face. He held up his hand to block the flashes from the photographers, but he was helpless to evade the questions hurled his way.

"Detective! Can you tell us how many there have been so far?"

"Are any of the abductions connected?"

146

"I have sources telling me that as many as a dozen children have gone missing."

Grant waved his hands, growing more irritated the longer they followed him to the door. "I don't have any comment on current investigations." He pushed through to the door and left the roving animals outside where they belonged.

But if Grant was hoping for sanctuary in the precinct, he didn't find much peace inside. Phones rang loud and intermittently. Officers scurried around their desks. Everyone was on high alert. And for good reason.

Lieutenant Furst was behind his desk, the phone glued to his ear. Mocks was already in the office, twirling her Bic lighter but keeping the flame at bay. She didn't like to do it in front of the bosses. She thought they might think it was weird. Grant had always told her it was too late for that.

"Yes, of course, Mayor," Furst said, nodding, then looked at Grant. "I actually have them in my office now. I'll call you back with an update as soon as I have one." He set the phone down, then pointed to the door. "Mocks?"

Mocks shut the door and the chatter, phone calls, and office machinery fell silent.

"If the press haven't given it away already, I suppose you can figure it out," Furst said, leaning forward. "We have an epidemic on our hands."

"I had a reporter ask if it was twelve?" Grant asked, his voice exasperated. "Is that true?"

"Fifteen," Furst answered. "From all around the state."

"We had another abduction reported while you were talking to the Givens girl," Mocks said. "Boy was taken at Hyde Park."

Even before Grant joined Missing Persons, he had never heard of anything like this happening before. Cases were always spaced out. In the two years he'd been with the unit, he and Mocks had only worked twelve legitimate abduction cases.

Furst rocked in his chair. "That's two for this precinct and another thirteen outside our jurisdiction. I've spoken with the other lieutenants to get a handle on any connections." He pressed a finger into the desk. "All victims were under the age of thirteen, with thirteen of the kids female and two male. The children's families have mixed backgrounds and ethnicities, as well as financial status. We have poverty to upper middle class." He sprung from his chair, walked over to his printer, and removed a stack of papers from the feeder. "So far none of the abductors have made any demands or ransom. The only pattern identified so far is the locations. All public places."

"Malls, parks, crowded stores," Mocks said. "All textbook grabs. It has to connect back to that website."

Grant took the papers from Furst and sifted through them while the lieutenant arched an eyebrow.

"The website involved in the Givens case?" Furst asked.

"Yeah," Grant said, skimming the notes, looking for anything that stood out, particularly anything about spiders, but found nothing. "Has it spread outside of Washington?"

"I haven't reached out to any of my contacts in Oregon or Idaho," Furst said. "So maybe."

"Cyber find anything yet?" Grant asked.

"No," Mocks answered.

Furst slammed his fist on the table, the scowl on his face accentuating the scars on his left cheek that ran from his eye to his jawline. "We have an epidemic on our hands!" He pointed to the bullpen. "I've got parents from all over the city calling in and asking if it's safe for their kids to go outside. Not to mention the press, Mayor, and Senator's offices calling the chief and torching our entire department! We need answers, Detectives. And we need them now."

"If Cyber is still trying to crack that website, then we have to work with what we have," Grant said. "AMBER Alerts already set up?"

"We managed to push out your two cases, Annie Mauer and Tommy Steeves, but the chief is holding off on sending the rest of the AMBER Alerts until we can figure out a PR standpoint," Furst said.

"Yeah, because waiting is going to make things better," Mocks said, scuffing her shoes against the carpet.

"You handle your job, Detective," Furst said. "And I'll handle mine."

"There is something else," Grant said. "When I spoke with the Givens girl, she mentioned spiders."

"You lost me," Furst said.

"That makes two of us," Mocks said. "Are you sure that means anything?"

"She was pretty worked up, but I think it's significant," Grant said, nodding to the phone. "It might be something to pass along to the rest of your contacts, Lieutenant."

"I will," Furst said, and took his seat, slowly calming down. "Listen, what I tell you doesn't leave this room." He lowered his voice and leaned forward even though no one outside could hear. "The mayor and Senator Pierfoy want this handled quickly. This is going to be national news, and if these kids aren't returned safely, then heads will roll. Don't misstep."

"We won't," Grant said. "Thank you, Lieutenant."

When Mocks opened the door, the cacophony of the precinct blasted their senses. The pair returned to their desks, Grant still holding the files from the other cases that Furst had printed.

Grant handed Mocks the first half of files once he finished taking notes, and she absorbed the information like a sponge after only a few minutes. She tore open another

Pop-Tart package while Grant tried to connect the myriad of information into something coherent. But aside from what the lieutenant had said, there was nothing. And no spiders.

"Hey," Officer Banks said, sneaking up behind Grant. "We got a hit on the kid from Hyde Park on the hotline." He rotated the piece of paper in his hands. "Guy was seen with a boy matching the description of the rusted eighty six Toyota Corolla off Interstate Five. He turned off on an exit to a town call Lynden, just south of the Canadian border."

Grant and Mocks both reached for their jackets, and Grant snatched the note from Banks's fingers.

"Get on the horn with that county's Sheriff's office and put out the APB for that car," Grant said. "And do me a favor and get a message over to Sam in Cyber; tell him to run this plate number against any names on his list from the website. He'll know what that means."

Mocks was three steps ahead of Grant, but he finally caught up with her at the door. She walked fast for her size.

"Why do you want Sam to run the name attached to the plate against his information?" Mocks asked.

Grant pulled the door open. "Because I want to confirm the abduction to the website. We need to narrow down who we're fighting."

13

*P*olice cars lined the street, and two officers were forced to move the barricade when Grant and Mocks arrived on scene. The altercation was undoubtedly the most excitement the citizens of Lynden had seen in their lifetime because the street was packed with pedestrians, searching for a better vantage point at the unfolding scene.

Grant parked behind a cluster of squad cars that blocked the driveway where Craig Johnson's rusted Corolla was parked. The house he sought shelter in was more of a trailer, but the way it had been cemented into the ground gave it a more permanent look.

"Sergeant," Grant said, tapping one of the officers on the shoulder. "I'm Detective Grant."

The sergeant was Grant's height, maybe an inch taller, and had an unsightly orangutan orange color sticking out from under his cap. He smiled at Mocks, exposing off-white teeth. "Detectives."

"Is the boy inside?" Mocks asked, ignoring the sergeant's gawking.

"We're not sure," he answered. "We can't get a straight

JAMES HUNT

answer out of the guy. What we do know is he has plenty of shotgun rounds and hasn't shied away from using them."

And almost on cue, a twelve-gauge barrel poked through the window and buckshot blew into the front yard and the hoods of the police cruisers, the cannon-like blast sending every officer ducking, eliciting a horrific gasp from the crowd that had gathered.

Grant poked his head up from behind the trunk of one of the cruisers and saw that the weapon had disappeared from the window. Mocks was tucked behind the car to his left with the sergeant.

"What do we know about the suspect?" Grant asked.

"He's a janitor over at Seattle General," the sergeant said. "He's worked there for almost twenty-five years. Up until four months ago, he had over thirty grand saved up in his account, but several withdrawals since then have emptied it."

"Doesn't Homeland usually flag large withdrawals like that?" Mocks asked.

"He didn't make a large withdrawal," the sergeant answered. "Over two hundred small increments were taken out over that time span."

"Smart," Grant said.

Dozens of guns were trained on Johnson's fortress, and every curtain was drawn on the windows. If this guy took the same class as kidnapper in the Givens case, then he knew the authorities' plan of attack. And if he didn't get what he wanted, then things could end in a big boom.

"How many entrances to the house do we have?" Grant asked.

"Two," the sergeant answered. "I spoke to the landlord to see if there was any other way inside, but there was nothing. We were going to infiltrate, but S.W.A.T. found traces of explosive wiring around the doors and windows when they got close. He's sealed himself in there nice and tight."

152

Mocks pulled Grant aside and lowered her voice so only he could hear. "This guy knows all of the tricks. The moment we go inside, he'll blow the whole damn place sky high. It's just another Mexican stand off."

Grant shut his eyes, trying to figure out a way inside, but there wasn't a move he could make that Craig Johnson wouldn't anticipate. *Except...*

"Sergeant," Grant said. "Do you have a communication line already open with the suspect?"

"Yeah, but he's not talking," the sergeant answered. "Our negotiator has tried, but the man won't budge until he gets what he wants."

"I have something that I think will work," Grant said.

"And that is?" the sergeant asked.

"Giving him what he wants."

The sergeant's face twitched like he was having a stroke, and Mocks offered the coyest little smile.

"What the hell do you mean we give him what he wants?" the sergeant asked as both Mocks and Grant ducked low on their way back to their cruiser, Craig Johnson still randomly firing his twelve gauge into the squad cars. Once inside, they shut the doors, staying below the dash with their eyes barely exposed.

Grant reached for the radio. "Dispatch, this is Detective Grant. I need you to patch me through to Captain Hill and Lieutenant Furst. Tell them it's urgent." He let his finger off the button of the receiver and Mocks shook her head.

"You planning on calling in a few favors?" Mocks asked. "Because that's the only way you're going to pull this off."

"You heard what the lieutenant said," Grant answered. "The mayor and senator want a speedy resolution to this mess. The longer this goes on, the lower their poll numbers drop." He looked at her and grinned. "I don't think I'm the one that'll have to call in favors."

"Detective Grant, you have Captain Hill and Lieutenant Furst on the line," dispatch said.

"What is it, Grant?" Hill asked.

"Captain, Lieutenant, I have an idea," Grant said.

Grant walked them through the plan, having to pause several times to interrupt the captain's objections, but Grant found it a good sign that the lieutenant remained quiet. It meant that he was considering it.

"And what happens when we give him what he wants?" Furst finally asked. "What's to make him think that we won't double cross him?"

"Because it wasn't in the class he took online," Grant said. "It'll throw him off balance. He's thinking he has to dig in and wait until he blows himself off the face of the earth, but this gives him hope. Plus with all the news vans, he'll know if something happened to the boy on television, we'd be crucified."

"You're goddamn right we will be," Captain Hill said.

"Sirs, I'm telling you if there was another way to get that boy, we'd do it. But the way things stand right now, there is only one outcome, and that puts both Tommy Steeves and Craig Johnson in body bags. My way gives us a chance to intercept him when he comes out of the house."

"He's right," Mocks said. "It's the only way."

Grant smiled at the vote of confidence from his partner, and the fact that she was on the same page only gave him more clout.

"If this goes south, your career is over," Lieutenant Furst said. "If one hair on the boy's head is out of place after the smoke clears, then you're done. The press, politicians, even this very department will gun you down. Same goes for you, Detective Mullocks. I need to hear the two of you say that you understand."

"It's not our careers we're worried about, Lieutenant,"

Grant said. "It's that boy's life. And this gives him the best chance to keep it."

"I still need to hear you say it, Detectives," Furst said.

Grant looked to Mocks, and the pair leaned close to the receiver. "We understand."

A pause, and then the captain spoke. "We'll contact the mayor and senator to bring them in the loop, though they won't be happy about it."

"Just tell them what I told you, sir," Grant said. "And make sure you tell them it's from me." He set the receiver down and jolted from another shotgun blast, Craig Johnson's incoherent rambling muffled through the car's cabin.

"So now what?" Mocks asked.

"Let's go find out what he wants," Grant answered.

The officers had already called the house phone, which the communication company had turned off due to lack of payment, but after haggling with a supervisor for twenty minutes, it was reconnected after the threat of a court order. Whenever someone was slow to move, that one usually did the trick.

Ordained by the mayor, chief of police, and a United States senator, Grant now had full control of the operation, much to the sergeant's dismay, who still thought the idea was ludicrous.

Grant got on the line and called the house. When Craig Johnson answered the first time, he screamed a stream of curses and then unceremoniously slammed down the receiver. The second time Grant called, he didn't pick up at all. Thankfully, third time was the charm.

"Mr. Johnson, please, don't hang up," Grant said. "I'm not here to bullshit you."

Labored pants filled Grant's ear and after a few seconds' pause, Craig Johnson spoke. "It's just more games. I know what you want, and that's me in a fucking body bag!" His

JAMES HUNT

voice was haggard and panicked, dangerous even without the twelve gauge clutched in his hands.

"Not this time," Grant said. "Tell me what you want. And it's yours."

Again Johnson paused, contemplating the authenticity of the offer. "I want the cops gone. And the helicopters."

Grant stepped out of the back of the S.W.A.T. van, and glanced up to the few choppers in the sky. Only one of them was Seattle PD. "I can only call back the police choppers."

"Bullshit!"

"Wait! Wait, wait, wait," Grant said. "I can get the FAA to clear the air space around the house, but once you start moving, that's as far as the guarantee can go."

Another pause. "And I want the cops on the street gone. No one around the house for half a mile."

"All right, we can do that," Grant said, not bothering to take notes because he knew the call was being recorded.

"And I want a car with ten grand cash in a duffel bag in the passenger seat," Johnson said, his voice growing eager the longer he spoke. "No one follows me out either. I leave, with the boy, and no one follows. I get a hint that someone's on my tail, and he dies. We both will. I don't care anymore what happens to me, get it?"

"Yeah," Grant answered. "I get it."

The call clicked dead, and Grant returned the phone back to the negotiator, who raised his eyebrows skeptically. "Any word on exactly how you're going to deliver on that, your holiness?"

"Yeah, like all good holy men do," Grant answered, getting out of the back of the van. "Talk to the boss."

Mocks stepped in stride with Grant on his exit, and he tossed his phone to her. "Call the captain. He should have Mayor Brugsby and Senator Pierfoy on the line by now. Tell

156

him we need the choppers cleared from the area and ten grand. We'll give him one of the squad cars to get away in, and I'll have the sergeant clear everyone back once the choppers are gone."

"And after we do all of this, what's the plan?" Mocks asked, dialing. "Catching him *is* still a part of the plan, right? Or is this your way of going out in a blaze of glory?"

"Did you ever go to a magic show when you were a kid?" Grant asked.

"Rick took me to one when we were dating," Mocks answered. "We didn't go back."

"It's all about sleight of hand. The magician gets you to focus on everything but the trick, and by the time you realize what's happened, you've missed it." Grant glanced around to the chaos around him. "This is the distraction. And when the pieces start to move, that's where you and I perform the trick."

"You didn't go to magic camp when you were a kid, did you?" Mocks asked, but before Grant answered the captain was on the phone, and Mocks recited what Grant had told her. Judging from her facial expression, it wasn't going very smoothly.

Grant grabbed hold of the sergeant and pointed to the surrounding officers. "I want every unit, sniper, and badge watching that house to retreat at least five blocks. And it needs to happen all at once on my command."

"Your command?" the sergeant asked mockingly.

"Yes, mine," Grant answered. "So don't worry about any blowback if things go wrong. None of the heat will land on you."

Begrudgingly, the sergeant spread the news, and Mocks tugged on Grant's jacket just before a cold breeze gusted their way.

"Mayor said he'll make it happen with the cash, and the

Senator is clearing the request with the FAA right now," Mocks said. "They said it shouldn't take too long."

"With the Senator's connections, I didn't think it would," Grant said, thinking about the offer the man had extended earlier that morning. He was sure the senator would pressure him even more to take the job now. If he was successful of course. "C'mon, we need to get ready."

Grant returned to the S.W.A.T. van, which had become the HQ for operations. "I need to see the schematics for the house." One of the officers retrieved it and spread it out on the table for Grant to examine. He switched his gaze from the blueprints to the house. "Is there any bushes or trees over here by this window?"

An officer decked out in tactical gear nodded, his helmet bobbing with the motions. "Yeah, we tried to position an officer there earlier, but once we discovered the bomb threat, we pulled our guys back."

Grant stepped outside and spotted the growth on the south side of the house. The trailer was wedged up against a cluster of other homes, which provided good cover. "What's the distance from the side of the house to the front door?"

"Eleven feet," he answered.

It was longer than Grant would have liked, and there was still the possibility that Johnson would wire the boy to blow like Mallory Givens's abductor. Though if he used the explosives for around the doors and windows, he might not have enough to make a vest. "All right, that's our play." He turned around to Mocks, who was already back in the van and examining the blueprints herself.

"I'll go around the north side, and we'll hit him from both angles," Mocks said. "If we catch him off guard, we can force his initial reaction to shoot us first." She let out a low breath. "This will go down really fast."

When she stepped out of the van, Grant pulled her aside,

out of earshot from everyone else. "It'll be helpful to have two people do this, but if you can't—"

"I'm in, Grant," Mocks said. "This guy may have taken some classes on how to abduct kids, but he hasn't had the firearms training we have. And besides," she smiled and punched his arm. "Maybe I'll get my own medal for this."

"Careful what you wish for," Grant said. "Let's grab some vests."

The Kevlar was bulkier than Grant would have liked, but he knew it was needed. There was something ominous about strapping on Kevlar. He didn't wear it in his normal day-to-day. He felt like he was tempting fate when he did. Like he was asking for a bullet.

Once they were strapped up, Grant noticed the hum of the chopper blades fading. He looked to the grey, clouded sky and watched them disappear. Senator Pierfoy had come through.

"Sergeant," Grant said. "Get your people back."

In the chaos of the retreat, Grant and Mocks slid up around the backside of the houses next to where Johnson was located and huddled in their position.

It wasn't until Grant was alone at the south end of the house that he realized he never said anything to Mocks before the pair parted. There was the possibility that he wouldn't come out of this alive, and if so, his last words to his partner would have been 'let's grab some vests.'

Not the most eloquent goodbye. He would have preferred something more personal. After all, they'd been together for over two years, and it was by far the most successful partnership he'd ever been attached to. Plus, he was fond of Mocks. She was the little sister he never had. And he knew she looked up to him, though he wasn't sure why. In many aspects, she already surpassed him in the position. She had the mind and tenacity for the job, and once she picked up on the subtleties of dealing with people, which was the only area she lacked, she'd be the best in the field.

Heavy thumps snapped Grant's attention back to the house. Johnson shouted, but the words were muffled through the trailer walls. Grant removed the 9mm Glock from his holster and inched to the front corner of the house, ducking below the only window he passed along the way.

The last few police cars disappeared down side streets, and the crowds of pedestrians were corralled away from the scene. The thump of the choppers overhead faded. Everything was falling into place. All that was left was the getaway car and the cash. But the quieter it grew outside, the louder it became inside the trailer.

Johnson stepped heavily, running around the house, screaming nonsense. He could be hopped up on drugs. He could have already killed the boy. But could haves always bounced at the bank. Grant needed to stick with what he knew, and that was Craig Johnson stepping out of that house and trying to kill anything that got in his way.

Grant drew in a breath as the brakes from the getaway car squealed to a stop just short of the driveway. The officer inside stepped out of the vehicle slowly, his hands in the air. Grant saw the outline of the man's Kevlar underneath the bulky coat.

Johnson cracked open the front door and Grant remained glued to the side of the house, out of sight.

"Where's the money?" Johnson said, his voice raspy from shouting.

The officer, moving slowly, reached inside the car and grabbed hold of a duffel bag. He opened it and exposed the cash piled inside. Grant couldn't see the exact bills, but it was more than enough to convince Johnson that it was legit.

Johnson had everything he wanted. The choppers gone. The officers retreated. The getaway car, and now the cash.

The trust was established. The only question that remained was if he would take the bait.

The officer placed the duffel bag back in the car and slowly retreated, keeping his hands in the air as he walked backwards to the end of the street.

Grant's mouth went dry. His tongue turned into sandpaper and it hurt to swallow. He panted quietly from his mouth: adrenaline, nerves, blood pressure, and heart rate all skyrocketed and bundled together in the pit of his stomach.

The front door swung shut and Grant inched to the edge, his back scraping up against the faded paint. He craned his neck around the front and saw the porch. He made eye contact with Mocks as she did the same, her figure even smaller with the distance between them.

He couldn't tell if she was nervous. She just gave a slight nod and then retreated behind the house. Grant did the same. More thumps echoed inside, and Johnson barked something, and the question of whether the boy was still alive was finally answered as Tommy Steeves screamed.

Grant gripped the handle of his Glock with both hands, his knuckles white from the tight hold. He raised the pistol in preparation to strike. His muscles grew taut with anticipation, his mind and body poised to act at the sound of that door. He had two, maybe three seconds to assess the situation before shots were fired.

The details of the plan faded from his mind. The moment consumed him. He clung to the element of surprise, his only advantage, and hoped it was better than Johnson's nothing-to-lose. Johnson could miss. Grant couldn't.

The front door's hinges whined, and Grant planted his foot past the plane of cover. It was all instinct now. His mind and body retrieved the years of weapons training, the hours spent at the range, and muscle memory. But there was no paper target when Grant turned the corner, no stationary dummy with a burglar painted on the face, no blanks in the chamber. This was the field, where your actions had real consequences. And when Grant saw Craig Johnson with a pistol to Tommy Steeves's head, Grant aimed for the one square foot space on Johnson's chest just above Tommy's head. That was his window.

Johnson turned and made eye contact with Grant. Everything moved in slow motion. He screamed something as Grant applied pressure to the trigger, and the man removed the barrel of the gun from Tommy's head and aimed at Grant.

The bullet jettisoned from Grant's pistol and connected into the right of Johnson's chest. He stumbled backward and another gunshot fired. Instantaneously, a sharp pain ripped through Grant's gut.

Grant tumbled backwards, and amidst the ringing in his ears from the gunfire, a high-pitch scream broke through. He smacked the ground and the wind was knocked from his lungs. A third gunshot fired, and Grant rolled to his side, a pressure in his head so intense that he thought his eyes would bulge from its sockets.

He looked to the porch where Mocks had Johnson cuffed on the ground. The next thing he saw was Tommy Steeves. He was crying and covered in blood. Grant just hoped it wasn't his own.

14

———

*T*he sirens and flashing lights flooded the street as every squad car and cruiser that had retreated returned in full force. Dozens of officers and a handful of paramedics rushed over to both Johnson and then Grant, who had managed to steady himself on all fours. He gasped for breaths and fingered the center of pain in his lower abdomen. It felt like it went through.

"I just need you to sit still for me a minute, Detective." The paramedic had thick eyebrows and a shaved head. He flashed a light in Grant's eyes and then gently patted the area on the vest where he'd been shot, then took his blood pressure. "Can you hear me okay?"

"Yeah," Grant answered, inhaling a deep breath through his nose. He glanced over to the porch to see what happened with the boy, but a cluster of officers and medics blocked his view. He couldn't even see Mocks.

"I need to get this vest off you," the paramedic said.

Grant slid off his jacket, grinding his teeth as another shot of pain spasmed from his abdomen. Velcro ripped apart from the connecting pieces of the vest, and he tossed it aside.

The paramedic ripped open Grant's shirt and examined the red blotch on his abdomen. The paramedic poked the injury, and Grant winced.

"No bruising," he said. "So that's good." The paramedic flipped the vest over and found the bullet that nearly traveled all the way through. He rubbed his finger over the flattened metal and shook his head. "Looks like someone was looking out for you today."

But was somebody looking out for Tommy Steeves? Grant pushed himself off the ground and leaned up against the front of the house to steady his wobbling legs. He spied his Glock in the grass and bent down to grab it, being mindful of the soreness in his stomach.

When Grant raised his head, the cluster of bodies had disappeared, and he saw Craig Johnson being wheeled toward an ambulance, paramedics keeping pressure on the gunshot wound to his body. And off to the side of the porch, with a blanket wrapped around him, was Tommy.

Grant exhaled with relief, and the tension melted from his body. Mocks sat with the boy, holding him as he sobbed. The paramedic grabbed Grant by the shoulders but he shrugged him off, stumbling over to the pair and dropping to his knees.

"Are you all right?" Grant asked.

"We're fine," Mocks answered.

The ambulance doors carrying Craig Johnson closed, and the vehicle sped away. The remaining paramedics carried Tommy Steeves toward the second ambulance, and Mocks looked down at Grant's exposed shirt.

"Showing off that six-pack?" Mocks asked, cracking a smile.

Grant buttoned up. "Hardly."

The paramedic walked over and handed Grant his jacket.

"You should really let us check you out. Make sure you're all right."

"I'm fine," Grant replied. "What hospital are they taking the suspect?" Grant meant to question him the moment he was medically cleared. If Craig Johnson survived, it was their first big lead.

"Northside Memorial," the paramedic answered. "They won't let you in until he's stabilized." He paused, then looked back at the boy. "God knows he deserves a worse punishment than death."

The sergeant cantered over, shaking his head and smiling. "That was some legendary shit, Detectives." He looked to Mocks, his pupils dilated. "I suppose I have you to thank for that twenty bucks I lost."

"Keep the thanks," Mocks said, taking a step back.

"I want every corner of that trailer searched," Grant said. "Anything you find, you report it directly to me, understand?"

The sergeant held up his hands defensively. "I got it, Detective. I got it. Hey, maybe the mayor will give you another medal for this one." He chuckled and left.

"I doubt it," Grant said.

"Yeah," Mocks said. "The next one is for me anyway."

The phone in Grant's pocket buzzed and he jumped. When he removed his cell, the number was blocked. "Hello?"

"It's a dangerous game you're playing, Detective," Senator Pierfoy said. "Don't let this win go to your head. The next time it might result in your resignation and a child zipped up into a body bag."

"The goal is to make sure it doesn't escalate that far to begin with," Grant said. "The officers that arrived on scene chomped down on the bit so hard that the suspect had no other choice. They pushed him. He pushed back."

The praise and kindness that Pierfoy exhibited earlier

that morning had disappeared. The amiable tone had transformed into disappointment. "And what are you pushing, Detective? Your own death wish? I hope you don't expect for me to bail you out every time you find yourself in trouble. I don't want our relationship to become muddled."

"No, Senator," Grant said. "We wouldn't want that."

"Find the rest of those children," Pierfoy said quickly. "I want whoever is responsible for this madness behind bars now!"

The call ended, and Grant shoved the phone back into his pocket. He wasn't sure if he was shaking from anger or if the adrenaline from the gunfight had yet to fade.

"What now?" Mocks asked. "It'll take a while for forensics to sweep the place."

"The girl at the mall," Grant answered, pulling on his jacket. The air had grown oddly cold. "Let's see if forensics is done analyzing that video."

* * *

WHILE GRANT SEARCHED THE TRAILER, Mocks called the precinct and got an update on the video. They got a hit on the suspect in the Annie Mauer abduction.

"Parker Gallient," Mocks said, walking up to Grant and flashing him the picture. "Convicted felon for grand theft, assault with a deadly weapon, possession, and endangering the life of an officer. He was released by the state six months ago, and his probation officer hasn't seen him since."

"Six months ago," Grant said. "That's around the same time that website was created. Any affiliates or addresses we can check out?"

"They're putting that together now," Mocks answered, "and we have some good news." Mocks clapped her hands together. "The chief finally authorized the rest of the AMBER Alerts. They're going to be pushed within the hour."

"Good," Grant said, removing the gloves after his sweep of the trailer. "Let's get Parker's picture to the media. I want his face plastered on every screen in the northwest."

"Already done. Find anything?" Mocks asked.

"Since it was a rental, we only tagged the supplies he brought with him. Looked like he planned on camping out for the next few days. He also had passports for both him and the kid. They looked legit." Grant crumpled the blue glove into a fist. "It could be what the others are doing." He bit his lower lip. "Sam give you an update on the website?"

"No, but I can call him while we're waiting on the Parker info."

"I'll wrap up inside and meet you back at the car."

With the precinct phones jammed from chaos that was the city, concerned parents calling every five seconds, Mocks dialed Sam directly. She had stolen his number from his HR files when Cyber started working on the website. It wasn't exactly protocol, but no one tried to stop her.

"Hello?" Sam asked.

"Hey, it's Mocks. We need an update on the site. Did you manage to cross reference Craig Johnson with any of the usernames?"

"How did you—never mind," Sam said. "Yes, I managed to link Craig to one of the accounts. He was one of the sixty that actually finished all of the coursework."

"Sixty," Mocks said, raising her eyebrows. "That'll help weed out the amateurs."

"I also tracked Parker's truck through the traffic cams after he left the mall," Sam said. "He dumped it at some restaurant south of downtown. It's where his trail ends. You want the address?"

"Yeah." Mocks recorded it in the memory bank and nodded. "Thanks, Sam. You have anything else?"

"Not yet."

"Keep digging." Mocks ended the call and leaned against the passenger door, waiting for Grant to finish. She glanced around the poor neighborhood, with its houses of peeling paint, dirt yards, and chain link fences.

Mocks didn't like being this far north. It wasn't far from here where she used to go on her benders. Days of no sleep, no food, and all the heroin she could handle. Her hand shook just thinking about it. She reached inside her jacket and retrieved the green Bic. She flicked it on and off, the flame wiggling over the metal hole. Her hand steadied when she held it. Every time.

Her old rehab group had called it a trigger. All those years of spoons and needles had left more than a physical mark. Whenever she was stressed or went through some adrenaline-fueled event like today, her hand wouldn't stop shaking until she grabbed the lighter. Her sponsor had told her once that her body was just looking for something familiar to help calm itself, but Mocks knew the real reason: her hand was always still as water when she wanted a hit.

Mocks didn't want the familiarity of the lighter. She wanted the familiarity of what came next: the high. Heroin, weed, Oxy, coke, it didn't matter as long as it made her feel good. She flicked the lighter a few more times and a gust of wind blew out the flame.

It was one of the biggest reasons she didn't want kids. And no matter how many times Rick pestered her about it, she just couldn't bring herself to say yes. It wasn't that she was afraid she would use again; those days were buried. She was scared that her kid would use.

In the support groups Mocks had attended when she finally got clean, a lot of the people had addicts as parents.

And there was strong evidence that suggested that certain genetic codes were more susceptible to addiction. She didn't want that for her kid. She didn't want that for anyone.

Grant stepped out of the trailer. "What'd Sam say?"

"He said sixty of the users actually completed all of the coursework. He also confirmed that Craig Johnson was on the list, and so was Parker Gallient, the one who took Annie Mauer. He traced Parker's truck outside of a restaurant on Seattle's south side," Mocks answered.

"Not the friendliest place for us," Grant answered, then gestured to the fist that held the Bic. "You all right?"

"Yeah," Mocks answered, tucking the lighter back inside her inner jacket pocket. "Let's get out of here."

Lunchtime traffic had picked up in the city, and it added an extra twenty minutes on their way to the restaurant. It was a seafood joint, but in Seattle, seafood places were a dime a dozen. Whenever one went out of business, three more took its place. Rick loved seafood. Mocks figured she was the only person in Seattle that hated it.

A heavy scent of fish blasted Mocks's senses the moment they stepped through the doors, and she gagged in her mouth loud enough to catch the attention of the table of middle-aged women to her left. They stopped eating, but Mocks simply followed Grant to the kitchen with the hostess, where the smell only worsened.

Once past the sautéed shrimp, steamed clams, and baked salmon, Mocks shoved Grant and the hostess aside and burst out the back door. Outside, she lifted her face to the sky and inhaled deep breaths.

"Thought you'd be used to that smell by now," Grant said, side-stepping a very shocked hostess, who looked at Mocks like she had grown a second head. "You've lived in Seattle for what? Four years now?"

"Three years, five months, three weeks, two days, thirteen

hours and some change," Mocks answered, sucking in another deep breath of cold coastal air. "But who's counting."

"This the truck?" Grant asked.

The hostess nodded. She wore all black, and her blonde hair had matching dark roots. "I didn't see who dropped it off. I asked around and none of the kitchen staff saw anything either."

Mocks finally lowered her face, the queasiness in her stomach easing now that she wasn't surrounded by fish fumes. She walked over to the truck, the doors closed. "You found it exactly like this?"

"Well, no," the hostess said, playing with her hands. "The door was open. I just thought maybe someone left it open by accident. So I just shut it." She took a step back. "Does this have to do with all those kids going missing?"

"Thank you, ma'am," Grant said. "We'll let you know if we need anything else."

Mocks walked around to the passenger side and slipped on a glove. She opened the door, then the glove compartment. "Nothing but trash." She checked under and behind the seats. Nothing but rusted tools and more fast food wrappers.

"Anything?" Mocks asked.

"Nope," Grant answered, shutting the door and peeling off his own glove.

"Grant," Mocks said. "I think we need to start looking at this realistically." She stepped around the truck's hood and leaned against the driver side tire-well. "There could be another dozen kids that are taken within the next twenty-four hours, or some that were taken that haven't even been called in yet. Whoever is behind this meant for it all to happen today."

"You think someone is pulling the strings?" Grant asked.

"Whoever built that website for all of those creeps to use had a specific purpose." Mocks watched Grant mull it over.

"You think it's a diversion?" Grant asked.

"Sleight of hand, right?" Mocks answered. "We need to figure out why all of this is happening today."

"All right," Grant said. "We'll canvas the street and see if anyone saw anything. Look for security footage, maybe we'll get lucky."

"After today, I think all of our luck might be out," Mocks said.

* * *

ONE OF THE detriments of being a detective in this century was technology. It was a gift and a curse. Their Cyber division could do so many things with tracking digital footprints. But in the self-absorbed age of selfies and social media, one hardly looked up from their phones. And that made finding witnesses hard. No one saw anything. Maybe Mocks was right. Their luck had run out.

Forensics arrived shortly after their canvas of the area, and the team looked used and abused. There were a limited number of forensic field units, and with the sudden influx of abductions, they were being called all over the city. Grant and Mocks left the team to their devices and drove back to the station.

Grant kept stealing glances at the timer on his watch. They were already past the four-hour mark. Time was tight. Time was always tight.

"You keep checking that thing like it'll tell you where to find our missing kids," Mocks said, her gaze cast out toward the window.

"It helps keep me on my toes," Grant said. "You have any secret theories you're keeping to yourself?"

"I think Rick is cheating on me," Mocks answered.

She tossed it out in the open so casually that it took Grant a minute before he could wrap his head around what she'd just said.

"Why do you think—"

"We haven't had sex in over a month," Mocks said. "We fight constantly. It's like I'm living with someone I don't even know anymore."

Mocks finally turned away from the window, and Grant got a look at her face. No tears. No lines of grief. Nothing more than a plain, stoic expression of realization. She'd been thinking about this for a long time. He'd thought something was off with her, and now he knew the cause.

"What are you two fighting about?" Grant asked.

Mocks twirled the Bic between her fingers. "He wants kids."

"And you don't?"

Mocks sighed. "It's complicated."

"You need to talk about it," Grant said. "This isn't one of those instances where you can just sweep it under the rug."

"We've tried," Mocks said. "I'll admit that I'm the one who gets defensive about it, but I just—I just…" She curled her fingers, shaking her hands, and then dropped them into her lap, lifeless. "I'm scared, Grant."

"Is Rick working today?" Grant asked.

"No," Mocks answered.

Grant flicked on the blinker and took the next left he could make.

"Grant, we don't have time—"

"If there is one thing you know about me, Mocks, it's that I am a master of time." Grant swerved between parked cars on the side street and looped back around to the highway that would take them to Mocks's apartment. "Before Ellen died, there were hundreds of times where I could have gone home for lunch, left work early, gone to work late, and the world would have kept on spinning. We get so caught up in fast forward that we forget to appreciate the pause button. And trust me when I tell you that now is one of those moments to hit pause."

"The clock doesn't stop for those kids," Mocks said.

Grant saw Mocks's high-rise in the distance. "I'm more than capable of researching the Internet by myself, and when I figure something out, you will be my first call."

The rest of the trip, Mocks remained quiet. She only said two words when he pulled up to the curb of the sidewalk outside her building. "Thank you."

"Talk to him, Mocks," Grant said. "Rick wouldn't cheat on you."

"How do you know that?" Mocks asked, looking at him with eyes as big as saucers. She'd never looked more like a kid than she did right now.

"Because Rick looks at you the way I looked at Ellen," Grant said.

Mocks smiled, shut the door, and disappeared inside the building. The action provided a small piece of hope that Grant clung to on the way back to the station. It was a hope that helped block out all the painful memories from his own past. The daily struggle to keep moving never ended.

The old phrase 'time heals all wounds' was only half true. Yes, they did eventually heal. But they also changed you; twisted you into something different than you were before. Everything was still functional and you were alive, but you were not the same. Scars never disappeared. They lingered until your last day.

The precinct was still surrounded by the press when Grant arrived, and this time he avoided their questioning altogether by parking in the compound lot around back. It was fenced off, and only authorized personnel were allowed inside.

Grant did a quick check in with Sam to see if he was able

to pull anything else from the website, but he said he was still trying to get through some of the firewalls and that he needed more time.

All that was left was to research what Mocks had brought up. It was a brilliant theory, and it made sense the more thought he gave it. He opened a handful of tabs on his browser and went to work on finding what was so special about today.

Grant started small, staying strictly within Seattle, and then when nothing came of that, he expanded to the entire state of Washington. The only note of value he was able to find was his own ceremony that had taken place that morning. No other large-scale events had made the news, no meetings or large gatherings. Today was just another Saturday in late March.

The chair squeaked as Grant leaned back. He drummed his fingers on the desk. There had to be another connection, something else that tied them together. They had three confirmed cases, if you included the Givens case, where the abductors took this class. So what connected them?

Grant stopped drumming his fingers. *Spiders.*

Grant cross-referenced spiders and Seattle, and he received several hits, many of them from Seattle arachnid groups, which there were more of than he would have guessed. But there was only one hit that connected what Mallory Givens had said to Grant's current predicament.

A gang from the Philippines had made their way to the western shores of the United States. And Grant knew just the man he could talk to about it.

15

When Mocks pressed the tenth floor button on the elevator, a million thoughts raced through her mind. Her left hand moved and she looked down to see it holding the Bic lighter. She stared at it a moment and then returned it to her pocket. If Rick was having an affair, if there was some woman in their bed, then she needed to face it without the crutch of her past.

Mocks had been clean for a year when they met. And it was around the time when her therapist and sponsor thought it would be okay for her to enter a relationship. She'd done the plant thing, then the animal thing, making sure she could keep both of them alive before setting her affections on anything human. Her sponsor had also recommended abstaining from sex for at least six weeks after the start of a new relationship.

She slept with Rick on their first date. It was one rule she didn't care that she broke.

And as luck would have it, Rick turned out to be the last new person she'd ever sleep with, though she didn't see it that way in the beginning. She remained guarded in their first few months together. The sex helped though. A lot.

Rick never pried about her past, but she knew he had questions. After all, she couldn't hide the scars on her arms from years of needles. When the day finally came for Mocks to reveal her past, it exploded from her lips in a stream of breathless, run-on sentences. Once she finished, she thought Rick might take off. She had prepared herself for that. But he didn't. He stayed. But it wasn't easy.

Mocks put Rick through every hell that she experienced. The backlash from all of those years she abused herself were thrust onto him. But no matter how dark it got, no matter what she said, no matter what she did, he stayed. And finally, those walls she'd built cracked. And while they didn't come tumbling down, a doorway formed, and Rick was finally allowed inside.

Through it all, Rick never pushed harder than she wanted. Anytime she said stop, he stopped. Anytime she told him she needed space, he waited. Whenever she got so angry she broke something of his, he kept quiet until she calmed down. He was the most patient man she'd ever met. She never understood why he stuck around. Probably the sex.

Their engagement was short. When Mocks was ready, he asked, and she didn't want to wait. She had found someone with an unshakable foundation, and there wasn't anyone else she saw spending the rest of her life with.

But the move to Seattle when she was offered a detective's position had taken its toll. The hours were harsher than she expected them to be, and the added celebrity that came with being a former addict, along with a partner with Grant's history, only added to the gossip.

The rest of the officers at the precinct eventually accepted her regardless of her past. She knew Grant had a lot to do with that. Everyone in the department respected him. When they were first paired together, the stories they told about his career in homicide aired on the side of legend. But when she finally met the man behind the myth, she realized that he was mortal like the rest of them. A very talented detective, but still a man.

And Grant was right. This talk was long overdue. When Rick had the kid conversation with her a few months ago, she didn't handle it well. And they'd both used work as an excuse to put it off. He'd been pulling doubles, and their only time together were the few hours when they shared a bed where the space between them grew larger every night.

The inertia of the elevator's stop made the bundle of nerves in Mocks's stomach rise, and then settle. The doors opened, and Mocks hesitated. She didn't want to take that first step. But that's what it took. That's how you did the hard things. You just placed one foot in front of the other. One at a time.

Mocks entered the hallway, her footsteps silent on the carpet. She passed her neighbors until she got to apartment ten-nineteen. They picked it because it had a beautiful view of the city, though she found herself admiring it less these days.

She fished the key out of her pocket and leaned against the door to listen for any movement inside. She heard nothing. The key went into the lock slowly, and in one quick motion, Mocks unlocked and opened the door.

A tiny hallway led into the kitchen with new stainless steel appliances and marble countertops. Rick liked to cook, but they'd eaten a lot of takeout the past month. Her heart pounded as she passed the kitchen, the front door still wide open.

Mocks examined the living room for any clothes. She expected to find a bra or lacy thong that wasn't hers, but there was nothing.

She turned from the living room toward the bedrooms and bathroom. The spare bedroom door was open, the same with the bathroom, but the master bedroom door was half closed.

Mocks froze at the low murmur of a moan. It was a woman's moan, soft and breathless. With a shaking leg, she took one step. Then another. And another. The noises grew louder the closer she moved.

Rage, fear, and adrenaline funneled through Mocks's veins, and by the time she reached the bedroom door, she held her pistol then kicked the door open.

"Jesus Christ!" Rick said.

Mocks kept the pistol at her side, and hot tears burst from her eyes as she heaved her chest up and down. "Wh— What are you doing?"

Rick frantically clicked out of the window pulled up on the computer screen and then hiked up his pants that were dropped at his ankles near the wheels of the desk chair. He tucked his manhood away and then turned to face his wife. His cheeks were flushed and slightly sweaty.

Mocks looked from Rick to the computer, then to their neatly made bed. She shook her head, the ball of nerves slowly unraveling in her stomach. "I thought… I thought…" She couldn't spit out the words.

Rick pointed to the Glock in her hand. "Were you gonna shoot me?"

Mocks stared at the gun, then holstered the weapon. "I thought you were sleeping with someone."

"What?" Rick leaned forward, scrunching his face in disbelief. He was about Grant's height, a little taller actually, but more muscular. His hazel eyes shied away from hers in embarrassment. He gestured toward the computer behind him, then shut his eyes and shook his head. "I didn't think you were coming home."

With the adrenaline gone, Mocks sat on the end of the bed. Her shoulders hunched forward and low, and she rested her elbows on her thighs. "I wasn't. Grant said that we needed to talk." She chuckled. "We probably need to do more than that."

Rick covered his mouth and stifled a laugh. He sidled up next to her, and his added weight bounced her up and into him. "I guess we haven't really been as upfront with each other like we normally are." He shook his head. "You thought I was having an affair?"

Mocks rested her head against his arm. "Sometimes I think it's hard for you to remember what it's like for the rest of us mortals who aren't accustomed to taking the high road. My mind just wandered."

He wrapped his arm around her and pulled her close. "We could not talk or not have sex for the rest of our lives as long as I knew you were still my wife. Though I would prefer at least a *little* sex."

"I feel like an idiot," Mocks said, burying her face into his shirt. He smelled like work. That heavy musk of sweat and thick wool from his fire jacket. She loved that smell.

"Hey." Rick turned toward her and cupped her face with both hands. "I love you. That is never going to change. No matter what. Do you hear me?"

"I hear you," Mocks said, and when she reached up to kiss him, they fell back onto the bed.

* * *

GRANT SUSPECTED it would be easy to get an audience with the ambassador. And he was right. A portion of Mujave's schedule was cleared within the hour. On his way toward the embassy, he called Mocks. After a few rings it went to voicemail, so he left a message. "Hey, I found a link between what

Mallory Givens said about the spiders and the abductions. I'm heading over to the ambassador's residence to find out more. Hope everything's okay."

Grant tucked the phone into his pocket and then flipped on the lights in his undercover sedan, traffic parting on the highway as his speedometer tipped towards ninety.

When Grant called the ambassador's office, he retained a level of secrecy for the meeting's purpose. He thought the ambassador would be more willing to meet with him under the premise that Grant had reconsidered the job offer.

The gates of the mansion opened after the security guard checked Grant's ID and badge number, then ran it against their registry of guests. There were no smiles during the interaction. All business from the guard.

Grant parked, and a young man escorted him from the driveway and inside the house. He wasn't sure if the man spoke English because the only words he said were "follow me" in a feigned American accent.

The inside of the house was elegantly decorated, but done simply and tastefully. Art, depicting Mujave's home of the Philippines, decorated the walls, and ornate furniture filled the rooms. The floor was marble, the ceilings vaulted, and Grant caught the glimpse of a chandelier in the dining room he passed. But in addition to the finer things, there were also three dogs that greeted him before he entered Mujave's office, all wagging tails and hanging tongues. Grant also noticed the number of children's toys scattered on the floors and over the expensive furniture. It made the building less of a structure of grandeur and more like a home.

"Detective!" Mujave jumped from his seat, that wide, warm smile on full display, the whiteness of his teeth contrasting against his tan skin. "It's so good to see you again, my friend." He took hold of Grant's hand, shaking it wildly, and after seeing the man's excitement, Grant started to regret the false pretenses of his visit. "Please, have a seat."

"Thank you, Ambassador." The dogs circled Grant happily, the Golden Lab hopping up onto the couch next to him.

"Happy, down!" Mujave said, laughing. "They get excited about new visitors."

"I don't mind," Grant said, scratching behind the Lab's ear.

"So," Mujave said, clapping his hands together. "I hope your visit brings with it some good news?"

Grant rotated the wedding band around his finger. "More questions than news, I'm afraid. It's about the other children that have been reported missing. I think it might be connected to something bigger."

The upbeat smile faded from the ambassador's face, and he leaned back. "I see."

"I spoke with a young girl from a previous case this morning that I believe is connected to the abductions from today." Grant made sure to watch the ambassador's face closely when he told him. "The girl's abductor said it was better the girl was with her than the spiders. I did some research about what that could mean and discovered a gang in the Philippines that identify themselves by spider web tattoos, and that they deal primarily with human trafficking."

"The Web," Mujave said. "There isn't a parent in the Philippines that doesn't know who they are." He stood and walked over to a cabinet behind his desk where he removed a crystal vase and two matching glasses. He brought both back to the sitting area and this time joined Grant on the couch, pouring each of them a quarter cup.

Grant wasn't much of a day drinker, but he found it best to go with the flow when prying for information. And after the first sip, he might have to ask where the ambassador got it. Not that he could afford it. "They're the group you wanted me to tackle in the international efforts, aren't they?"

"Yes," Mujave answered, taking a sip. "There have been over ten thousand missing children reported over the past five years in my country. Only a fraction of them are recovered. Some are killed, and the ones that survive their reprogramming are sold into sex trades around the Pacific." He wiped his mouth with the back of his hand and paused. When he finally looked up, he pointed to a painting in the office. "That's my village."

Grant turned to see it. It was a beautiful scene. Right on the beach, with trees shading the sand and the tide coming in. Huts lined the beach, a few fires going, and the village people walking about. But the whole painting was built around a young woman, ankle deep in the surf. She had a basket on her head, and her tan skin glistened in the fading sun. She was beautiful.

"Looks like a wonderful home," Grant said.

Mujave smiled. "It was. In fact, that was where my interest in politics began." He pointed toward the picture, walking closer to it. "I ran for local office in my village, that was almost twenty years ago now." He sipped. "I put together a sort of neighborhood watch. Any capable young man joined, finding that there was safety in numbers. We were a modest sized village. Only a few thousand, but still small enough to become targets for the Web." He loosened his tie, his presence growing more informal with every swallow. "We had limited guns, but a few of the men had spent time in the Philippine version of the National Guard. I had the local police give them special privileges, and we created a security schedule and had a twenty-four hour patrol of the village. It made people feel safe." He shook his head. "It didn't last long."

"The gang attacked you?" Grant asked, rotating the crystal cup in his fingers.

"I boasted about the initiative," Mujave answered. "I wanted other villages to join. I wanted us to band together. When leaders of the Web heard about my efforts, they decided to bring me down a notch."

Mujave sank into the couch cushions. He didn't blink and hardly moved a muscle. "I can still see them as clearly as the night they arrived. They came in full force: automatic weapons, armored trucks with mounted fifty-caliber guns. They mowed us down like cattle. They torched the houses, raped the women, and stole what they wanted. I managed to get my wife and a few others out to the water in the dark of night." Mujave's eyes watered. "They were bloodcurdling cries, Detective; screams only possible in the fires of hell. But that's what my village turned into that night. By morning, there was nothing but ash and blood." He drained the rest of the liquor and set the empty crystal on the coffee table. "Those people died because they believed I could protect them. They died because I boasted that we were untouchable. I made a promise to myself that day that I would bring them down. That I would make the children of my country safe."

Grant drained the rest of his own drink and sat the empty crystal next to Mujave's glass. "If you're leading international efforts to hunt this group down, then you'd need to be working with the FBI for anything domestic on the U.S. side."

"That's right," Mujave said.

"I need to know who your point person is on that case," Grant said. "I think the Web has grown more sophisticated with their tactics."

"You already know the point person on that front," Mujave said. "You worked with him to get my daughter back. Special Agent Hickem."

"Dad?"

Mujave and Grant turned and saw the ambassador's daughter hovering at the door, the pack of dogs circling and begging for attention.

"Dalisay," Mujave said, smiling. "Come here. I want you to meet your rescuer."

The girl was timid, her head down as she walked. Grant forgot it had only been two days since they found her in that house. At eleven years old, she'd experienced more heartache than any child should have to bear. Her week-long captivity was not a pleasant one, but Grant had found her just in time. One more day and the man would have killed her.

"Thank you," Dalisay said, keeping close to her father.

"You're very welcome," Grant said.

"Why don't you go and play with the dogs out back," Mujave said, giving her a kiss on the cheek that brought a shy smile. "I think they're getting restless."

"Okay. C'mon, Happy!" Dalisay sprinted back into the hallway, the Golden Lab barking and chasing after her, the others following suit.

Once the noise of his daughter's voice faded, so did Mujave's smile. "The therapists say it'll take time for her to process everything that happened."

"I never saw the medical report," Grant said. "Did everything come back all right?"

"Yes," Mujave said. "Thank God."

Medical report was the discreet method of asking if the girl may have been abused or raped. Avoiding those scenarios depended on authorities finding the children quickly. He glanced down at his watch. The timer ticked past six hours.

"I'd like to speak with Agent Hickem," Grant said. "See what intelligence he has on the gang stateside. Could I get his information?"

"For you, Detective Grant, I'll set up a meeting personally."

"Thank you, Ambassador," Grant said. He declined another drink, and Mujave agreed it was for the best. Once outside, Grant tried Mocks's cell again, and this time she answered.

"Hey," Mocks said, sounding slightly winded. "You got something?"

"Yeah," Grant answered. "I just finished my talk with the ambassador. I've got a new lead. Everything go all right with Rick?"

"Yeah," Mocks answered. "It went great."

"I'm heading back to the precinct," Grant said, getting into his car. "Meet me there." He hung up and drove to the exit, where the guard opened the gate and let him out. It was the second time today Grant had used favors in a case. It wasn't his normal protocol on the matter, but he was running out of time.

Grant's phone buzzed. It was the precinct. "Detective Grant."

"Hey, it's Sam. I had a breakthrough with the website."

Finally, some good news. "What do you have?"

"The man who took the girl at the mall, Parker something? I managed to track the IP address he used when he logged into the website. All of the other users got rid of theirs, but his is still operational."

"What's the address?" Grant scribbled it down, sloppily. "Thanks, Sam. Good work." Between his meeting with the ambassador and Sam's breakthrough, things were starting to come together. Now, he just needed to find out where Parker Gallient was hiding Annie.

16

_W_hen Grant returned to the precinct, Mocks was already waiting out back where the press couldn't bother her. The horde of news vans and reporters had grown larger now that the major networks were jumping on the bandwagon. The whole nation had their eyes on the state of Washington, and they weren't going to turn away until this was over.

"Hey," Mocks said, climbing into the car, shivering under her bulky coat. "Sam filled me in on Parker."

"The ambassador set up a meeting with the FBI team handling the gang stateside," Grant answered. "We're going to his office."

Mocks clicked her seatbelt into place and raised her eyebrows. "I'm sure they're going to love us snooping around their backyard."

"The lead investigator was the same agent I worked with on the ambassador's daughter's case," Grant said. "I'm hoping we can come to an agreement."

"And if that doesn't happen?" Mocks asked.

"Then we use the leverage we have with the address,"

Grant answered. "I'm sure they'd be willing to work with us for some intelligence on one of the gang's safe houses." Which Grant was assuming what the house was for. That, or some type of post for their trafficking.

The FBI office wasn't far from their precinct, and Grant found some street parking near the building's entrance. He stepped out of the car, zipped his jacket to the collar, and tucked his hands in his pockets to avoid the cold.

Grant wasn't sure what to expect from the FBI's field office, but it definitely wasn't what greeted him. Old and molding carpet, walls with paint peeling off in long strips, a ceiling with flickering fluorescent lights and yellowed tiles. Even his college dorm wasn't this bad.

"Don't let the federal budget fool you. It's not as glamorous as they make it out to be." Special Agent Chad Hickem was bigger than Grant remembered and when he took hold of Grant's hand and gave three firm pumps, he thought his arm might fall off. "I figured it was only a matter of time before the ambassador tapped you."

"Good to see you again," Grant said, then turned to Mocks. "This is my partner. Detective Susan Mullocks."

"I didn't think they let ogres join the FBI," Mocks said, her tiny hand swallowed up by Hickem's as they shook.

Hickem laughed. "I got a special exception. C'mon back."

The office was small, and the 'back' was suspiciously close to the front. Eight other agents occupied tiny desks, all of them buried in their computer screens or jotting down notes while on phone calls.

Hickem's tiny space was more cramped than the rest, though Grant attributed that to the man's size. No nameplate or personal items adorned the desk. Just a few pens, files, and a laptop covered the top. The desk was functional, like the man who sat behind it.

"I need to know about all of your operations with the

gang called 'The Web,'" Grant said, fishing out his phone. He pulled up the email with Parker's picture. "Specifically this guy."

Hickem grabbed Grant's phone, studying the picture. "He doesn't look familiar, but then again, the gang has been recruiting like crazy lately."

"How crazy?" Mocks asked.

"When I first started working this case eighteen months ago, we had their numbers stateside estimated at around a dozen. But recent tally suggests that they've blossomed to nearly one hundred in the state of Washington alone," Hickem said. "We know they have contacts and movers down the entire West Coast all the way into Mexico. The majority of their imports come through Seattle. For now, it's still their base of operations."

"Have you done any investigations into how they're growing?" Grant asked. "And more specifically how they're communicating with one another?"

Hickem rested his meaty arms on the table, shrugging. "Burner phones mostly. They've tapped into the local home-less population for a lot of their new recruits, which is perfect for them. The homeless don't have ID, are hard to identify, and will take pretty much anything you give them. They've also purged some of the smaller gangs in the area. There was a bad turf war about six months ago on the southern coastline of the city. They made our local gang-bangers look like elementary school bullies."

"I worked on a case after helping you with the ambas-sador's daughter, and I think it's connected to what's happening with all of these abductions today," Grant said.

"An hour ago I thought the same thing, but all of our intelligence is telling us that our guys have been quiet," Hickem said.

"These people are running an international sex trafficking ring and the only thing they're using is burner phones?" Mocks asked. "I don't buy it. They've got a hand in this, and someone specific is pulling the strings."

Hickem raised one of his very large eyebrows. Everything about the man was huge, even his inquiries. "And what makes you think that?"

"Someone created a website that teaches people how to abduct kids," Grant answered before Mocks could be any more cryptic. "And it covered everything. How to earn their trust, stay below the radar, places to look, where to abduct, the most effective methods of how to evade authorities; it was incredibly thorough."

"We haven't run across anything like that in our investigation." Hickem pointed back toward the only space that didn't have a desk in it, which was taken up by filing cabinets. "Everything we've gathered so far is in those cabinets. You're more than welcome to take a look at them. It'd be quicker than getting you clearance for the files we have on the servers."

"We don't have that kind of time," Grant said. "Especially if these guys are as organized as you say they are." Grant reached into his pocket and removed the paper that contained the address Sam gave him. "Do you know this place?"

Hickem looked it over, shaking his head. "Hey, Billy!"

Another agent stopped in Hickem's doorway, leaning against the frame. "What's up, boss?"

Hickem handed him the paper. "Is this on any of our Web posts that we have around the city?"

"Nope," Billy said. "Not in our records." He looked at Grant. "You guys found this?"

"One of our cyber techs did," Grant answered.

"So you're telling me we have the address of a currently operational Web station?" Hickem asked.

"That's what we think," Mocks answered.

"All right," Hickem said. "What do you want?"

"An introduction," Grant answered. "You get the credit for the bust of Seattle's worst bad guys, and we get to know what they know. No questions asked."

Hickem smiled. "You could have brought in your own S.W.A.T. team for this, yet you chose to come here and hand this to the FBI. You must hate paperwork, Detective."

"I hate scumbags who snatch little kids," Grant said. "We have a deal?"

Hicken leapt from his chair and stepped around the desk. "We leave in twenty. All right, boys!" He whirled his finger in the air, as if he were corralling the wagons. "Let's strap up!"

Grant and Mocks stepped aside as the office workers transformed from pencil pushers into a field-ready unit almost instantaneously. Mocks leaned in, whispering. "Are you sure about this? I don't know if the captain is going to like another showy public display of police force. Not to mention the mayor and the senator."

"Annie's been missing for longer than six hours," Grant answered. "We haven't had any hits from her AMBER Alert. And if she was taken by one of these people she could be down in California by now."

"But is this the right move?" Mocks asked. "We should check on the suspect in the hospital. Tommy's abductor."

"He's still unconscious," Grant said. "Someone put a bullet in his back that damaged his kidneys." He gave Mocks some side-eye.

"Dangerous line of work, kidnapping," Mocks replied. "They should have read the fine print." She paused. "And thanks for today. I needed it."

"I'm just glad you and Rick are fine," Grant said. "He's a good man. No reason for you to worry about nothing all day. I need your mind on the case."

"You think we'll find something with this Web crew?" Mocks asked, her face skeptical.

"It's the best lead we have right now," Grant said. "We just need to keep pressing forward."

"Weren't you the one who told me it's best to take a step back every once in a while to take a look at the bigger picture?" Mocks asked.

"All right you two," Hickem said, strapping on his bulletproof vest. "We don't have any extra gear, so I hope you have your own."

"We'll make do," Grant said. He headed for the door and Mocks followed.

"I think this is one of those times where you should take your own advice," Mocks said as they made their way to the car.

"Well, that's the great thing about being the person who gives advice, Mocks. I get to choose when and how I take my own medicine."

"That just sounds like a bad combination."

Hickem drove like a madman, but Grant kept pace with the FBI van weaving through traffic. Not that Grant minded the speed. Every second that ticked away on Grant's wrist lowered their chances of success. Once they reached the twelve-hour mark, the odds of a successful retrieval dropped in half after every subsequent six hours.

Mocks had reached for the green Bic lighter in her jacket and was already performing the ceremonious flick of the flint to calm her nerves.

Grant followed Hickem off the highway and toward the shambled structures that comprised the south side of Seattle. Broken windows, barred doors, and graffiti were common sights.

Vagrants shuffled along the sidewalks, swallowed up in their large coats, their hollowed faces and blank stares cast toward the pavement. A group of kids played on a rusted swing set, chasing one another in yards devoid of grass. Much like the rest of the neighborhood, it was nothing but dirt and trash.

Politicians had used the south side as a campaigning platform for years. They promised to clean the city up, but once elected, the neighborhood became a distant memory. There were other worries and issues to think about: the drug and homeless epidemic, and now the human-trafficking problem. But Grant knew it was all connected. You pulled one string, and one hundred others followed with it. The only challenge was figuring out which string unraveled it all.

Hickem slowed and veered off the road. Once he stopped, his agents filed out the back. Grant parked behind them.

Hickem loaded a round into his shotgun. "The house is a few blocks up the road. The moment they see us coming, they'll dig in. This is your last chance to back out. You two may have seen a lot of shit, but this is going to be different. I promise you."

"We can handle ourselves," Grant said.

Hickem shook his head. "Have it your way." He grabbed two earpieces and a pair of black masks. He handed Grant and Mocks one each. "You'll need to wear both."

Mocks lifted the mask. "Seriously?"

"These people don't know who we are, and you want it to stay that way," Hickem said. "They are worse than the Mexican cartels when it comes to payback."

Grant and Mocks did as the man said, and once their faces were covered, Grant opened his trunk, and he and Mocks strapped on their own protective vests, grabbing some extra magazines out of Grant's duffel bag that he kept stocked for such occasions. He fingered the bullet still lodged in the Kevlar from the raid on Craig Johnson. He hoped he wasn't tempting fate again.

"Listen," Grant said. "We need to follow their lead. I've seen them in action before, and they know what they're doing."

"You think we're gonna be in their way or something?" Mocks asked. "Or have you forgotten the pair of detectives that saved that little boy earlier today, or the little girl yesterday?" Her tone was laced with sarcasm, but Grant didn't want to take any chances.

"Hickem is right," Grant said. "We're walking into something we've never experienced before. I don't know how bad it'll get."

Mocks went quiet, and then after she finished the last strap that secured her Kevlar, she quietly spoke. "I've seen bad, Grant. Whatever's in there, I can handle it."

A few of the homeless looked up from their feet as Hickem led the charge. Grant's heart pounded in time with their quick footsteps, and the activity reminded him of the lack of food he'd had over the past two days. He hardly ever ate during an investigation, and with the number of cases he'd had stacked lately, he was practically fasting. Adrenaline would kick in though. That he was sure of.

They reached a crossroad, and Hickem stopped thirty feet before the turn, holding up his fist, halting the crew. He signaled for the rest of the team to head around back, and then motioned Grant and Mocks toward him.

"You two stay on my six the entire time, understand?" Hickem asked.

"We won't get in the way," Grant answered.

"I'm not worried about you getting in the way," Hickem said. "I'm worried about you getting shot." He leaned closer. "The moment we turn this corner, they'll have a line of sight on us, so brace for impact."

And whatever hell Grant thought would rain down on him didn't even come close to what happened next.

Two men stood guard on the house's front porch. AK-47s hung from their shoulders. It was one hundred feet between the street corner and the house, but when the gunfire started, it felt much closer.

Bullets spit from the automatic rifles and tore into the concrete and asphalt as Hickem rolled left behind a low-lying concrete wall that was once a perimeter fence. Grant and Mocks followed, the sound of every gunshot pounding in their chests.

"Just stay down!" Hickem said, then squat-walked a few feet forward. He shot straight up and returned fire, his movements quick and mechanical. He squeezed off a half dozen rounds, and then retreated back behind cover.

Gunfire erupted to Grant's left, and when he turned, he saw that Mocks had stood and fired as well. He yanked her down, and another barrage of gunfire vibrated through the wall.

Hickem walked over and gave both of them a shove. "I don't need any cowboy shit."

"No," Mocks said. "What you need is cover fire. We know how to shoot."

"She's right," Grant said. "We can help."

It was impossible to study Hickem's facial expressions behind the black mask. But with his eyes focused on Grant, the detective knew he was considering it.

"All right," Hickem said. "Wait for my mark." He quickly turned back to the edge of the wall, and Grant and Mocks coiled in position.

Shouting replaced gunfire as Hickem craned his neck back toward Grant, holding up three fingers, counting down. On one, Grant and Mocks jumped from cover and fired into the converging gang.

The first two shots hit nothing but the side of the building, but once Grant had a better view of the situation, he adjusted his aim to the trio of thugs near the front porch. With the gang's attention focused on Grant and Mocks, Hickem sprinted forward and dropped the trio with three quick strikes.

Hickem turned back to Grant and Mocks on their sprint and held up his palm. "Stay back!" The rest of Hickem's unit crawled up the side of the house and they stormed inside.

Grant pressed his head against the rough grain of the concrete wall and checked the ammunition he had left in his magazine. A piece of cloth blocked his vision and he adjusted his mask to count the remaining bullets. Five left.

Mocks lifted her mask up, her face flush from the added heat. "I can't see a damn thing with this on." She wiped the sweat from her forehead.

"Put it back on," Grant said. "We don't know when this is going to be over." More gunshots echoed from inside the house, along with the crash of glass.

The earpiece in Grant's ear came alive with chatter, and Hickem repeated the same order over and over. "Man down. Man down. Suspects fleeing south."

Grant poked his head over the wall and saw three gang members heading their way. He pushed himself to his knees, the majority of the wall still providing cover from his chest down, and opened fire.

The first two bullets went wide right, but the third made contact with the rear gang member's leg. The front two members returned fire, and Grant ducked just as Mocks stood. "No!"

But before he pulled her down, she opened fire, her mask still pushed high on top of her head as the fleeing gang members got a good look at her face. Empty casings ejected from her pistol and Grant yanked her back down.

Grant poked his head over the top, and the gang member he shot crawled on all fours, the automatic rifle still in his hand. He shoved Mocks, who adjusted the cloth over her face. "C'mon."

He leapt over the side, pistol aimed at the suspect. "Freeze!"

The gang member stretched his arm to aim his rifle and Grant fired just to the left of the man's hand, forcing the suspect to stop. Grant planted his knee into the man's lower back as the suspect groaned and rambled in a foreign tongue.

Mocks moved closer and pressed the end of her barrel against his forehead. "Don't move, asshole."

The man looked up and flashed a smile that was riddled with gold and silver teeth. Tattoos covered his face, neck, arms, any portion of his skin that was exposed. Some of them were words in another language, others were of women, but the majority were spiders. They crawled all over his body, and when he laughed, the web on the left side of his cheek crinkled.

"We saw you, bitch," he said, looking at Mocks. "You're dead. You know that? You're fucking dead!" He laughed again, and Grant shoved his face into the dirt.

"Detective!" Hickem's voice boomed outside the house, and Grant let the man go. He walked over, his agents close behind. "You two all right?"

"We're fine," Mocks answered.

Grant kept his eyes locked on the suspect on the ground, the blood from the man's calf staining the dirt and dead grass crimson. "Yeah. We're fine."

"I have medics on the way," Hickem said. "One of our guys took a bullet, but he should be fine. We've got a few more inside."

"There were two that got away," Mocks said.

Grant nodded. "Looks like they were heading west. Not sure where to though."

"I know where. To tell their friends what happened and

come back with more trouble that we're not equipped to handle right now." Hickem looked down at the suspect. "Get him over to the driveway with the others. We'll sort this mess back at the office."

Grant peeled the gangbanger off the dirt and kept the man upright on the walk toward the front. He glanced back at Mocks a few times, and Grant shoved his face forward. The ambassador's story suddenly surfaced in Grant's memory. All of the death and destruction the Web brought upon anyone that opposed them. It was a fate he wanted to avoid.

17

*T*he interrogation room at Hickem's headquarters became a revolving door. Grant watched from the one-way glass as the FBI Special Agent worked over each of them, one by one, doing everything he could within the lines of the law, and even stepping over them a few times.

But each interrogation was only met with the same blank stare and same indigenous curses. None of them were giving up anything. Not even their names.

They denied the weapons and ammunition that were found inside the house. They denied the charges against conspiracy to kill law enforcement. They denied the drugs and the fact that they had inhabited a foreclosed building.

"This is a waste of time," Grant said. "These people would rather die than give up any of their own."

Mocks sat in the corner, working overtime on her Bic. "I wouldn't have a problem with that." Her eyes were focused on the newest suspect inside the room, who just so happened to be the man Grant had shot.

Grant walked over and placed his hand on her wrist, and she stopped. "Are you all right?"

Mocks pulled her hand back. "We need to go back and search that house."

"The other gang members are probably already there," Grant said. "It's too dangerous."

"C'mon, Grant," Mocks said, irritated. "You've seen it; these guys aren't going to turn over, no matter what we throw at them. They're loyal. We need something else."

Grant looked down at his watch, and the timer rolled over to eight hours. "We'll need to be quick about it."

Mocks pocketed the lighter and hopped off the table she was sitting on. "Then we better go before Captain America tells us otherwise."

They slipped out of the room, and one of Hickem's agents stepped in their path on the way to the front door. "Don't want to stick around?" he asked. The man was a little shorter than Grant, but much wider, and it looked like he was all muscle.

"We still have a case to handle," Grant said. "Tell Hickem that if he finds anything to give me a call. And tell him I'll do the same." Grant sidestepped him, and Mocks followed quickly.

The ride over was quiet. Nothing but ambient traffic noise flooded the cabin of Grant's sedan. He glanced in the rearview mirror, half expecting to see Hickem's armored truck barreling down after him, but he was nowhere in sight.

"All units, be advised," Dispatch said, cutting through the silence. Grant and Mocks swiveled toward the radio. "AMBER Alert recovered in northern Skagit County. Adolescent girl. Dead on scene."

Grant tightened his grip on the wheel, praying it wasn't Annie Mauer. His stomach tightened into knots. He couldn't lose her. Not this one.

"Suspect's name is Bart Malliby, also dead on scene. An

accomplice is believed to have escaped, be on the lookout for—"

Grant turned the volume off. Not their suspect. Not their girl. Neither of them said a word for a moment, but Grant still felt the anger simmering, deep beneath the surface. His breathing quickened, and his knuckles whitened against the black steering grip.

"Goddammit!" Grant punched the dash, and the radio's receiver was knocked from its perch.

One of his knuckles cracked and bits of blood dotted the leather of the wheel and the dash. His hand ached, and he cursed under his breath. He veered left and maneuvered around a slow-moving van in the middle lane and took his aggression out on the accelerator.

"We have to stop them, Mocks," Grant said, all of his concentration focused on the road, changing lanes, picking up speed, getting to the headquarters as fast as they could. "We can't let them get away with this."

"I know," Mocks said. "And we will." She placed a hand on his wrist. It was her turn to bring him back from the edge. "But it won't do us any good if we wreck before we get there."

The lump in Grant's throat slid back down to his stomach, and his heart rate slowed. He took three deep breaths, exhaling slowly. By the time they returned to the house in the south side, the anger had dulled but hadn't disappeared.

Grant parked the car in the corner, and they walked the two houses to the gang's headquarters. Blood and bullet holes marked the carnage from earlier. On autopilot, Grant unholstered his pistol and took the first steps up to the porch, his eyes darting between the broken windows.

There were no cars out front, no signs that anyone had returned. Maybe Hickem was wrong. With the breach, the gang could have written the house off as a lost cause. But if that was the case, then there most likely wasn't anything of value left behind.

The conditions inside the house weren't better than the exterior. While the outside was riddled with bullet holes, the inside was littered with trash and ratty furniture. But it was the smell that made it unbearable. No central heat flowed, so a musty chill lingered in the air. Every breath Grant drew muddled his lungs with crap.

"I'll start looking in the back, and you check the front," Grant said. "If you hear anything, come and get me, and I'll do the same."

"Fine by me," Mocks said, stifling a cough. "Sooner we can get out of here, the less time I'll have to spend in the shower scrubbing myself clean."

Grant stepped around empty beer bottles and was mindful of the used needles that littered the ground. He thought about asking Mocks if she was okay being around that stuff, but he decided against it. Of course it bothered her. She was an addict in the middle of a drug den.

The rooms in the back were small. Bare mattresses were shoved in corners, and more food wrappers and bottles littered the floor. What carpet wasn't covered in trash was stained in what Grant figured was a mixture of booze, blood, and semen. The walls were decorated with pictures of naked women. A dartboard hung at the end of the hall-way, and the misses were marked with tiny holes on either side.

But each room Grant checked had nothing more than the one before it. He wasn't sure what he would find, and he wasn't sure what he hoped to find. Maybe a manifesto, some type of communication, anything. If this gang was involved in the mass abductions, or even orchestrated them, then there had to be a paper trail somewhere. The Web wasn't just flying by the seat of their pants.

"Grant!" Mocks said, her voice excited. "I've got something."

Grant sprinted from the last bedroom and up the hall. He found Mocks in the living room, hunched over a laptop with her gloves on. He walked over, his heart racing at a breakneck pace. "Where'd you find it?"

"It was stashed under a floor board underneath the couch with a brick of coke," Mocks answered, her keys gliding over the keyboard with one gloved hand. "Along with this." She held up a small notepad with a bunch of symbols etched over it.

"What is it?" Grant asked.

"Don't know."

Car doors slammed outside. Grant and Mocks turned to the broken windows. Three sedans were parked in the street, and three men in suits and sunglasses stepped out. The wind gusted one of their jackets open and exposed the dual shoulder holster underneath, and they openly carried AK-47s strapped to their shoulders.

"We've got to go," Grant said, closing the lid of the laptop and backtracking down the hallway.

Mocks followed on light feet and before they reached the first bedroom down the hall, the front door groaned as the men entered, and a flood of unintelligible voices followed. If they came for the laptop, then it wouldn't be long before they realized it was gone.

Grant pulled Mocks toward the end of the hall and the dartboard, and they escaped out of sight just as the first gangbanger entered the hallway. The voices grew louder, and the crash of furniture thundered their haste.

Grant fumbled with the doorknob to the back door. It was locked. Footsteps in the hall grew closer. Mocks removed her pistol. Grant shook the door lightly. It was flimsy material. He shouldered it, and the wooden frame splintered as he stumbled into the backyard.

The noise gave them away, and heavy footsteps chased them down the hall as Grant and Mocks sprinted into the backyard, heading for the gap in the wooden fence. Grant stopped to let Mocks pass through first, and during his pause, three armed men funneled out the back door. They screamed, raised their rifles, and fired as he ducked behind the fence.

"Don't stop, Mocks!" Grant pulled out his pistol on the run, the laptop still clutched under his arm. Mocks's legs blurred together in her quick, short strides, and Grant's own legs burned as they pounded against the pavement.

The small grid of houses where the gang lived had narrow alleys, forcing the pair to run single file. More gunshots fired, and Grant felt a wave of heat and air brush his left ear. He waited for the pain of a bullet, but none came as he followed Mocks around the next corner that spit them out onto the sidewalk of a four-lane road.

Heavy traffic sped back and forth, and Grant spun around to get a pulse on their pursuers. He watched two of them spill out onto the sidewalk a few houses down, their rifles raised.

With pedestrians and civilians outside in broad daylight, they opened fire. Grant and Mocks sprinted into traffic, Grant tweaking his ankle from the sudden burst of speed.

"Jesus Christ!" Mocks said, barely able to keep her feet as Grant pulled her across the road.

Cars laid on their horns and brakes screeched, but it all ended once the gunfire reached the road. Bullets tore apart trucks, sedans, vans, any vehicle that was in the gang's path. Grant didn't look back until they reached the other side.

His lungs burned, and the muscles in his legs turned to

jelly. Mocks gave him a shove and pointed back to the thugs still trying to cross the now standstill, traffic-jammed street.

The pair sprinted between two houses in an old development and entered another grid-like maze of tight alleys and sharp corners. Clothes hung on lines to dry, most of them still wet from the constant drizzle.

Gunfire echoed behind them, but it sounded farther away now. Grant reached for his phone and dialed Dispatch, reporting their location. "Shots fired at 53rd South and Connolly Ave. Suspects are heavily armed. Medical units needed onsite."

Grant skidded to a stop the moment the words left his mouth, and Mocks only made it a few more feet before she stopped to rest, too. The cold air was like breathing ice, and every breath was painful.

"There are still people trapped back there," Mocks said.

Grant ripped off his jacket, wrapped the computer inside, and then stuffed it under the small space beneath the house to his left.

"Ready?" Mocks asked.

Grant removed his pistol and nodded. "Let's go."

The crash of metal and screams echoed louder on their return to the highway. In the last narrow alley before the road, Grant had a view of the street and its chaos: Screams. Gunfire. Smoke. Panic.

Grant and Mocks rushed into the violence, their pistols aimed at the gang that had unleashed so much hell.

Smoke drifted up from the hood of a wrecked truck, a young man unconscious behind the wheel. Grant veered to check on him and found the man's forehead crusted with blood. He checked for a pulse and felt the faint beat of life. Grant started to move him but froze when he made eye contact with a gangbanger through the passenger windshield.

The shooter opened fire and Grant yanked the young man from the driver seat. Bullet holes redecorated the truck, and Grant dragged the unconscious man backward to the safety of the sidewalk.

The jammed cars provided plenty of cover, and Grant found most of them abandoned. He rounded the hood of a Ford Mustang, and another gangbanger appeared around the van's rear.

Grant charged before the shooter fired and tackled him to the pavement. Both of their weapons fell to the asphalt and the thug rolled left, using the momentum to mount Grant and then wrapped his meaty fingers around Grant's throat.

Grant's airway closed. He punched the man's sides as he choked for breath. The tattooed face above him blurred. His arms fell to his sides, and the mounting pressure in his head slowly faded. A numbness spread from his neck to his hands and feet. And that's when he saw them.

His wife, Ellen, and his unborn child, Annie. The daughter he never had a chance to meet had red hair like her mother and blue eyes like him. She was smiling, reaching out to him. And just before they touched, she was gone. Vanished into nothing, just like in the car accident that had altered Grant's life forever.

The thug's limp body landed on top of Grant, the heavy man suffocating his lungs still gasping for air. He shoved the body off and rolled to his hands and knees. There was a muffled noise in his ears, like someone shouting underwater. His vision cleared, and when he craned his neck to the noise he saw Mocks huddled behind a car, evading gunfire.

"Grant!" she screamed between the gunshots, and he stumbled to his feet. He made it two steps before he stopped and reached for the AK-47 that belonged to the thug. He tucked the butt of the rifle under his arm and blinked away the last few black dots from his vision. He crept alongside the van and craned his neck around the front bumper for a better vantage point.

Two shooters. Automatic rifles. Grant motioned for Mocks to stay down. He retreated a step, his head still fuzzy from the fight, and then jumped straight up, slamming his elbows on the van's hood to steady his aim before squeezing the trigger.

The recoil from the automatic rifle pounded against Grant's shoulder in rapid succession. The power of the weapon caused his aim to drift, but the distraction alone was enough to give Mocks the needed time to escape the piece of Swiss cheese that used to be a Mazda.

Mocks leapt behind Grant and the van, and the trail of bullets followed her. The tires exploded, and the windows shattered as Grant and Mocks kept low on their retreat behind another cluster of cars.

The pair stopped at the driver side door of a BMW, the rear bumper smashed from a collision. Grant saw the man he'd dragged to safety still unconscious on the sidewalk. But aside from him, the street had turned into a ghost town.

"You all right?" Mocks asked.

Grant nodded. "Thanks for bailing me out back there."

"I thought it was the chivalrous thing to do," Mocks answered.

Grant peeked over the BMW, the pair of shooters closing in. There was nowhere left to run. "How much ammunition do you have left?"

Mocks removed her magazine. "Four rounds."

Grant reached for his phone and texted Sam a message: **yellow house off of 53rd, computer under the house wrapped in my jacket. Pivotal for case against the Web.**

Grant clicked send in case they didn't make it and then pocketed the phone. Vibrations rattled through the Beemer as gunfire grew louder. Glass shattered and rained on their shoulders. Mocks and Grant kept low, waiting for any lull in gunfire to make a move. The pair made eye contact and with hellfire raining down, Grant realized Mocks could be the last person he saw on this earth. Dying next to your partner didn't sound so bad though.

"Ready?" Grant asked.

Mocks nodded. She inched toward the hood while Grant went to the trunk. He paused at the rear blown-out tire now sitting on its rim. Grant held up his hand, counting down from three, two, one.

Grant stood, lifting the rifle's sight to the gangbangers to his left. Blood splattered over the man's suit and he flew backward. He saw Mocks in his peripheral, the four quick strikes from her pistol, and she ejected her last magazine. She was empty. He pivoted his aim and knew that he wouldn't make it in time before they gunned her down, but he had to try. Just as he squeezed the trigger on the thug who had Mocks in his sights, something stole his attention. A siren. Lots of them.

"Grant!" Mocks said, and pointed to the cluster of squad cars down the road.

The surviving gang members retreated into the crevices of their slums, firing randomly as the police formed a perimeter. Grant and Mocks quickly fished out their badges as officers converged on their location. Grant lowered the rifle then tossed it on the Beemer's trunk, his hands raised as the officers circled him.

18

*T*he aftermath from the gunfight made the south side look more like a Middle Eastern warzone than a community in Seattle. People watched from the windows of their houses while pedestrians snapped pictures on their phones and streamed video to the web. The show of police force in the area was impressive, and officers scoured the area looking for the gang but found no one.

"Detective Grant." An officer exited one of the alleys between the houses, the same one that had taken his statement on what happened. He was thorough, though his mechanical method of questioning was tedious. He held up the jacket and the laptop wrapped inside. "This what you were looking for?"

Grant sat in the back of a squad car, his legs hanging out the door and the sole of his boots grinding glass into the asphalt. He held a cup of coffee in his left hand that he hadn't touched. He liked the warmth, but not the caffeine. Despite the fatigue, he was still wired from the gunfight. A light twitch in his right hand revealed his frazzled nerves.

"Yeah," Grant said.

The officer unwrapped the jacket from the laptop and returned it to Grant. He held up the laptop. "What do you want me to do with this?"

"Get it to Sam Braddock over in Precinct Eighteen," Grant answered, shaking the crud from his jacket. "Tell him it has to do with the website and that I need a summary of everything that's on that computer." He tapped the top of the screen. "There is also a note on there with some symbols. I don't know what they represent, but they might be a password."

Grant was thankful the young officer had a notepad out, jotting everything down. "Got it. Anything else?"

"Tell him to hurry," Grant answered.

"Yes, sir." The officer jogged off and disappeared into the clusters of policemen, paramedics, and from what it looked like, the FBI.

Mocks appeared with her own cup of coffee and leaned against the back of the van. "How you feeling?"

"I'll be better once we find our kid," Grant said, looking down at the coffee that had cooled significantly. He dumped the brown liquid onto the pavement just as Hickem and his agents arrived.

"What the hell was that, Grant?" Hickem asked but didn't bother waiting for a response. "You realize that your little stunt will send these people underground? You may want to find these kids, but I want to bring down their organization, and God knows how much you fucked all of this up!" He pointed his large meaty finger right between Grant's eyes.

"Did you get anything from the interrogations?" Grant asked.

Hickem's stony expression reddened. "No."

"And I don't suspect that'll change anytime soon," Grant said, stepping out of the car and straightening his back, which gave a dull crack. "You've never gotten anything from interrogations of Web members, have you?"

"No," Hickem answered.

"Then why the hell did you even agree to take us over there?" Mocks asked, her own face reddening now. "You almost got us killed, and you got one of your own guys shot!"

The left corner of Hickem's mouth curved up his cheek. "Our protocols are clear about when I'm allowed to engage and utilize resources for a raid. It's only by approval from my superior or special circumstances." A more amiable expression appeared. "I was able to file this one as a special circumstance."

"Unbelievable," Mocks said.

"I'll be able to use your names in the report, and when my boss asks why two Seattle detectives were part of a sting, I'll get to tell them it was because the ambassador called me, and that's my get out of jail free card." Hickem crossed his arms, shifting his glance back and forth between the two. "Getting the jump on those guys allowed us to confiscate a lot of guns and a lot of drugs. And because we took a pivotal crew off the street, the whole organization will have to shift. And when people shift, they make mistakes." Hickem straightened. "I intend to capitalize on those mistakes."

"Well," Grant said, sliding his jacket back on, parts of the inside wet from the ground. "I'm glad we could help you in that matter. C'mon, Mocks." The pair walked through the crowded street and did one final check-in with the lieutenant on scene to make sure they didn't need anything else.

"You're all set, Detective Grant," the lieutenant said. "And maybe next time when you're going to be in my neighborhood, give me a heads up? I'll schedule my guys for overtime in advance." He cracked a playful smile, and Grant patted him on the shoulder.

"Will do," Grant answered.

Once they were out of earshot and closer toward the car, Mocks spoke up. "I'm assuming you didn't tell Hickem about the laptop on purpose."

"I don't need him confiscating evidence for his case when we can use it for ours," Grant said. "He used us, and now we've used him. I'd say that makes us even."

Mocks smiled. "That's why you wanted that officer to go and get the laptop." She shoved him in the side quite hard. "You needed to establish chain of evidence."

Grant fished out his keys and stepped around to the driver side of his sedan. "Want to make sure we have a case that sticks." He climbed inside, but when he slid the key into the ignition, he didn't turn it on.

Mocks noticed the pause as she clicked her seat buckle into place. "What's wrong?"

Grant twisted the gold wedding band. "I saw them when that gangbanger was choking me." He kept his eyes glued to the metal. It was cold to the touch and damp from the moisture outside. "I saw their faces clear as day." He smiled. "Even my daughter's." When Mocks didn't respond, Grant looked over and then he shook his head. "I know I sound like a crazy person."

"You're not crazy," Mocks said, then after a pause, she added, "What did she look like?"

"Annie?" Grant asked.

"Yeah."

Grant closed his eyes and leaned his head back against the seat rest. "She had red hair like Ellen. Her eyes were like mine." He smiled. "Everything else was all Ellen though. Ears, nose, skin." Grant opened his eyes. "Ellen always said that I was her anchor and that she was my ship. I always thought it was silly, but after she died, I realized what she meant. There were places that I could only go with her. And there were storms that she could only weather with me." The smile faded from Grant's face, and his voice grew very quiet. "The perfect pair."

Mocks placed her hand on Grant's shoulder. "It's good to have those memories. And it's good to be that close." And then she dug into the meat of his shoulder with her nails. He winced and she leaned closer. "Do not chase that feeling again."

Grant shook his head, confused. "What are you talking about?"

"I know what it's like to have something make you feel good when there isn't a whole lot to feel good about," Mocks answered. "Heroin did that for me for a long time, and I've got the scars to prove it. But there are other highs in this world that are just as dangerous. And I don't need you turning into an adrenaline junkie so you can chase visions of your wife and child. You've still got work to do." She let go of his shoulder, and the pinpoint pressure from her nails left indentations in the jacket.

He understood what she meant, because the thought had crossed his mind more than once. He wanted to see his wife again. He wanted more time with the daughter that he never had the chance to hold. He wanted the life that he envisioned before the accident.

"We should head back to the precinct," Grant said. "See what we've got from the AMBER Alerts while—"

"Unit thirty-five, please advise, Craig Johnson is out of surgery and stabilized. He has been cleared by the doctors for interview."

Grant snatched the receiver that still lay on the floor-board after his outburst from earlier. "Copy that, Dispatch. Tell the hospital we are on our way." He clicked his seatbelt into place and cranked the engine to life.

"I meant what I said," Mocks said, shifting in her seat. "Chasing after it will only get you killed."

"I know," Grant said, putting on his seatbelt. "But there are worse things."

* * *

THE FLUORESCENT LIGHTS reflected off the polished tile of the hospital, highlighting the white floors and walls. Nurses walked by with clipboards, their sneakers squeaking with every step. Grant tapped his finger impatiently at the nurses' station while Mocks sat in one of the chairs in the waiting area.

"All right, Detective." The nurse behind the desk returned his badge and a visitor's sticker. "The patient is in room two-twelve."

Grant slapped the sticker on his front jacket pocket and slipped his badge back around his neck. He walked around the station and Mocks followed. He spied the room guarded by an officer. It was standard protocol for someone like Johnson to have protection. Pedophiles weren't popular with any group of people.

"Let me know if you need anything, Detective," the officer said after Mocks stepped inside.

"Thank you," Mocks said, and then shut the door.

Grant sidled up to the left side of the bed, and Mocks went to the right. Johnson slept, but there wasn't anything peaceful about it. The bed sheet was pulled up to Craig's waist. The hospital gown they put him in lay flat against his thin body. Wispy, lightly browned hair sprouted from the top of his head. His cheeks were hollow and curved into his mouth. His eyes were closed, and the machines hooked up to his body beeped in rhythmic intervals. Grant gave the bed a light rattle.

Craig's eyes fluttered open, and when he saw Grant and Mocks hovering over him, the machine monitoring his heart rate beeped wildly. He pressed himself deeper into the mattress as if he could melt into the sheets and escape.

"W-what do you want?" Craig shifted his eyes between the detectives, his mouth ajar and running his tongue over his thin lips.

"We never formally met," Mocks said, breaking the ice. "I'm Detective Mullocks, and this is my partner Detective Grant. We're the ones who shot you." She smiled, but Grant kept his expression stoic. Whenever Mocks took the lead, Grant played the strong, silent role.

"I-I want my lawyer," Craig said, his tone lacking confidence. "I have a right to—"

"Not you," Mocks said. "Kiddie rapists get a special exemption on lawyers."

"The website," Grant said. "Who told you about it?"

Craig Johnson burst into tears. "Please, I didn't do anything to the boy. I promise you. I swear to god nothing happened."

"But something was going to happen," Mocks said. "Wasn't it, Craig? That's why you took the kid, why you wanted to shuffle him up north across state lines. We saw the passports. You must have spent a pretty penny on those."

Grant leaned closer to Craig's face, his shadow slowly covering Craig's figure, blocking out the bright lights of the room. "Who told you about the site?"

Another wave of sobs erupted from Craig, tears bursting from his eyes as he mumbled unintelligible words through his blubbering.

"You're gonna have to repeat that," Mocks said. "I didn't catch it."

"I met him at the park I go to," Craig said, regaining some ability for coherent speech.

"Where you abducted the boy," Grant said, finishing the sentence.

Craig nodded. "He told me he could help give me what I wanted. He said no one would ever find out if I did exactly what he told me to do." He shut his eyes, squeezing out a few more tears. "So that's what I did." He sniffled and opened his eyes, looking at Grant. "He never gave me a name. Just a card with the website information."

"Where's the card now?" Grant asked.

"I-I destroyed it," Craig answered, shrinking deeper into his pillow. "He told me to." His Adam's apple bobbed up and down when he swallowed. "The man was... frightening."

"What'd this guy look like?" Mocks asked.

"Older white guy. Grey hair. It was longer, down to his neck, but I only saw what wasn't covered with his hat," Craig said. "He wore sunglasses too."

"What about scars, tattoos, birthmarks, anything like that?" Mocks asked.

"I can't remember," Craig answered.

Grant wrapped his hand around Craig's throat, and the beeping skyrocketed. "We need something more than a geriatric who gave you a card to throw away."

Craig thrashed in his bed, but weakly so, like a piece of prey that knew it was caught. He tried to speak, but Grant's grip was too tight.

"What was that?" Grant asked.

"Spiders," Craig said, his eyes wide. "Spiders on his hand. Three of them, crawling over a black web. They were all black." Grant let him go, and Craig bawled.

Grant turned to leave and Mocks followed. She caught up to him halfway down the hall.

"Put out an APB for an older white male, grey hair, with three spiders over a black web," Grant said. "We need to follow up with Sam, see what he has so far on the computer."

"Hey," Mocks said, blocking his path before they reached

the elevator. "Are you all right? That wasn't your normal tough cop."

Grant held up his watch, the timer ticking toward ten hours. She looked, then stepped out of his way, and he pressed the down button and they descended to the first floor.

"You don't have to keep reminding me that this is urgent." Mocks crossed her arms, staring straight ahead. "You don't have a monopoly on wanting to successfully complete our cases. Last I checked, we were still partners."

The elevator doors pinged opened, and Grant had a clear view to the automatic glass doors at the hospital's entrance where a few members of the press had clustered, waiting for him outside. Grant sighed. "Great."

"I'll handle it," Mocks said, stepping in front of Grant on their exit. The doors opened and the press immediately swarmed them.

"Detective! Do you have any leads on who could be behind these abductions?"

"Did the suspect survive the altercation at the house?"

"How many more children are at risk?"

Mocks held up her hands. "We're currently following several leads in regards to the abductions. We don't have any further information to provide you at this time. Thank you."

The horde of reporters slowed their pace to a crawl, and Grant's patience grew thinner. All of the frustration, fatigue, uncertainty, and stress of the past two days reached a tipping point.

One of the reporters veered from Mocks and thrust a microphone in his face. "Detective Grant, have you used some of the tactics on current suspects that you used during the altercation with Brian Dunston two years ago?"

The comment stopped Grant dead in his tracks, and Mocks turned to try and intercept, but she was two steps too slow. Grant smacked the microphone out of the reporter's hand and shoved him hard in the chest, sending him to the pavement.

Camera lights flashed quickly and the rest of the reporters captured the moment with video and sound as Grant cocked his arm back and hardened his hand to a fist. Before he struck, Mocks stepped in his way.

She shoved him as hard as she could, throwing all of her five-foot, one-hundred pound frame into it that only moved Grant a few inches. Another round of camera flashes and questions polluted the air, but Mock's sudden action was enough to snap Grant out of his rage.

The pair turned and hurried to the car, the reporters following, with Mocks stuck in the middle of it, waving her hand and saying that they weren't taking any more questions and they didn't have a comment.

The reporters pressed against the side of the car, and Grant reversed out of the parking spot as Mocks blocked her face from the cameras peering inside. Grant floored it out of the parking lot and, thankfully, they didn't try and follow.

"What the hell was that?" Mocks asked, slapping the dash. "Do you have any idea what you just did?"

The rage receded from Grant's mind, but the memories of the night from two years ago poured into his consciousness. Flashes of blood appeared on his knuckles. Brian Dunston's blood. His screams. His pleas for mercy. His pleas for forgiveness.

"I'm sorry," Grant said, his breaths quick and shallow. His heartbeat accelerated and his head spun. He slowed the car and pulled over to the side of the road, the rest of the traffic blaring their frustrations for the inconvenience. He shifted into park, but left the engine running. He kept his hands tight on the steering wheel. He needed to hold onto something. He couldn't slip back into that madness again. Not now.

"They shouldn't have asked you about that," Mocks said, her tone softer. "That reporter deserved what he got and what he would have gotten. But that's not how it'll be spun on the six o'clock news. And that's not how the captain will see it."

Grant cursed under his breath and shut his eyes. "It was stupid. I know. It's just…" He looked at Mocks. "I'll never really know."

Mocks shook her head, confused. "Know what?"

"What my daughter would have sounded like. Who she would have grown up to be. I'll never know what kind of father I would have been. And it's a question I'll never be able to answer."

There was a time when he'd thought he could find those answers when he transferred to Missing Persons. He wanted to believe that he could help ease his own pain by easing the pain of others. But he still felt the loss. It was as sharp today as it was two years ago.

"No," Mocks answered. "You won't." She leaned closer. "And that's the burden of the living, Grant. That's what makes life hard, and dirty, and wonderful all at the same time. It's that pain that gives us strength. It's given you strength, and while you may not feel it in your own life, others have felt it. I've felt it. It'll never leave you, I know. But don't let the pain swallow you up." Mocks laid her hand over his on the wheel. "The pain can't define you, because then it controls you."

Grant rested his forehead on the crest of the steering wheel and shut his eyes. His insides were on fire, and the sucking pain in his chest pulled him inward. He wanted to fight it, but he'd been fighting it for a long time. He was tired.

"We still have to find Annie Mauer," Mock said. "She still needs us."

Annie. Grant lifted his head. He glanced at his watch. The timer ticked away seconds with impunity, a steady reminder that time was the master of all.

Grant shifted into drive and pulled back out onto the road. "We'll head back to the precinct. See what Sam was able to pull off the computer." He just wasn't sure how long he'd still have his badge when he arrived.

19

_T_he press had doubled around the precinct. Grant and Mocks parked in the back to avoid the circus. Grant lingered in the car after Mocks had gotten out. She knocked on the window, and he held up his hand.

Grant closed his eyes, took a deep breath, exhaled, and counted to three. There wouldn't be anything pleasant waiting for him inside, but he had to face it. He stepped out of the car and followed Mocks inside. After three steps, the captain spotted them heading to Cyber.

"Grant! Mullocks!" Captain Hill's cheeks wobbled in sync with his flabby neck, his skin flush red. "My office, now!"

"Captain," Mocks said. "We're—"

"I said now, damnit!" Captain Hill turned on his heel and marched back toward his office. The rest of the department had gone quiet, and it wasn't until Grant and Mocks were halfway to his office that everyone resumed their activities.

Grant was the last to enter and he shut the door, sealing them inside. Lieutenant Furst was in the corner with his arms crossed. Hill had plopped in his chair and leaned forward.

"I received a call from the station manager at Channel Four news asking me if I had a comment about the assault that one of my detectives performed on one of his reporters," Hill said.

"Sir," Mocks said. "You have to know that—"

"Shut it, Mullocks!" Hill thrust a finger in her direction, then pivoted his aim toward Grant. "Every news camera in this city is looking for the inside scoop on these abductions, and the last thing this department needs is its officers losing their cool under pressure. Do you have any idea the scrutiny we're under right now? No one feels safe. No one wants their kid to be taken, and every single person across the state is counting on us to end this."

Hill leaned back in his chair, the rant taking the breath out of him as he sucked down a few gulps of air, his forehead dotted with beads of sweat.

"Captain, this is bigger than just the abductions that were reported," Grant said. "We have reason to believe that a crime organization that calls itself The Web is involved in these abductions and the overall trafficking of sex workers through the entire West Coast."

"I don't give a shit if it's the goddamn Illuminati," Captain Hill said. "I want. Those kids. Back!" He slammed his fist on the desk and knocked the phone off.

Lieutenant Furst kept quiet. Grant waited for him to speak up, but it never came. Not that he blamed the lieu-tenant. Grant was a dead man walking, so it didn't matter what he did next.

"You don't let me finish this case, and there'll be more than just my assault on the six o'clock news," Grant said.

Hill lowered his voice. "Watch your tone, Detective."

Grant walked to Hill's desk, getting in his face. "I'll tell that reporter who asked me about Brian Dunston exactly what he wants to know. How you helped falsify the report of what happened that night. How you intimidated him to not press charges. And the best part of the story? It's true."

"You are way out of line!" Hill's cheeks wiggled and reddened. Spit flew from his mouth.

"Let me finish this case," Grant said. "You know that we're still your best bet to find those kids."

"Detective Grant," Furst said. "This isn't—"

"The only reason you're pissed about that reporter is because it reflects badly on you, Captain," Grant said. "You wouldn't give a shit if I hadn't been recorded. You only care when it disrupts your afternoon nap. So if you really want to save your ass, then let me and my partner do our job."

It was bold, but it was Grant's only play. He knew Hill would suspend him and an investigation would be ordered. Any superior officer would have done it under normal circumstances. But this wasn't normal.

The captain calmed a bit, and Grant knew it had worked.

"You will have to answer to the charges filed against you," Hill said. "I will keep the wolves off your back until this is done, but after, you turn in your badge. And if you fail, then all of this comes crashing down on your head." He looked at Mocks. "Both of your heads."

Grant turned on his heel and stepped out before any more stipulations were thrown their way. Grant got the time he needed. Now he had to deliver.

Mocks walked quickly by his side on their way back to Cyber. "You know they're going to run that story in the news no matter what. Everything from that night will be made public."

"I know," Grant said. "But it's like you said." He looked down at her. "I can't let it define me."

Mocks snorted and then stopped at her desk to retrieve a fresh Pop-Tart from its packaging. She ripped open the top and devoured it in three bites. "God, I was starving." She wiped her mouth with the back of her sleeve. "Sometimes I wonder if I substituted Pop-Tarts for drugs." She shook her head. "Still not sure if it's the healthier option."

Grant chuckled unexpectedly, and it helped calm the nerves. He felt steady now, more purposeful. The mission was clear, and they had good intelligence. Now they just needed the head of the snake.

When they arrived at Cyber, Sam had three laptops open on his desk: his own, the one that belonged to Stacy West's fiancé, and the laptop they had retrieved from the gang's headquarters in the south side.

"Tell me you have something, Sam," Grant said, sneaking up behind him.

"Well, I have made progress on the site," Sam said, pulling up a spreadsheet and list of names. "I've managed to locate all the IP addresses used by the usernames on the website and have even matched a few more real names, though none of them have been close in location to where the other kids were abducted."

"Send them out to the precincts where they're located anyway," Grant said. "Have the officers bring them in and search their homes. They might get lucky and find something."

"I don't think it'll be hard for them to get a warrant in our current environment," Mocks said.

"What about the laptop from the gang?" Grant asked. "Anything?"

"Oh-ho," Sam said, his voice low and throaty. "You could say that." He held up the blue note pad that Grant had taken along with the computer. "It's Cebuano, one of the main languages of the Philippines. This whole laptop is programmed to only accept, and react, to that type of language. It's even embedded into the coding, which I have never seen before."

"What do you mean?" Mocks asked.

"Coding is like math," Sam answered. "It's universal. And while different programs have specific languages, the language is the same in the program regardless of the country it's in." He lifted the laptop. "But this little tart has had its hard drive tweaked to have the Cebuano language embedded in its core coding."

"So what does that mean?" Grant asked.

"It means it's been a pain in my ass," Sam answered.

"There is something on that computer The Web doesn't want anyone to see," Grant said. "There has to be a location, some date, something that tells us where this is all going." *If it hasn't already happened.*

"I'm working with a translator from the State Department, but it's just slow going," Sam said. "I'm sorry."

"We don't need sorry," Mocks said. "We need evidence."

"I can give you what I have so far," Sam said, reaching for a notepad. "I wrote everything down that I've decoded." He gave a sheepish grin. "Sorry for the messy handwriting."

Grant handed the pad to Mocks once he realized he couldn't decipher the chicken scratch. Mocks looked it up and down. "These are just random pairs of numbers."

"That was in a folder titled 'hilo,'" Sam said. "Which translates to venom in English. Most of the files on the computer follow some type of spider theme."

"Let me see," Grant said, taking the notebook from Mocks. He counted down the paper. There were eight sets. "All of them came in pairs like this?"

"Yeah," Sam answered.

"GPS coordinates?" Mocks asked.

"It fits the length for longitude and latitude," Grant said. "Sam, type the first one in." Grant handed the paper back to Sam and he opened up a GPS. The first pair of coordinates zoomed in on the coast of southern California.

"Could be drop off points for shipments of women coming in from the Pacific," Grant said. "Try another one."

The second set of numbers was a location off the western coast of the Baja peninsula.

"Keep going," Grant said. "There has to be one closer to Seattle."

"Wait! I got one," Sam said. "Forty-six, forty-six, fifty-nine, dot, sixty-four, ninety-six North. One-twenty-four, five, forty-six dot thirty-one, twenty-eight West."

The map zoomed in on the southern coast of Washington State, and Sam expanded the image. "It looks like it's in the heart of Grayland Beach State Park."

"Secluded, off a main highway, thick cover from the trees, no coastal lights," Grant said. "Nighttime when that park is closed, it would be the perfect drop off point for smugglers."

"Looks like the others are all south of Los Angeles," Sam said. "This is the closest one to Seattle."

"We still don't have a time," Mocks said. "It could have already happened."

Grant shook his head. "No. They'll wait until after the twelve-hour mark when they know authorities will start to pull back on searches. I bet that's when they'll move the kids. Plus it'll be dark." Grant checked the time. "It's six-thirty now. Sun sets in an hour, and the park closes."

"I'll tell the captain," Mocks said.

"No, tell Lieutenant Furst. He'll be able to put a S.W.A.T. request together faster," Grant fished out his phone and dialed Hickem. "I'll get reinforcements. We're going to need a lot of bodies for this one."

THE ORANGES and pinks of the sunset had vanished by the time Grant and Mocks arrived at the park. Clouds rolled in

225

and blocked the stars and moon, pulling a blanket over the night sky. It made perfect conditions for smugglers and made it harder for Grant, Mocks, Hickem, and his team to locate the bad guys.

In addition to Hickem's FBI team, the Seattle Chief of Police ordered four S.W.A.T. teams down with them. With everyone accounted for, their group totaled fifty. Grant wasn't sure if it was enough.

Mocks shut the trunk of the sedan and loaded a fresh magazine into her service pistol, then holstered the weapon. "You think our kid will be here?"

"Maybe," Grant said. "We'll know soon enough."

Mocks nodded, her fingers twitching after she inserted her earpiece. She joined the clustering group of S.W.A.T. and FBI agents while Grant lingered behind.

As Grant placed his own earpiece on, he felt different. The usual steel winged butterflies hadn't appeared. Instead he saw the vision of his daughter, Annie, the same vision from the gunfight with the gangbangers, and a wave of calmness washed over him. Despite Mocks's warning, all he thought about was seeing her again.

"Detective Grant."

Grant looked up to see Hickem standing in front of him. The FBI agent raised an eyebrow, his body encased in the same gear as the raid at the house. He didn't even bother washing the blood off. "I suppose we go into this thing on an even playing field."

"Yeah," Grant said. "You could say that."

"You probably won't get any credit for this bust," Hickem said. "Seeing as how you've run into some discipline issues lately."

"It wasn't a discipline issue," Grant said, giving Hickem a shoulder bump on his way past. "It was a lack of it."

Grant, Hickem, and Mocks led the way as their teams

followed them through the woods. The going was slow, methodical, none of them sure if the gang members were here already or what they would find.

They reached the edge of the forest where the stretch of sand touched the ocean, the sound of waves rolling onto the beach. Hickem inched over to Grant. "This is as good a vantage point we're going to get." He lifted a small GPS device. "The coordinates you found are fifty yards to the south. From here, we'll be able to see any movement coming in and out of this forest."

"No one moves unless I give the command," Grant said, then looked at Hickem. "I wouldn't want you to get in trouble if things go south. Plausible deniability."

"Whatever makes you feel better, boss," Hickem said.

And then they waited. Grant checked the timer on his watch every few minutes, which only made the time pass slower. Thirty minutes, then an hour, then two, which tipped them over the twelve-hour mark. This felt like Grant's last shot. If he was wrong, he'd end his career with a loss. And what was worse, Annie wouldn't come home.

"Movement," Hickem said, whispering into his radio. "Two hundred yards in the surf."

Grant lifted the pair of binoculars. He didn't see it at first, the waves were too high that far out, but a break in the surf exposed three boats.

Engines rumbled farther down the beach, and Grant pivoted toward the noise. Two large trucks had rolled out onto the sand.

"The pair of dump trucks are surrounded by two dozen armed hostiles," Hickem said. "Could be more in the boats. Everyone stay put until we have confirmation of the cargo. Units seven, ten, and nine, go ahead and move into firing position."

A series of copies echoed over the radio, and tiny movements in the trees gave way to their motion, but to someone on the beach, it looked like nothing more than the wind rustling the branches.

The three boats crested a wave and then killed their engines, riding the surf onto the shoreline where they were greeted by a handful of the men who'd arrived with the trucks. Huddled masses swayed in the small dinghies, but even in the darkness, Grant knew what they were: women taken from their homes in the Philippines and brought to the States to be sold into sex trafficking.

But where were the kids? Were they in the boats as well? In the trucks?

"We need to move in now," Grant said, lowering the binoculars and turning to Hickem. "We can't lose them."

"We wait until they're out of the boats," Hickem said. "It'll give them less opportunity to run with their merchandise out in the open."

Grant grabbed Hickem by the collar, and the trained FBI agent with over a decade's experience in the field quickly raised a pistol to Grant's temple, his eyes calmly locked onto Grant's.

Mocks didn't move a muscle in Grant's peripheral, and despite the gun to his temple, Grant didn't release Hickem from his grip. "That's not merchandise. Those are people. Girls scared out of their minds, and if they're out in the open, then they become targets. These people don't care about those women's lives. They might even shoot a couple themselves just for fun."

"They're starting to unload," Mocks said.

Hickem lowered the pistol, and Grant let go of the man's collar. He nodded. "All right, Detective. We'll do it your way." He turned his attention down the beach and reached for his radio. "All units, you have authority to engage. Priority one is the safe retrieval of the victims. Let's move!"

228

Grant, Mocks, and Hickem stayed on the edge of the forest, and before they made it halfway, gunfire broke the silence of the night.

Rifle muzzles flashed in the dark with every gunshot, their bullets zipping through the air like deadly fireflies. Grant broke out into a sprint, pistol aimed in the thick of the gunfire. The chatter from the radio in Grant's ear was nonstop.

Mocks disappeared into the throng of S.W.A.T. agents and darkness. Grant's only focus was on finding Annie. A bullet splintered the tree trunk to his left. He flinched but held his fire. He was still too far away for a clean shot. He looked to the water and saw only one boat beached. The other two were being pushed back into the water, along with the women inside.

Grant broke from the safety of the trees and sprinted to the boats. He shot the first thug in the back and he splashed into the water. The second thug ducked underwater, and Grant fired two random shots into the waves.

Night had turned the ocean into black soup, and he couldn't tell if he hit his target. Grant waded out farther and the waves lapped at his chest. He reached for the rope of the nearest dinghy when the gunman broke the water's surface to his right.

The high water and waves slowed Grant's motion, and he narrowly blocked the knife that slashed at his neck. The thug screamed in his native tongue, his eyes as black as the water around them.

The thug clawed at Grant's throat, their arms locked together as Grant kept the knife away from his jugular. Grant thrust his forehead into the thug's nose, and the man's grip loosened.

Grant knocked the knife away and dunked the gang-banger underwater. He thrashed wildly while the waves pounded Grant's face, his nose and eyes burning from the salt water. The thrashing faded, and then the body went still. Grant's muscles remained taut, and he gasped for breath as though he had been held underwater himself. When he let the body go, it drifted to the surface and floated in the waves.

A thick cord circled the entire outside of the dinghy, and Grant grabbed it with both hands, trying to spin the boat around so the bow faced the shoreline, cutting through the surf easier.

In the chest-high water, Grant couldn't get the needed leverage to turn the boat, and the gunfire from the shoreline worsened. The girls in the dinghy screamed as bullets entered the side.

Salt water dripped down Grant's face, and he saw the tiller engine strapped to the dinghy's stern. He pulled himself up and over the side and landed awkwardly on a pair of bodies.

The boat rocked up and down from a wave that knocked Grant off balance on his scurry toward the engine. He grabbed the cord to start it and yanked hard. The engine spun but didn't catch.

Bullets thumped into the side of the boat again, and this round of gunfire triggered a bloodcurdling scream from one of the girls. Grant turned and saw three women rush to the girl's aid, but she lay lifeless and still. It was too dark to see the extent of the injury, but judging by the way she wasn't moving, Grant didn't think she was alive.

Water flooded the boat, and Grant noticed the holes in the sides. He yanked the cord again, then a third and fourth time. His shoulders burned, and the water in the boat reached his shins. "C'mon!" He snapped the cord back hard and the engine cranked to life. He revved the throttle and jettisoned north, away from the gunfire.

Bullets followed for a moment but stopped once they

were out of range. The wind whipped at Grant's face, and the air froze the water to his body. He shivered and got his first good look at the girls.

All of them looked foreign. And most of them were older. Annie wasn't among them. Grant turned around and wondered if she was in the first boat, or the third. She might even be in the trucks. He kept the throttle open all the way to the shore, and the dinghy thumped into the sand, skidding forward until the propeller ran out of water. Grant killed the engine as the dinghy collapsed to the left. The girls remained in the boat.

They were frozen by fear, shivering in a huddled mass. Gunfire down the beach stole his attention and Grant hopped out of the boat. "Just stay here. You'll be safe as long as you don't move!"

One of the trucks had crashed into the trees, but the radio chatter confirmed some of the gang members had thrown down their weapons. He looked back out into the water farther off the shore and saw the third dinghy disappearing into the surf.

Sprinting in the sand was like running in slow motion. Grant's legs stiffened and sank with every step forward. The fighting had concentrated at the second dump truck, where the remaining gangbangers had huddled inside. The chatter in his ear said something else, but it was muddled. Everything was so loud, so many people talking at once. It was hard to keep up with what they were saying.

Grant spied Mocks in the line of officers and agents that circled the truck. Weapons were raised, and no one moved. The rear of the truck was unoccupied, Hickem the closest to the opening.

"Exit the vehicle!" Hickem said. He stood closest to the truck's ramp. Grant had no idea how many hostiles were inside. "Drop the weapons and step out, now!"

Shouts erupted from the inside of the truck, voices echoing off the metal walls. It all sounded like nonsense, but then Grant thought he heard English, and that was when a man burst out the back and crawled his way up the side, a woman close to his front with a gun to her head.

"Get back!" The gunman kept his back to the truck and the pistol trained on his hostage. In the darkness it took a second for Grant to recognize him, but it was the face he was looking for, the one who'd taken Annie: Parker Gallient.

"You take another step and I will blow her fucking brains out!" Parker had a white patch of cloth over his hand, which held the woman's throat. She moaned and sobbed, tears and snot dribbling down her face.

None of Hickem's men moved, and neither did S.W.A.T. Everyone's weapons followed Parker like a magnet, Grant's included. Parker inched up the side of the truck slowly, his eyes wandering in every direction.

"Let her go!" Grant said, sidestepping in the sand and separating himself from the cluster of officers.

"I said get the fuck back, man!" Parker pressed the pistol harder into the woman's skull and she let out another wail. "Don't you get it? It's all shit! It's all fucked now! Everyone and everything!"

Grant's arms were stiff and his mind tired, but he still had a good shot. It wasn't as clean as he wanted it to be though. It was too tight.

"Where is Annie Mauer?" Grant asked.

Parker scrunched up his face. "Who?"

"The girl you abducted from the mall," Grant answered. "Is she here? What'd you do with her?"

Parker laughed. "That bitch is done, motherfucker!" He shook the woman in his arms. "She's already somebody's new plaything."

Grant noticed some of Hickem's men move toward the

back of the truck where the rest of the gang members still resided. His grip tightened over the pistol. "Where did you take her?" Flashes of Ellen and his own Annie flooded his mind. A voice in his head pressured him to take the shot. *It's his fault. Shoot him.*

"That's not part of the rules, man," he said, the gun still pressed to Annie's head as he reached the door of the truck. "And you can't break the rules."

Grant inched closer. He separated himself from the rest of the group by three feet. The voice continued its whispers, and rage slowly trickled toward Grant's trigger finger. His daughter should have never died. His wife should still be alive. It was all Dunston's fault. He should have pulled the trigger that night, too.

"Where's Annie?" Grant asked, his whole body trembling. *Shoot him. He deserves it. Just like Brian Dunston deserved it.*

Parker reached the door, keeping the woman pulled close. He sniffled. "My last chance was a long time ago." Parker reached for the door handle.

Grant squeezed the trigger. The bullet penetrated Parker's chest, a red bloom forming over his shirt. The woman screamed, but it was drowned out by the roar of gunfire that thundered inside the back of the truck.

Hickem screamed into the radio. "Hold your fire! Hold your fire!"

Officers charged Parker and S.W.A.T. dragged the woman from the scene. The radio in Grant's ear was loud now. It was Hickem. He was screaming.

"We need medics!"

Grant suddenly felt hollow and cold. He remained frozen in the same stance, and it wasn't until Hickem rushed past him that he finally lowered the weapon.

"I told everyone they had hostages!" Hickem said, running back toward their cars. "I never gave the order to shoot!"

Grant turned toward the rear of the dump truck. The officers and agents near the truck's back end had lowered their weapons. Two of them dropped to their knees. One vomited.

Grant took a step forward, but an arm held him back. Mocks appeared in front of him and she shook her head. Tears formed in her eyes.

"Don't look, Grant," Mocks said.

The cold and hollowness spread through Grant's body. He stepped around Mocks, walking forward like a zombie. He dropped his pistol in the sand on the way. His mouth went dry.

Life was sucked from him, and he felt cold. And weak. He shivered. When he turned the corner and looked inside the back of the truck, his stomach twisted into knots and he collapsed to his knees. "No." He shook his head, tearing up. "No, no, no."

Amongst the bodies of the gang members were women. Shot and killed by the very poachers that abducted them from their homes to sell them into the sex trade. But that wouldn't happen anymore. Nothing would ever happen to them again.

Another voice filled Grant's head. It was Parker. The one he'd shot. What did he say? Something about rules. Yes. That was it. You couldn't break the rules, not without consequences. Grant couldn't imagine a worse consequence than this.

20

*E*very single gang member that wasn't being shoved into a body bag was on their knees with their hands cuffed behind their backs and bags over their heads. Hickem didn't want to take any chances.

"They're really that vindictive?" Mocks asked.

"Last year, one of my guys was on a sting operation down in northern California," Hickem answered. "It was supposed to be a clean break after it was done, his last mission and then he rides off into the sunset. Everything went according to plan, and my guy entered Wit-Sec and moved to Hawaii." He looked Mocks in the eye. "The Web found him and cut him to pieces. The coroner told me they took their time."

Hickem rejoined his team, and Mocks walked farther north up the beach. She avoided the back of the dump truck. They were still removing bodies. She couldn't stomach looking inside again. She almost lost her lunch just thinking about it. But Grant...

Mocks found him alone, sitting on the ground with his back propped up against one of the trees. He hadn't said a word since he saw the aftermath of the shooting. He hadn't even reacted. No tears, no anger, nothing. It was like he shut off. In their two years together, she had never seen him like this. But from what he had told her about what happened after his wife's accident, this could have been what it was like.

"Hickem told me they're going to send most of the suspects to their federal office and process them there," Mocks said. She looked back out to the ocean. "They called the Navy and Coast Guard to look for that dinghy that got away, but it'll be tough sledding to find them out there, especially since it's night. Hickem thinks that they may have just gone farther south and beached at another location."

Grant just kept his head forward. He didn't move a muscle, didn't react to anything she said. He was a zombie.

"None of the victims in the back of the truck were kids," Mocks said. "And they're confident the boat that got away was another load of women from the islands. Our girl wasn't here." Mocks squatted and looked him in the eye. She grabbed his face and shook her head.

"This wasn't your fault," Mocks said. "Do you hear me? Those women didn't die because you pulled the trigger. They died because a sick group of animals plucked them from their home and shipped them overseas to be sold as slaves." She pointed back to the cluster of workers that had gathered on the beach. "Do you know how many we saved tonight? Thirteen. That's what you did, Grant. That's what we did."

Even though Grant looked at her eyes, Mocks wasn't sure if he saw her. The darkness gave his eyes a hazy, blind look. Mocks let go of his face and dropped to her knees.

"Grant, you can't put yourself through this," Mocks said. "These were extraordinary circumstances. Do not go down that rabbit hole."

And then Grant finally saw her, and a chill ran down Mocks's spine. As an addict, she had been around enough

people who were out of their mind to know when someone
had gone too far, when they reached that point when reason
was no longer an option, when chasing the satisfaction was
all that mattered.

"I won't be a detective for much longer," Grant said. "It's
over for me, Mocks." His voice was stoic, calm, and he
glanced over to the crime scene. "You should start separating
yourself from me. I'll do what I can, but you'll get a lot of the
heat regardless."

Before she could speak, he was up and disappearing down
the beach, away from the scene, away from the bodies, away
from his partner. Mocks lingered on her knees, hoping he
would turn back, but he didn't.

Mocks rejoined the rest of the officers, and Hickem asked
where Grant was. "I don't know," she said, and then nodded
to the gangbangers being loaded into one of the S.W.A.T.
vans. "Think I could get a ride back into town?" Mocks
asked.

"Sure," Hickem answered. "We leave in two."

Mocks ended up in the back of one of the S.W.A.T. vans
crammed with officers. She was the only woman in the
bunch, not something that she wasn't used to, but the fact
that Grant wasn't by her side irked her. She knew he was
right though. No matter what happened moving forward, he
couldn't turn back the clock. The women were dead, and that
was as final as it got.

Hickem dropped Mocks off a few blocks from her apartment, and she flipped the collar of her jacket up to block the
wind funneling through the streets of downtown. Even after
almost four years in Seattle, the weather still chilled her
bones.

The homeless man outside the Starbucks in front of her
building was bundled up under blankets and newspapers.

She couldn't see his face to tell whether he was sleeping or not, but she slid a dollar next to his head.

Mocks's phone buzzed when she stepped inside the elevator. She knew who it was. The captain wanted an update, and more importantly, he wanted to know where the hell Grant was. She ignored it. Enough shit had been dealt with for one day.

The heat of the building made her sleepy and by the time she reached the tenth floor, she could barely keep her eyes open. She stumbled down the hall in a daze and fished the keys out of her pocket. She yawned and singled out her apartment key to unlock the door, but stopped.

The front door was ajar, the lock broken. The fatigue lifted from Mocks's mind and she dropped the keys and retrieved her pistol, aiming at the crack in the door. She looked up and down the hallway, but she was alone. Her heart rate spiked, and she slowly opened the door.

"Rick?" Mocks asked.

The living room was trashed. Cushions had been ripped. Lamps were overturned, casting ominous shadows over the walls. Glass from picture frames littered the carpet along with stuffing from the couches. But what was more disturbing was the silence. No one was home.

Mocks walked quietly, her arms extended, the pistol guiding her movements through the rooms. Her boots pressed slowly and methodically into the carpet as she scanned the apartment in a grid.

She turned the corner of the hallway and saw the bedroom door open. Her hand became unsteady as she drew closer, passing the spare bedroom, which was also open and empty. And then the bathroom. Empty.

Every step forward on the carpet cracked what resolve she had left. She couldn't stop thinking about what Hickem had said about one of his former agents being cut into pieces. This couldn't be happening. This wasn't real.

Mocks paused at the entrance to her bedroom, her hands trembling now as she lowered the weapon, and it dropped to the floor with a muted thud from the carpet.

The bedroom had been untouched. The bed was made. All of the pictures still hung on the walls, and there was no one inside. But what caused Mocks to scream and drop to her knees was a picture of Rick. She recognized it immediately. It was from their honeymoon, because he was so sunburnt. Drawn over the photo was a picture in black marker. It was a spider web.

GRANT WASN'T sure how far he'd walked when he finally stopped, but he couldn't see the lights of the crime scene anymore. By now most of the people had packed up, and everyone was gone save for a few forensic techs.

He turned into the woods. His shoes crunched on dead leaves and branches, and he nearly twisted his ankle on a rock through the dark path. His eyes had adjusted to the lack of light a little and it was still hard to see everything, but he just needed to move.

Grant distracted himself with memories of his wife, and he was thankful she couldn't see him like this. If she knew about the things he'd done, how much blood was on his hands after she had passed, he wasn't sure if she'd even stick around.

Why did the girl's name have to be Annie? Out of all his cases, not one of them shared his daughter's name. Why this one?

The phone in his pocket buzzed, but he ignored it. It was probably the captain, or the chief of police, or the senator asking him what the hell happened. Tomorrow morning's news would have his picture plastered over every television and computer screen in the northwest, along with a caption that read, 'Rogue Detective's Actions Leave Dozens Dead.'

The acid crawled up from his stomach and Grant stopped, hunched over, and vomited. He nearly hit his shoes, but he managed to miss them at the last second. Hot bile lingered on his tongue and just when he went to wipe his mouth, another round spewed up like a geyser.

When his stomach emptied, Grant's insides burned and cramped, and the stink of the puke made him gag. He spit to try and get rid of the taste, but it still lingered.

The phone vibrated, over and over and over, and finally Grant reached for it. He was about to throw it when he saw the name plastered on the screen. It was Mocks.

"I can't—"

"They took Rick," Mocks said, her voice panicked and quick. "He's fucking gone, Grant."

Grant paused, his mind trying to catch up with the information. "What are you talking about?"

"I just got home, and the door was broken down and the place is torn up." Mocks spoke quickly, her words running over themselves. She was scared. "And there was a picture taped to our bedroom mirror. It was a spider web, Grant. They have him. I don't know what to do."

With his insides still aching from the vomit, Grant broke out into a jog toward the car, fumbling in his pocket for his keys. His mind shifted gears, back into work mode, the switch easier to flip than he thought. "Call Hickem. He's more likely to take your call than mine. Find out what happened to Parker Gallient."

"Why?" Mocks asked, sounding like she was fighting back tears. "What the hell would he know?"

"If he's still alive, I think he'll talk," Grant said, starting the engine. "He was the only non-Filipino in the group, which means he wasn't born into it. And after today, he might feel differently about his loyalty to the gang."

"Do you think Rick is still alive?" Mocks asked. "And don't bullshit me, Grant."

He hesitated. The first instinct was to blurt out that he thought Rick was dead. But he forced himself to pause, to think it over. There was no guarantee that was true. Especially if they took him recently. They probably wanted to question him, see what he knew about Mocks and himself. That could take time, especially if they took him to a remote location.

"If he is, he won't be for long," Grant said, doing his best to not sound completely hopeless. "Call Hickem and find out where Parker is. I still think he's our best bet. The moment you know, call me and I'll meet you there."

"Where are you now?" Mocks asked.

"I'm still at the park," Grant answered. "Just got into my car."

Mocks paused for a second. "I need you, Grant. All of you. And that means putting behind whatever shit you're going through and helping me get this done. You know we don't have a large window to get him back alive. I need the old you. Please, Grant."

Grant held the phone with this right hand and he glanced down at the gold wedding band. He kept it as a reminder of a past and pain that drove him to find kids and return them to their parents. He attributed his success to that pain, and he now had a new well of pain to draw from. He closed his fingers and formed a fist.

"I'm here, Mocks," Grant said. "Call me when you know something."

"I will."

The call ended and Grant shifted into drive. He pulled

out of the parking lot and back onto the highway that cut through the park. The road markers lit up as he drove, and more than once, Grant looked down to the wedding band.

When Grant was a boy, his parents used to take him to church on Sundays, and then afterward they'd go out to lunch with the rest of the family. He always had so much fun; not from the sermon and church, but the time spent with family. But toward the end of those days, Grant always felt something haunting him. It was like an unseen doom, a fear of the unknown that accompanied the next day.

Maybe it was because Monday was back to school, and Sunday night meant the end of the weekend and fun. But Grant felt that again. Except this time there was no family, no lunch, no church. The doom was real, and the consequences of the unknown would be damning. He just hoped that those consequences would only fall on him and not what remained of the people he cared about. If they did, he might not make it out of this alive.

21

With Hickem's unit just a few blocks from Mocks's apartment, it didn't take her long to find out where Parker Gallient had been taken. Mocks phoned Grant and told him to meet her at Seattle General.

Everything felt like a dream. Her movements were slow and lethargic, like she wasn't in control of her own body. But it was real. Rick was gone. The Web took him. And if they didn't find him quickly, he could die.

Traffic was light due to the late hour, and when Mocks pulled up to the ER, she parked the car in the drop off lane.

"Excuse me," a nurse on a smoke break outside called out to Mocks. "Ma'am, you can't park your car there."

Mocks flashed her badge and jogged inside without a word. She checked in with the nurse at the front desk, where she impatiently tapped her toe. The waiting area was empty, and the gift shop across the hall was closed. They were the only two on the floor.

"The patient is in room two-fourteen," the nurse said. "It looks like he's being prepped for surgery though, I'm not sure you'll be able to see him."

Mocks snatched the visitor's badge from her grip and sprinted toward the elevator and up to the second floor. She reached for her phone and called Grant. "Hey, how far out are you?"

"Five minutes," Grant answered. "I just got into downtown."

"They're prepping him for surgery," Mocks said as the door slid open. "I'm going to try and get in before they put him under."

"All right," Grant said. "I'll see you soon."

Mocks pocketed the phone and immediately spotted the officer outside the door of the room where their suspect was located. The officer was young, tall, and lanky. When he held up his hand, his fingers were bone thin.

"I'm sorry, I can't let you in there," he said. "Orders from the Chief of Police himself."

"Listen, I don't have time to do the run-around with you, but if you don't let me inside and talk to that man, more people will die," Mocks said.

The officer glanced down at her hip and she frowned in confusion. It wasn't until she looked down herself that she realized her hand was on the butt of her service pistol. She let go and stepped back.

"You have to let me in," Mocks said. "Call anyone you need to, but I'm going in that room."

The officer squinted. "Wait. I know you. You're Detective Grant's partner."

"I am," Mocks answered.

"Sad to hear about what happened with that reporter. Grant's a good man." The officer looked down both ends of the hall and then back into the room. He leaned in close and dropped his volume to a whisper. "Listen, I'm really not supposed to let anyone in. But I can give you five minutes, and then you have to bolt. Understand?"

Mocks patted him on the shoulder on her way past, but she stopped when he grabbed her arm.

"And, hey, next time you see your partner, tell him that Officer Sturgeon says thank you." The young cop gave a half smile. "He'll know what it's for."

"He'll be here soon," Mocks said. "And thank you." She shut the door behind her, and Parker Gallient jolted in his bed. A large bandage was over his chest and shoulder where Grant had shot him, and a few red lumps were on his face where the cops had hit him when he resisted. Both hands were cuffed to the railing of the bed, and he was hooked up to a few machines. He wore the same clothes from a few hours ago.

"Who the fuck are you?" Parker asked, his voice cracked and groggy.

Mocks removed her badge, then her holster with the pistol, and set them both down on a table on the other side of the room.

Parker wriggled in bed. "What the hell are you doing?" He looked to the door. "Hey, guard!"

"He's not going to bother us," Mocks said. "It's just me and you for a few minutes. I've got questions. And I want answers."

Parker coughed, then laughed, but it was short-lived. "Bitch, whatever you think you can do to me, The Web would make it ten times worse."

Mocks pressed her palm into the bandage and pressed down. "I do love a challenge."

Parker groaned and his face reddened. "God fucking dammit! You fucking bitch!"

"My husband was taken by your people, and I want to know where he is," Mocks said, adding more pressure the longer she went without an answer.

"I don't know where they took him! I've been here!"

"Bullshit!" Mocks removed her palm and then punched the wound. Parker screamed and then hacked and coughed, saliva dripping from his lower lip. Mocks raised her fist once more. "Where is he?"

"Just stop! Stop!" Parker wheezed a few more breaths and then slammed his head back into his pillow. "They might have taken him up to the mill."

"What is that?" Mocks asked.

"It's where I had to drop my girl," Parker said. "Sometimes we have to make special trips up there, but only for certain occasions. Only when he wants something."

"When who wants something?" Mocks asked. "Your boss?"

"I don't know if you could call him the boss," Parker answered. "The guy who pulls the strings, maybe. It's like his special workshop or some shit."

"Where's the mill?" Mocks asked, her fist still cocked back.

"You take I-5 north until you hit Timber Creek Road. Follow that till it forks and take a left. It's a dirt road. After that, you'll run right into it."

Mocks lowered her fist but then thrust her finger in his face. "If I have to come back here because you lied, The Web will be the least of your problems."

"I doubt it," Parker said.

Mocks retrieved her gun and badge and when she reached the door, Parker called out to her one last time.

"If they have your husband, then you might as well write him off as dead," Parker said, taking a swallow. "And if there is anything left of him, it won't be pretty."

Mocks opened the door and then slammed it shut as she walked to the elevator. When she reached the first floor and the doors opened, she saw Grant jogging into the lobby.

"I know where he is," Mocks said without breaking her stride.

Grant fell into line with her and the pair walked back to her car, which was closer as it was still parked in the drop off lane. Grant got behind the driver's seat, their natural rhythm already in play as Mocks tossed him the keys. She thought it was good that they were back in sync. He had his head on right. He was focused.

"Did you get anything beside the location?" Grant asked, starting the car and speeding out of the drop off area.

"Yeah," Mocks answered. "We don't have a lot of time."

* * *

MOCKS FLICKED the green Bic lighter on and off on the entire drive north. Grant pushed one hundred on the interstate. Aside from a few truckers, they were the only ones on the road.

Grant wished that there was something he could say to help her, but he knew that the only cure for what ailed her was action. She needed to move. She needed to do something other than think. What Mocks had in her head was the right direction, and Grant just had to keep her on that path.

"I've been up here before, you know," Mocks said, the flame on her Bic wiggling from the heat blasting through the vents. The temperature had dropped significantly in the late hour, and Grant didn't object to the warmth. "When I was using. Came up here all the time when I wanted to go on a bender. Nobody asked questions up here. Nobody cared what happened to you."

"You having flashbacks?" Grant asked, watching her reaction through his peripherals.

Mocks let the lighter's flame disappear and shook her head. "No." She turned to Grant. "This is what you felt, wasn't it? That night you beat the man that killed your pregnant wife. The rage, the purpose, the fear, all of it controlling you, pushing you."

"Yes," Grant answered.

"I had that feeling every time I wanted to get high," Mocks said. "Sometimes I look back on those days and don't recognize that person. And other days I remember her very well."

"And today?"

Mocks paused. She looked down at the lighter and gave the flint another flick, which brought the flame to life. "Today I'm going to get my husband back."

A few more miles down the road, and Grant pulled off the interstate. The city was far behind them, and their new environment was thick with trees.

"You ever think the Givens girl would have led to all of this?" Grant asked as they turned off the paved road and started making their way onto the dirt path.

"I didn't see a lot of this coming, Grant," Mocks answered, then quickly changed the subject. "Parker said it was an old abandoned sawmill."

The prospect sounded more ominous than hopeful, and Grant wasn't sure if they'd find Rick in one piece. He followed the two-lane road until it forked and turned left as Mocks instructed.

The dirt from the road swirled in the headlights, which was the only source of light back here. And from the dips and bumps in the road, it didn't look like anyone had used the road in a while. "We should have four-wheel drive for this," Grant said.

"Cut the lights," Mocks said. "I don't know how much farther it is, and I don't want them to see us coming."

Grant would have objected, but Mocks made a solid

point. He turned off the lights but slowed his pace to compensate for the lack of sight.

"Call Dispatch," Grant said. "Let them know our location."

Mocks reached for her phone. "No signal." She scanned the radio for their channel. "Dispatch, this is unit thirty-five. We are forty-five miles north of Seattle. We turned west off of I-5 onto Timber Creek Road and followed it down to the fork where we took a left. We're currently checking out an abandoned sawmill. We need units on standby, over."

Static crackled back.

"I repeat, this is unit thirty-five, we are—"

"Mocks," Grant said, stopping the car. "Look."

Mocks leaned forward and squinted. A dark outline took shape in a clearing in the forest. "Yeah. Looks big enough to be a sawmill." She noticed a glow from the backside of the building. "We should park here and walk up."

Grant tucked the car near a cluster of trees and bushes and when he tossed some branches over the top, you couldn't even see it from the road unless you knew it was there.

Together, Grant and Mocks kept to the tree line and off the road on their approach. The glow grew brighter, and Grant noticed a second glow through one of the windows on the lower level of the mill. The light was orange, almost like it was from a fire, the way it moved and swayed against the glass.

Mocks paused when they reached the edge of the trees just before the clearing began. Grant crouched next to her, one knee planted in the dirt. No cars or guards from what he saw, but that didn't mean there weren't people inside.

"Grant," Mocks said, glancing down at the tip of her boots. "If Rick is dead and the guys who did it are still inside, you have to let me decide for myself what to do." She looked up, her eyes big and wide like a child asking her father for permission. She always looked so small whenever she did that.

"It won't make you feel better," Grant said. "No matter what you decide. But it is your decision to make."

"Thank you." Mocks cleared her throat and then motioned toward a side door that was the farthest away from the flickering light inside the sawmill. "Let's go."

The pair kept low on their sprint into the clearing. Their figures blended into the night, and the cloudy sky provided further cover.

Grant nestled up against the edge of the building, the wood rough and cold against his shoulder. He panted heavily from the short run, his body already tired from the long day. He peered around the corner, and the coast was clear all the way to the door. Grant stepped around first and Mocks followed, watching his back.

When Grant reached for the door handle, he found it locked. He turned to Mocks and shook his head, and they moved on to the next entrance. They passed under the window where the light was strongest and fought the urge to peek inside. They knew it wouldn't be the best vantage point anyway.

The next door was locked as well, and when they circled around to the east side of the sawmill, Grant stopped at the corner, Mocks bumping into him from the abrupt halt.

There was another building, a small trailer like you'd find at a construction site. Lights were on inside, and Grant figured that was the source of the second glow he saw in the car.

Grant motioned toward the structure, and Mocks nodded. He made one last scan to ensure the coast was clear and then sprinted toward the front steps. The plummeting temperature revealed their breaths with each pant.

He pressed his ear to the door, listening for movement,

but heard nothing. He grabbed the doorknob and gave it a twist. Locked. Grant tapped his shoulder and then pointed toward the door. Mocks nodded and moved into position, gun raised.

Grant knew the cold would make the contact worse, but he gritted his teeth and rammed the door with all his weight. The frame cracked and Grant tumbled onto the floor. Mocks followed inside, pistol raised. But the place was empty.

Mocks stepped inside and shut the door. Her arm fell to her sides, the pistol hanging loose in her hand. "What the hell?"

While the outside resembled a trailer for a construction site, the inside was a completely different story. Ornate wooden furniture lined the walls, and a plush rug gave accent to the hardwood floors. Paintings decorated the walls, pictures of nature in all its elements. One photo caught Grant's eye. It was a small ship in the middle of the ocean during a massive storm. The waves tossed the ship about, the dark skies spitting rain and lightning. Grant saw the tiny figures aboard the ship, no larger than ants in the grand scope of the sea, clinging to dear life as they fought against the enormity of Mother Nature.

A leather couch was at the far end of the trailer, and on the opposite end was a desk, which Mocks immediately searched. She skimmed papers and then hastily tossed them aside.

"These are the same documents we found during the Givens case," Mocks said. "They're immigration forms, except these ones have been filled out already. Names, date of births, Social Security Numbers."

Grant picked up one of the paper stacks and saw that each of them had pictures paper clipped to them. They were all girls. Young girls. "Jesus Christ."

"Wait," Mocks said. "Look at this." She raised the paper so Grant could see. "You know who that is?"

"No," Grant answered.

"Sophie Mathers," Mocks answered. "She was one of the reported abductions today." She flipped to the next set of papers. "And this one, Mary Hives, she was reported missing today too."

Grant took the papers from her, shuffling through until he found the picture he was looking for. "Annie." Name, height, weight, hair, and eye color, all of her personal information filled out. Except, like the other girls, their names had been changed on separate forms. She wasn't Annie anymore. She was Beth Myers. From Canada.

"All these forms," Mocks said. "These are legitimate documents. Federally stamped and everything." Mocks set the papers on the desk, shaking her head. "The Web has contacts in the federal government."

Grant set Annie's documents down. "The kids are here. They have to be."

They opened the rest of the drawers and Mocks found a set of keys. "Think it's for the mill?"

"Let's go find out," Grant said.

Grant watched Mocks's back while she tried different keys until she found one that worked. In one swift motion, she stepped inside and covered the right while Grant filed in after, covering the left.

But like the trailer, the place was empty. At least with regard to people. The flicker of light that Grant had seen through the dirtied window was from kerosene lanterns that hung from the walls and support beams. The building was old, but the equipment looked brand new. Fresh steel blades gleamed from the lamplight, and Grant pressed his finger into one of the teeth. It pricked blood.

"Grant," Mocks said.

He turned and saw her standing next to a long table with straps to keep someone tied down. A smaller table sat next to it, covered in what looked like medical instruments that rested over white cloth. Tiny incision cutters, large clasps, braces, knives, and pieces Grant had never even seen before.

Mocks walked to the end of the table and picked up one of the instruments. Fresh blood shimmered off the steel, and Grant looked down at the floor beneath the table. Sawdust had been dumped in patches, but there were still a few stains of blood that they had missed.

"We don't know if this was him," Grant said, although he wasn't sure if the expression on his face matched the hopeful tone.

A muffled moan to their left caused both Grant and Mocks to aim their pistols in a dark patch of the mill. They stepped toward it slowly, Grant reaching for one of the lanterns on the way to help light their path.

A door, boxed into the corner of the room, concealed the source of the noise, and when Grant opened it, the lantern revealed a staircase that traveled beneath the mill. Mocks held the door while Grant stepped down first, the wooden stairs groaning from the descent.

The lantern's light only protruded a foot into the pitch black, and Grant descended slowly, unable to see what his nose could smell. The scent was unmistakable. Years in Homicide had left the stench of human waste and blood in his nose, and whenever he got a whiff of it, all of those memories flooded back to him. And judging from the light gasp that Mocks quickly muffled with her hand, he knew she understood what it meant.

Whispers drifted out of the darkness, along with the scraping of metal on concrete. When Grant took his last step and stood on the basement floor, the lantern illuminated the first girl chained to a metal bar in the corner. She couldn't have been older than ten, and her hair was messy and greasy. Dirt smeared the girl's cheeks, and she was curled up in a ball in clothes too big for her small body.

Grant stepped toward her and then noticed another girl next to her. She was chained to the same bar and in the same ragged condition as the girl before. Grant guided the lantern along the edges of the room, more girls and one boys chained to the metal pole that ran along every wall in the basement. They were all here. Even Annie. "Oh my god."

A groan came from under the stairs and when Grant shone the light in the area, Mocks rushed over.

"Rick," Mocks said, gently patting her husband's bloodied face. He lolled his head back and forth in an unconscious dream, and Mocks yanked at the chain and irons clamped around his wrist, tethering him to the wall. "Rick, can you hear me?"

Grant checked on the kids while Mocks attended to Rick. Their ages ranged a bit, but from the count, it looked like they were all of the kids reported in the abductions today. Some of them were awake, others asleep. Needle marks scarred the arms of the unconscious ones. They were drugged, but they were all alive.

"This must be one of their transition sites," Grant said, but he was surprised there weren't more. And the fact that Rick was brought here where the kids were kept felt strange. All of this, combined with the fact that the trailer out back felt more like a home than an office, he began to think that this place was special to someone.

"Grant," Mocks said, reaching for the ring of keys that had gotten them inside the mill. "Help me get him up." She had to try a few of the keys before she found the right one, and Mocks and Grant dragged Rick to the foot of the stairs where they propped him up against the wall.

Grant held up the lantern and got a better look at the rest

of his body. His face was cut up, along with his left arm. A large bandage was over his right thigh and another wrapped around his abdomen. The cuts looked deep, and the paleness of his cheeks meant he'd lost a lot of blood. But he was still breathing, for now.

"We need to get him to the car," Mocks said.

Grant turned to the rest of the kids. "We need to get them out of here. They wouldn't leave them down here without supervision for long. If they—"

Footsteps thumped above and a door shut. A pair of muffled voices spoke, and Grant immediately blew out the light. He helped Mocks drag Rick back under the staircase, and there they hid.

The voices mumbled in casual conversation, but when the communication ended abruptly along with their footsteps, Grant knew they were found out.

The footfalls started up again, but the voices remained silent. Grant lifted his weapon. With the lantern snuffed out, Grant followed the sound of their feet.

Grant froze, his muscles aching and irritated from the concentration and energy it took to remain so still. The girls that were awake sobbed quietly to themselves. They knew what the return of those footsteps meant. The Web had done their work well.

The footsteps ended, and shadows and light fell down the staircase through the open door. Grant knew they couldn't see him, not when it was this dark. He had to be patient, to wait for them to come down. Right now he had the element of surprise. There were no more than two, and from the silence, he knew they hadn't radioed anyone.

Slowly, Grant's eyes adjusted to the darkness, and he saw Mocks in his peripheral, closer to the foot of the stairs. She had her pistol aimed at the door.

"Whoever's down there, come up now," a voice said in broken English. "You have ten seconds."

Grant and Mocks remained quiet. The breaths through Grant's nose grew stronger and faster. His heart rate spiked. The first flash of Ellen and Annie pierced through the fog as the adrenaline rolled in. He gripped the pistol tighter, and the vision grew stronger. For a moment, he lost where he was, the visions overwhelming. A gunshot fired, and the girls screamed.

More bullets fired down the stairs, and Grant tucked himself underneath it with Mocks and Rick for cover. The door slammed shut and Grant hurried up the stairs, knowing that if they didn't move now, then they'd die in the hole they dug for themselves.

Grant shoulder checked the door open and spilled out onto the floor. He immediately spied the first gunman to his left and fired three rounds into his chest.

The second gunman fired from the door, the distance causing him to miss as Grant ducked behind the table with the straps for cover. Once he was outside, Grant screamed down to Mocks. "He's on the run!"

Grant sprinted to the door, pausing at the exit before he peered outside into the night. Heavy breaths misted in the cold air and his fingers were numb against the pistol.

Still pressed against the wall, Grant craned his head through the open door and watched the gunman fire from the steps outside the trailer.

"Got you," Grant said. He spun around the cover of the wall and planted his knee and foot on the ground, firing into the door of the trailer that the gunman had just entered.

Grant pushed himself up and sprinted toward the trailer. Glass shattered from the window to the left of the trailer door and a rifle muzzle was thrust outside. It fired blindly as Grant sidled up flush with the trailer wall.

The rifle disappeared back inside, and Grant kept his breathing as quiet as possible. He inched toward the stairs, moving as softly as he could. The goon inside didn't make any effort to be quiet though, and Grant tried to keep tabs on him by the sound of his feet shuffling across the hardwood floors.

Grant placed his foot on the first step of the staircase, then the second. He could shoot through the flimsy walls, but the projection of the bullet would drastically change once it penetrated the trailer, so there wasn't even the guarantee that he would hit his target.

Grant threw the door open wide and crouched low in the entrance. He only had three seconds to assess the situation, aim his weapon, and fire the trigger before the goon unloaded on him, but he felt the recoil of the gunshot in his hand just in time.

Blood splattered over the man's chest and the phone fell from his limp hand. Grant rushed over and picked up the phone. The person on the other end was speaking another language, but Grant didn't stay on the line long enough to decipher it. He hung up and immediately dialed the precinct.

"This is Detective Chase Grant," he said, looking down at the man he'd just killed. "I'm with Detective Susan Mullocks, and we're north in the timberlands off of I-5. We have hostages, minors, up here at an old abandoned sawmill. I've taken out two guards, but they have more on the way. We need S.W.A.T., the National Guard, anyone with guns, and we need them up here now."

"Hold on, Detective, where exactly are you?"

"I don't have the exact coordinates, but I'm calling you from a landline, so there has to be cables running out here somewhere," Grant said. "Look for any old lines that run off of I-5 into the timberlands that are around an old mill. If that doesn't work, I'll just leave the phone off the hook and you can trace this call. Just hurry."

Dispatch tried to respond, but Grant had already set the phone down and was halfway out the door when he stopped. He turned back to the goon and patted him down, taking his rifle and ammunition. He spotted the web tattoo on the gangbanger's neck and wondered how many more of these scumbags existed. But what he wanted to know more than anything was the identity of the man in charge. The master weaver, connecting all of the different threads together.

Grant returned to the cellar where Mocks had managed to get half the girls out of their shackles, all of them clustering near the base of the stairs and cringing when Grant appeared. He imagined it would be a while before they trusted any man that came near them.

"I called for backup, but the gang member managed to call reinforcements as well," Grant said.

Mocks kept her eyes focused on the locks around the girls' ankles and wrists. "Did Dispatch give you an ETA?"

"Didn't stick around for one, but it could be a while," Grant said. "We need to get these kids out of here before whatever Web reinforcements show up."

"Here," Mocks said, tossing the keys to Grant. "Start helping me get them uncuffed."

Grant and Mocks worked their way around the room, and once the kids were freed, Grant helped Mocks drag Rick to the staircase. "We'll get him up first," Grant said. "We can hide the kids in the woods until backup arrives."

Grant scooped Rick up under his arms and heaved him up the first couple steps while Mocks clumsily grabbed his legs. Both were careful not to damage what was already broken on him, but it was difficult with the random cuts and spotty bandage work.

Rick groaned, and his lifeless head and limbs flopped

around on the way up the stairs, but they managed to set him by the door without any major incident. When they returned downstairs, the kids that were awake had huddled in the corner, some of them dragging the unconscious ones with them.

"I know you're scared," Grant said. "But I'm a detective, and I'm going to help you." He gestured to Mocks. "So will my partner." Mocks gave a friendly wave, and Grant approached Annie, slowly reaching out his hand. She recoiled slightly, but Grant didn't give up. "Trust me."

Annie switched her glance from Grant's hand to his face, the exchange going back and forth a few times until she finally clasped onto Grant's pointer finger.

"All right then," Grant said, smiling. "Let's go."

With the first girl separating herself from the pack, the others followed. Grant led those that could walk up the stairs and out of the side entrance of the sawmill and into the woods. He led them deep into the brush until they couldn't even see the mill anymore. Grant marked the spot with some large branches but made sure nothing stood out.

The girls and boy huddled close to one another, and Grant knelt down to whisper at them. "Don't move, okay?" He held up his hands. "I'll come back, but you have to stay." He slowly backtracked through the woods and prayed that their backup arrived before the rest of the goons did.

Grant helped Mocks carry the four kids that were unconscious out of the mill, leaving Rick for last. Grant was glad to see that the kids were still huddled exactly where he'd left them, and also by the fact that he was able to find them again.

Mocks lay her kids down, and when she turned, Grant stopped her. "Stay here," he said. "I'll go and make the last trip."

"I don't think so," Mocks said, taking a step forward, but

Grant stopped her once again, this time with more force. "I'm not letting you go back in there alone."

"And I'm not leaving these kids out here in the woods alone," Grant said.

Mocks forcefully removed her arm from his grip, and she gave him an adolescent snarl. "Then I'll go back and you stay with the kids."

"You didn't want me to bullshit you, remember?" Grant asked, his temper flaring. "Fine. The chances of Rick surviving are slim. The chances of these kids surviving as long as they have someone to protect them is high. You can't carry Rick by yourself. If things turn south before I can get back, I'll ditch him in the woods and cause a distraction." His anger calmed. "I'll bring him back. I promise."

"All right, Grant," Mocks said, her voice shaking. "Don't let me down."

Grant sprinted away and made sure Mocks didn't follow. Lights flashed to Grant's left the moment he reached the tree line, and he ducked behind a large pine and craned his neck around the side. They were cars. And they weren't police.

Gang members exited the vehicles, all armed with automatic rifles, and each one of them looking as though they wanted to blow something off the face of the earth. He watched the gang walk toward the other side of the mill where the trailer was located. There were at least ten, more than enough to mow down Mocks and the kids. Grant drew his pistol, his body scraping the bottom of the adrenaline well to push him just a little further, then sprinted toward the mill door.

Voices bounced off the old machinery, but they came from the other end of the mill. When he found Rick, the wounds on his legs and arms were bleeding again. It oozed from the bandages when Grant picked him up and dripped on the floor. A trail wasn't something Grant wanted to leave, but he didn't have time to clean up after himself.

All that mattered now was getting Rick out and making sure the thugs didn't find Mocks and the kids.

The dead weight wore Grant down, but when he heard the angered shouts inside the sawmill, another shot of adrenaline kept the fatigue of his muscles at bay. He burst into the woods as the thugs exited the mill.

With an added two hundred pounds of dead weight, Grant couldn't be as quiet as he wanted, pulling Rick through the forest, and so he decided to go with the flow. He reached for his pistol and fired into one of the trees.

The thugs in the clearing immediately honed in on Grant's location and fired their automatic rifles into the woods, hoping to get a lucky shot, but they came up short. He pulled Rick a few more feet and then tucked him behind a cluster of rocks and shrubs.

More gunshots stole his attention toward the entrance of the forest as Grant covered Rick with branches and leaves. He maneuvered away from Rick, firing into the woods to draw the thugs toward him. He trekked northeast, as far away from Mocks and the kids as he could manage.

Bullets and gunfire filled the night, splintering tree trunks and pounding eardrums. Flashlight beams penetrated the darkness and forced Grant to zigzag through the forest.

After a few minutes, Grant found a large oak that he hid behind and kept quiet. There were two thugs that were close. Grant crouched low at the tree's base, his knees pressed against his chest. He took quick, shallow breaths as they neared him. Grant's ears pricked up at the sound of crunching leaves on his left. He aimed the pistol, ready for the thug to walk right by him.

Ellen and Annie filled his thoughts, and Grant knew he'd see them soon. He felt the cold metal of his wedding band,

and when he saw the thug's boot step into his line of sight, he made his move.

Grant jammed the end of his pistol into the thug's gut and squeezed the trigger. The thug coughed blood over Grant's face and then collapsed. When Grant saw the lifeless body beneath him, he experienced an emotion associated with death that he never would have said aloud. He felt good.

Gunfire from the thug's partner forced Grant back behind the tree, and Grant stole the dead thug's assault rifle. Vibrations from the bullets on the opposite side of the tree trunk hit in rapid succession, and he curled himself into a tight ball to avoid getting hit.

A break in the gunfire allowed Grant to spin from cover and pump four rounds into the goon's chest. The rifle thumped quickly against Grant's shoulder. The shells dispensed onto the forest floor, covering his feet until the magazine had emptied. Grant tossed the rifle aside and then reached for his pistol, firing into the night. Someone was screaming now. It was him.

Grant's throat grew raw from the bloodcurdling cry, and when the gunshots ended and nothing but his voice remained, he collapsed to his knees. Bullets entered the tree and ground next to him, but Grant didn't move.

He let the gunfire surround him, the inevitable fate of death circling. He saw Ellen and Annie as clear as day. They were calling out to him, beckoning him to come and join them in the abyss. He was so close.

But then the faint wail of sirens pulled Grant back and ended the barrage of gunfire. It sounded far away at first but grew louder.

The flashlights from the thugs turned off, and through the thicket of trees and shrubs, Grant saw red and blue lights flashing. He planted one foot in front of him and went to push himself up when a sharp pain bloomed from the back of his head and planted him face first into the dirt.

The ground felt uneven and the world spun. He couldn't feel his legs or arms anymore. His vision went in and out, but just before it went completely black, he saw a pair of shoes. And then another sharp pain in the back of his head. And then black.

22

*T*hrobbing, aching, numbing pain. It started in the very back of Grant's skull, spread down his back, and went straight through to his heels. His hands and feet tingled with pins and needles. It was dark. Pitch black.

Grant lolled his head back and forth a few times, disoriented and unsure if he was sitting down or standing up. He wasn't sure if it even mattered anymore. Had he died? And if he had, where was he now?

It'd been a long time since those Sunday church and family days, and Grant wasn't sure if salvation was in his cards. He thought of the women in the back of that truck who were gunned down by the mindless thugs that stole them from their homes. Dead because Grant pulled the trigger.

A door opened, and a blinding white light accompanied it. Grant turned his head away, his eyes shut tight.

"Don't look so melancholy, Detective. Brooding doesn't suit you. You don't have the stature for it."

The voice echoed, like it was at the end of a tunnel. But it was loud, closer than Grant would have liked. He tried to speak but fumbled with his tongue. It was heavy, like a piece of metal or concrete.

"Drink," the voice said. "You've had quite the past few days."

A straw was thrust into Grant's mouth and he sucked down the liquid greedily, draining it until nothing but air sprayed his tongue. He licked his lips and his vision cleared. He blinked rapidly and when he moved his legs, he realized he was bound.

Rope cut into his ankles and wrists, and the chair he was tied to rocked as he tried to wiggle free. And as he did so, one of the chair legs bumped into something. Grant looked down, his eyes unsure of what he'd just seen. It was another leg. But it wasn't his.

Grant examined the rest of the floor. More legs. More arms. More bodies. Dozens of bodies. They were naked and covered in lime. Decomposing, bits of flesh rotting from the bones and atrophying muscles. Their mouths were agape and their eyes open. He was sitting in the middle of a graveyard.

"I hope you don't mind the company," the voice said, but this time the voice had a body attached to it. It stood in front of the large white light that cast his entire body into shadow.

And that was when Grant noticed the walls around him and the steep slope on which the voice stood. The grave he was in had already been dug, and he was willing to bet that he'd be joining the bodies soon enough.

Grant had been stripped of his clothes, his badge, and his gun. He sat naked and bound, shivering and sweating in a pile of death, waiting for his turn to die.

But slowly, the thoughts of how he arrived came together. Grant remembered the thugs he was with in the woods; he remembered the gunshots, and then the police sirens. But he had never heard that voice before. It was well spoken, older, and very American.

Did Rick and Mocks make it out okay? Did the kids that he had pulled from that cellar make it out alive? Did Annie? He glanced back up to the voice as the man moved closer.

"Who—" Grant's voice cut out, and he lowered his head. He sounded so weak, so tired. He cleared his throat and lifted his head to try again. "Where is my partner?"

"Oh, we'll get to her in a minute," the voice said, making his way down the slope into the pit. "But first I just want to take a minute to congratulate you. It's not every day someone is able to disrupt my plans so vehemently. This was supposed to be a special day for me, but I'm afraid you've ruined it." The closer he moved, the larger he grew. Well over six feet, with quite a bit of girth around his mid-section.

"Half of the city's police officers will be looking for me," Grant said. "Even if you kill me, they won't stop until they've caught you, and after what I found in that sawmill, you're going to be in jail for a very long time."

The man stepped around to Grant's back and chuckled. "If the police ever found me, the kids at the sawmill would be the least of my worries."

Thick, meaty hands gripped Grant's shoulders and he felt paralyzed, helpless as slow, firm circles were rubbed into his skin.

"Quite the body on you," the voice said, and then leaned down and whispered into Grant's ear. "I don't usually go for something so seasoned, but it would be a shame to waste you."

Grant rolled his head away and the voice laughed, slapping his shoulders hard.

"Just poking a little fun," the voice said, circling Grant, who continued to shiver. "You are quite too old for me. Though I understand I'm in no position to talk."

And then, when the man turned and stopped where the light caught his face, Grant got his first good look. He was old, to be sure, but nothing like he would have imagined. The man was preserved, like the dead bodies around him. The decay was slow, and the old man had done what he could to delay it, but in those efforts he only accentuated what he had tried to hide.

The old man did have hair, but it was slicked back. And he wore a wife beater and a fine gold watch on his wrist, with a few rings on his fingers. His pants and shoes were expensive, and he looked down at Grant like a piece of property.

"Some of these are men that you killed, and others…" The old man circled his hands in the air. "Well, occupational hazards."

The questions made Grant's head hurt, and he shut his eyes to try and focus on the matter at hand. And that was trying to get out of this alive.

The old man smiled and then walked back up the slope. "You have two options, Detective. The first is to rot in this pit with the rest of the dead. The second is to accompany me to dinner. I have quite a few questions to ask you, and I was hoping to get the answers from you personally. What do you say?"

Grant shook his head. "You think you will get away with this, but you're wrong. I've gotten this close, and my partner will too. You're going to lose."

The old man stopped at the top of the slope and looked back down to Grant, a sad smile on his face. "Detective, I have been doing this longer than you have been alive. I'm sorry to say that you're late to the party. And if there is one thing I'd hope you'd learned by now, especially judging by your predicament, it's that I don't lose. Ever." He walked away, out of sight, but then called out at the last minute. "I await your answer in the morning. Good night, Detective Grant. Sleep tight."

The door clanged shut and the spotlight shut off, casting Grant back into darkness. He couldn't see the bodies on the floor anymore, or even his own legs. He had reached the underworld. And he had just met the devil.

23

TWO YEARS AGO

*C*igarette smoke filtered through the air, and forced laughs masked the fatigue and loneliness of the late hour. The clock on the wall ticked closer to last call, and the bar's patrons swayed back and forth, beer bottles and glasses grasped loosely in their hands, everyone doing their best to numb the realities that waited for them after the tab had been paid.

Neon lights of pinks blues and reds illuminated the yellowed walls, stained from decades of heavy smoke, and the cracks along the concrete floor. Someone had flipped the old jukebox in the corner to a Moody Blues song, "Nights in White Satin."

The lyrics drifted between the empty barstools and slurred conversations. A woman on the far end of the bar near the exit threw her head back and cackled at something a man in a trucker hat said.

Like the bar itself, the people inside it were broken and decayed. Some on the inside, some on the outside, some both. But everyone shared in commiseration of forgetting the past. Or in the case of Detective Chase Grant, gulping down enough liquid courage to face it.

A slew of empty glasses covered the stained wooden bar top in front of Grant. He scrunched his nose as he caught another whiff of mildew that drifted up from behind the bar. He sat hunched over as he examined the remining whiskey of his eighth drink.

Liquor slushed through his veins, and he swayed on the bar stool. Drunkenly, he picked at the wedding band on his left hand, the metal warm from his skin. His eyes watered at Ellen's memory, but he quickly blinked them away. He was almost there. Just a few more. He drained the glass, then ceremoniously slammed it on the bar.

Ice ejected from the glass and shattered on the floor. He felt eyes on him, and caught the bar tender throwing a heavy side eye. The bouncer at the front door pushed off his stool, crossed his arms, and stared Grant down from across the room. But Grant simply partnered the empty with its fallen comrades and pushed the sweaty bangs of black hair off his forehead, slicking his wavy locks backward.

"Hey." Grant motioned to the bartender, his tongue heavy. "Whiskey."

The barkeep turned his head toward Grant as he wiped down a glass, then up to the clock on the wall that ticked past one-thirty a.m. "Sorry, buddy. You're done."

Grant exhaled and rubbed his eyes. Everything blurred and the liquor that had flowed so freely now turned his muscles to stone. He sagged on the barstool, and when he attempted to move his foot slipped. He smacked his hands on the bar for support, but body and gravity conspired against him and he landed hard on his side.

The floor shifted like a ship deck as Grant pushed himself to his hands and knees. His stomach lurched, and he forced himself to his feet before he puked. He closed his eyes and focused on breathing, and keeping that whiskey in his stomach.

"Hey." The voice was accompanied with a heavy slap on Grant's shoulder. "Let's go, pal."

Grant lifted his head and the bouncer hovered close. At six feet tall, Grant rarely had to look up to meet a man's eye, but the bouncer had a good four inches on him, and the man was as wide as he was tall with a hand more grizzly bear than human.

"I said move it, buddy," the bouncer said, shoving Grant toward the door.

Grant frowned and knocked the security guard's hand off him. The bouncer reached to put him in a choke hold, but Grant wriggled free and took hold of the bouncer's wrist and gave it a hard twist left. The bouncer wailed, and Grant took hold of the thick man's neck and slammed him onto the bar, keeping pressure on the wrist.

Gasps replaced the idle conversations and the Moody Blues drifted through the bar without interruption. The bouncer struggled under Grant's hold, but quickly stopped his squirming when Grant applied pressure to the wrist he kept locked straight behind the man.

Grant saw the bartender reach for his phone. "You calling the cops?" He reached inside his jacket and removed his badge. "They're already here."

The barkeep put the phone down, then slowly raised his hands in submission. "I don't want any trouble."

Grant leaned forward. "I do." The whiskey pushed his thoughts into that dark corner of his mind that he'd circled for the past week. He knew what was there, and he knew what would happen once he stepped inside. And now he was finally too drunk to care.

Grant shoved the bouncer off the bar, and the big man stumbled a few steps before he got his feet under him. The bouncer's chubby cheeks glowed red, and he rotated the arm that Grant had kept pinned. He took an aggressive step forward and Grant opened his jacket and grabbed the butt of his service pistol. "Don't, asshole."

The bouncer froze, joining the mannequin-esque stature as everyone else. "Nights of White Satin," ended, and the bar fell silent.

Beads of sweat appeared on Grant's forehead. His eyes were dry and burned from the constant layer of smoke. All his concentration and focus was on the bouncer. "Back. Off."

The bouncer tossed a glance to the barkeep, and Grant followed the man's line of sight. The barkeep, still with his hands in the air, motioned toward the door. "Just go."

Grant stepped forward, circling the bouncer, keeping his hand on his pistol. He retreated backward toward the exit and caught the blurred expressions of horror and fear on his retreat. What Grant saw in those drunken eyes was the same look Grant wanted to see in *his* eyes.

Outside, an icy burst of air cooled the liquor-laced sweat. He leaned forward when he walked, the whiskey swaying him left, then right on the way to his car. He fingered his pockets for his keys and yanked them out.

Grant missed the keyhole to the door twice, scratching the paint, then dropped them to the asphalt. Angry, he snatched them up, unlocked the car, and crumpled into the driver seat.

A laptop rested in the passenger seat and he turned it on. He searched the Seattle Police Department database for Dunston's address, and started the car as the computer searched. When it appeared, he plugged it into the GPS, shifted into reverse and peeled out of the parking lot.

Grant's knuckles whitened over the black steering wheel, and his fingers itched for the pistol under his jacket as he turned off Interstate Five into a small neighborhood on the northwest side of Seattle.

Single family homes sat clustered together on either side of the street. Small front yards were filled with a variety of flowerbeds, children's toys, bicycles and patio furniture. Cars filled the driveways and street parking, everyone home and asleep on the late weeknight hour.

Grant drove slow, checking the house numbers on his left. He counted upward, and he eased on the brakes as the house came into view. No toys or bikes in the yard. No manicured garden or lush green grass. No decorative fare that revealed the owner's personality. It lacked the charm that flowed throughout the neighborhood.

Grant pulled over and parked. He shut off the engine and closed his eyes. His heart pounded quickly, violently. His liquor-soaked mind searched the darkness, needing that last piece of rage to leap over the edge. And he found it.

A memory of his wife, Ellen. She was at the piano in their living room, sitting awkwardly due to the massive swell of her belly. She placed her hands on the keys and played. It was the song they danced to at their wedding. As she played, she turned to him and smiled, then sang very softly. She rarely sang, said she hated her voice. Grant loved it.

And then the playing stopped, and she placed her hand on her stomach. She laughed and beckoned him over. She reached for his hand and replaced hers with his over her stomach. A light bump smacked Grant's palm, and he smiled. It was the first time he felt his daughter kick.

No more than a handful of moments define a man's life. We'd like to think it's more, but the truth is there are only a few. For Grant, that was one of them. It was the most surreal moment of his life to date.

Grant opened his eyes. Memories were all that were left now. He clung to a past that looped repeatedly in his mind, like a favorite movie. But he could never know what came after the credit rolled. Anything more was fiction. They were gone.

Grant removed the detective's badge from his neck, tossed it into the passenger seat, pulled the 9mm Glock from his holster, and stepped out of the car. He flipped up his collar, blocking the wind and his face from view. He kept his head down and the weapon close to his side. He stopped at the door and jiggled the handle. Locked. He holstered his pistol and reached inside his pocket and removed the lock pick, but dropped it clumsily on the floor. The whiskey had cost him dexterity. But he didn't need much, just enough to pull the trigger.

He maneuvered the pick in the lock and wiggled it until the click of the tumbler sounded. He pocketed the lock pick set, and the door groaned reluctantly as Grant pushed it open.

Light from the streetlamp on the corner behind him spilled into the foyer and cast Grant's shadow deep into the house. Grant stepped inside, quietly.

The house was shotgun style, and a hallway led toward the back. The long stretch made the house feel small, the living and dining area crammed together and backed up into the kitchen.

Grant followed the hallway to the bedroom where the door was open. He paused at the entrance and saw Brian Dunston asleep in his bed.

Rest had eluded Grant since the accident. Every time he closed his eyes, all he saw was Ellen's crushed and mangled body on the coroner's table. The swell in her stomach gone, along with the life that was carried inside. His baby girl. His little Annie.

Grant stormed into the room, and Brian Dunston woke before Grant reached the bed. Dunston jolted backward, but despite Grant's intoxicated state, he was still quicker than his half-asleep prey.

Grant punched Dunston's nose and the crunch of bone and cartilage muffled Dunston's wail as blood spurt from his nostrils. He hoisted Dunston by the scruff of his neck and tossed the man to the floor.

Dunston's legs tangled in the sheet as he scurried backward on the carpet and rammed into the dresser. He thrust his hand up and outward, blood pouring from his disfigured nose. "Please, stop."

Grant didn't listen. The man could scream and beg and cry, but Grant wouldn't stop. He raised his fist as rage and anger fueled his assault, bringing down fist after fist onto Dunston's body.

Bones crunched, skin ripped, and blood spilled. Small, warm splatters of blood splashed on Grant's face and body. Dunston lifted his arms, weakly defending himself, but Grant's six-foot, two-hundred-pound frame worked Dunston's body into pulp.

Slowly, with every punch, Dunston's wails lessened, and his arms dropped to his sides until he lay lifeless on the floor. But Grant refused to let up.

His fingers ached, and his arms grew heavy. Grant landed one final crack across Dunston's face, then stumbled back to the bed where he collapsed on the edge, catching his breath.

Dunston lay on the floor, lifeless, wheezing from the rib that had punctured his lung. Blood soaked his now misshapen face. The left eye had swollen shut, his lips puffed outward, and his nose bent sharply to the right. With his one good eye he looked to Grant. "Please." Blood dripped from his mouth. "Stop."

Grant pushed himself from the bed and lifted Dunston from the carpet, slamming his body against the wall. "Do you know who I am?" The whiskey kept its firm grip on his mind.

Dunston's head lolled back and forth between his shoulders like a pendulum, and Grant slammed him against the wall a second time. "Look at me!"

Propelled either by fear or by adrenaline, Dunston lifted his head and used the wall to help steady himself. His one opened, bloodshot eye fell upon Grant's face. He nodded. "I know you."

"Good." Using one hand to hold Dunston up, Grant fished out his pistol and pressed it against Dunston's forehead. "You took everything from me." His lip quivered, and hot tears gathered at the corners of his eyes. He sniffled, pulling in the snot dribbling from his nose. "You don't deserve one more second of breath. No charges?" He scoffed, his tone thick with lunacy. "If the judge won't bring justice, then I'll do it myself." Grant curled his finger over the trigger. Dunston shivered and whimpered, but he kept that one good eye locked on Grant.

Grant had been in shootouts before. He'd even shot a suspect. But he'd never been this close. It had never been this personal. But he had a right, didn't he? Any natural law granted him this vengeance. An eye for an eye. A life for a life. And Dunston didn't just take one life; he took two.

"Do it," Dunston said, barely able to move his lips anymore, his jaw possibly broken. "I deserve it." A tear fell from the corner of his good eye and cut through the blood on his cheek.

Grant's body tensed. His finger froze on the trigger.

Pull it.

Ellen flooded his mind, her mangled, bloodied, broken body on the cold steel of the coroner's table.

Pull the trigger.

Grant's whole body shook, the pistol vibrating against Dunston's skull.

Finish what you came to do.

Grant barred his teeth, spit and foam squeezing through the tiny gaps as he grit his teeth.

Kill him.

His trigger finger spasmed, but still no shot.

Kill him.

The voice grew louder.

Kill him!

"AHHHHHH!" Grant shoved the pistol so hard into Dunston's forehead that his skin ripped and fresh blood poured down the front of his face. Dunston cried and shut that bloodshot eye, bracing for the end. And just when Grant was about to pull the trigger, just when he was about to kill the man who'd killed his family, the pistol fell to his side and Grant let Dunston crumple into a sobbing heap on the carpet.

Grant paced in a tight circle, his head down, the pistol still in hand. "Fuck!" He kicked the foot of the bed and spun back around toward Dunston. He lay there, wheezing and sobbing, bleeding over himself and the carpet. The man was two steps from death and Grant couldn't find the grit to finish the job.

Grant looked to the pistol in his hand, his finger still on the trigger. He couldn't kill the man who'd take all the joy and happiness from his life. He couldn't do what needed to be done. He'd failed.

The pistol slowly raised, Grant's hand moving with a mind of its own. He closed his eyes and shivered when he felt the steel against his temple. He saw Ellen. He even saw Annie. They were smiling, laughing. It was an image of a future that didn't exist. Or maybe it could? All Grant had to do was pull the trigger to find out. He could be with both of them.

Grant scrunched his face tight. *Just do it,* the voice said. It was nothing more than a light tickle in the back of his mind. *If you can't avenge them, then join them.*

Ellen and Annie continued to laugh. They wanted him there. He wanted to be there. All it took was one quick pull of his finger. Less than a few ounces of pressure separated him from his family.

Grant pressed the barrel harder into his skull. His arm shook. He wanted to do it, but his finger wouldn't listen to his brain. *Pull the trigger, Grant.* Tears leaked from the corners of his eyes. *Pull it.* Grant's finger twitched. He screamed, all of the rage and pain he'd felt since the accident roaring in defiance. And then he dropped the pistol to the carpet.

Grant gasped for air, unaware he'd been holding his breath as he stared at the pistol on the floor. And then, all at once, the past two weeks replayed in his head. The call from the hospital, identifying the body, the funeral arrangements, the wake, the two caskets lowering into the ground, one of them empty because the wreck was so severe that there wasn't anything left of his daughter to bury.

Deep, rolling sobs bounced his shoulders up and down, and tears dripped onto the carpet. "I miss them," Grant said aloud. "I miss them so much."

Dunston didn't respond. He just lay there, pulling in slow, rattling breaths. Grant stumbled out of the bedroom, leaving the pistol, and headed toward the front door.

A tightening, souring pit formed in Grant's stomach and he hunched forward as he approached the door. The acid bile crawled up out of his stomach and he barely made it out of the door and into the yard where he vomited in the dirt and grass.

The hot, barely digested whiskey burned even worse on the way out, and Grant produced two more rounds of vomit onto the front lawn before his stomach emptied.

Once finished, Grant fell back onto the grass. He glanced

up to the night sky. He hoped they couldn't see him right now. He hoped that Ellen had turned away the moment he stepped into that house. He'd lose his badge for this, though he didn't think he'd go to jail. There wouldn't be a jury out there that would convict him, not for any hard time. At least he didn't think so.

Grant was certain of only one thing, and that was the fact that his life had changed course. Whatever he would have been, whatever he could have done, it had been altered. Fate had flipped its coin, and Grant's future had landed on the losing side.

Like the memory of feeling his daughter kick for the first time, this was another moment that would define him. A hopeless moment, with no other future than to rot in a bar, numbing the pain until he felt nothing. He reached for his phone and called Captain Hill. It was time to face facts. It was time to pay the price for his pain.

PRESENT DAY

*B*lue and red lights flashed in the night. Police cars and ambulances crowded the small clearing around the old saw mill and clogged the dirt road that led back to the highway. Dozens of flashlights lit up the thick forest that circled the mill. Dogs barked, looking to catch a scent.

Mocks turned from the lights and back to Rick. She kept hold of his hand while the paramedics checked his vitals and rushed him toward the ambulance on the stretcher. She jogged alongside, squeezing his hand tight while his remained limp.

"Hook up an IV and let the ER know we'll need a transfusion once we arrive." The paramedic examining Rick looked to Mocks and his voice softened from the robotic orders he gave his partner. "You riding with us?"

Mocks examined the deep, long cuts on Rick's arms and legs. Haggard bits of flesh hung loose, and the white gauze used to stanch the bleeding were soaked with blood. "Yes."

"Detective Mullocks!" Lieutenant Furst jogged over, his

tie loose around his neck and dark circles under his eyes as he stepped in time with Mocks and the paramedics.

"Did you find him?" Mocks asked, slowing to a walk as they neared the ambulance.

"Not yet," Furst answered, catching his breath.

"Where are the kids?"

"Someone from Child Services is taking care of them now, and their families are being notified." Furst placed his hand on Mocks's shoulder. "Take care of Rick. There isn't anything else you can do right now."

"But Grant—"

"Would want you to go."

Mocks sighed. "That's what got him into trouble in the first place."

"I'll call you the moment we find anything," Furst said.

Mocks nodded and stepped up into the ambulance, the paramedics shutting the doors behind her.

"Let's go!" The paramedic pounded on the front wall near the driver seat, and the ambulance sped forward, siren wailing.

The ambulance wobbled on the dirt road, and Mocks kept one hand on Rick and the other on the stretcher to keep herself steady. Rick's oxygen mask fogged with every breath as the pair of medics dressed his wounds.

The ambulance lights accentuated the pallid color of Rick's skin. He'd lost so much blood. "Will he make it?" She squeezed Rick's hand harder.

The paramedic tossed a red stained cloth into the waste bucket. "I don't know. If he does, he might lose his leg. The blood loss has impaired circulation to the body. And those cuts are deep enough to have caused nerve damage."

Mocks nodded slowly. The ambulance hit a pothole and they rocked left and right and she gripped Rick's hand and the stretcher harder to keep her balance. She watched Rick's eyelids flutter as the paramedics applied the tourniquets to his wounds. She wasn't sure how much blood he had left.

The nearest hospital was a local branch of Seattle General twenty minutes away. The ambulance pulled into the ER drop off, and Mocks jumped out with the paramedics as they wheeled Rick through the open doors.

"I've got a priority!" The paramedic said, a few heads turning in the ER lobby to their left.

A pair of nurses stepped in stride with Mocks and the medics down the hall. "We have room six set up for a transfusion, we're getting the doctor prepped for surgery. What are we looking at?"

"Blood loss, multiple lacerations to limbs, possible concussions and organ failure," the medic said, slowing as they maneuvered Rick's stretcher to enter the room. Mocks went to step inside, but the nurse thrust out her arm.

"Ma'am, it's better if you wait out here."

Mocks stepped forward, buckling the woman's stiff arm. "I need to be with him."

With at least fifty pounds on Mocks, and six inches in height, the nurse tossed her back into the hall aggressively. "We need to get him ready for surgeory. The doctor will be down in a minute to give you an update. We don't have time to babysit." She disappeared into the room, and shut the door.

While Mocks hadn't been to many ERs for situations like this, she expected a little more compassion when dealing with patient's family members. But she understood the situation. They needed to do their work, and they needed to do it quickly. So Mocks let the nurse have her small victory, and she watched through the tiny window as the medics and nurses blocked her view of Rick as they prodded him with needles and hooked him up to machines.

Her hand twitched and she reached for the Green Bic

lighter inside her jacket. When she looked down at her hand, she stopped. Blood shimmered under the florescent hallways over her knuckles. Rick's blood.

Mocks flicked the flint, repeating the motion absent-mindedly until her hand steadied. She paced back and forth in front of the small window, her mind racing about Rick, Grant, the Web. She needed to do something. If she couldn't help Rick, then she might be able to help Grant. Because there was someone here who she could speak with.

Mocks pocketed the lighter and headed back down to the ER station, flashing her badge. "I need a room number for a patient. Parker Gallient."

The nurse had a plain face, and pale. Her small, beady eyes looked at Mocks and she frowned. "He's on the fourth floor, room four hundred nine, but—"

Mocks sprinted to the elevator, clicking the up arrow repeatedly. She stepped inside, squeezing between a pair of orderlies on their way out, and hit the fourth floor button.

If Gallient was willing to give up the location of the saw mill, then he might know of other locations important to whoever was running this game. She had to narrow down where they'd taken Grant. But that was if he was even still alive.

Mocks pushed the thought from her mind. No, Grant was alive. He had to be. They would have found his body by now, and no body meant they took him alive. No reason to drag a dead detective's heavy corpse to another location when you can just leave it in the woods. They probably want to know how Grant found the place, and dead men were harder to interrogate.

The elevator doors pinged open and Mocks's stomach soured. A cluster of officers stood outside Parker's room. Yellow police tape covered the door and circled the officers in the hallway. She jogged over, ducked under the tape, and pushed her way to the front.

Forensics was already on scene. A flash from a camera captured the bloody sight of Parker's lifeless body on the hospital bed. His head was turned toward the door and Mocks saw his expressionless face, his eyes still open. Blood stains covered his chest and stomach and dripped from his arm where it collected into little puddles on the floor.

The bandage that concealed Parker's spider web tattoo had been ripped off, and the ink had been blacked out. Blood rolled down over the hand in thin strips, and Mocks backed away from the scene.

It was the Web. Had to be. They really could reach *anyone* at *anywhere* at *anytime*. Mocks knew they had a contact inside the federal government, it was the only way they could have got their hands on those documents they found. But now Mocks shifted thinking.

The Web could have other moles on the ground. Hell, they could have people in at her own precinct. She needed to find out how far it went, and she'd have to be careful moving forward. The death toll was climbing, and she didn't want to add any more bodies to the count.

Owen Callahan tapped his finger on his knee in exasperation. He didn't want to be out this late. He should be home, in bed at this hour. But complications were a part of the business. And he had no intentions of losing so close to the finish line.

His blazer was undone, and his growing gut spilled forward into his lap. He glared down at it with disgust. One thing he hadn't envisioned in his senior years was the reality of the body you were stuck with. Modern medicine could only do so much. And every day that passed only intensified the longing for his own youth.

He caught his reflection in the driver side window in the sedan's backseat. The tightened skin, the lifted cheek bones, collagen and Botox injections, all feigning the appearance of youth. His thick head of shoulder-length hair had greyed, which was the only aspect of his age he enjoyed. He thought it made him look distinguished.

Owen tired of his reflection and looked to his bodyguards up front. They rarely spoke. And even though they followed whatever command was given, sometimes he felt like they were more prison guards than protectors.

One of the spider tattoos on the driver's neck crawled out of the shirt collar and Owen looked down at the tattoo on his own hand. Three black spiders were inked into his skin, a forced show of good faith. It was The Web's branding. And once you were in, there wasn't any getting out.

Of course Owen knew the stakes when he signed up. He wouldn't have taken the risk if the reward wasn't worth it. And while his association with The Web presented challenges, the benefits far exceeded the costs.

The SUV pulled into the driveway of one of the several mansions in the neighborhood. Most of Seattle's rich and powerful didn't know a world beyond their butlers, chauffeurs, maids, or private chefs. And while some of them earned their fortunes by getting their hands dirty, none were dirtier than his own.

The driver opened Owen's door, and he stepped out. He glanced back at the fountain in the center of the circled driveway that accented the extravagance of the house and rolled his eyes. All show. No substance.

The front doors opened and Owen was escorted inside with his two men, who left their rifles in the car. When dealing with the general population, Owen found it hard to build rapport when his associates had such firepower. Not that they'd need them here anyway.

The butler stopped at the open study doors and gestured inside. Owen entered and saw the walls were lined with bookshelves, though he doubted the senator had read anything in this room.

"Owen," Pierfoy said, forcing a smile and a nervous chuckle. "Good to see you again." The senator extended his hand, but Owen ignored it.

"Is it?" Owen sat in one of the leather chairs that circled a large coffee table made of solid oak, then reached for the open box of cigars. He clipped the end off, struck a match, and puffed smoke. He closed his eyes as the tobacco filled his senses. "You always did have the good stuff."

Pierfoy took a seat in the chair next to him. "I'll send you home with a box."

Owen tapped the end of the cigar and ash fell to the carpet. "I'll need more than just the smokes today."

Pierfoy looked up from the freshly sprinkled ash. "What else do you need?"

"The laptop," Owen said, taking another drag. "The one those detectives stole."

Pierfoy opened his arms in a display of helplessness. "Owen, that computer has already been logged as evidence. It's out of my hands."

"No, it's not," Owen said. "In fact, I would say it's very much in your hands, but I'd be happy to have my associates chop them off to alleviate your responsibility." His face grew hazy in the smoke. "Then you'd be free and clear."

Pierfoy's cheeks turned pale, and he cleared his throat with a nervous twitch. "There's no need for such talk."

"Or maybe it's not your hands that need to be taken from you." Owen shifted in his chair, the leather groaning from his weight. He gestured the cigar toward the senator. "How old is your granddaughter now?"

Pierfoy's face reddened, the fat beneath his chin wiggling. "Do you have any idea what I've done for you? Access to federal documents. Forgery. I've kept the FBI off your back for longer than anyone could have done. You wouldn't even be here without me."

"I think you have that backwards," Owen said. "I didn't contribute all of that money to your campaign for documents or helping me evade the authorities. I could have done that on my own." He twisted the tip of the cigar into the armrest of the chair, snuffing out the fire. "I bought you because I wanted a puppet. So when I tell you to do something, you do it."

"Owen, the cyber technician with the Seattle PD has already been in contact with a translator for the State Department," Pierfoy said. "It's been recorded. That can't be undone."

"I don't care what you think can't be undone." Owen pressed his palm to the top of his head and flattened his hair as he ran his hand all the way back to his neck. He quickly cracked his neck left in frustration, stood, and walked to one of the bookshelves while Owen's bodyguards stepped into the den and then closed the door behind them. "Anything I wanted."

"Owen, I—"

"That's what you told me. Remember that? It was enough money for you to run whatever type of campaign you wanted. And don't pretend like you didn't know where the money was coming from. You knew who I was. You knew what you were getting yourself into. Saying anything less would be a lie. And I knew you'd keep your word. Want to know how?"

The senator reached for the crystal glass on the coffee

table. He sipped the brown liquor and then leaned back in his chair. "How?"

"Because you're a United States Senator," Owen said proudly, straightening his back and puffing out his chest. "You've built your reputation on the values and ethics of a nation that loves families, barbeques, and apple pie. You know who your biggest demographic was in your win for the Senate seat? Voters aged thirty-five to fifty-five. Voters with families, Senator. Families who would be shocked to learn about who you're in bed with."

"You expose me, and you'll go down with me," Pierfoy said, a snarl in his lip.

"My fall is much shorter than yours," Owen said. "Plus I still have The Web, and all the money and influence it provides. But you, Senator, would evaporate into nothing."

Owen moved intimately close and pulled up the sleeve that hid his spiders. He examined them and lifted it for the senator to see. "I have done things for this organization that still give me nightmares." He dropped the arm, and the senator cowered. "I want that laptop."

The bodyguards sidled up on either side of Pierfoy's chair, and the man held up his hands, padding the air to try and keep the wolves at bay. "All right. All right. I'll get it back for you. Somehow."

Owen smiled and smacked the senator's thigh. "Excellent." He stole the glass of liquor from the Senator's hand and took a sip. "Mm, that's good." He reclined back in his own chair. "Where are we at with the legislation?"

The pair of bodyguards remained on either side of Pierfoy's chair, and he stayed low in the seat. "My aides have packaged it up nice and tight. It will be presented to the House next week. I've put together the necessary votes for it to pass."

"And you're confident in the congressmen you've selected?" Owen asked.

"Yes," Pierfoy answered, reaching for the folder on the coffee table. "Page ninety-three to ninety-four." He slid it toward Owen. "That's where your clause was inserted."

Owen opened to the suggested page, and there it was in black and white. "Very good." He snapped the binder shut and tossed it back on the table. "I need the vote date moved up."

Pierfoy laughed. "And I suppose you want a meeting with the President as well to discuss your concerns personally."

Owen shrugged. "I don't think we'd have much to talk about. I voted for the other guy. But if it's on the table?"

Pierfoy's smile faded. "Congress isn't in session until next week. It's the earliest I can get the vote to happen."

"As majority leader, you can call a special session," Owen said. "Call it."

"And bring more attention to the legislation?" Pierfoy asked. "I don't think it's best to highlight it any more than I already have."

"But that's the best part about our democratic process, Senator." Owen stood and buttoned his jacket. "No one will care. Let me know when you have the laptop and have pushed up the vote date." He walked toward the door but stopped when a picture caught his attention.

It was of the Senator's family, his entire family: wife and three children with their spouses, and six grandchildren, all lined up in matching outfits in the wilderness. It was incredibly folksy, good election bait as the Senator liked to say. He pointed to the only granddaughter in the bunch. Couldn't have been older than nine. "She's beautiful." Owen turned to Pierfoy whose cheeks had lost their color. "Oh, and I'm going to need one last thing from you before I leave."

Pierfoy swallowed, sinking into his chair, his eyes glued to the picture in Owen's hands. "What?"

"The Detectives that were assigned to those abduction cases, the ones that spoiled that fresh shipment of girls the other day, I want to know more about them."

"Why?" Pierfoy asked, slightly surprised. "The woman is going to be taken off the case and you've killed Grant, right?" He leaned forward. "Haven't you?"

Owen set the picture back on the mantle and tucked his hands into his pants pockets. "Tell me more about Detective Chase Grant."

Mocks paced the hallway outside of Rick's room as he was prepped for surgery, her cell phone glued to her ear. The doctor had gone inside ten minutes ago, and Rick still hadn't been wheeled to the operating room, and Rick's body was still blocked from view by the nurses inside and the call went to voicemail.

"Hi, you've reached Sam. I'm not available at the—"

"Shit." Mocks ended the call and dialed the precinct, where she was lucky enough to have Banks pick up the phone. "Hey, it's Mocks. I need Sam. He's not picking up his cell."

"Let me find him," Banks answered.

"Hurry." Mocks chewed on her nails and glanced into the narrow window again. The doctor was talking a lot. She didn't like that. She didn't like the wall between her and her husband. She didn't like that she couldn't be in the room with him. He shouldn't even be in that room at all.

"Found him," Banks said. "I'll put you through."

A quick dial tone, and then one ring before Sam answered. "Hey, Mocks—"

"Where are you at with the computer we got from The Web?" Mocks asked.

"I just got off the phone with the translator at the State Department," Sam answered. "It's done."

Mocks exhaled a sigh of relief from the good news. "Listen, I need you to sift through the data and compile every piece of property the Web has listed on that hard drive. Cross reference that data with sawmills located within Washington's state lines. All of them. Most of them were probably shut down years ago, so you'll have to dig. Look at tax receipts. Those will be the most reliable records."

"Mocks, there is a lot more on here than just property information," Sam said. "I decoded bank accounts, schedules, Social Security Numbers, fake identities. It's a gold mine."

"Grant's missing," Mocks said. "He takes priority."

"What about the rest?" Sam asked.

"Start making a backup of the files." Elevator doors opened at the end of the hall, and a few officers stepped out, catching Mocks attention. She turned away, and lowered her voice. "Listen, the guy who gave us the location of the sawmill where we found those kids is dead."

"What?" Sam asked, his voice a gasped whisper.

"I think the Web has influence on the department, but I don't know how far it goes or who's involved. But I don't want to lose that data."

"It'll take some time to back up the hard drive, and while the files are being copied I can't use the original file," Sam said. "So what do you want done first?"

"The files for Grant," Mocks said without hesitation. "But the moment those are done you copy it, got it?"

"Yeah, I got it."

"It's going to be a long night for both of us," Mocks said. "Let me know the moment it's done." She hung up and brushed the bangs off her forehead where a headache began to take shape.

"Mrs. Mullocks?"

Mocks spun around, white-knuckling the phone. The doctor held a clipboard to his chest, his cheeks drooping, giving off the impression of a hound dog with glasses. She nodded, her tongue tied.

The doctor pulled her aside and kept his voice low. "Your husband's injuries are severe. Particularly along the left leg. The cut is wide and to the bone. From what we can see so far, there has been nerve damage and a significant loss of blood."

"The paramedics said that," Mocks said, then swallowed. "They also said that he might lose the leg."

"He might lose both."

Mocks's knees buckled slightly and she reached for the wall for support. The headache immediately disappeared, but a sinking, nauseating smell took its place. She shook her head. "What, um, what are the chance of that happening?"

"That's what I wanted to speak with you about," the doctor answered. "We can attempt surgery on both legs to try and save them, but the injuries are so substantial that it's going to take at least six hours on an operating table to repair the damage."

Mocks paused, waiting for the inevitable downsized.

"But the bloodloss to your husband has put a lot of pressure on his heart over the past several hours. If we try and push him to far he could die."

"Christ." Mocks's own heart pound harder, and the floor felt like it was starting to shift under her feet. She closed her eyes, trying her best to think everything through. "What are the chances of him—" She swallowed "—Dying during surgery?"

"Forty percent," the doctor answered."

The reality of Rick's future settled into her mind. He'd have to quit the fire department, and that would kill him. Not being able to do all the things he loved would be a blow she wasn't sure he could handle. She wasn't sure if *she* could handle it. But none of that matter if he didn't survive.

"Save his legs," Mocks said, looking up at the doctor. "I don't care what you have to do. He'll be able to cope with limited movement, but he can't lose them. Please, Doctor." She clutched his arm, squeezing hard.

"I'll do everything I can, Mrs. Mullocks," he said.

Rick's door opened and a team of nurses wheeled her husband out. And the doctor left to join them. He was still unconscious. Mocks followed a few steps before they disappeared through the double doors at the end of the hall and out of sight.

Mocks shivered and she took a seat in one of the plastic chairs that lined the hallway. She rested her elbows on her legs and leaned forward, placing her face in her palms, the phone still clutched in her right hand. It was all too surreal. And it was her fault.

When she was an addict, she'd hurt people before, but nothing like this. Most of the damage was to herself, and it made the burden less heavy. But to do something like this to Rick, the one person she loved more than anything in this world... That could break her.

Mocks walked to the waiting room, trying to hide the tremble of her hand. Rick's fate was in the doctor's hands now. Grant's was in hers. She hoped her hunch about the sawmills was right. The mill where Rick and the kids were kept was special to somebody. And she was willing to bet there were more places like it.

The forests were chock-full of abandoned sawmills near the rivers. She imagined most would have been closed for a long time, some of them so off the grid people didn't even know they existed anymore.

Reclusive and forgotten, they were the perfect place for an organization to handle any business they wanted kept hidden from the public eye. She took a seat in one of one of the plastic, waiting room chairs, and bounced her knee nervously. Using her phone, she researched everything she could find about the Web.

Most of the news articles that she found were written in another language, but the pictures included were graphic enough to tell the story without words. One article, written by an American reporter six years ago, revealed entire islands no longer under the control of the Philippine government.

By controlling sovereign Philippine land, along with the surrounding waterways, the Web was a nation unto themselves.

Mocks scrolled and read, distracting her mind with research. After an hour she set the phone aside and rubbed her burning, bloodshot eyes. A table with coffee, cups, cream and sugar beckoned her toward it and she poured a fresh cup.

Until she had Sam's data everything was just a hunch. She tried to think of what Grant would do, how he would work the case in her shoes, and a memory surfaced from their first week together.

A little girl had gone missing, seven years old, taken from her school bus stop. They'd interviewed the kids that saw it happen, though nearly all of their stories differed in some regard. But there was one little boy who stayed quiet, and they'd spoken to him last.

Once interviews were over they drove back to the precinct, and Grant asked her what she thought. Out of all the kids they spoke to there were a few common elements, and that the abductor was a man, in a white truck.

"You don't sound convinced," Grant said.

And she wasn't. "That last kid we talked too. He said it was a car. Not a truck."

"You believe him?" Grant asked.

"He was the only one that had a different story."

"That's not what I asked."

Mocks sighed. "He pointed out a bumper sticker on the back as well. NRA. Probably for the rifle association. I don't think he would have made that up."

"And what does your gut tell you?"

"My gut is telling me it's time for lunch," Mocks answered.

And that was when Grant changed his tone, and looked over to her as they pulled up to a spot light. "In our line of work you have two things: Facts and Instincts. You can't be a detective without using both. When your instincts start to match up with the facts, follow it. And trust it."

Mocks stared into the Styrofoam cup steaming with coffee, Grant's words lingering in her head. Her gut lined up with the facts. She just needed to trust it.

She turned back to the waiting room, taking small sips of her piping hot beverage. Three other visitors sat in chairs, waiting for nurses and doctors to tell them what happened with their loved ones.

A woman kept her purse in her lap, twisting the handle and staring at the same patch of carpet, biting her lower lip. An elderly man, his chin pressed hard into his chest that lifted him up and down with each heavy, snore filled breath. And a younger man, massaging his temples with his eyes closed. Each of them had their own worries, their own fears, absorbed in their own worlds.

Her phone buzzed and she glanced down at the screen. It was the lieutenant. "What'd you find?"

"We retrieved blood splatter in the northeast quadrant of the forest around the mill," Furst said. "We think it might have been Grant's."

Mocks's heart sank, and she paced a tight circle on the waiting room floor. "A body?"

"No," Furst answered. "Not yet. We're calling off the search team for now."

Mocks grimaced. It wasn't 'for now,' it was for good. Unless they had new evidence to warrant a new search, they weren't going to spend the manpower needed to scour that large of a search field.

"Detective," Furst said. "There are some things we need to discuss. I'm getting calls from the Mayor and Chief of Police. They want to know what happened up here. And the press are chomping at the bit for a statement from us."

"Can it at least wait till morning?" Mocks asked.

"I'll see what I can do," Furst said.

"Thanks, Lieutenant."

The call ended and Mocks checked the clock and paced the floor, her mind racing through the scenarios and her stomach grumbling. She'd kill for a Pop-Tart.

Her left hand trembled and she reached for the familiar feel of her green Bic lighter. But when she flicked the flint, her hand continued to shake. She let her thumb off the flint, and took a breath before she tried again. But still, her hand shook.

Mocks frowned, flicking it repeatedly in frustration, each time harder than the first. "C'mon." She grit her teeth. Her cheeks reddened. "Piece of shit!" She slammed the lighter on the ground, then kicked it across the room where it smacked violently into the wall. The room fell silent, and when Mocks looked around, all three pairs of eyes were locked on her. She snarled. "What?"

The woman returned to twisting her purse handle, the old man closed his eyes again, and the young man watched TV. Mocks stomped out of the room and two nurses passed, their eyes falling to her still shaking hand. She tucked the hand in her pocket to avoid any more stares and walked over to the nurse station, knocking on the desk to catch the attention of the woman with her nose buried in her phone.

"Can you tell me how much longer Rick Mullocks will be in surgery?"

"We don't have a way to check in with the doctors while they're operating," the nurse answered, shaking her head. "Let me check his file and see what the timeline was."

"They said it could take a while," Mocks answered before the girl could swivel away in her chair. "I was just hoping for an update."

The nurse forced a smile and folded her hands on the desk. "I'm sure everything is fine, ma'am. If you can just take a seat—"

"Everything is not fucking fine!" Mocks slammed her fist on the desk. It could have been the nurse's tone, the smarmy smile, the way it felt like her concerns were being dismissed or the stress of the past few days from the case, but Mocks felt the frayed ropes of her sanity unravel. "My husband is on a fucking operating table and I don't know if he'll be able to walk again when he comes out!"

The nurse's face flushed red, but before she opened her mouth, or Mocks rammed her fist into it, she stepped away. She needed air.

The automatic doors opened and Mocks zipped up her jacket in the frigid early morning air. She crossed her arms walked until the sidewalk ended on the side of the hospital.

Alone, Mocks lowered her head, fighting the tears. It was all too much. In one night she could lose her husband and her partner. The urge to use took hold of her thoughts. One little hit and it'd all go away. She knew it would. It was one of the reasons it had taken her almost three years to sober up.

But there was one pivotal difference between Mocks then, and Mocks now. And that was the people in her life.

The ones she loved, the ones she cared about, the ones that she couldn't let down. Grant had kept his promise and got Rick out of there alive, saving herself and the kids in the process. She wasn't going to let him down.

* * *

THE MOMENT OWEN RETURNED HOME, he shed his blazer and tossed it on a chair. He was glad to see the mess in the living room had been cleaned up and the furniture returned to their normal positions. He unbuttoned the cuffs of his dress shirt and rolled up his sleeves, then turned around to the pair of bodyguards still following him.

"Find something to keep yourselves busy," Owen said.

The pair complied, and Owen disappeared down the hallway opposite of his protectors. The narrow cut through opened into a bedroom with high ceilings like the living room and was one of the few places inside his converted home with windows. And it had a beautiful view.

A clearing in the trees revealed a waterfall gushing over a ledge. The violent white water spilled to the rocks and river below, and then drifted toward the sea. Such a powerful element water was, and adaptable. It could cut through rock, topple cities, and swallow ships, yet be as gentle and nurturing as a mother. It was a vile and giving creature. Owen thought of himself the same way.

Owen shifted his gaze from the waterfall to a door on his left. It was late, but she was a night owl, and he hoped she still be awake.

A spring appeared in his step as he walked toward the fantasy that lived on the other side. A world he'd created just for him. And it wouldn't be much longer until that world grew larger. He unlocked the door and stepped inside. "And how are we doing this afternoon?"

A young girl, ten years old, with light brown hair and hazel eyes looked up from her coloring book. She wore a yellow dress that accented the soft brown of her skin. She didn't smile. She didn't cry. It wasn't the ideal reaction, but apathy was better than tears.

"I'm good," she said, her young voice high-pitched and soft. "How are you?"

Owen smiled brightly, his skin drawn tight from all those plastic surgeries. He hated that feeling. It only reminded him of his age. The opposite effect of the surgery's purpose.

"I'm well, Izzy, thank you for asking." Owen joined her on the floor, and the girl returned to the picture where a princess appeared in the window of a castle. A young knight looked up to the young maiden, standing outside the castle's wall. "That's a beautiful drawing."

"Thank you," Izzy said, a happy tone to her voice.

Owen pointed to the princess. "Is that you?"

"Mmhm," Izzy answered.

"And who is that?" Owen asked, pointing to the knight.

The girl kept quiet and shrunk inward. She stopped coloring and lowered her head.

"Izzy," Owen said, keeping his voice calm and kind. "You can tell me. Who is it?"

The girl sniffled and, keeping her head down, answered, "My rescuer."

Owen nodded and then placed a comforting hand on the girl's back. She trembled at his touch. "It's all right, Izzy. Shh, shh, shh. Nothing to be upset about." He lifted the girl's chin. Her cheeks were wet with tears, but she made no sound.

"Are you going to have special time today?" Izzy asked, her little voice thick with phlegm and grief.

Owen smiled and then wiped the tears from her face. "No, sweetheart. Not today." He bent over and kissed the top of her head. "Not today." Owen laid on his side, and watched her finish her drawing. She didn't look at him while he sat there, nor did he expect her too.

A transition of trust took time, and he hoped that his current display of self-control would help strengthen that trust. It was all about layering, reshaping the girl's mind to accept that what he did to her wasn't just normal, but good. It was a process, but it was one that he enjoyed.

He played with her hair for a bit, letting the smooth silky strands run through his fingers. She didn't shudder when he touched her that time, another improvement. And while she didn't talk much, he continued to ask her questions, the one word answers slowly morphing to longer explanations the longer they spoke.

"Well, it's getting late my sweet," Owen said, kissing the top of her head once more. "Time for bed." He picked her up and placed her under the covers, pulling them up close to her chin. He cupped her cheek, and smiled. "Sleep tight, love." He held her tiny hand in his, kissed it, then walked out, shutting the light off on his way.

Owen locked the door, then returned to his own bed, his body sagging from the long day. He needed rest. Tomorrow would be just as worse. He disrobed, and climbed into bed, naked, thinking of those detectives and his conversation tomorrow. But despite the circumstances, he was excited.

For over thirty years, Owen had been abducting children, and when his relationship with the Web began almost a decade ago, it propelled him into a new level of power. It was an authority he reveled in, but he was so isolated. No one to speak with, no one to challenge him.

But this detective had managed to do what no other authority figure could, and currently he was locked below, his mind no doubt wondering whether he would live or die. And depending on the answers Owen received, it could go either way.

25

*L*ight broke the darkness, and exposed Grant's naked body tied to the chair he'd sat in all night, or forever long it'd been since that door was closed. He squinted, the brightness painful to his sensitive eyes. Was it the old man from last night? Had he come to finish the job?

The light exposed the sea of corpses that lay stacked at Grant's feet. The sight of the rotting flesh accentuated the throbbing pain at the base of his skull. Those bodies had screamed at him last night, demons from his past clawing their way to the present. But now everything was quiet and he was convinced the lack of sleep left him delirious.

Two pairs of hands removed the restraints that kept Grant in the chair and dragged him over the bodies toward the light. He caught the blank stares of a few, their jaws slack and tongues rolled out with their eyes open. He wondered if the dead could still see, and what they would tell him if they could speak now.

Once out of the pit, the blinding whiteness of light began to fill in with his new surroundings. He noticed the hardwood floors that scraped his knees and feet. He lifted his head and saw paintings hung along the hallway.

There was a picture every few feet, mostly of nature. Flowers, rivers, beaches, and forests. Some had people, others contained animals, and some were barren of anything but plants. Life ahead of him, and death behind.

The pair of men that carried him were dressed in suits. But Grant saw the spider web tattoos creeping up their necks from behind their collars. The old man who visited him last night had tattoos like that, but on his hand. He was the spinner of the web Grant had found himself caught in, and what an intricate web it was.

Grant was dropped in a room completely furnished with a bed, dresser, and nightstand. The bed was made, and a pair of slacks, a dress shirt, and a belt and socks were laid on top of the comforter. A pair of shoes rested on the carpet directly underneath, and a jacket hung on the closet door handle.

Naked and filthy with dirt and sweat, Grant turned back to the pair of thugs that had dragged him to the room. They stood expressionless, their hands on the assault rifles that were strapped over their shoulders. Both of their heads were shaved, and Grant suspected that if they smiled, he'd get an eyeful of silver and gold.

"Wh—" Grant choked on his own voice, his throat dry and hoarse. He took a dry swallow and cleared his throat. "What do you want?"

"Shower," the guard on the left said, then pointed to the clothes. "Dress."

The two words were Grant's only direction. Slowly, he pushed himself off the carpet and leaned against the dresser for support once on his feet. He hobbled to the bathroom, his joints stiff and aching from the night in the chair.

There was no curtain for the shower, no privacy of any kind. A mirror revealed the guard directly behind him. The thug's expression was hard as stone. Grant looked at him through the mirror and arched his eyebrows. "Did you bring the sponge?"

With the joke lost on his captor, Grant stepped toward the shower and turned on the faucet. He cranked the temperature to hot and let the water cleanse him. With a bar of soap, he scrubbed the dead off, rinsed, and then dried himself. When he stepped back into the bedroom and reached for the clothes, he found that they were all in his size.

Once dressed, he checked himself in the mirror. He didn't recognize the face of the man staring at him, but he recognized the type of attire he wore. All black. Funeral colors. He absentmindedly went to rub his wedding ring, and when his fingertips touched only skin, his heart skipped. He turned to the goon, his fists clenched, but the man only motioned over to the dresser.

It was there Grant caught the gleam of his wedding ring. It had been cleaned and polished. He picked it up and placed it back over the pale circle of flesh where it had resided for over a decade.

The thugs grabbed Grant by the arm and thrust him into the hallway. With one thug leading and one behind him, Grant was sandwiched into the narrow hallway as they walked single file until it opened into a large dining room.

A long, wooden eight-seater table was adorned with plates, silverware, and breakfast. Eggs, steak, bacon, fruits, and orange juice. The food steamed on their plates and a servant poured water into a crystal glass from an even larger crystal pitcher.

The goon behind Grant elbowed him forward, and Grant was escorted to the seat to the right of the head of the table.

"Good morning!"

The old man from last night entered through a different hallway to Grant's left. He was dressed in similar garb, though the colors were lighter. Grey slacks, and jacket, and a pale blue shirt. A matching pocket square accented the shirt, and a gold watch flashed on his left wrist. He was clean-shaven and had slicked back his long grey hair.

One of the guards pulled back the old man's chair for him and he took a seat, reaching for the napkin and placing it in his lap. "It's been a busy morning." He grabbed a fork and knife and cut into the steak. It bled onto the white porcelain. With a chunk of meat at the end of the fork, the old man gestured to Grant. "Everything fit? I'm afraid I had to take some calculated guesses with the attire. But I thought the color suited you just fine." He took a bite, and then the servant returned with a bottle of champagne that he poured into both of their glasses.

The old man reached for his glass the moment the servant was done and held it up. "To Detective Chase Grant. Seattle's favorite son." He forcefully clanged the crystal glasses together and then sipped, closing his eyes and offering a satisfied moan. "Delicious."

Grant didn't touch the food despite the growling of his stomach. He stared absentmindedly at the old man who acted like Grant was a long-lost friend come to chat over dinner and catch up on old times.

The old man caught the stare and dabbed at the corners of his mouth. "I hope your bunk mates didn't cause you to lose your appetite?" He shook his head and tossed the napkin back onto his lap. "Honestly, Detective, I thought you were made of stronger stuff."

"You leave me in a pit of bodies, dress me up like some doll, and bring me here," Grant said. "If you plan to kill me then—"

"I told you I had questions for you, but I need your mind sharp, and it'll be hard for you to do that on an empty stomach," the old man said, cutting off another piece of steak. "Eat."

Grant eyed the knife, and then looked to the guards. Both had their guns aimed at him with their fingers on the trigger. He'd be dead before he made the throw. And so, with his stomach grumbling and no idea if he would be granted a next meal, Grant picked up the utensils and dug in.

The moment the first bite touched his lips, everything except satisfying his hunger disappeared. He devoured the steak, took two helpings of eggs, emptied the glass of orange juice, and the juice from the cantaloupe and watermelon dribbled down his chin with every bite. His plate was taken from him only when he leaned back in his chair.

"Glad to see you have your appetite back," the old man said.

Grant dropped his fork and pushed the plate away. "It was a fine last meal."

"It doesn't have to be." The old man adjusted the belt around his girth that looked a little bit tighter than before. "I've been doing this for a long time, Detective. Longer than your career in law enforcement. During my tenure, there have been eighteen detectives that have come and gone who've tried to catch me. All eighteen failed." He pointed a meaty finger at Grant, which curved from arthritis, and remained still as water. "You're the only one who has ever found me."

"Others will pick up where I left off," Grant said.

"And they already have. But they won't be successful." The old man picked between his teeth, fishing out a sliver of steak, and then wiped his finger clean on the napkin in his lap.

Grant eyed the champagne. Real champagne from France, not like that sparkling wine most people buy. The butler returned and poured the old man another glass. "Celebrating something?"

"As a matter of fact, yes," the old man said, picking up the champagne. "It's a special day for you, Detective." He sipped, the bubbles in the glass still fizzing.

The pair of body guards stepped closer to Grant and the hot trickle of sweat appeared under his arms. He grimaced.

The old man looked at Grant. "You don't remember?" He smiled, his eyes locked on Grant as he sipped from the glass again, then set it down, smacking his lips. "Detective, I'm surprised. You always seem to have such a handle on things." He leaned forward. "It's your two year anniversary."

Grant winced and a whisper tickled the back of his mind. It goaded him into anger, the same anger that filled him the night he attacked Brian Dunston.

The old man frowned, feigning sympathy. "I know it must be hard to talk about. It was a dark time for you. You were angry. Violent. Death will do that to you." The old man reached out a hand and touched Grant's arm. "You must miss them so much."

Grant lunged, but the thugs stopped him before he could even raise the piece of silverware. A heavy thud knocked Grant's head forward and he slammed onto the table, one of the rifles pressed into the back of his skull.

The old man looked up to the guards pinning Grant down. "Still a sore subject apparently."

Grant's cheek smooshed against the table cloth, and he writhed underneath the goon's hold. "Talk about my family again and I will kill you."

"You're not a killer, Detective," the old man said. "Not in the brutal sense anyway. Which begs the question I've wanted answered since the moment I found out who you were." The old man lowered his head to meet Grant's gaze, and then laid his head on his arm, like he was having pillow talk with a lover. "Why didn't you kill him? That man, Brian Dunston. You went to his house, beat him to a pulp, but let him go. He killed your family. Albeit it was an accident, but still."

Grant thrashed more violently, the fork still gripped in his hand that was pinned at the wrist.

The old man raised his eyebrows. "He was right there! You could have gotten what you wanted, but you let it slip away." He shook his head. "Why deny yourself what makes you happy?"

"Killing you would make me happy," Grant said, the pressure from the rifle barrel growing in the back of his skull.

"And having my associate put a bullet through that handsome face of yours would do the same for me," the old man said. "But you're my insurance." He sat up and leaned back into his chair. "I need a bargaining chip in case I'm unable to retrieve what I need. Not that your partner has the imagination to find me, but I don't like to take unnecessary chances." The old man nodded to the hallway.

The thugs yanked him out of the chair and punched Grant's stomach, which dropped the fork from his hand. The second blow to his face numbed his body, knocking the fight out of him.

The goons dragged him back to the room and tossed him onto the carpet, then shut and locked the door. Grant rolled to his back and rotated his jaw, the left side of his face tender from the hit. He lifted his head and saw the shadows of the thugs in the hall through the bottom door crack.

Grant really *had* forgotten it'd been two years since that night he'd gone to Brian Dunston's house. But he hadn't forgotten what transpired. There was still anger there, still resentment. The old man's questions resonated in his mind.

Why didn't he kill Dunston? He was drunk enough, mad enough, and on the right side of morality, wasn't he? The man had ruined his life. And even though it was an accident, that didn't make Dunston any less guilty, nor did it ease Grant's pain. So what held him back? What stopped him?

Absentmindedly, Grant reached for his wedding ring and gave it a twist.

* * *

MOCKS SAT HUNCHED in one of the plastic chairs of the waiting room, her arms crossed, and her head cocked forward at an angle she'd regret for the rest of the day. She slept while nurses walked past and the television played a rerun episode of "Friends."

"Mrs. Mullocks?"

Mocks jerked her head up sharply, blinking away what little sleep she managed to get. She pushed herself up, rubbing her eyes, her mind and body feeling like they were filled with lead. "Yes?"

A Doctor came into view as Mocks lifted her head. Rick's doctor. She jumped from the chair, and clutched his arm, her heart racing a mile a minute. "Is Rick all right?"

The doctor smiled. "He's stabilized now. The surgery went great."

Mocks wrapped her arms around the doctor's waist and squeezed him tight. "Oh my god, thank you so much." She pulled herself off of him and wiped her eyes, waving her hands. "I'm sorry. I didn't mean to attack you like that."

"It's all right," the doctor said. "And I'm happy to report that we managed to repair most of the damage to his legs and arms. He'll be spending a lot of time in physical therapy to get his range of motion back, but we're confident he'll be walking around again in a few months, though he will have limitations even after the therapy."

But at least he'll be walking, Mocks thought. "Thank you,

Doctor. Thank you so much." She wiped her nose and cleared her throat. "Can I see him?"

"I'll take you back."

Mocks followed the doctor past the rooms and her stomach twisted into knots in anticipation of seeing him. She focused on her breathing and the fatigue from the past few days vanished as the doctor led her inside his room.

"I'll leave you two alone, but if you need anything just flag down one of the nurses."

"Okay," Mocks said, turning back toward the doctor, tears filling her eyes. "Thank you again."

"You're very welcome."

Rick was still asleep as Mocks approached. Wires and tubes traveled out from underneath his hospital gown, and the machines monitoring his vitals beeped in a reassuring cadence.

Mocks gently touched Rick's arm, his skin warm against her fingertips. Tears rolled down her cheeks freely as she bent down and kissed his forehead.

Rick's eyes fluttered open and he looked up at her. "Susie?"

Mocks smiled and cupped his face. "Hey, baby. How are you feeling?"

Rick groaned. "Tired."

"I bet." Mocks brushed the bangs off his forehead. "The doctor said you'll need some physical therapy. The cuts were deep, and you had some nerve damage."

Rick opened his eyes. "How bad?"

Mocks kissed his lips, glad to feel his warmth again. "Let's just take it one hurdle at a time, okay?"

Rick pinched his eyebrows together, and he stirred, the machine monitoring his heart rate beeping in faster intervals. "Grant. I saw him. Last night. What hap—"

Mocks pressed her hand into his chest and lowered him

back down onto his pillow. "There was a shootout after we found you and the kids. Grant disappeared into the woods and acted as a distraction." She paused. "He's still missing."

Rick looked at the bandages on his arm. "The people that did this took him?"

"Yeah," Mocks answered.

"Christ." Rick closed his eyes, shaking his head. "You think he's still alive?"

It was a question Mocks had pondered since the police arrived at that mill. She was hopeful, but that nagging realism wouldn't remove its claws from her thoughts. "I don't know."

Gingerly, Rick reached for her hand, his grip so weak she barely felt his touch. "If you need to go, then go."

Mocks tightened her grip on his arm. "I almost lost you. I'm not leaving you here alone."

"If the roles were switched," Rick said. "And Grant was here, and you were missing, what would he do?"

Mocks drew in a deep breath, which was followed by a sigh riddled with anxiety and relief. She nodded, and then kissed Rick again. "I'll be back as soon as I can. I love you."

"I love you too," Rick said.

Mocks turned to leave, but then stopped when she saw Rick's belongings on a nearby table. His clothes, wallet, and phone were among the items, but there was something else inside too. She sifted through his belongings, and smiled when she felt the bulky face of the watch.

"What are you doing?" Rick asked, struggling to lift his head to watch her.

Mocks faced him, clipping the watch around his wrist. "Mind if I borrow this?"

"Uh, sure, but—"

"Get some rest," Mocks said. "I'll see you soon."

A nurse entered the room as Mocks left, and the moment

her foot stepped into the hallway, she shifted gears. With Rick alive, she focused on the case.

Mocks pressed the down arrow for the elevator then sifted through the settings of Rick's watch. Thankfully, it was digital, and when she came upon the stopwatch she clicked it. The clock was on. And she was already behind the curve. She needed was a starting point.

She picked up her phone and dialed Sam. The phone rang six times before dumping her to voicemail, and as the elevator doors pinged open, she stepped inside and tried again.

"C'mon, Sam," Mocks said, tapping her foot impatiently. "Pick up."

Another voicemail.

Mocks hung up and when she stepped outside the hospital she only made it a few steps before she stopped and closed her eyes in frustration. No car. She'd ridden to the hospital in the ambulance. She spotted a taxi near the entrance and jogged over.

After a bribe of twenty bucks convinced the driver to start his shift an hour early, Mocks gave him Sam's address. Luckily, traffic was light, and the ride over didn't take long. Mocks tried Sam's number a few more times before giving up entirely, and when the taxi pulled up to his apartment building she tossed the cabbie another twenty and didn't bother waiting for change.

Mocks pressed her palm into the buzzer for Sam's fifth floor apartment, letting it linger before she removed it. No answer. She double-checked the name to make sure she had the right number, then tried again. Still nothing.

She hugged herself, and rubbed her arms, quickly pacing the stretch of sidewalk in front of the apartment door to stay warm. Seattle wasn't known for it's warm, embracing mornings. "C'mon, Sam. Wake up!"

Mocks smacked the buzzer once more, but when a woman came out of the building she darted inside, flashing a badge at the startled lady and scurried to the elevator.

The building was older and rundown. Mocks always thought that the Cyber unit made good money, but judging from the musty hallways, faded paint, and trash littered on the floor, she wasn't so sure. The elevator doors pinged open and Mocks stepped onto Sam's floor, which was more of the same from what she saw on the first.

Mocks turned the corner and spotted Sam's apartment number. She pounded her fist against the door, rattling the whole wall. "Sam, open up!" She knocked on the door again. "It's Mocks, I need to talk to you."

She waited, but after a minute of no answer, she twisted the doorknob and it gave way. She cracked the door open, slowly. "Sam?"

The lights in the apartment were off, and the shades were drawn on the windows. Mocks stepped inside, the place smaller than she expected, and much cleaner. She expected to see pizza boxes piled up and beer cans strewn about the place. But that could have just been her when she lived alone.

The foyer to the front door opened into the living room, and the kitchen was adjacent on the left. Two doors rested on the left and right of the living room, both closed. "Sam? It's Mocks. You home?"

Silence answered and Mocks removed her pistol. Something felt off, her instincts sounding the alarm. Flashbacks of Rick's abduction played in her mind. Every where she looked she expected to find a spider web drawn. But this was different. Her apartment was trashed. Sam's wasn't.

Mocks approached the door on the right of the living room first. She gave the knob a twist and it opened, exposing the bedroom that was just as tidy as the living room. She entered, checking under the bed, then the closet, but found nothing.

She stepped out, pistol still gripped with both hands, her grip tightening as she crossed the living room to the second door. She reached for the knob, giving it the same slow twist as the bedroom door. She pushed it open and as the door widened it exposed the bathroom tile, then the sink and mirror. Then the blood on the floor next to the tub and an empty pill bottle.

"Sam!" Mocks holstered her weapon and rushed to the tub. Sam's head rested lifelessly on his shoulder. Dried vomit covered his chest and chin. She checked his pulse, his skin still warm. But he was gone.

Mocks closed her eyes, fighting back tears as she dialed the precinct. "This is Detective Mullocks. I'm at 372 North Highland Road, apartment five-ten. I have a body. Male, early thirties. Homicide is needed on scene."

"Copy that, Detective. We'll send a unit over to assist."

Mocks hung up and sat on the tile, leaned up against the wall at the foot of the tub. She stared at Sam's pallid cheeks and lifeless eyes, and then she cried. Death followed her wherever she walked now. The Web had long reaching fingers, and they'd taken another life that tried to bring them down. She thought of Rick, still back at the hospital. He had an officer guarding his door, but so did Parker Gallient, and the last time she saw him he shared Sam's lifeless stare.

Anger slowly took the place of grief, and Mocks wiped her nose and removed a glove from inside her jacket. She picked up the pill bottle, and checked the label. Pain pills, prescription. They were in Sam's name, but they were old. She recalled him having an appendicitis last year. Could have been from that.

The forensic unit arrived twenty minutes later and Mocks waited in the living room while they removed Sam's body. Most of the evidence was tagged and bagged when Marcus and Franz, the pair of homicide detectives from her precinct, arrived.

"Hey," Marcus said. "How you doing?"

Mocks nodded, her arms crossed over her chest. "I'm all right."

"Dispatch said you found some pills?" Franz said, already making his way toward the bathroom.

"Yeah," Mocks answered. "Prescription."

A forensic tech exited Sam's room. "Detectives, I've got something." He placed the open laptop on the kitchen counter, which already had a document pulled up on the screen.

Marcus and Franz walked over, blocking the laptop from view. Marcus wiped his mouth, and shook his head. "Jesus Christ."

Mocks wedged her way between Marcus and Franz, shaking her head. "There's no way that's real."

The suicide note was short, and to the point. A few lines described Sam's guilt, how he was working for the Web, feeding them information about the abduction cases, and finally returned the laptop he'd been working on with Grant and Mocks. Apparently that had been the last straw.

"Pills, note, no sign of forced entry," Franz said. "It's gonna be hard to prove anything else, Mocks."

"Bullshit. You passed Sam every day on your way back to your desk," Mocks said. "You're really gonna tell me that the guy who brought donuts in every payday was suicidal? That he was working for a crime syndicate? C'mon." She gestured around the place. "The Web killed him."

"Calm down, Mocks," Marcus said.

"Grant, Sam, Rick," Mocks said, listing off the names. "It's all connected. This is just more shit to throw us off the trail, to keep us from stop digging." She stepped close to Marcus.

314

"Sam was deciphering the laptop. He was working with the State department. Why would he go on record deciphering the computer and leave a paper trail like that if he was working for the Web?"

"Mocks—"

"Call the State departemtn," Mocks said. "They'll confirm what he was doing. I'm telling you that—"

"Mocks!" Franz said, pointing to her pocket, the phone buzzing and flashing through her jeans.

She ended her rambling, and checked the caller. It was the precinct's number. "Mullocks."

"Mocks, it's Banks, the Captain wants you to come into the precinct."

"I'm in the middle of something right—"

"The Chief of Police is here," Banks said, then lowered his voice to a whisper. "You need to come in. Now."

Mocks exhaled an irritated breath. "All right." She hung up and stepped between Franz and Marcus on her way out, and paused. "Sam didn't kill himself." And as she left she just hoped that she could prove it.

26

*G*rant ran his fingers along the cracks of the doorframe, searching for any opening he could use as leverage, but found nothing. He opened the drawers of the dresser, but all were empty. No frames or pictures on the walls, and the bedframe was a single piece of metal.

The bulb inside the lamp on the nightstand was encased in the plastic orb that was too bendable to break, and the lamp was cordless, so no wires. The only viable weapon was the mirror. But he would have to break it, and with the round-the-clock guards outside his door, he couldn't do it quietly enough to avoid detection.

But what halted the quest for escape altogether was the small camera he found in the back corner of the room. It wasn't larger than a nail, and the only reason he saw it was because he'd been staring at the wall for the past hour. Curious, he searched the bathroom and found another camera in the top corner of the shower.

The bedroom door opened and Grant stepped out of the bathroom. Two of the guards entered, followed by the old man who sat on the edge of the bed, smiling. "You looked like you were getting restless. Thought I'd check-in."

Grant crossed his arms and lingered in the bathroom doorway. He eyed both the guards, noticing their fingers on the triggers of their rifles. "Lack of privacy's concerning."

The old man unbuttoned his jacket and crossed his legs rather femininely. "Don't flatter yourself, Detective. You're too old for my taste."

"What do you want?"

"Conversation." The old man spread his arms open in a giving gesture. "I've seen some repressed behavior over my lifetime, but you're something special," he said. "The anger over your wife's accident is powerful." He leaned forward and smiled. "It helps to talk about it." He shrugged. "What else do you have to do?"

"My wife is—"

"Dead." The old man held up a finger. "Yet you still refer to your wife as if she was alive. 'My wife was,' not 'is.' And family implies children, and while Ellen—"

"Don't say her name." Grant's voice cracked and his eyes watered. He hated that the bastard knew about her. He hated how weak he felt when the old man spoke about her. He was exposed. He was vulnerable. And the old man knew it.

"Your wife," the old man said, slower, "was pregnant, but you weren't really a father yet." The old man crossed his arms, staring at Grant like a vet examining a sick dog. "It must drive you mad not knowing what it would have been like to be a father. After all, you're a detective, a seeker of knowledge, striving to answer the unanswerable. To find the lost. To seek the truth among the lies." The old man uncrossed his legs and clasped his hands together between them. "I'm sure you would have been a good father." He scoffed. "Better than mine at least."

And that was where Grant noticed his opening. He

watched the old man's expression morph from playfully inquisitive to stoic. If Grant's weak point was Ellen, the old man's was his father.

"He was a mean son of a bitch." He looked up at Grant. "A drunkard. Whiskey was his favorite. But he never hit me when he was drunk." The old man spoke the words inquisitively. "Growing up I always thought that was strange."

"Your father worked at a mill," Grant said.

The old man smiled and wagged his finger. "You're not a disappointment, Detective." He crossed his arms and chewed on the corner of his lower lip. "Sometimes I think it was the job at the mill that made him so angry. But even despite the beatings, the curses, and the drunken rages, I still wanted the old man's affection." He laughed. "I used to take him lunch before I was old enough to start school. My mother would pack a basket for him, and I'd run up from the house. It was a two-mile walk, daunting for such a young boy, and I was such a small thing. Each day I told myself, 'today he'll look at me. Today he'll finally give me a smile, or a wave, or brag to his co-workers about me.' But it never happened. If I wasn't a bottle of whiskey or my mother's pussy, I wasn't of any use to him."

Grant listened to the familiar slip into nostalgia. He'd been in enough interrogation rooms to know when a suspect wanted to talk, wanted to confess. The old man wouldn't have come in here if he didn't have something to say. He suspected the thugs around him didn't make for good conversation. And if the old man was going to kill Grant regardless, it didn't matter what came out of his mouth. The secrets wouldn't leave this room.

"Someone else noticed me when I came to the mill, though," he said. "One of my father's friends. He was a thin man, but tall, at least to the likes of a boy. He had a thick beard and coarse hands. They were so calloused and rough."

He grazed his cheek absentmindedly. "I'll never forget those hands."

The old man's finger lingered on his cheek, and then he wiped the dazed look off his face. "Of course I didn't realize what he was doing at first, nor did I care. I finally had the admiration of a father figure that I had always wanted. I don't know if my father ever knew about our interactions, but they carried on for some time."

The more the old man spoke, the faster the wheels in Grant's mind turned. If he was as good a predator as Grant thought, then he would have positioned himself early on in a career that would have granted him access to children. A social worker, maybe. Or teacher. And back when he started to live out his pedophile fantasies there was no Internet or social media to aid in catching him. Grant bet the old man missed those days.

"So how did you do it?" the old man asked, a smile on his face. "I know the laptop gave you loads of help, but your chase started before all of that."

"The website," Grant answered. "The one you created that attracted all of those pedophiles. I caught one of your students."

"Oh, yes, the woman." Owen shook his head. "Out of all of them she showed the most potential. Talented but arrogant. An attribute I was willing to forgive, but alas, you stumbled on her too soon."

"You wanted the abductions to happen on the same day," Grant said, more thinking aloud now. The detective protocols were set firmly within his mind, and once they started it was hard to shut them down. "Why? Confusion?"

Owen puffed out his lower lip, and gave an 'eh' expression. "Partly. It was more of a challenge for myself. And it was also a test for a few, to see how they performed. With the entire state of Washington on alert, there would be eyes everywhere. If all the abductions were successful, it wouldn't have just been a new way of kidnapping, it would have given me what I needed."

Grant racked his brain, pulling out the old files from that case, trying to keep the old man talking. "Mallory Given's abductor mentioned something to me before she died. Said she should have waited like the others."

"She got greedy." The old man frowned, suddenly angry as he stood and paced around to the foot of the bed. "Patience wasn't her strongest virtue." He turned to Grant. "Do you have any idea how difficult it was to coordinate all those abductions? And that bitch tipped you off before I even pulled the trigger."

"Why look for outsiders?" Grant squinted, trying to connect the dots. "You had an entire organization at your fingertips that could have taken whatever kids you wanted."

"Abductions in the Philippines are easy, especially on the more rural islands," the old man said. "But the Web couldn't just start applying their snatching methods stateside and expect to have any sustainability. I taught them my methods: seduction, abduction, escape."

"If you taught them what you knew, then what would they need you for?" Grant asked. "You made yourself obsolete."

"Exactly." Owen ran his finger over the pattern of the comforter on the bed. "I don't plan on doing this forever, Detective. But in order for me to ride off into the sunset I needed a replacement. Someone with a mind like my own to take up the mantle. Another me. Not an easy task I might add."

Grant arched an eyebrow. "Looking to retire?"

The old man gestured to himself. "I am approaching my golden years." He slapped his stomach. "Hell, I'm in the middle of my golden years." He grimaced. "And it's not all its cracked up to be, I'll tell you that much." He looked Grant up and down. "Despite all of my money, all of the power, all of the influence I carry, I'd give it all up to have my youth again. I look at you and see nothing but possibilities. But my future, well, there's one inevitable looming in the distance."

"You in a jail cell," Grant said.

The old man offered a coy smile. "You never stop do you, Detective? It's admirable, but pointless. But I suppose that's why you were the one to find me. Out of all the others, you persisted. It took a pained, and broken man to catch me." He crossed his arms. The old man's eyes wandered over the room walls. "I'm just as trapped as you are, Detective. Forced to hide my desires from public view. If I ever revealed who I am, and the things that I want, I'd be burned at the stake. But, then again, most people hide who they really are. Pretending to be something that they're not. Like you." He gestured to the hand with Grant's wedding ring. "It's been two years and you still wear it. But it's not who you are anymore." The old man stood and stepped closer to Grant. "Let me show you who you are. Let me give you what you want."

"You have no idea what I want," Grant said.

The old man smiled, then turned toward the door and once out of sight, the old man hollered back. "Don't be afraid to step off that ledge, Detective. You might find you enjoy the fall."

* * *

THE RIDE back to the precinct was filled with anxiety. She knew the captain wanted answers about what happened last night. But it could be something else. Something worse. A message that needed to be delivered in person.

Had they found Grant? Was he alive? The questions raced through her mind and her stomach twisted into knots the longer she thought about it. When the officer of the squad car she rode with back to the precinct slowed, she pushed the thoughts out of her mind. Grant had to be alive. She could feel it.

At the precinct, the press core outside had nearly tripled from her last visit. The officer rode the brake through the crowd of cameras, microphones, and flashing lights as the reporters scraped against the car. It wasn't until a pair of officers forced them back that they were able to park. But the moment Mocks stepped out of the car she was immediately swarmed.

"Detective! Do you have a comment about the operation down south on the coast late last evening?"

"What about the accusations made against your partner in regards to the assault on Brian Dunston two years ago?"

"Any word on whether more abductions will take place?"

"What's the condition of the children that were rescued last night?"

"Who was behind all of those abductions?"

Mocks kept her head down and her mouth shut. She shouldered the precinct doors open and was glad to rid herself of the questions and cold.

Her entrance was noted by every officer's turn of the head as she walked past. It felt like death row, and the captain's office was the gas chamber. And when she opened the captain's door and saw his face, she didn't think her demise was out of the question.

"Shut the door, sit down, and shut up," Hill said, pointing to the chair in front of his desk.

Mocks did as he asked, though her lips wiggled in defiance.

Captain Hill looked rough, more tired than she'd ever seen him. But she suspected that getting reamed by the Chief of Police in his own office wasn't helping with his complexion, or the press circling outside for that matter.

"You're being put on administrative leave effective immediately," Hill said. "Three weeks, with pay, to take care of your husband and his recovery."

"You're fucking kidding me," Mocks said.

Hill thrust a finger at Mocks, his cheeks reddening. "I told you to keep that mouth shut, Detective! Do not test my limits. This is as good a deal as you're going to get."

"What deal?" Mocks asked. "Captain, there is some serious shit going on. Grant's still missing, Sam was just killed, and we don't know who is running The Web stateside."

"That gang is no longer your concern, and neither is the search for Detective Grant's body," Hill said. "And as far as Sam, his death is officially being ruled a suicide."

"Bullshit!"

Hill slammed his fist on the table repeatedly. "Enough, enough, enough! Evidence was found on Sam's laptop that connected him to the same dark sites that The Web was operating on. He was a mole. He gave the Web back their laptop. Then he killed himself out of guilt. End of discussion."

Mocks laughed, the chuckle hysterical. "You're a fucking idiot."

Hill squinted his eyes, the same flushed appearance still on his cheeks. "Excuse me?"

Mocks leaned forward, raising her voice. "I said you're a fucking idiot."

"I want your badge and your gun on my desk, now!" Hill said.

Mocks stood, angrily removing the Glock and slammed it down, followed quickly by her badge.

"You will be reviewed by the ethics board to ensure that

no misconduct happened during your investigation, and once that investigation is complete, the Chief of Police will decide whether you will continue to be employed with this department," Hill said, taking her badge and gun and placing it in a desk drawer. "You're lucky to even have that opportunity after the shit you and Grant pulled."

"He's still out there," Mocks said. "And you're just sitting here on your fat ass doing nothing!"

Hill slammed both palms onto the desk and lifted himself out of the chair. "I'm getting calls and visits from people that I have never gotten in thirty-five years on the force. We retrieved the missing children. We did our job. Now drop it. Before you get yourself killed."

The pair lingered in angered silence for a moment and then Mocks retreated toward the door. "When does the next search for Grant start?"

"Lieutenant Furst will be handling that," Hill said. "Take care of your husband, Mullocks. Be thankful for what you have. And get the hell out of my office."

Mocks ripped the door open and it slammed against the wall on her exit. There wasn't a pair of eyes in the precinct that didn't watch her stomp to her desk and grab every file they had so far in regards to the case. If the captain and chief of police wanted to stop her then they'd have to lock her up.

A hand touched Mocks's shoulder and she spun around, snarling to a surprised Anthony who jumped backward.

"Sorry," Anthony said, cowering a few steps back. "But I need to talk to you."

"What is it?" Mocks asked.

Anthony was one of the cyber techs that worked with Sam. The pair hadn't had much interaction with one another since Anthony had heard Mocks's comment on the man's weight. Mocks didn't remember saying it, but apparently there was a walrus comparison thrown in.

"Sam left this for me last night when I came onto the night shift at midnight." Anthony held up a small thumb drive. "He said that it was important I give it to you in case…"

Mocks cocked her head to the side. "Did Sam say something to you?" She snatched the drive out of his hand before the big man got cold feet, and prayed it was the data she needed to find Grant. "What do you know?"

Anthony waved his hands, looking around the precinct in quick glances as he backed away. "L-look I don't want any trouble. I just wanted to give that to you. I have to go."

She watched Anthony scurry back to cyber, and Mocks ended her quest for the case files and bee-lined it out of the precinct and back through the hordes of reporters. She didn't hear the questions they shouted at her. She wasn't even aware of any pictures that were taken. All she thought about was continuing the case and finding the person responsible. And she'd bet her last dollar that if she found that individual, she'd also find Grant.

*G*rant looked from the bed sheets to the mirror on the wall. If he removed the mirror and put it on the bed, he might be able to shatter a piece off without making too much noise.

But there was still the problem of the cameras. He could tear them down, but there might be others he hadn't seen. And the moment he did, the old man would know something was up. It just didn't give him enough time.

The bedroom door flung open and the old man's body-guards burst inside. They ripped Grant off the bed and shoved him into the hallway. When he didn't move, they jammed the end of their rifles into his back, jolting him forward.

The violent escort continued through the hallway, the thugs prodding Grant along when he slowed. They passed through the dining room from earlier and entered another passageway, which fed them into a living room with high ceilings, at least thirty feet.

Grant's shoes clacked against the tiled floor as he separated himself from the goons. The furniture had been pushed to the walls to make space for a large, clear plastic tarp in the center of the room.

The guards motioned to the tarp, and before they prodded him forward, Grant stepped over it freely. He knew what it was for; easy cleanup. The sheet crinkled under Grant's shoes and he stopped when he reached the middle. He turned back to the guards, waiting for them to pull the trigger. But they kept their rifles lowered and aimed at the floor.

"So much pain."

Grant turned left and saw the old man leaning against another hallway exit. There was something near his feet, a red container with a nozzle. It was a gas can.

The old man examined and picked at his cuticle. "The past two years have weighed heavy on you, Detective. But today is a new day. Today I relieve you of the burden of your wife and daughter's deaths." He snapped his fingers and the pair of thugs disappeared and returned, dragging a body with a bag over its head, hands and feet bound behind his back.

Whimpers penetrated the black mask, the cloth moving with each breath. The thugs dropped the man at Grant's feet, and then dropped a tire iron that clanged against the plastic covered tile. Their delivery complete, both Web members retreated from the tarp, but kept their thousand-yard stare.

"In my line of work, you learn about people," the old man said. "You discover who can bear the weight of purpose, and those that are crushed by it." He paced the perimeter of the tarp, heels clacking rhythmically against the tile. "You are one of the rare few that can take it, Detective. But you haven't decided how it will transform you. You have yet to choose a path. But that ends today."

Another whimper and sniffle filtered through the captive's mask. Grant shifted his eyes to the tire iron, then back to the old man.

"Go on," the old man said. "He won't bite."

The thugs raised their rifles, one aimed at Grant, the other at the man curled on floor. Grant knelt, then slowly reached for the mask. His finger grazed the man's chin, and he recoiled from the touch like a frightened animal. With one quick strike, Grant ripped the mask off, and cold terror flooded through him at the sight of Brian Dunston's face.

Dunston blinked rapidly, shaking his head, wiggling over the plastic tarp. His cheeks were red and stained with tears. His lower lip quivered and he squint his eyes shut hard, his forehead creased with thick lines as he sobbed.

Flashbacks from the night two years ago surfaced in Grant's memory in rapid, lightning strikes. He recoiled, falling backward. The tarp crinkled as he frantically scrambled away from the man that had killed his wife and daughter.

"I wouldn't go much farther," the old man said. "The moment you step off that tarp, they'll shoot you."

Dunston lifted his head, opening his eyes, looking at Grant, but not seeing him. "P-please." He shivered uncontrollably. "I w-wanna go h-home."

Grant looked to the tire iron at his feet, then to Dunston and the tarp. He connected the dots, and shook his head. "I won't do it."

"Don't pretend like you didn't want this." The old man pointed an accusing finger at Grant. "It has festered in your mind like a disease, rotting your brain of everything else. This is your chance to cut the cancerous tumor out of your life!"

Dunston rolled helplessly from side to side. His breaths

were quick and shallow. He looked at Grant again, this time squeezing his eyebrows together in confusion. "You? No. No, please. I never told anybody about what happened that night." He looked to the old man. "I don't know what they told you, but I—"

"Quiet." The old man picked up the gas can and walked to the edge of the tarp. He dropped the can and it thumped onto the tile, the fuel inside sloshing back and forth. "You have two options, Detective. The first is to pick up that tire iron and bash Dunston's head until he's dead. The second involves this gas can and a match."

Dunston wailed, his mouth agape as he thrashed wildly over the tarp. "It was an accident! I just fell asleep. I'm sorry! I'm so s-sorry."

Grant clenched his fists, and they shook. He couldn't take his eyes off the tire iron. The little voice emerged from the depths of his memories. The one that was so angry after Ellen's death. The one who wanted Dunston dead.

Do it. For Ellen. For Annie.

Grant remembered the funeral, the days and weeks afterward where he cried and drank and did anything to numb the pain, all the while his mind circling the vengeful thoughts of murdering Dunston for his crimes.

It's your right. Kill him.

"It's all right to want it," the old man said, a smile in his voice. "We're raised to believe that acting out our desires is a bad thing, but it's not. It breathes life into our souls, makes us feel invincible."

Ellen filled Grant's mind. Then Annie. He saw them, smiling together, laughing, playing. What would she have said? What would she tell him to do? He fumbled through the darkness, searching for her voice. And then, just when he felt himself tire, he heard her. *Let go.*

Grant uncurled his fists, his muscles relaxed. He looked to Brian Dunston who trembled and cried, fearful of the judgment Grant would cast. But he simply walked toward the man, knelt, looked him in the eye and spoke the words he should have said a long time ago. "I forgive you."

Dunston scrunched his face in pain and wailed, nodding as he cried. "Thank you. And I'm so sorry. I'm sorry about your wife, and your little girl. You don't know how many times I wished—"

One of the thugs poured gasoline from the nozzle, drowning Dunston's words and when Grant tried to intervene the second shoved him back. Dunston gagged from the putrid fuel and choked, unable to pivot away from the stream of fluid. He spit, shaking his head, and then vomited, retching over himself and the tarp.

The last few drops of fuel dripped from the can and the thug tossed it aside, then stepped back. Dunston's clothes had darkened, now soaked with fuel. His hair flattened against his skull, and he kept his eyes shut to shield himself from the stinging gas. He splashed in the small puddles of fuel that had collected in the crinkled tarp, and he continued to cry out.

The old man reached inside his jacket pocket and removed a packet of matches. He rattled them in his hand. "The smell of burning flesh isn't something that ever really leaves you. It's unique." He broke off a single match. "Have you ever smelled burning flesh, Detective?"

"What I did to him before, it was wrong," Grant said. "It was just an—"

"Accident?" The old man asked. "He fell asleep behind the wheel of his rig. Was it an accident that he decided to drive with minimal sleep? Was it an accident that he didn't pull over when he started to get tired? Don't mistake an accident for carelessness, Detective."

The old man struck the match against the backside of the packet, and the flame came to life. The fire wiggled, pinched between his finger, and was mirrored in the old man's eyes. He stretched the flame toward Dunston. "Don't feel bad if you lose your lunch. I did the first time too."

"Stop!" Grant thrust out his hand, and the old man froze, the flame hovering above Dunston's gasoline-soaked body. Grant picked the tire iron off the tarp, and the old man pulled back his hand. "I'll do it."

"There we are!" The old man blew out the flame and tossed the burnt match aside. "I knew I'd pull it out of you eventually." He motioned for his bodyguards to step off the tarp. "Give him room, boys. Give him room." The old man clapped his hands together and rubbed them vigorously. "Swing away, Detective."

The sweat from Grant's palm loosened his grip on the metal as it grew warmer from his touch. He readjusted his fingers and stepped closer to Dunston, who shivered with every crinkle of the tarp.

The puddle of gas around Dunston's body rippled when Grant stepped in it, the tips of his shoes only one inch from Dunston's body. He lingered there, searching for the grit to spare the man from a fiery death.

"Second thoughts?" The old man held up the matches and gave them a rattle.

Dunston sobbed, and Grant knelt near Dunston's head. He placed a gentle hand onto Dunston's shoulder and for a moment the man's trembling ceased.

"I'm sorry for what I did," Grant said. "It was an accident. I knew it then, but I didn't want to believe it. I didn't want to feel it." He dropped his voice to a whisper. "I'm sorry for this." Grant stood and raised the tire iron high above his head, pausing.

Dunston shook his head. "N-no. Please don't—"

Grant slammed the end of the tire iron onto the top of Dunston's skull and the man flattened to the tarp, jerking convulsively. A small pool of blood collected where Grant had struck him, and Dunston garbled nonsense, his head lolling back and forth. He raised the tool again and then cracked it against Dunston's skull once more, this time exposing brain.

Dunston's body continued to spasm, but the garbled words ended. His eyes bulged from his skull and he took deep breaths that sounded like he was breathing in fluid. Blood spilled from his mouth, and the spasms worsened.

Grant's hand and arm melded to the piece of iron. He struck again, repeatedly bringing the tire iron down harder, faster than the previous blow. Bone broke and blood splattered, each blow covering Grant's face and body with warm bits of Brian Dunston.

Rage took hold at the sight of the carnage and Grant screamed. Something primal surfaced in those moments as the heavy tire iron cut through what was left of Dunston and reached the tarp and tile, and a mound of mush lay where Dunston's head once rested.

Blood, brain, and bone sprayed outward in thin, stringy lines. Grant tossed the blood-soaked iron aside and stumbled back, panting, and collapsed to his knees,.

The old man clapped, slowly, and stepped onto the tarp. "Well done, Detective! Well done!" He stopped short of Dunston's body and leaned over. "I would say that the punishment fits the crime. He smashed your family with a semi-truck, and you smashed his head with a tire iron." The old man chuckled playfully. He inched intimately close and crouched to meet Grant at eye level. "Doesn't it feel good to get what you want?"

Grant lifted a shaking hand to his cheek and smeared the specks of Brian Dunston into thick streaks. He still felt wild, angry, but when he spoke his voice was soft, quiet. "I'm going to kill you."

"No," the old man said, his tone stoic. "You won't." He stepped off the tarp and then motioned to Dunston's body. "Clean up that mess. It's poor manners to leave things like that lying around. After all, you're still a guest. For now."

A few of the reporters followed Mocks down the street, but after a few blocks of her silence they ended their pursuit. Her apartment was close to the precinct, so she walked the rest of the way, the thumb drive burning a hole in her pocket as she broke out into a jog, checking the timer on her watch that ticked upwards of two hours. But in reality she was already passed the ten-hour mark in regards to Grant's disappearance. Time was tight.

Once at her building, Mocks raced to the elevator and then up to her apartment. She loaded the drive into Rick's laptop and opened the files. Dozens of folders appeared, and she scrolled down until she found one with her name on it. She opened it and another series of subfolders appeared, along with a document that was titled 'Read Me.'

Mocks,

I've compiled the list of locations you wanted here in this folder. The drive also contains a complete copy of the laptop's entire hard drive. I wanted to give you the backup as a safety. Hopefully we won't need it. If you have any questions, let me know.

Sam

Mocks leaned back in the chair and exhaled relief. She'd need to turn this over to Franz and Marcus. It was more proof that Sam didn't kill himself. But that would have to wait. Grant took priority.

Mocks returned to the folder and clicked on the one titled "Sawmills." Sam had done his work well, finding five mills that intersected with GPS coordinates found on the Web laptop. She clicked through the links, which detailed the sale and tax history for each.

Most of them were foreclosed, shut down during the Great Depression, and never recovered. But of the five mills that intersected with the Web GPS coordinates, four were purchased by one of the Web's dummy corporations. The last one was purchased by a private buyer.

Mocks drilled down on more information for that particular mill and discovered that aside from the tax documents, there were no other records that Sam could find that showed the property even existed. No name of the buyer, no record of purchase accept for the taxes on the land.

It was the perfect place to hide what didn't want to be found, and Mocks was willing to bet that was where the bastard in charge was. And if he was there, so was Grant. She needed to get there, and fast.

But despite the information, and her eagerness to bust down some doors, she knew that place would be heavily guarded. And at the moment she had no badge, and no gun except for the spare revolver in the closet. It was a pea shooter compared to what she'd be up against. She needed more guns. A lot more.

* * *

GRANT'S JACKET sat to his left on the bed. Blood splattered the sleeves and lapel. Brian Dunston was all over him. His hand trembled and he pumped it into a fist until it steadied. He reached for his wedding band, his fingertips smearing a few specks of blood over the gold, giving it a brownish hue.

Grant had visualized killing Dunston for a long time. He'd repeatedly replayed the night he'd beat the man to a pulp. Hours were wasted trying to figure out why he couldn't pull that trigger. He was angry. Weak. Helpless. And now that he finished what he set out to do that night two years ago, he felt empty. There was no sorrow for the man's death, but no joy. No relief. He was numb.

And if this was what he felt, then what was the point of all of it? Dunston's death was the one thing that was supposed to make him feel something.

Grant stood and stumbled to the bathroom. He caught his reflection in the mirror. He was a stranger in his own skin. A murderer.

Streaks of Dunston's blood had dried onto the stubble of his unshaven face. He turned on the hot water nozzle on the sink and splashed his face, rubbing vigorously. The streaks of red faded, red droplets running down his face and neck. He reached for the soap and scrubbed.

The blood's heavy metallic scent filled his nostrils, and he grew antsy, panicky. His stomach churned. It wasn't just the smell of the blood, it was the knowledge of how it got there, and who it belonged too.

Vomit crawled up his throat and he lunged for the toilet. He dropped to his knees and hunched over just in time. His throat burned and he gave another dry heave at the scent of his own stink, then quickly flushed the toilet. He pushed himself up and ripped off his shirt and pants, stumbling backward into the wall. He tossed them aside and reached for the shower handle. He cranked it on hot, but stepped in before the temperature had a chance to rise.

Dozens of tiny red lines trailed down his legs, cutting

through the white soapsuds. The water grew hotter and burned Grant's skin, his shoulders and back growing red from the heat. But he didn't adjust the temperature. He wanted to be cleansed. He wanted for all of this to be done.

Grant removed the wedding ring and scrubbed it as well. It slipped from his hands and clanked to the tub's bottom. He quickly squat and snatched the ring before it rolled down the drain. And as he clutched in his fingers, he cried.

He missed Ellen. He missed her more than he could bear. He wanted to hear her voice again. He wanted to watch her play the piano, her hands moving gracefully over the keys. They were supposed to die many years from now; together. That was the plan.

But plans had changed. The situation was hopeless. And a hopeless man might as well be a dead man.

* * *

THIRTY MINUTES into climbing up the mountain, despite the chill in the air, and Mocks was soaked with sweat. Her muscles ached and cramped. Apparently spending the night in a hospital chair didn't provide the best circumstances for thorough REM cycles. But even if she had gotten a good night's sleep, it didn't change the fact that she was outside. And she hated the outdoors.

"Not having any fun?" Hickem smiled, climbing on her left, he and the rest of his unit cloaked in tactical gear. They didn't seem as bothered by the weather or the climb.

"Not my idea of a good time," Mocks answered, her breathing labored.

Hickem nodded to her boots. "I can see those haven't been thoroughly used. They look brand new."

They were. Well, not brand new per se. Rick had bought them for her for Christmas in the hopes that if she got out into nature more often, then she might enjoy herself. She didn't.

"Not much farther," Hickem said, then nodded with his head, his boot crunching on leaves and twigs. "There should be a small ridge up ahead. We'll have a good view of the compound from there to see what we're dealing with."

Mocks turned back to Hickem's unit. "You sure you and your guys will be able to handle this? If this place is what I think it is, then security will be tight."

Hickem gave a quick glance at the men behind him. "I have a former Navy SEAL, a Green Beret, two Marines, and a Secret Service officer." He adjusted the pack on his back and the rifle in his hands. "I like my chances."

Mocks raised her eyebrows. "Big dicks swinging. How refreshing."

"My wife telling stories again?" One of the men behind her asked, which triggered a series of chuckles.

"I'm pretty sure she was talking about me, fellas," Hickem said. "And make sure to tell your wife I'll see her this weekend, Garcia."

"Just make sure you mow the yard this time," Garcia said. "I need to get *something* out of this deal."

The laughter was light hearted, but laced with nerves. Mocks took it as a good sign though. She imagined it was how they coped before going on a mission like this. You'd have to be insane not to be nervous. She was.

Once they crested the top of the hill, Hickem paused, and the rest of the unit followed suit. He clicked his radio, keeping his voice low. "Jim, I need recon of the compound."

A figure broke from the group and banked left out of Mocks's peripheral. She crawled to the very edge of the ridge to get a better look. Slowly, she lifted her eyes above the steep slope, her mouth dropping slowly.

What may have started out as a sawmill now looked more

like a modernized castle. A twelve-foot wall acted as the compound's perimeter. An armed guard patrolled atop the wall, and she ducked back below the ridge before she could be seen. She lay flat on the cool, damp soil. The radio crackled in her ear, the report coming in.

"Compound is heavily fortified," Jim said. "I count eight guards on perimeter patrol, and two more that entered the compound. Total number of known combatants sits at ten."

"Copy that," Hickem said. "Best course of entry?"

"Southeast corner," Jim said. "Poor visibility from the high ground, and good cover on approach. Two guards on that location."

"Hardware?" Hickem asked.

"AKs, M-16s, and AR-15s," Jim replied. "Side arms on most of them. No explosives or heavy artillery visible. Helipad and chopper on the northwest corner."

Hickem hand motioned to his unit and they scattered. Three of them pulled left, while one went right. Hickem crawled to Mocks and kept his voice low. "Stay here." He reached for the side of his pack and removed a satellite phone. "If shit gets bad, use this." He removed a piece of paper from his pants pocket and folded it into Mocks's palms. "If I give the word, you call the number listed on that paper named Alpha One and provide them with the go codes associated with it. They'll know what it means."

"So I just sit here?" Mocks asked, expecting her duties to extend a little farther than secretary duty. "I did bring a gun, you know."

"And you only use it if someone shoots at you," Hickem said. "I don't need you in line of fire. Stay put. Stay still. And stay quiet."

Before Mocks responded, Hickem was gone. She pocketed the codes and satellite phone and removed her revolver.

She exhaled a slow, rattling breath. It was the calm before the storm, and it was going to rain hard.

* * *

GRANT SAT ON THE FLOOR, his back against the wall, the towel he used to dry himself from the shower still around his waist. The fresh clothes remained untouched on the bed, and he'd taken his wedding ring off and rolled it between his fingers.

The emptiness inside had grown. It was worse than right after Ellen's accident. At least then he could fill the void of her absence with work and a simmering rage. But with Dunston dead, that rage and that drive had been carved out, and there was nothing to replace it, except for the old man.

Grant circled that thought, his mind defaulting to detective mode, sifting through what he'd learned. He found it odd that the old man was white. The Web, who seemed to value only keeping their own in the group, had allowed an outsider to ascend high within their ranks, which could have been out of the need for growth.

The Web needed contacts in the States to grow their trafficking business. The old man provided insight to the area and more sophisticated ways to skirt the laws. After all, the old man had designed the website, searching for his heir to the throne.

The ring slipped from Grant's fingers and rolled onto the carpet. His hand felt lighter without it. But there was more weight to the band than just the metal it was made of. A guilt-riddled past, soaked heavy with pain, had dragged him down. And while Dunston's death relieved him of some of his weight, the memory of his family remained.

Burying himself in his work provided the needed escape to avoid the necessary pain of dealing with his grief. But his endeavors weren't fruitless. He'd recovered more abducted children than any detective in the history of the Seattle PD. That had to have counted for something. But those victories came at the cost of his own healing. And as a result, he never had a chance to move past the pain of his loss.

And now, sitting in a room in the middle of nowhere, he had run out of time and no one to blame but himself. He hoped Mocks would be okay, and that Rick had survived his injuries, and that the kids were returned to their families. At least they had a chance.

Grant reached for the ring on the carpet when his ears perked from the sound of a light pop. It was muffled, and distant, but distinctive. *A gunshot.* He jumped, moving to the rear of the room, pressing his ear to the wall. The pops grew louder and more frequent.

Grant turned to the bed, tearing off his towel, and quickly dressed. Shouts preceded and followed the gunfire now, along with the heavy, hurried thump of footsteps. Grant finished the knots of his shoelaces and then wrapped the towel around his fist and sprinted into the bathroom.

He cocked his arm back and rammed his wrapped fist into the mirror. Vibrations rattled his bones all the way up his shoulder, but the glass didn't crack.

The gunfire shifted to outside his hallway. Grant cocked his arm again and hit the mirror. Fault lines traveled from the epicenter of contact and tiny bits of the mirror fell to the sink.

Grant hit the glass again, and the cracks deepened and multiplied. He unwrapped his hand and reached for one of the larger pieces that had fractured off. Blood pricked from his fingers as he removed the jagged shard from the mirror just as the bedroom door slammed open.

Gripping the serrated mirror wedge, Grant spun around as boots entered his room. He remained hidden behind the bathroom wall, poised to strike. A rifle barrel broke the plane of his vision and he knocked the weapon down while ramming the sharp mirror tip forward and through the tender flesh of a throat.

Blood erupted in quick spurts from the thug's neck, but quickly faded into a dribble as another rushed around the corner.

Grant lifted the body to shield himself from gunfire, a high-pitched whine deafening him after the gunshots. He shuddered from the heavy percussive blasts, but training overrode fear and he lifted the stolen rifle, aimed, and pumped three rounds into the suited chest of the second thug who fell backward onto the floor.

Large pools of blood soaked into the carpet, and Grant froze, aiming the rifle at the room's entrance. He stiffened, waiting for another thug to rush inside, but no one else followed. He lowered the weapon and checked the bodies.

He lifted a spare magazine for the AK-47 and a knife for when the bullets ran out. Armed, Grant entered the hallway rifle first. The narrow space made it difficult for him to maneuver with the rifle in firing position, and the echo of gunfire and screams kept his head on a swivel.

Grant followed the maze-like hall to the same living room where he killed Brian Dunston, finding everything perfectly back into place after he was forced to drag the body outside and dispose of it. He was thankful for the tarp, which was thick enough to mask the smell.

Grant quickly passed the room and entered another hallway. It was short, a sharp left up ahead that blocked the pair of Web thugs waiting for him on the other side that surprised him and opened fire.

Bullets obliterated the edge and forced Grant farther back. Grant dropped to his knee, making himself a smaller target, then pivoted around the corner and squeezed the trigger.

The first bullet entered the thug on the left's stomach, and the second connected with the right thug's left thigh. Both dropped to the floor, but not before firing helplessly into the air as Grant tucked himself back behind cover.

The groans continued, and it meant one was still alive. Grant stood, took a breath, and then spun from the wall's edge and pumped three rounds into the surviving thug.

Grant pressed forward, the rifle raised and the gunfire growing closer. He stepped over the bodies and blood, and the hallway opened up into a foyer filled with a half dozen Web members. Their backs were turned, their focus on an enemy outside.

Grant tucked himself back behind the wall and considered his approach. He might be able to take out three before the others noticed, but that wasn't ideal. He glanced back to the pair of bodies in the hall.

Keeping his head on a swivel, he searched their jackets, hoping to find some heavier artillery. And after turning over the second body, he did.

Grant fisted the grenade in his right hand and hurried back toward the open room. He pulled the pin on the explosive, the lever squeezed tightly in his hand. Three were clustered together, and Grant tossed the grenade in their direction. Two of them heard the thud of the grenade's landing but realized the cause of the noise too late.

The blast left another high-pitched ringing in Grant's ears, but the moment after the vibrations from the blast rippled through his chest, he stepped into the living room, engaging the remaining thugs who were caught off guard by the explosion.

Blood covered concrete, and smoke plumed into the air, the three thugs lifeless and in pieces. Grant entered the chaos and pulled the trigger. Three rounds dropped the first target and he pivoted left toward a second and fired another spray of three rounds. He swept the room methodically, always moving, always alert.

A Web member burst through a cloud of smoke to Grant's right and knocked the rifle from his hands. A knee slammed Grant's gut and he doubled over, but raised his arms in time to block the right hook to his face.

Grant countered with a leg sweep, which missed as the thug jumped, then stepped back. Grant jabbed, but the goon sidestepped him, taking hold of Grant's arm and pinning it behind his own back.

Pain radiated from Grant's elbow, shoulder, and wrist from the harsh twist, and the thug mumbled something in Cebuano. The thug kicked the back of Grant's knees, and he hit the floor, his arm still pinned. A shimmer of steel caught his peripheral and Grant thrashed to escape the hold, but couldn't as the blade drew closer to his throat.

A gunshot thundered, and the grip on Grant's arm loosened. He spun around, the thug's brains spread over the floor from a head shot, the knife meant to cut his throat still in the thug's hand.

"Room clear," Hickem said, stepping through the front entrance, scanning the area through the sight of his rifle.

Three more men followed, all dressed head to toe in tactical gear. They passed without acknowledging Grant, and it wasn't until Hickem grabbed hold of Grant's shoulder that he realized he wasn't hallucinating.

"You must have nine lives, Detective," Hickem said.

Grant shook his head in disbelief. "How?"

Footsteps echoed at the entrance along with a light panting, and Mocks jogged inside, her face sweaty and red. "Thank God." She sprinted to Grant and slammed her body into his, wrapping her arms around his torso.

"What the hell are you doing here?" Grant asked.

"Long story," Mocks answered, and before she could continue, Hickem's men returned.

"Rest of the house is clear, boss. Chopper's gone."

"Shit," Hickem said. "All right. Let the FAA know and see if they can track it in air space." He shook his head and looked to Grant. "Why don't you take a seat, Detective. It'll be a while before backup arrives."

Grant dropped the rifle to the floor and found a seat on a chair that had a few bullet holes in the back. He lowered his eyes to the dead bodies on the floor, Hickem's men picking at them with their boots like vultures nipping at a carcass.

"Grant?" Mocks asked, taking a step toward him. When he looked at her, she was concerned, her hands huddled together. "Are you all right?"

His time spent here in captivity replayed in his mind in fast forward, and he twisted the wedding band on his finger, fresh blood on it. He shook his head. "No."

"What happened?" Mocks asked. "Did you see him? The person in charge?"

"I saw something." Grant thought about the old man, but what he wanted to put into words sounded absurd. How did you stop something so calculated, manipulative, and evil? How were you supposed to kill the devil?

29

*T*he chopper landed outside another compound thirty miles from the previous site. Owen kept quiet on the journey over, contemplating his next move. He looked at the laptop that the Senator had arranged to be returned to him. The only way someone could have found that place was if they had the computer sitting next to him. Which meant someone made a copy.

The trouble must have been caused by Detective Grant's partner, the former drug addict. And now Grant was alive, Owen's home destroyed, and a team of federal agents hunting him down. He didn't have much time.

The chopper bounced harshly upon landing, and Owen unclipped his seatbelt and ducked his head as he exited. Three Web members met him on his approach, and equipment was already being removed from the site and into trucks.

"How much longer?" Owen asked.

"Ten minutes." The man who greeted Owen was shorter than him, but as wide as a redwood. All muscle, with enough brains behind the thick skull to be dangerous. Unlike his

Philippine counterparts, the only tattoo on his skin was the mandatory spider web that he placed on the left side of his neck.

"And we have the assets I requested?" Owen asked, stepping inside the compound, which was smaller than the previous location. Owen rarely visited this site since it had no living quarters. It was primarily used for storage. And if the detectives had caught on to his sawmill renovations, it wouldn't be long before they found this one.

"They're inside," he answered.

"Get Senator Pierfoy on the line for me," Owen said. "Now."

"Yes, sir."

Owen took a seat on one of the crates still inside while the dozen or so Web members hulled everything out. Drugs, weapons, documents, computers, it was one of their more important waystations in regards to inventory. But they had places like this stashed all over Washington. He didn't have the resources to clear all of them, so he focused on the important ones. He sacrificed the drugs and weapons, a hefty cost that his counterparts in the Philippines wouldn't like, but the data was more important. He didn't want to leave any more evidence than what the detectives already had.

"Sir, the senator."

Owen grabbed the satellite phone and pressed it to his ear. "Someone made a copy of the laptop."

"That's impossible," Pierfoy answered, his voice crackly through the earpiece. "We cleared the records between the State Department and the police technician that worked on it. I don't know how they could have the data."

"Because you waited too long to get it back," Owen replied through gritted teeth. "For your sake, I hope you didn't lollygag on the vote in Congress."

"I've requested a special session, but it'll take a few days for the process to go—"

"That's the wrong answer, Senator." Owen dropped the phone to his side and walked across the room. A man, woman, and young girl were bound and gagged, blindfolds over their eyes. They shivered, mumbling through the tape over their mouths. Owen singled out the young girl and ripped the tape from her mouth, and she whimpered in pain. He thrust the mouthpiece to her lips. "Say your name."

The girl's lips moved, but it took a few seconds before words finally escaped. "K-Katie Pierfoy."

Owen pressed the phone back to his ear. "Did you catch that, Senator?"

"You fucking piece of shit!" Pierfoy screamed. "Let her go! I swear to god if anything happens to her—"

"Her blood will be on your hands," Owen said. "So unless you want me to ship your granddaughter back to you in pieces, I suggest you find me every copy made of that laptop's hard drive and nail down a date for the vote by the end of the day."

Owen ended the call and tossed the phone back to his associate. The senator understood the message. And if he didn't, then it would sink in after the first bloodied finger removed from Katie's hand arrived on his front doorstep.

Owen cupped the young girl's cheek. She shuddered at his touch, but he shushed her. Her mother sobbed and her father screamed. He knew they heard what he said. He wanted them to hear it.

"I hope your grandfather loves you," Owen said, rubbing his thumb against the smooth young cheek. "And if he doesn't, then I promise I will." He kissed her forehead, then replaced the tape over her mouth.

Owen stepped back outside as the rest of the crates were cleared out. "Load the family into my car. Send the rest of the cargo on the boats and get the other locations cleared. We'll only have the opportunity for one shipment."

"Yes, sir."

Owen climbed into the passenger seat of the lead truck, and the driver pulled forward. He calculated the potential financial windfall from this new interference. It would be costly. But if he could stop the hemorrhaging, he'd still have enough left for his arrangement with The Web. Though he'd need an extension on his timeline for a replacement, a request that he wasn't sure would be granted considering the rapid deterioration of events. But if the Senator pushed the legislation through Congress, it might be enough to buy Owen out of the doghouse.

But what plagued his thoughts the most was Grant. The haggard detective was troublesome and, even worse, smart. He needed to wipe the board clean, start fresh; easier said than done.

Owen clicked his seatbelt into place and rubbed his temples. There was an answer in front of him that he just wasn't seeing, a solution staring him in the face. And then it hit him.

A wide smile tightened Owen's unnaturally smooth skin, and he laughed, nodding in satisfaction. He only needed to pull one string, and everything else would fall into place. He leaned back, more relaxed now, and closed his eyes.

* * *

WHILE MOCKS CAUGHT GRANT up with what happened after he was taken, it didn't take long for Hickem to discover what Grant had already known after a thorough sweep of the house. The place was wiped clean.

"Not a single goddamn hair," Hickem said, his voice thick with irritation. "Computers, security footage. Even if we manage to get a print somewhere, I don't think it'll give us a hit in the database. I haven't seen a scrubbing this good since the cartels down in South America." He turned to Grant, who was still sitting in the same chair in the living room after he saw Mocks. "But they don't leave survivors. That's where our boy slipped up. What do you know?"

Mocks sidled closer to Grant's side and placed her arm on his shoulder. "Give him some breathing room. I'm sure there's paperwork for you to fill out."

"And it's as tall as Mt. Olympus," Hickem replied. "But I want to know what he knows. And I want it now."

Grant remained seated. "Was there a child here?"

"Yeah," Hickem said.

Grant shut his eyes, and exhaled. The old bastard was cocky. He looked outside to the forest beyond the compound's concrete wall. The place was secluded, hard to find. "He's smart, well organized, equipped, violent, and cunning." Grant stood and weaved around the carnage of the dead Web members still on the floor.

"But what does he want?" Hickem asked. "What's the man's end game?"

Grant sifted through his conversations with the old man. He was rushed. Worried. And tired. He was nearing the end of his watch. Grant turned to Mocks. "Did you find out who he was working with on the inside?"

"Inside what?" Hickem asked.

Mocks fidgeted with her fingers. Grant knew she wanted to reach for her lighter. He wasn't sure why she didn't do it. "No, but whoever it is must be high in the chain of command." She turned to Hickem. "We think there's someone in the State Department working for the Web."

"Christ!" Hickem said, his angered voice echoing to the high ceilings. "And you're just telling me this now?" Hickem paced in a circle, muttering curses to himself. Finally, he paused and took a breath. "All right. I want you two debriefed back at my office. I want to know everything you know. Got it? I think I've earned it after our little field trip today." He motioned toward the door. "Wait outside."

Grant followed Mocks out front and looked back at the structure briefly. It was larger than he expected, more militaristic. He imagined Hickem's men had a hell of a time trying to get inside.

Mocks stopped at the edge of the clearing and leaned against a tree. She finally reached for the lighter in her pocket but didn't flick the flint.

"I'd kill for a cigarette right now," Mocks said, turning toward Grant. "I gave them up in rehab. Every time I smoked one, it just made me want a hit of something stronger. I guess that's just the way my brain works." Mocks twirled the lighter in her fingers.

"What is it, Mocks?" Grant asked.

"I think the chief is being influenced to cover up Sam's death. They want to make it look like a suicide."

"What?" Grant asked. "That's insane, Sam wasn't—"

"I know." Mocks paused, running her hands through her short brown hair. "Grant, I don't know who we can trust. And right now, neither of us have a badge."

Grant arched an eyebrow, this tidbit missing from their earlier talk.

"Captain put me on a leave of absence," Mocks said. "Told me that I was too close to the case. It came from the Chief himself. Since the kids were found, they want this chapter closed. They don't want to deal with The Web anymore."

"I think it goes higher than the chief," Grant said.

"Mayor?" Mocks asked.

"The mayor wouldn't be able to get that kind of access to the State Department," Grant answered. "It'd have to be someone from Congress. Maybe a senator."

"Pierfoy?" Mocks asked, skeptically. "That's a dirty bed to lie in, even by a politician's standards."

"The Web has a lot of money," Grant replied. "I'm willing to bet the old man funneled money into whatever federal coffers he could. Campaigns are expensive, and in return, their candidate turned a blind eye." Grant thought more on it and furrowed his brow. "Pierfoy wanted me out of the detective unit after the Givens case. Told me he wanted to head a special drug unit."

"So what do we do?" Mocks asked. "If the Senator really is the contact this guy has, then I don't know of anyone else we can go to. The Chief isn't going to risk sticking his neck out, not after taking my badge."

"We can trust Hickem," Grant said, turning back to the compound. "He's brash, but he takes his work too seriously to be swayed by outside politics. And the way he's pursued The Web, he's caused them too much trouble."

"So we have some guns on our side, but we need more than that," Mocks said. "Who do we go to?"

"The ambassador," Grant said. "But we need to take a closer look at the hard drive and see what else we can find. Maybe we can unearth the connection between the old man's sudden need to speed his agenda along and what is on the computer. There's obviously something on there he didn't want us to see. We need to find it."

30

$\mathcal{H}$ickem's field office transformed into a data center as Mocks passed the thumb drive to each of his agents, everyone making a copy. Grant circled the group as the information downloaded.

"We need to look for something beyond the obvious," Grant said. "We know they have drugs, and guns, and women, and right now all of those pieces are moving. But we want the big fish. We want the man pulling the strings."

Mocks removed the drive from the last computer. "Following the money will be a good indicator. Bank accounts and transactions happening stateside and offshore."

"It'll be large amounts," Grant said. "This guy is looking forward to riding off into the sunset. We need to figure out where that sunset is falling."

Hickem's unit clustered their desks together. Everyone was assigned specific folders to search, and Grant borrowed a spare laptop to help.

Grant started with land property The Web owned, and then connected some of the purchases through offshore accounts. The Web had banks all over the world. Caymans,

Swiss, China, South America, and a few private institutions within the United States where the cash flow was more moderate, hovering in the millions.

But the offshore accounts, that was where their real money was. In total, The Web's cash tipped over half a million dollars, with a yearly revenue stream of the same amount. He followed the cash streams and found their main sources of revenue.

The largest source of income came from trafficking. They had thousands of locations around the Pacific, and it looked like they were starting to branch out into Eastern Europe. But their entire web of intricate and connected locals was more than any single agency could handle. This was a nation in and of itself, and their gospel had spread farther than what Hickem and the ambassador were aware of.

Smaller sources of income came from drugs and weapons smuggling in southeast Asia and along the U.S. West Coast and down into Mexico and Central America. The total money from these endeavors only made up a third of The Web's total revenue, but it had grown significantly over the past five years, doubling their profits.

The Web was connected, they were flush with cash, and they were everywhere. Grant wasn't looking at an organization, he was looking at a plague.

He returned to the property folder and drilled down further on their real estate. They owned all the land where they had operations for their brothels, each of them under a separate dummy corporation that Grant suspected was tied to a parent company.

Grant scanned the different regions of The Web's extended global network, and when he arrived at the Philippines, he noticed that large groups of islands in the southern portion of the country had been sectioned off. The description for each transaction simply read 'under development.'

Grant returned to the bank accounts and searched for any corresponding withdrawals or deposits in the area and found that tens of millions of dollars had been dumped into the southern Philippine islands over the past three years. And all the receipts for the deposits were marked with the same ambiguity as the description of the land itself.

"I think I've got something," Grant said.

Every head perked up, and Hickem was the first to hover over Grant's shoulder, followed quickly by Mocks.

"What am I looking at?" Hickem asked.

"A string of islands in the southern Philippines," Grant answered. "It's been flagged by The Web, and I'm assuming it's a stronghold of theirs."

"It is," Hickem replied. "They've been giving the Philippine government more trouble than they can handle. We've had reports of entire islands being taken by The Web. They're smaller pieces of land, but the Philippine government doesn't have the resources to get them back."

"I read about this," Mocks said, leaning closer. "With the resources at their disposal, they can outspend the budget for the Philippine military."

"They don't receive any foreign aid from the U.S.?" Grant asked.

"They do," Hickem said. "But what they do with that money, I'm not sure."

"This is where he wants to go. This is why he wanted the laptop back so badly." Grant swiveled around in his chair. "He kept talking about creating a place where he didn't have to hide. Where he could be himself, openly."

"If the U.S. government found out about this, they'd have a field day," Hickem said. "Not to mention the press."

"We need to call the ambassador," Grant said. "Bring him in on this. He has the weight and clout we need right now to get this in the open. He'll know who we can trust with the information."

"Agreed," Hickem said. "We're going to need all the help we can get."

A phone buzzed, and Mocks reached for her pocket in a knee-jerk reaction. When she stared at the screen and frowned, Grant knew something was wrong.

"What is it?" Grant asked.

"The number is blocked," Mocks answered, slowly lifting the phone to her ear. "Hello?" Her face grew stoic, and she handed the phone to Grant.

"Who is it?" Grant asked, taking the phone from her hand.

"Senator Pierfoy."

AMBASSADOR MUJAVE, Grant, Mocks, Hickem, and Pierfoy were the only people present for the meeting. They met at Mujave's home, in his study, behind closed doors, the entire wing of that section of the house vacant. No one could hear them. It was Pierfoy's demand, which included a sweep of the room for any bugs. Once his people said it was clear, he spoke.

"You have to understand my motives," Pierfoy said. "I thought I could do a lot of good once in office. To reach this level of power, you must shake hands with unsavory characters. Of course, now, looking back, I wish I'd done things differently."

"You knew," Mocks said, her mouth downturned, disgust on her face and disdain in her voice. "You fucking knew what they were doing to kids and women."

"And I'm willing to face the consequences of my actions,"

Pierfoy said, his back stiffening. "But I'm not willing to let my family pay for them."

"So what does he want?" Grant asked. "In exchange for your family?"

"I created a piece of legislation," Pierfoy answered. "It's sandwiched in with more boring details, but the portion that benefits him deals with the United States budget on foreign aid. More specifically in the Philippines."

Grant and Mocks exchanged a glance. Grant turned back to the senator. "And because he was a major contributor to your campaign, he threatened to blackmail you by going public if you didn't." Grant shook his head, betting that the old man had kept that one in his back pocket for a long time.

"Yes," Pierfoy answered, leaning forward. "Please." His eyes misted and his cheeks reddened. "My granddaughter... she's only nine."

"It's a powerless feeling, isn't it?" Mocks asked. "Unsure if your children or grandchildren will survive."

Pierfoy snarled and wiped his eyes, turning away to reach inside his jacket for a tissue. "And what would you know about survival?"

"What's his name?" Grant asked.

"Who?" Pierfoy asked.

"The man who funded your campaign," Grant said. "The stateside leader of The Web. What. Is. His. Name?"

Pierfoy hesitated like he expected the question, but still hadn't decided how to answer. After a pause, he settled on his answer. "Owen Callahan."

"We'll have to verify that," Hickem said. "And because of the nature of this meeting, we'll need to get a few things down on paper."

"No," Pierfoy said firmly. "Not until I have my family back."

Mocks stepped into the neutral zone between the two

parties. "You don't have anything to negotiate with. You lost all credibility the moment you got into bed with that piece of slime."

"And what would you know of all the things I've done?" Pierfoy said, becoming defensive. "I've passed more legislation for this state than any senator in history. I've funded and reformed the foster care system, I've added more money to the budget for children and families, I've promoted businesses to become more sustainable. I have given my life to public service, and I will not be lectured by a former drug addict!"

"That's enough," Grant said, his voice calmer than the expression on his face. "Whatever you did, whatever good you thought you could bring, doesn't negate the bad."

Pierfoy petulantly turned his head away and crossed his arms. "And you would know all about that, wouldn't you, Detective Grant?"

"No man is without sin," Mujave said. "We must move forward."

Grant exhaled, nodding. "We need to lure Owen out. Take him before he has a chance to escape again." He turned to Pierfoy. "You'll demand to see your family. A last request before you fly to Washington. You want confirmation that they're alive, and you'll want him to be there in person as a show of good faith. It'll be at an airfield of our choosing."

Pierfoy nodded. "If that's the angle we go, then so be it. The moment I have my family, I'll sign whatever documents you want."

"And you will resign your post as Senator effective the moment your family has been returned," Mujave said. "You will make a public statement about your deeds and be taken into custody by Agent Hickem." He stood and crossed the room, shoving his face into Pierfoy's. "And if I learn that you had anything to do with my own daughter's disappearance, you will not be able to hide behind the law. Not from me."

Pierfoy kept his head down, unable to meet Mujave's gaze. Eventually, the ambassador turned away, leaving the room and slamming the door shut behind him.

"So you call Callahan, give him your demands, and then we set up a sting." Hickem clapped his hands together and then rubbed them vigorously. "Easy-peasy."

"Make the call," Grant said. "Now."

Pierfoy sheepishly reached for his phone and dialed the number. He walked to the corner of the room, but Grant moved close enough to ensure he heard every word. The senator followed the script, but when he chose the airfield, they hit a snag.

"No," Pierfoy said, shakily holding his ground. "It will be under—" Color drained from his face. He trembled. His voice thickened with rage. "Don't you dare touch her! Leave her alone! I said leave—"

A scream pierced through the phone's speaker, a young girl's scream, and Pierfoy pulled the phone from his ear and winced. After the scream vanished, he leaned back into the call.

"No! Don't—" And then Pierfoy stopped, his body hunched over, and hung up the phone. He turned to Grant. "He demanded that we meet him at an airfield in the northwest portion of the state. It's a private airfield."

"His airfield," Hickem said, snorting. "Did he give you coordinates?"

"He'll text them to me." Pierfoy's voice was a whisper, his cheeks still white as a sheet.

"And he'll be there?" Mocks said. "Callahan?"

Pierfoy nodded.

"We'll confirm the airfield with satellite imagery," Hickem said. "I can call a few favors over at NORAD. There's an airman I know that owes me a favor." He exited the office, leaving Grant, Mocks, and Pierfoy.

Pierfoy collapsed into the nearest chair and buried his face into his palms. Grant almost felt pity for the man, but the emotion was fleeting. Everyone reaped what they sowed, and time had a way of catching up with people.

"It'll stay with you forever," Grant said, and Pierfoy looked up. "You won't be able to sleep, or eat, or enjoy anything again. It'll follow you until your last days, which I don't imagine will be very long once you get behind bars."

"Grant," Mocks said, grabbing hold of his arm and pulling him back. She kept her voice low. "We need to give a copy of that drive to Mujave. If something happens during the raid, we'll need insurance. And he's our best bet."

Grant looked to Pierfoy, who had his eyes locked on the two of them, then quickly flitted away once he realized Grant saw him.

"All right," Grant said. "We'll make it a priority. We need to let Hickem know." Grant started for the door with Mocks following behind, but when he reached for the handle, Pierfoy called out to him.

"He's more terrifying than you know," Pierfoy said. "You may have spent some time with him, but that doesn't mean you really understand him. It doesn't mean you haven't seen him at his worst."

"You're probably right about that, Senator," Grant said. "But he hasn't seen my worst either."

*I*t didn't take long for Hickem to verify the airfield's existence, as well as the name Pierfoy had given. Owen Callahan was a Washington resident whose father worked at a sawmill that had mysteriously burned down, taking the lives of nearly every man that worked inside, including Callahan's father.

The story matched what the old man had told Grant during his captivity, and it was enough to confirm Pierfoy's admission as true. They had the bastard's name along with a photo, albeit a much younger version. Owen couldn't hide anymore. The old man was exposed.

Hickem kept the team to engage Owen at the airfield small, only expanding his core unit by another four, and only by men who Hickem trusted with his life. With Grant and Mocks in the mix, it brought their total offensive numbers to twelve. If they counted Pierfoy's security detail, then that number jumped to fifteen.

The meeting was scheduled only two hours after Pierfoy's call, and they arrived at the airfield early to wire the senator so they could listen to his conversation. Once

Callahan and his men were exposed, Pierfoy's code phrase was "take care of my family." After that, it was all up to Hickem's men.

The airfield was bare bones. Nothing but a strip of grass in the middle of a forest. But the surrounding trees provided good cover. Hickem even had a drone sweep the area to make sure Callahan didn't have any men hiding in the woods for an ambush. The sweep came back clean, and all that was left to do was wait.

Both Grant and Mocks were given assault rifles for the mission, though Mocks looked uncomfortable as she handled the weapon. Grant almost told her to just use her side arm, but after Hickem made the comment of getting Mocks a BB gun, he thought better of it. The only way she was going to give up the rifle after that comment was with her cold, dead hands.

Hickem was kind enough to offer them Kevlar for the mission, and made sure to emphasize the need to have them returned in the same manner in which they were given; without any bullets lodged inside them.

Grant peered through the binoculars, finding Pierfoy's plane parked off the runway near an old hangar. The staircase was down, and he heard the old Senator breathing nervously through the microphone. He lowered the binoculars and jabbed Mocks in the shoulder.

"You all right?" Grant asked.

"I'm fine," Mocks answered, her voice short and irritated.

Grant hadn't brought it up before, and he was hesitant to do it now, but thought it a good idea. "It's better if we take him alive."

Mocks looked at Grant. "And you think I won't?"

"You almost lost your husband," Grant replied. "That's not something that's forgiven quickly."

"There could be a lot of gunfire," Mocks said, looking

through the sight of the rifle. "No telling what could happen once the bullets start flying."

Before Grant had a chance to reply, the thump of helicopter blades sounded overhead. Three choppers descended on the airfield, close to Pierfoy's plane, blocking the Senator on the strip.

"Heads up, everyone," Hickem said. "We take out the choppers first, and then move in. Team three, you have lead position."

"Copy that."

Hickem had split up their forces, putting the majority closer to Pierfoy's plane in hopes that Callahan would try and box Pierfoy in, and it worked perfectly. With the other teams in place closer to the combat zone, Hickem, Mocks, and Grant were onsite only as backup.

Pierfoy exited the plane, escorted by his security detail, and Callahan showed himself once Pierfoy was on the grass. Grant lifted his binoculars to watch the exchange. Callahan brought eight men, and Grant saw a few bodies with bags over their heads on the center chopper. It was Pierfoy's family.

"Well," Callahan said, his voice catching on Pierfoy's hidden mic. "There they are." He gestured to the center chopper. "I bid you good luck on your trip to D.C."

"I want to see their faces," Pierfoy said. "I want to talk with my granddaughter. After that, I'll be on my way."

Callahan lingered but finally acceded to the request. The bodies were pulled from the chopper and their masks taken off. Pierfoy rushed to the young girl and the pair cried together.

"Are you all right?" Pierfoy asked. "Are you hurt?"

"I want to go home," the little girl said. "Grandpa, please!"

Callahan's men ripped the girl from Pierfoy's arms and she screamed, dragging her and the parents back to the chopper. The senator remained on his knees as Callahan walked over.

"So, I held up my end of the bargain," Callahan said. "Now it's your turn."

Grant shifted his gaze toward the Secret Service behind the senator. None of them had their weapons out, which irked him, especially with Callahan's men so openly armed. It went against their training to be in such a vulnerable position. Something was wrong.

Pierfoy lifted his head, his eyes red, sniffling and wiping his nose with his jacket sleeve. "All right."

Hickem wiggled on his stomach. "Stand by."

Pierfoy turned his head toward Grant and his muscles tensed. Through the binoculars, it was like the senator was looking directly at him. Grant waited for Pierfoy to give the go-code. But that's not what happened.

"There are twelve of them," Pierfoy said. "Sixty yards toward the western tree line, and then to the north twenty yards nestled in the woods. They're heavily armed, and there is a drone in the area."

"Shit!" Hickem said, pushing himself off his stomach and sprinting along the tree line. "You two stay back!"

Gunfire immediately descended upon Hickem's men, and Grant pivoted the binoculars to the battle on the tree line. A rustle stole his attention to his right, and when he looked up from the binoculars, Mocks had sprinted off, heading straight for Callahan.

"Mocks!" Grant jumped up, following her, and raised his rifle.

Exposed and in the open, the only advantage the pair had was the distance between them and The Web. Grant caught up to Mocks and yanked her arm back.

"We need to circle around," Grant said, pulling her from

her set path. "Hickem will want to try and box them in! C'mon!"

The chopper blades whirred as one of Callahan's aircraft lifted off, and Mocks followed Grant's lead. The pair fired intermittent blasts on their run, Grant's vision shifting between Pierfoy and Callahan.

The world narrowed through the scope of Grant's rifle, and he concentrated his fire on the airborne chopper. His shots missed wide left, then right, but he connected with the windshield just before the aircraft ascended out of reach. It did little to stop the pilot's advancement. And as the chopper turned, Grant got a good look at the fifty-caliber gun on its deck.

Grant lowered the rifle and focused on the sprint to the hangar. "Get to cover!" He sprinted around Mocks, pulling on her shoulder. He glanced over to the plane and choppers still on the ground.

The senator had disappeared back into the safety of his plane, but he caught a brief glimpse of Callahan as he took shelter inside one of the helicopters.

The chopper with the mounted gun turned to Hickem's men on the north side of the airfield. Gunfire thundered into the forest, tearing apart trees, kicking up dirt, and laying waste to anything in its path.

Screams pierced the radio as Hickem's men maneuvered to evade the gunfire. Grant's legs cramped on the run, and he limped the last few steps to the backside of the hangar, slamming into the rusted metal siding.

Mocks sidled up beside him, her eyes toward the chopper. Toward Callahan. "He hasn't taken off yet." Her voice was breathless. "We can still take him."

"It's too dangerous," Grant said. "The best move for us is to stay alive. That's why he wanted to lure us here. To wipe us out so we couldn't talk."

Mocks stepped around Grant and reached for the hangar's back door. Grant pressed his hand against the door and leaned his weight against it to block her.

"Don't," Grant said. "It's not worth it."

"He cut up my husband. I'm not letting him get away with that." Mocks knocked away Grant's hand, then ripped the door open.

"Mocks!"

Gunfire pounded the air beyond the hangar walls, and the radio chatter intensified. She sprinted through the hangar, rifle raised, and Grant followed. She was faster than him, her short legs blurring as they neared the front. Grant heard Hickem give the order to fall back.

"Mocks, stop!" Grant said, but his request fell on deaf ears.

Mocks shoulder-checked the front hangar door open and fired into the pair of helicopters. Grant was ten feet behind and raised his rifle to cover her from a pair of Web members that sprinted from behind a chopper. Grant brought the crosshairs over a chest and stomach and quickly pulled the trigger.

The stairs of Pierfoy's jet were still attached, and Grant yanked Mocks behind them for cover. He looked up to the sky and reached for a fresh magazine as he ejected the empty.

"If that fifty-caliber sweeps back around, we're both dead," Grant said, noticing the blades were still thumping farther down the airfield, chasing Hickem's men. "We don't have a lot of time."

Mocks reached into her pocket and removed a grenade. "I get this between the choppers and it could take both out."

"No," Grant said. "They're too far part." He gestured to the chopper on the left. "Take out the front one. It'll force them to funnel."

The chopper whined as the engines whirred, and Grant

craned his head over the stair's banister. Mocks pulled the pin then stepped out from behind her cover and chucked the grenade.

They both ducked, and screams preceded the heavy rumble of earth from the blast. Grant lifted his head and lunged for Mocks before she could go alone. "Wait!"

"Let go!" Mocks ripped herself from Grant's hold and sprinted away from the stairs, firing into the second chopper.

Grant followed but struggled from his awkward position on the stairs. It cost him a few seconds, and by the time he tailed Mocks, she was past the smoldering wreckage of the first chopper.

"Mocks!" A Web member circled around the back, closing in on her blind spot at eight o'clock. Grant aimed quickly and connected with a head shot. He looked to the sky, the thump of the third chopper returning to its grounded brothers.

Wind blasted Grant's face, and he squinted as Mocks drew closer to the chopper ready for takeoff, firing impotently into the windshield. The glass was bulletproof, the bullets bouncing off the surface.

The chopper's sliding deck door opened and a rifle appeared. Shots were fired, and Mocks was flung backward, dropped to the grass.

"No!" Grant aimed, but before he could squeeze the trigger, the harsh pelt of bullets struck his chest, flattening him on his back. Wind rushed over his body, and he rolled in pain. He lifted his head and saw two men drag Mocks's body onto the chopper. Grant reached for his side arm and lifted a shaking arm to fire. The door shut as the chopper took off and like the windshield it was bulletproof.

They disappeared behind Grant, but not before the second chopper with the mounted machine gun descended upon him. Grant jumped to his feet, and the heavy thump of gunfire propelled Grant faster toward the hangar.

Bullets nipped at his ankles, tearing through Pierfoy's jet in the process. Grant leapt through the hangar door, landing on his belly and covering the back of his head as the high caliber bullets tore through the hangar's old and rusted sheet metal.

The thump of the choppers faded, the gunfire ended, and the world fell silent. Slowly, Grant lifted his head, his stomach and chest sore, and when the adrenaline subsided, he suddenly found it hard to breath. He took quick, shallow breaths, avoiding the pain of a deep inhale that his body desperately wanted to take.

Static crackled in Grant's ear, and he pressed the receiver on his communication link. "Hickem? Anyone copy?"

Only static answered back. Grant forced himself to sit up and heard movement outside the hangar walls. He limped to the wall next to the hangar door and peered through one of the bullet holes left behind by the fifty caliber.

A pair of Pierfoy's Secret Service detail stepped out of the fuselage to examine the damage. He reached for his side arm, the rifle still lying out in the grass.

Grant waited until both Secret Service members had their backs turned and then he stepped from cover. "Freeze! Place the hands on the back of your heads, turn around, and walk slowly toward me."

Both Secret Service members complied. Grant kept his pistol trained on his new hostages, but his eyes flitted up to the open plane door.

"Come out, Pierfoy!" Grant said. "It's over!"

No answer.

Grant ordered the pair of guards to drop to their knees, and he tossed one of them a zip tie. "Tie his hands behind his back." Once the serviceman's partner was restrained, Grant bound the second serviceman. He did the same to their ankles, leaving them on their sides.

After a quick pat down and removing their fire arms, Grant moved to the stairs, his pistol still aimed up at the open door. A breeze cooled the sweat on his forehead as he ascended the stairs. His abdomen spasmed, his body brusied from the bullets, but the Kevlar had done its job. He pressed forward, then paused at the dark entryway to the plane.

"Last chance, Pierfoy!" Grant said. "Callahan is gone." One bodyguard remained, and the last thing Grant wanted was a shootout with a Secret Service officer.

With still no answer, Grant stepped inside. He sidled up next to a small counter and cabinet before turning into the main aisle that stretched down the plane's middle. He inched toward the edge, then carefully peered around the side.

It was a narrow glance, but Grant spied a few bodies huddled all the way in the back, tucked behind chairs and seats.

"I didn't have a choice," Pierfoy said, shouting from the back. "He had my family. What was I supposed to do?"

"You made your bed a long time ago, Senator. It's no use backpedaling now." Grant peered around the edge again, growing bolder and inching farther. He needed the remaining bodyguard's location. His field of vision widened with each inch and when he spotted the pistol between a pair of seats, it fired.

Grant ducked and crouched lower, bits of wood falling over his head and shoulders with every gunshot. Five more shots, and then they stopped. Grant brushed some of the debris off his face and repositioned himself near the aisle's edge.

"I'm not going to let you dismantle everything that I've built," Pierfoy said. "The only way you're getting me off this plane is in a body bag."

Grant closed his eyes, controlling his breathing. The shooter had limited mobility with the pistol wedged between the seats. If he moved left fast and far enough, then he had a shot.

Grant scooted closer to the edge, ignoring the pained fatigue his body whimpered along with the daunting task of what came next. One step at a time. That's all he needed to do.

Grant spun around the corner's edge and the serviceman fired, missing Grant's shoulder by a hair. Grant aimed toward the source of gunfire and squeezed the trigger. Recoil from the shots jerked Grant's wrists in three quick strikes, and shrieks pierced as the gunfire rose from the rear of the plane. And then quiet. Just like that.

Grant pressed forward, pistol still aimed at the serviceman who lay lifeless on the floor, his eyes scanning the rest of the plane. Pierfoy's family held up their hands, the father shielding his wife and daughter.

Pierfoy stood next, and when Grant approached the Secret Service man, he saw a small river of blood roll into the aisle.

"You three, on the back wall," Grant said, pointing to the family. "Stay on your knees and place your hands on your head. Do not move unless I tell you to."

The family quickly complied, the mother and daughter still crying. When Grant arrived at Pierfoy, the old senator kept his hands at his side. His face drooped, as if defeat had finally sunk its absolute claws into his back.

"So," Grant said. "Do you want to walk out that door? Or do I need to get you that body bag?"

The senator slowly raised his arms.

32

*G*rant moved Pierfoy and his family off the plane,
leaving the body of the Secret Service agent where
he lay. With the investigation that was sure to
follow, Grant didn't want to cause himself any more grief by
adding tampering with evidence in addition to the charges
accompanied for shooting a federal officer.

With the family off the plane, Grant checked the radio
one last time, hoping some of Hickem's men survived. "Agent
Hickem, this is Grant, can you hear me?" He paused, waiting
for a response. He checked the communication link, making
sure everything was plugged in and turned on. It was. "I say
again, this is Detective Grant. Is anyone out there?"

A burst of crackling static, and then garbled nonsense.
Grant's heart leapt at the noise, and he took a half step
toward the tree line.

"Grant," Hickem said. "You still there? Grant?"

"I'm here," Grant answered. "Are you all right?"

"I'm fine, but my men are injured. I've radioed for a
medical evac."

"Where are you now?" Grant asked, pivoting three-sixty, but saw nothing except grass and trees.

"About a mile north of the airfield," Hickem answered. "I'm staying put with my guys. What's your situation?"

"I have Pierfoy along with his family and security detail," Grant answered. "Callahan is gone. He took Mocks."

Hickem remained silent for a moment. Then, with a steady tone, he replied, "She'll be all right. She's too ornery to die."

The medical unit landed twenty minutes later, and Grant kept an eye on Pierfoy and company while the medics fished Hickem and his men from the forest. Or at least what was left of them.

Six had died. The other three were injured, including Hickem himself, who had a gash on the back of his left calf, which he conveniently forgot to mention until after his men were taken care of. He'd duct-taped the flap of meat back to the rest of him. The piece of muscle was at least the size of a steak.

The injured were taken first, Hickem staying behind with Grant, and another chopper arrived to pick up the bodies. While they waited, Grant pulled Hickem aside to give him the news about the Secret Service man he'd killed.

Hickem's face went slack, and he nodded. "It's not going to be easy for you when this is all over."

"It was never going to be easy," Grant said. Though he honestly didn't think he'd still be alive anymore. He was supposed to die back in Callahan's bunker. But how much more would he have to endure before that wish was granted?

While Hickem spoke about next moves, Grant didn't listen. His thoughts drifted to Mocks, wondering if she was still alive. She was wearing a vest, and the gunshot looked to hit her in the chest over the protection. But with Owen as your warden, survival didn't mean necessarily mean you'd stay in one piece. Flashes of Rick struck his mind, the gruesome cuts of jagged flesh over his body. The same could be done to her. Or worse.

"Grant," Hickem said, nudging his arm. "Did you hear what I said?"

"What? No," Grant answered. "Sorry."

The chopper descended, and Grant's stomach drifted upward from the inertia. Their vehicles were tucked away off the side of the highway. State troopers blocked traffic and the chopper landed directly on the eastbound lanes of Highway Ten.

"I can hold off on my report until I get a medical update on the rest of my men," Hickem said. "Which means I can keep the death of the Secret Service officer off your back from an official standpoint. But I can't prevent Pierfoy from going to the press, which I'm sure he'll do the moment he has his lawyer. They're going to paint you as the bad guy. Even though you're not."

Grant understood. The Secret Service officer was just doing his job, protecting the man the people had elected. The chopper jolted on the landing, and Grant unclipped his seatbelt and removed his headset. Hickem followed him to the car, the blades of the chopper winding down.

"He'll ask to trade something for her," Hickem said. "And when he contacts you, which you and I both know he will, you need to tell me."

Grant opened his driver side door without a word and then shut himself inside. Hickem tapped on the glass as Grant started the car. He lowered the window.

"Call me when it happens," Hickem said. "I want to hear you say it."

Grant exhaled. "I'll call you."

"Good," Hickem said, leaning away from the window. "What are you going to do until then?"

Grant kept his foot on the brake and shifted into drive. "We know his name now. Which means I've got homework to do."

* * *

POLICE TAPE COVERED Grant's door when he returned to his apartment, which he tore off and threw in the trash the moment he stepped inside. His place was small, tinier than the house he had with Ellen. But a studio was all he needed. He never entertained, and the only time he was at home was when he slept, and sometimes not even then. He'd pulled more overnighters at the precinct since Ellen died than all his years combined before her accident.

Grant sat at his desk and opened his laptop, immediately going to work. He Googled Owen Callahan and a few hits popped up, including the article about the fire at the sawmill they had noted earlier. But aside from an announcement of his birth at the local hospital, there wasn't much else.

From there, he typed Owen Callahan into the police database, and he was glad to find that his administrative privileges had yet to be turned off. The department had probably thought he was dead.

The name got a few hits, but it wasn't the Owen Callahan that Grant was looking for. He clicked on alias tabs and found a report filed over a decade ago with a connection to a cold case from the early eighties that was reopened. Which would have put Owen in his mid to late twenties.

The cause for reopening the abduction case was the discovery of the victim's body by a pair of hikers. A series of storms had blown through the previous week, and investigators believed that the constant rain and wind unearthed and exposed the young girl.

A DNA test confirmed the body was in fact the young girl who went missing years prior, and the detective who took over the case was Roger Hayfield. Grant remembered the name but never interacted with the man. He was still studying for his detective's exam at the time, and Hayfield worked at another precinct north of Seattle.

The body of the girl that was abducted was in the foster care system, so Hayfield began interviewing individuals who worked for the department of children and families at that time.

Most of the notes from the interviews were vague, Hayfield noting that the witnesses had hazy or foggy memories. By now, most of them were retired or dead. But a few mentioned a name, and they all said the same thing: Owen Callahan was such a lovely young man. So Hayfield tracked Callahan down.

At the time, Callahan was still working at the DCF in Seattle and had moved up to director of his division. Hayfield's notes on him were detailed.

Interviewee was oddly calm and overly sympathetic to the situation, though from interactions observed of him and his staff, it was normal behavior. Some sociopathic tendencies noticed. Loves attention, dominating with his presence, likes to be in control, which explains his current position. Says he's retiring soon.

Hayfield never got past anything more than a hunch about Callahan. But Grant continued to explore the old man's history. His school records revealed a bright student, A's and B's in all his classes. He excelled in social studies, and his college transcripts from Washington State revealed a double major in psychology and social work. It was the perfect path suited for his pedophilia.

After graduation, he found an entry-level position within

the foster care system. Grant followed his career through a series of paperwork, and his stomach lurched when he discovered where Callahan had spent most of his DCF career.

The bastard had weaseled his way into a quality assurance position, which granted him access to the children's facilities all around the state at any given time for 'surprise inspections.'

Grant clicked through some of the reports Callahan prepared, then cross-referenced those reports with the disappearances of children within the foster care system.

On average, around one hundred kids bolted from the foster care system once they were old enough to hold a job, and before the age of the Internet highway, it wasn't hard for kids to do so.

To have an idea of how many kids Callahan might have taken, Grant measured the number of kids classified as 'runaways' the decade before Callahan's employment, and then during. The numbers weren't drastically different in regards to total numbers, but there was an obvious increase in children disappearances.

Year over year during Callahan's stint in quality assurance, the average number of children classified as "runaways" was at plus twenty percent, which averaged out to be ten more kids a year. Which meant that Callahan picked out a new kid almost every month. All of them under the age of twelve.

Grant leaned back in his chair, slamming the laptop shut. His phone buzzed, and even though the number was blocked, he knew who it was. "Is she still alive?"

"Yes," Owen answered. "And if you want her to stay that way, then I want something from you."

"What?"

"A copy was made of the hard drive from the laptop you

stole. I want it back, and any other duplicates."

"We know about the islands," Grant said. "Your paradise is finished. There is no way that legislation Pierfoy created for you will pass now that he's been arrested. It's over."

"There is always a way out, Detective," Owen said sharply. "We just might not always like where it leads."

"Where do we meet?"

"I'll text you the coordinates. Come alone, and bring me what I want."

The call ended, and Grant let the phone linger by his ear. This was where he was supposed to call Hickem. But Grant knew the old man was too smart to get caught on his heels now. If Grant brought help, Mocks would die.

Grant gathered his things, along with his revolver and extra boxes of ammunition. He still had his vest, along with enough gas in his car to make the trip. He removed the hard drive from the laptop and placed it in his pocket when his phone buzzed. It was Lieutenant Furst.

He wasn't sure how the lieutenant had discovered that Grant was out of the compound. Pierfoy must have already gone to the press. His first instinct was to ignore it, but the lieutenant had always been a friend, and it wasn't like Grant had to tell him where he was or what he was doing. "I know you probably have questions, but—"

"Is Mullocks with you?" Furst asked, his voice quick and breathless.

"No," Grant answered, avoiding telling Furst that Mocks had been taken. Hickem must have not told him yet. Not that he had a reason to.

"Shit," Furst said. "She might already be gone then."

"What are you talking about?"

"Someone took Rick from the hospital," Furst answered. "They cut the power, and when the generators were still running, someone killed the officer watching his room. If the gang went after him again, then they might be going after her too."

Grant hung up the phone before Furst wasted any more time. He had to get there quickly. But the old man wasn't the only one who had tricks up his sleeve. Grant had a few surprises as well.

33

*G*rant eased up on the brakes, and the mechanism squealed as the car crawled to a stop. Dust kicked up from the tires drifted over the vehicle. Grant looked up to the sky. The sun was shining through the clouds. He recalled that it was sunny the day of Ellen's funeral. The worst days always had good weather.

The sawmill was visible from where Grant parked off the side of the road, or at least what was left of it. Long black scorch marks traveled up the walls. Empty holes replaced the windows, and half the roof had collapsed at the rear of the structure. Wild growth had consumed most of what remained of the mill.

Aside from the mill itself, Grant saw no one outside. He turned left and right on his walk up, searching for either Callahan or his henchmen in the woods, but the forest was quiet. Nothing but gusts of wind and a few birds chirping in the trees.

A side door near the front of the mill was open. Looking at it from the outside, Grant would have thought it was the entrance to some kind of beast's lair.

Grant didn't bother removing the revolver on his approach. He was on Callahan's turf now. Grant only had one card to play, but he wasn't sure if the old man would take the bait.

Grant entered the mill, and solid beams of light from empty spaces where windows once stood pierced the darkness. Dust and insects drifted in the long beams, but Grant remained in the shadows. He spotted Callahan at the rear of the mill, right before where the roof had collapsed.

Callahan was dressed in a black suit, a red pocket square the only bit of color on his attire. He wore no tie, but the outfit was suited for a funeral. Grant spotted Rick tied to one of the remaining pillars. He was unconscious, and his chin dug into his chest. Grant wasn't sure he was alive.

A pistol in Callahan's right hand hung limply at his side. His left hand held a green Bic lighter.

"That doesn't belong to you," Grant said.

Callahan flicked the lighter, and the flame brightened the darkness that had swallowed the old man. He kept his eye on the flame as it wiggled. "I've always been fascinated with fire." He lifted his gaze to the mill. "It was my first love. I suspect that if I hadn't become what I am now, I would have turned to arson. There's something beautiful in the way that it cleanses."

"Where's Mocks?" Grant asked, his hand itching for the revolver in his holster. He knew he could draw on the old man faster than Callahan could pull the trigger, but Grant knew Callahan wouldn't be alone. His henchmen were here somewhere. Hiding.

* * *

CALLAHAN LET his thumb off the lighter and cast himself back into darkness. He raised the pistol and aimed it at

Grant. "I'm sure you've done your research, Detective. You can guess where we are, what I did here."

"This was the mill your father worked at," Grant replied. "The paper said it killed every man inside."

"Including my father and that friend of his I told you about," Callahan said. "You see as I got older, my once-great admirer lost interest in me. I was no longer his type, and I can't tell you how much that hurt me. I'm sure my adolescence amplified that pain, but it was agonizing."

Callahan stepped forward, still glancing around the inside of the mill. "You know, I never thought I'd come back here." He shivered. "Such cold memories."

"They blamed it on a cigarette that caught fire," Grant said.

"Everyone smoked back then, and with all of this wood, all it took was a little bit of gasoline and one of my mother's Lucky Strikes. I did it in the morning, when everyone was still getting ready for the day. There was only one door, which I sealed shut."

Grant furrowed his brow. "That wasn't mentioned in the article."

"Why would it be?" Callahan asked. "The mill had been cited for poor ventilation, hazardous work conditions, and on several occasions, the foremen had to remind the workers not to set any logs by the door." Callahan shrugged. "During the fire, one happened to be near and fell. It was well planned, and no one would have suspected a high school student back then to enact something to terrible."

"So you got what you wanted," Grant said. "Like you always do."

"But it was more than that, Detective," Callahan said. "It was the first time in my life that I realized the only way to get what you wanted was to take it. And it was a lesson that I still carry today." He pointed at Grant. "It was a lesson I tried to teach you, but it didn't stick."

Grant fidgeted. He still hadn't spotted Mocks. And the closer Callahan walked to him, the stronger the smell of gasoline became.

"I do wish the whole place would have just collapsed onto the bodies," Owen said, longingly. "But I suppose I could still finish the job."

"You're not getting the drive until I have both Rick and my partner," Grant said.

Callahan stepped back, retreating until he made it all the way to where Rick was restrained. He pointed the pistol at Rick's head. "I think not."

"I made copies," Grant said. "You kill either of them, and you'll never find them." He fished the drive out of his pocket. "There is a folder on here that lists the number of times it's been copied, so you'll know how many you'll need returned to you."

"Copies?" Callahan asked. "You've grown too big for your britches, Detective." He tapped the barrel of his pistol against his chest. "I'm the one holding all of the cards here. I have your partner, and your partner's husband. Who—" he turned to look back at Rick, "—has looked better."

"No hostages, no drive," Grant said.

"Delaying the inevitable," Callahan said. "Someone took a page out of the class that I taught." He smiled, shaking his head and pleasantly delighted with himself. The old man removed the pistol from Rick's head and then holstered the weapon. "All right, Detective. If you want to play quid pro quo, then we'll do it your way." He stuck out his hand. "Drive, please."

Grant hesitated, but then tossed it to Callahan, who snagged it from the air. There was a trash can to his right and he dumped it inside.

"Now you let Rick go, and give me Mocks," Grant said. "Once they're both safe and long gone from here, I'll tell you where the other copies are located."

Callahan folded his hands in front of his body and rocked back and forth on his heels. "Do you know what I really wanted, Detective? It wasn't the drive. It was you. You don't think I don't know that Hickem is still alive? You don't think I don't know that Pierfoy will fold and spill everything he knows about me to the authorities? My days here in the States are over. There's no changing that."

Grant's heart beat faster as Callahan opened his left hand and exposed Mocks's lighter. He reached inside the trash can and removed a piece of paper.

"What I wanted most of all was to come full circle," Callahan said. "I started my criminal life here, and this is where I want it to end. And seeing as how you have been the only detective to have ever bested me, I thought it appropriate to have you burn as well." He flicked the lighter and the paper caught fire. He dropped it into the trash can and the orange flames danced. "Goodbye, Detective."

Callahan knocked the trash can over, and the flames inside caught quickly as the old man dashed for the door. Grant sprinted toward Rick, who was only a few feet from the flames.

The fire travelled in thin lines where fuel had been poured, and it spread quickly through the dry structure. Flames consumed the walls and pillars, fighting their way to the ceiling and the second floor.

Smoke filled the mill and climbed up and out of the windows. Grant coughed and shielded his nose and mouth with his shirt, but the acrid fumes filtered through. He jumped over the growing flames and skidded to a stop where Rick was tied. He reached for the knife in his pocket and cut the zip ties from Rick's ankles and the back of his hands.

Heat reddened Grant's face, and his body broke out into a thick sweat as he lifted Rick by the armpits and dragged him toward the door.

Ambers drifted through the air, and the darkness that had filled the mill was replaced by the agitated flames that feasted on what remained of the structure. Smoke continued to build, and Grant's chest cramped from the fumes.

Grant exited the mill, dragging Rick's body as far from the structure as he could until his legs collapsed from under him. Every breath choked him. His throat and lungs burned. He rose to his hands and knees and glanced back at the burning mill.

Smoke flooded through the windows, blacking out the sky above, and bits of what remained of the roof were already crumbling away.

Disoriented, Grant stood, then stumbled in a half circle, but stopped abruptly when he saw Callahan and his henchmen standing on the edge of the clearing near the trees.

The old man was smiling, and his pair of bodyguards kept their rifles aimed casually at the structure. His presence was sobering. Even if Grant went back into the flames and pulled Mocks out, Callahan had no intention of letting them survive. This was just another game. Strings to pull on his playthings to entertain, then dispose of when they no longer amused him.

Grant sprinted back toward the flaming structure, the heat unbearable as he rushed through the wall of smoke at the door. A thick filter of fumes darkened even the fires inside, and Grant stumbled blindly, every breath choking him.

"Mocks!" Grant said, his voice raspy. "Mocks!"

The first floor was consumed with fire, but the second had yet to fully catch. He blindly found the stairs to his left, remembering the location of the stairs prior to the fire. He hunched over on his ascent, hearing the wooden steps groaning and bending with his weight. He avoided the handrails, flames already crawling up the top. A few of the steps had caught fire as well, and Grant jumped over them to the second floor.

Grant hacked up a spat of phlegm that felt like one of his lungs had dislodged. He wheezed in crippling short gasps and was forced to shut his eyes to shield himself from the smoke.

Finally, Grant lifted his head and forced his bloodshot, watering eyes to open. The collapse of the roof had consumed most of the second floor. But near the back wall on her side and tied to a post was his partner.

"Mocks!" Grant crawled forward, unable to stand anymore, his hands and feet gliding over the hot wood, covering him in soot. Loud cracks and pops filtered through the air, and Grant knew the place wasn't going to stand for much longer.

Grant fumbled for the knife in his pocket and untied the rope around Mocks's ankles and wrists. She was unconscious, a gag in her mouth. Thank god she was so light, because as Grant wrapped his arms around her, his body groaned in defiance.

A loud crackling caught Grant's attention, and he turned toward the stairs only to watch them collapse. And as the stairs gave way, the floor buckled.

The disruption sparked another burst of embers that rained over Grant and Mocks. He pulled Mocks close and shielded her body. The roar of the flames, the crack of wood, and voices in his own mind blocked out the ability to think. He glanced down at Mocks's face, which had darkened from the soot. He couldn't let them die here. Not like this.

A faint ray of light where the smoke escaped through a

window illuminated the hazy veil of fumes and flames. Grant grabbed hold of Mocks and the rope and yanked her toward the window. Twice Grant was forced to stop, his body convulsing. Oxygen deprivation was taking hold, and nearly all of his vision had blacked out. Only a small keyhole of clarity remained to guide him forward.

Another loud crack, and the floor jolted and the roof lowered. Grant hastened his pace. Five feet away. Then four feet. Then three. Another round of coughing paralyzed him and he lost his grip on Mocks's shoulder. He lost feeling in his feet and legs. Numb fingers fumbled clumsily over Mocks's shirt and he pulled her forward, but only for a few inches before he lost his grip again. Grant's lungs turned to bricks, and he breathed short, lifeless gasps that worsened the dizziness.

The floor rumbled again and flaming debris fell over Grant and Mocks. A crack in the roof appeared and offered another escape for the smoke. The thick black pea soup lessened a bit, and Grant took hold of Mocks once more.

They were less than a foot from the window now. One final push, every muscle in his body breaking down, and the insides of his chest burning and melting into nothing from the fire and smoke around him.

Grant stood next to the open window, gulping as much air as he could in the small sliver of space below the column of smoke escaping the same imprisonment. He reached back for Mocks and pulled her head out into the open. He wasn't sure if she was even breathing, and he wasn't in sound mind to check.

A fifteen-foot drop stood in the way to their freedom. Bushes lined the ground, and they would soften the blow a little. The roof groaned, cracked, and gave way again, this time dropping a foot before stopping.

Grant pulled Mocks to the edge, then tied the rope back

around her wrists. He lowered her body over the side feet first, keeping hold of her hands in the process, then when her arms were stretched as far as they would go he grabbed the rope and lowered her until the rope ran out, turning the fifteen foot drop into four feet. Grant let the rope go and Mocks's lifeless body crumpled into the bushes with a thud.

The building trembled beneath Grant's stomach and he pushed himself to his hands and knees. He lingered at the edge. Another groan from the roof, and it finally gave way. Grant jumped from the ledge of the window and his body tensed before impact.

He landed feet first, and his left leg cracked as he crumpled into the grass and bushes. He screamed, but his voice was drowned out by the crash of the mill as it caved in on itself.

Grant whimpered and examined his leg. He couldn't see the extent of the injury with his pants still on, so he reached for his knife and slashed the fabric. Once the cloth was removed, it revealed a large bruise on the front quad of his left leg. He poked it and he screamed as his leg barked in anger.

He hacked and coughed, and then his stomach soured, and he turned to his side, retching a pile of bile that was as hot and black as the smoke he'd just inhaled. He spit, but was unable to rid himself of the taste, and collapsed. His lungs ached, and his brain buzzed from the lack of oxygen.

Slowly, Grant lifted his head and spotted Mocks sprawled out in a lifeless mess in the bushes. He forced himself to sit up, a sharp pain running from his leg all the way up his left side. He leaned to the right, putting all his weight on that side, keeping his left leg as straight and as immobile as possible.

But even the smallest movement triggered pain, and before Grant was even able to lift his butt off the ground, he was forced to stop. His will had smoldered into nothing, like the mill that nearly burned him alive.

Shouts made him lift his head, and it triggered another jolt of pain. His leg was already swelling from the fracture. The shouts drew closer, and he remembered the pair of bodyguards with rifles next to Callahan on the other side of the mill.

Grant forced himself up. He hobbled toward Mocks and grabbed her arm, too weak to pull her any other way, and dragged her deeper into the forest.

It was slow, and painful. Mind-numbingly painful. Every limp forward stabbed knives into Grant's body. And just before the pair of shooters stepped around the mill, Grant hid Mocks behind the cover of bushes and he dropped to the ground next to her, muffling his pained noises and concentrating on not giving away their position.

The pair of guards continued to chat back and forth, and their voices were soon drowned out by the thump of helicopter blades. The wind from the aircraft gusted smoke into the forest where Grant and Mocks were hidden, and Grant knew his window was short.

Grant shifted his weight back onto his right leg as he used the tree trunk next to the bushes to help himself up. The smoke blew through like a hazy fog and once again choked the breath from Grant's lungs.

But the smoke provided cover, blinding Grant and the gang members to a visibility of less than a foot. Grant remained quiet and listened for the sound of footfalls. He clutched the knife in his hand, his arm coiled to strike. A rifle's barrel entered his view, and Grant spun around, leading with the tip of his knife, and found the thug's throat.

Blood spurted out in a geyser, warm claret covering Grant's face in a splatter as the thug clawed at Grant's arm. The man dropped to his knees, gurgling his last few breaths.

Grant snatched the rifle from the ground and immediately raised it to the hazy fog that still covered the forest floor.

Grant limped forward cautiously, his finger over the trigger. The chopper blades wound down and the smoke began to clear.

A shadow appeared to his left and Grant turned fast, too fast. The pain in his leg caused him to collapse and groan. The incident caught the thug's attention and he turned and fired, missing Grant as he fell.

From the grass, Grant raised his rifle and squeezed the trigger until the shadow dropped to the ground. The thump of helicopter blades ended, and Grant rolled to his side, hacking up another wad of black phlegm. He stood, using the rifle as a crutch as he approached the still-burning mill.

Grant crept along the side and slowed once he neared the edge. He craned his neck around the side and got one look at the chopper before the guard and pilot spotted him. They shouted in Cebuano, and Grant fired, squeezing the trigger before he had gotten the chance to aim properly.

The first four bullets missed, but the next three connected with the pilot, and then the next four dropped the co-pilot. Grant then swung the rifle's sight toward a stunned Callahan, rushing from the chopper's tail toward the deck, but the old man wasn't faster than Grant's trigger finger.

Two bullets entered Callahan's side and he tripped to the ground, sprawling out on his belly, moaning from the gunshot wounds. Grant checked left and right, making sure there weren't any more surprises, but when no more gunshots sounded, he figured the coast was clear.

Grant lowered the weapon and limped toward the old man still wallowing on the ground. He watched Callahan try and reach inside his jacket, but Grant fired another shot close to the old man's body and he stopped.

Two red blotches covered the bullet holes in Callahan's

left side, and blood dripped onto the grass, some of it smeared from the way he wallowed on the ground.

Grant walked over, the pain in his leg displayed in full with each grimace of his face. By the time he reached the old man, Grant couldn't even hold the rifle up anymore.

Callahan sucked air, his mouth reddening with blood. "So," he coughed, and specks of blood fell onto his chin and white shirt. "Finally come to slay the devil?" He frowned and another spat of hacking, this round more vicious than the previous one. He clutched his side where his wounds were, gingerly grazing his fingers over the holes, then winced upon contact and retracted his hand. "Go on then, Detective."

"You've abducted and molested children," Grant said. "Murdered, ripped apart families, shuttled drugs and sex slaves for profit. You don't deserve a trial. A cell would be too good for you. Even with the knowledge of what they'd do to you in prison."

"I'm sure I'd get mine," Callahan said. "But you want to do it yourself. Take my lesson and make it come full circle." He nodded to the rifle. "Or are you too weak to stomach it?"

Grant looked at the rifle that hung from his fingertips, then to the deck of the chopper. A can of gasoline was on board. Grant dropped the rifle and reached for it.

"No!" Callahan held up his hand as Grant soaked the old man with fuel from head to toe.

Grant emptied the can, tossed it aside, and then retrieved Mocks's green Bic from Callahan's jacket pocket. He gave the lighter a careful flick, mindful of his fuel-soaked hands, and watched the flame sprout from the top.

"You were right," Grant said. "It does feel good to get what you want."

Grant tossed the lighter onto Callahan's body and stepped back as the old man caught fire. He writhed on the ground, screaming, rolling to try and put the fire out, but he was covered in too much fuel.

The odor of burnt flesh and charcoaled clothes was nauseating, and watching the old man's flesh melt and blacken made him sick to his stomach. But he watched the old man until the screams and movement ended. And when it was over, Grant turned around, limping back toward Rick and Mocks and the collapsed, smoldering sawmill.

34

*T*he hospital machines beeped in a steady rhythm, which Grant found to be a comforting sign, considering they were hooked up to him. He'd slept for most of the day, but with his leg in a cast, there wasn't much else he could do.

He jiggled his left wrist and tugged against the cuffs that kept him in the bed. That didn't help his mobility either. He glanced over to the door where the pair of officers watched his room. He rested his head back onto the pillow and closed his eyes.

He'd been stuck in the room for almost three days now. He'd had visits from nearly everyone, even the ambassador, but there was still one he was waiting for. A hard smack to Grant's right shoulder opened his eyes.

"Hey."

The expression on Mocks's face was stoic. She stood there, dressed in a blue blouse, and her hair brushed off her face and tucked behind her ears, those green eyes focused on him. The oxygen tank was at her side, and the mask in it hung limp in her hand.

Both of them still had trouble breathing from the smoke inhalation, though Mocks's was worse because she was unconscious. The doctors said the gag around her mouth saved her life because it blocked most of the smoke from her lungs.

And then, without a word, she lunged forward and wrapped her arms around his neck. He slowly reciprocated, giving her a gentler squeeze than he received, and she sniffled into his shoulder.

"You owe me a new lighter," Mocks said.

Grant laughed, and it triggered a spat of coughing, and she lifted her oxygen mask in a peace offering gesture.

"Want a hit?" she asked.

"No, no," Grant answered, coughing and waving her off. "I'm fine."

"I had to check with the doctors to make sure there wasn't anything addicting in here," Mocks said, looking down at the tank. "I suppose this is one thing that I'm supposed to be addicted to."

"Breathing is important," Grant said. "How's Rick?"

"Some of his stitching had opened up, but no further damage to report," Mocks answered. "He would have come, but the cops made him wait in the hall. I think the only reason they let me inside is because they knew we were partners. That, and I didn't have my gun on me." She smiled, but it faded. "What do you know so far?"

Grant shrugged. "Not a whole lot. My attorney told me he's confident the D.A. will drop the charges, and if I do time, it'll be minimal."

"The media has turned your story into a circus," Mocks said, shaking her head. "Channel Three tracked down Ellen's parents. They didn't comment though."

Grant didn't think they would. He hadn't heard from them since the funeral. He wasn't the only person who blamed himself for Ellen's death. "The nurse keeps asking me if I want to watch it on the television. But I'll have plenty of time for that when they release me from the hospital."

"House arrest?" Mocks asked.

"Yeah," Grant answered. It was the best he could have hoped for, considering all the laws he broke. Murder by coercion was still murder. "What about you? You get to keep your badge?"

"The lieutenant is making a strong case for me," Mocks answered. "I might get bumped down to traffic, but I'm not sure. Depends on how much trouble they think I caused."

"Well then you're off the force for sure," Grant said.

She punched his arm again.

"You hungry?" Mocks asked.

"Starving," Grant said.

Mocks removed a packet of strawberry frosted Pop-Tarts from her pocket, and Grant chuckled as she handed him one.

"You're unbelievable," Grant said.

"What?" Mocks said, biting into her pastry. "I was going through withdrawals." She closed her eyes and let out a satisfied moan as crumbs sprinkled onto her shirt.

After the treats were eaten, the silence lingered. Grant knew that his detective days were over, and that meant he didn't have a partner anymore.

"It's not right," Mocks said, her eyes reddening. "You didn't do anything wrong."

"I did plenty wrong," Grant said. "And it's high time I paid for it."

Mocks quickly grabbed hold of his hand, and tears fell from the corner of her eyes. "I will always have your back, Grant. No matter what. You tell me what you need and I'm there. No questions asked." She squeezed, and her voice dropped to a whisper. "What do you need?"

Grant felt the mist growing in his own eyes and engulfed her small hand in his. "I've never worked with better. It's an honor to leave the force knowing that."

Mocks fell forward, resting her forehead on his shoulder, and she sobbed. Grant wrapped his arm around her and kissed the top of her head.

"Thank you, Grant," Mocks said, pulling her head back and wiping her nose with her shirt sleeve. "For everything."

A knock stole their attention, and they both looked to see Lieutenant Furst lingering in the doorway. "Detectives."

Mocks wiped her eyes quickly, and Grant did the same.

"I was hoping to have a minute with you, Grant," Furst said. "If now's a good time?"

"It's all right," Mocks said. "I should go." She looked to Grant and smiled. "Bye, partner."

"Bye, Mocks." Grant watched her leave, the oxygen tank handle gripped in her hand as she rolled it behind her.

"What is it, Lieutenant?" Grant asked.

Furst kept his hands behind his back. "How's the leg?"

Grant examined the cast. "Still broken."

Furst approached Grant's bedside and revealed the folder he'd been hiding. It was thin, only a few papers inside. "The official charges filed against you. Thought you'd want to look at it."

"Dead men usually don't get to see their certificates," Grant said under his breath, opening the folder. He sifted through the pages. There weren't any surprises. Murder, withholding evidence, use of unnecessary force. With every line, he totaled the number of years a maximum sentence would carry if he was convicted. Grant would die in prison.

"Most of it is to just make an example," Furst said, trying to sound reassuring. "There's been such a public circus about this whole situation that the D.A. can't appear to be going soft on you. Especially with the exposure of the corruption in the Senator's office. Heads are rolling."

"And how far do you think mine will go?" Grant asked, handing the folder back to Furst.

"Hopefully not far," Furst answered.

Grant drummed his fingers on his chest and drew in a breath, his lungs still rattling from the smoke. The doctors told him it would take a week or so before his lungs were fully cleared. They'd done what they could from a surgical standpoint already, sucking out some of the crap when he first arrived.

"What's happening with Pierfoy and the Chief?" Grant asked.

"Charges are being brought up, and there is a huge audit running through the State Department right now," Furst answered. "The Attorney General will be handling the case personally."

"And Ambassador Mujave?" Grant asked, hoping the man would have some weight in the proceedings.

"He's being consulted on matters," Furst said. "He's using the momentum and spotlight to have Congress appropriate more funds and new legislation to combat the problem. He's making headway."

"That's good." If there was one man who deserved to lead the charge against what remained of The Web, then it was Mujave. With the organization's main contact on the state-side dead, the remaining members went underground, but most of them hadn't moved fast enough. What news Grant did catch centered on Hickem and his now fifty-man operation gutting locations based off the data from the hard drive. It was like shooting fish in a barrel.

"And our deal is still in place?" Grant asked.

Furst nodded. "The D.A. won't file any charges against

Detective Mullocks so long as you claim responsibility and sign the statement admitting it."

"Good." It was the only card Grant had left to play. And if he could shield Mocks from any further legal torture, then he was glad to put it on the table. "She can never know about it, Lieutenant. If she did, she'd try and unravel the whole ball of yarn."

"I can only keep it quiet until the D.A. makes the statement public," Furst said. "You're sure you don't want to warn her first?"

Grant looked at the leftover Pop-Tart he'd yet to finish. He'd loved working with Mocks. Their relationship had gotten him through more dark times than he cared to admit. Without her, he wouldn't have survived after Ellen's death. Even with the transfer to Missing Persons. He leaned on her for so much. And it was the smallest things throughout their day together that he loved the most.

The Pop-Tarts, the quirky remarks, the eye rolls, and that green Bic lighter of hers. Grant knew once she was back on the force she would use what happened and become a better detective than he ever could be. She loved the job. She loved her family. And a person who'd been through as much as she had deserved a chance to grow. Grant couldn't think of a better way to say goodbye.

"She'll be furious with me," Grant said. "But it's for the best. She's the only family I have left, Lieutenant. And I'll do whatever I can to protect her." He looked away from the pastry and back at Furst. "It's what we do for the people that we love."

Furst nodded, and the pair shook hands. "It was an honor working with you, Detective. The department will be lesser without you."

"Thank you, Lieutenant."

Furst disappeared and Grant was once again left alone in

his room, cuffed to the bed and waiting for the inevitable circus of a trial that was just around the corner. It would be hard, painful to watch his history and life thrust into the spotlight. But perhaps this was his final punishment. One last trial before he could finally let it all go. His hands were tired of holding on so tight. They ached. He wanted to rest.

* * *

FOUR MONTHS Later

The office was neatly organized. Elegant touches were thrown in where it could be afforded: an ornately designed wooden table, paintings, new carpet, all designed to give the space an air of superiority. But all Grant felt was anxiousness.

He sat at the long table, a window outside his view into a world he'd been limited in seeing since his release from the hospital. House arrest wasn't terrible, but that tiny apartment grew smaller every day.

Grant shifted his weight to the right in the seat. The cast had been taken off last month, but his leg was still stiff and sore. He was glad for the summer weather and its warm temperatures. Winter would be harder now, but he would deal with it.

The door behind him swung open and his lawyer stepped inside. "Sorry to keep you waiting, Mr. Grant."

"I've waited this long," Grant said. "A few more minutes won't hurt anything."

Jake Wilber was a younger man, eager to prove himself in his profession. He was only a few years removed from law school, but he was smart. He contacted Grant personally when he heard of the case and offered to represent him pro bono. Grant knew it was more for the publicity than the kindness of his own heart, but the man had done his job well.

"I just got the final approval of your statement by the D.A.," Jake said, flipping through the papers and signing a few. "All we have to do now is sign on the dotted line and have you read the statement to the press." He pushed the papers across the table, along with a pen, and smiled. "And then it's all over but the crying."

Grant examined the papers, reading through the statement for the thousandth time. Words had been cut, and changed, and rearranged so many times that he couldn't remember what the original version looked like anymore. He signed the documents, dated them, and turned them back over to Jake, only keeping the one page that contained the actual statement he would need to read.

"All right then," Jake said, neatly organizing the stack of papers. "Ready?"

Grant nodded and pushed himself out of the chair. He reached for his cane, and Jake opened the door for him as he walked down the hallway and out to the front of the building where a horde of reporters anxiously awaited his appearance.

The pair stopped at the door, and Grant heard the murmur of the crowd outside. Jake adjusted Grant's tie and brushed off the shoulders of his suit jacket.

"I'll introduce you, then you make the statement, and then I'll be answering any questions they throw at you," Jake said. "No matter what they ask, don't take the bait. The moment you're done reading off that piece of paper, you come right back inside. Got it?"

"I never answered their questions when I was a cop," Grant answered. "I'm sure as hell not going to start now."

"All right then," Jake said, taking a deep breath as if he had been the man on trial for the past four months. "Let's go."

Jake opened the door and a surge of camera flashes blinded them on their way to the podium that had been set up a few feet from the door. Jake led the way and Grant filed in behind him, leaning on the cane for support while he waited his turn.

Jake held up his hands, stemming the flow of questions. There must have been fifty reporters crammed onto the tiny lawn.

"Thank you everyone for being here today," Jake said, raising the volume of his voice. The incoherent stream of questions ended. "My client will be making a brief statement in regards to his recent trial, and then I will be available to answer a few questions."

Jake stepped aside, and Grant stepped up. A roaring click of pictures greeted him and he placed the single piece of paper onto the podium, smoothing it out on the surface. He placed the cane on the inside of the podium and gripped the sides for support.

"Thank you," Grant said, clearing his throat. "Four months ago, I was part of an investigation that involved the abduction of a young girl. During the process of that investi-gation, and once the child was safely recovered, it was discovered that the abduction was part of a larger ring of abductions around the state. Those investigations led me to work with multiple agencies, including the FBI, and my involvement extended beyond normal Seattle PD Detective responsibilities that resulted in casualties, injuries, and destruction of property." Grant looked up from his paper, every eye in the crowd focused directly on him. "I want to make very clear that my actions were not directed by any authority of local, state, or federal levels. I acted alone. Despite direction from my superiors, I ignored their orders and followed leads how I saw fit, and at my discretion. Those acts resulted in the unfortunate incidents that I was charged with during my trial. And despite the jury's decision of not guilty across all charges of manslaughter, I will be carrying out my probation sentence for obstruction of justice for the next two years, as well as the mandatory service hours. For all of those who were affected by my actions, I know there is no apology that can ease the suffering of those involved. However, I still wish to extend my deepest condolences to those affected, and hope that I will one day be forgiven. Thank you."

Grant took hold of his cane, grabbed his statement, and turned away while the reporters raised their microphones, everyone shouting questions at the same time. Jake quickly stepped in Grant's place and shouted for everyone to calm down before he singled out the first reporter to field a question. Grant was inside, shutting the door behind him before he could hear what it was. He was done.

* * *

Two Years **Later**

The road curved and wound through the mountains. The lush green forests provided the scenic tour that only the wilderness of Washington could offer. Traffic on the highway was non-existent, and Grant steadied the wheel of the rented U-haul. He rotated his left foot, his ankle finally free of the tracker he'd worn during his probation. He was glad to be rid of it. And he was glad to be out of Seattle.

He'd saved enough money during his time at the department to live off until the press circus died down. It had taken six months, but when it was finally over, a weight lifted off Grant's shoulders. He could walk down the street and become lost in the crowd. New scandals broke and other troubles begged for the media's attention. Grant was old news. And he couldn't have been happier about it.

While serving his probation and working off his community service hours, Grant found a part time job down at the docks. He'd never had much experience in that kind of work before, but he enjoyed the work outside. The constant movement of manual labor kept his mind occupied.

But at night, when he was at home and alone in his apartment, his mind would wander. The passage of time lessened the anxiety, but it never truly went away. The occasional nightmare of Ellen's accident, or the death of Brian Dunston, or the deaths of all those Philippine women still chased him. They would always haunt him.

It had taken almost a month before Mocks forgave him for the deal he brokered with the district attorney. Grant purchased her a new lighter and a Costco-size order of strawberry frosted Pop-Tarts, which helped speed up the process.

Mocks remained on Missing Persons after her administrative leave was over, which Grant was glad to hear. And Rick had done well enough in his physical therapy to return to work last year with the fire department. You couldn't even notice his limp anymore.

The exit sign for Deville appeared, and Grant veered off the highway. It was still ten miles until he reached the small town, and Main Street was so short that he nearly passed it.

Only a handful of buildings comprised downtown, and Grant pulled into a parking space in front of the office that had "Deville Realty" painted in faded white letters on the window.

A bell chimed when Grant opened the door, and an older woman with grey hair, coke bottle glasses, and a friendly smile sat up from her desk.

"Can I help you?" she asked.

"My name is Chase Grant. I spoke to you over the phone about the property?"

"Mr. Grant!" She smiled and extended her hand. "So good to finally meet you in person."

It was one of the rare occasions where Grant had met someone who knew his full name and still welcomed him with a friendly demeanor. It was the main reason he picked Deville to start over. He wasn't even sure if they had cable out here.

"We have the place all ready for you," she said. "Would you like to go look?"

"That'd be great."

Grant followed Jane Carr's old Chevy Silverado down a side street, and after a series of left and right turns down dirt roads, they arrived at a small house nestled amongst the forest.

It wasn't much to look at, and it needed quite a bit of TLC, but it was dirt cheap and in the middle of nowhere. Two of Grant's only requirements.

"I didn't get to clean up outside as much as I would have liked," Jane said, pointing toward some old rusted relics the previous tenants had left behind. "But I promise you the innards of the house are in much better shape."

Grant stepped inside and was glad to see she was right about the conditions. The floors had been cleaned and swept, the kitchen as well. The appliances were old but were in good working order. The living room and bedroom contained the musty scent that most old buildings provided. The place wasn't much larger than the studio he held back in Seattle, but the view had drastically improved. Nothing but beautiful greenery, instead of the concrete buildings he was forced to look at through his tiny bedroom window in Seattle.

"There were some stains in the tub that I just couldn't scrub out, but I assure you everything has been sterilized," Jane said. She walked over and handed him the key. "Do you need any help moving in? I'm afraid my back isn't of much use, but I could call my husband."

"No, thank you," Grant said, sticking the key into his pocket. "I'll manage."

"All right, then. I'll let you get settled. Utilities are all set up, and the bill comes on the fifteenth of the month. If you need anything, please call."

"I will. Thank you, Mrs. Carr."

With the old lady gone, Grant started moving in the boxes from the truck, using the dolly for the couch and dresser. His belongings didn't even fill up half the truck, and it took him less than an hour to lug everything inside, and only another two to unpack.

He saved the bedroom for last where there was only one remaining unopened box. He sat on the edge of his bed, staring at it, knowing that he'd have to go through it sooner or later, and putting it off would only prolong the inevitable.

He opened the box and pulled out the first thing on top. It was a picture of Ellen. One of their wedding photos. The box was full of the old mementos he'd kept in storage after the funeral. Her parents took most of her belongings, but he made sure to set aside a few things that he wanted to keep.

It wasn't much. A few photographs, a necklace he bought her for their tenth wedding anniversary that she never took off, letters and cards that she'd written him over the years, and the ticket stub to the movie they saw on their first date together: Mission Impossible II.

The box was nearly empty save for one tiny box nestled in the corner. Grant removed it and clutched it in his hands. He hadn't opened it since he retrieved Ellen's belongings from the coroner when he identified her body. He'd nearly thrown it away a dozen times but could never follow through with it.

Nestled inside was Ellen's engagement ring and wedding band, and despite the years in storage they still sparkled in the lamplight. Grant glanced down to his own wedding ring and set the box down. He twirled the band around his finger, and then looked to the picture of her in her wedding dress.

"I've never stopped thinking about you. Or Annie. Both of you are always on the tip of my tongue and the forefront of my thoughts. I miss talking to you. I miss hearing you laugh. I miss holding your hand." Grant teared up, and he wiped his nose, sniffling. "I thought keeping you buried and focusing on my work would be enough to keep going, but it wasn't. I never grieved, because I didn't want to let the pain go. I tortured myself with questions I'll never know the answers to. Who our daughter would have grown up to be, what kind of a father I would have been, what would have happened if I had told you not to drive that night." His lips quivered, and the tears fell. "But I just can't do that anymore. I love you but," He scrunched his face and cried. "I have to let you go, Ellie."

Grant pulled off his wedding ring and placed it over the pair of rings inside. It fit perfectly around Ellen's rings, forming a protective circle. He snapped the lid shut and returned the contents to the box, closed it, and placed it in the closet.

Grant went to the bathroom and splashed water on his face, wiping away the tears and snot. His eyes were bloodshot and his nose was red. The dark circles under his eyes and the lines on his face had aged him. A few grey hairs had finally sprouted through the thick black mane on his head. He looked older. He felt older.

He looked down at his left hand and the pale circle of flesh that was the only remaining sign of his wedding band. He dried his face and then walked to the back yard where he sat on one of the folding chairs the former tenants had left behind.

The sun was setting, and golden rays penetrated the trees.

Grant closed his eyes and let the warm summer evening sink in. Birds chirped, and there was a light breeze on the air.

He didn't know if it was God, or nature, or the fact that he had finally let himself look ahead to a future that was his own, but his mind had calmed. He had longed for a sense of peace, and now, after four years of pain, it had finally come.